C000228113

Kim Sherwood is an author a [...]
the University of Edinburgh. [...]
the Bath Novel Award and the [...]
Year, was shortlisted for the [...]
Award, and longlisted for the Desmond Elliott [...]
Kim was shortlisted for the *Sunday Times* Young Writer of the
Year Award. Sherwood is the author of the new *Double O* series,
expanding the world of James Bond for the Ian Fleming Estate.

Praise for *A Wild & True Relation*

'This book is a rarity – a novel as remarkable for the vigour of
the storytelling as for its literary ambition. Kim Sherwood is a
writer of capacity, potency and sophistication' **Hilary Mantel**

'Employing lusty couplings, a brooding hero and a tender
young heroine, Sherwood plays knowingly with the romantic
genre ... By both undermining and indulging the genre, it
seems Sherwood is having her delicious contraband cake and
eating it, too' **Suzi Feay, *Guardian***

'Breathlessly swashbuckling ... both full-blooded historical
fiction and thoughtful literary deconstruction, both elements
immaculately researched. You can take pleasure in her
punchy plotting and flamboyant nautical descriptions' ***Daily
Telegraph***

'[Sherwood] adopts the dramatic conventions of the 18th-
century adventure novel to spin a tale of secrecy, betrayal
and law-breaking on the open seas, while cleverly subverting
those same codes to reveal an inherently feminist agenda ...
champions rather than elides the female voice, giving her
heroine the right to both speak and record the truth about her
life' ***Harper's Bazaar***

'Smugglers, pirates and some cameos from some well-known writers – what's not to like! It presents swashbuckling action alongside reflections on authorship, agency and the powerful question of who gets to write history' **Fiona Mozley, Booker shortlisted author of** *Elmet* **and** *Hot Stew*

'I loved this tremendous book and devoured it in two days. Vividly imagined, relentlessly entertaining, rich and resonant in scope and context, it's both a thrilling adventure and a vital witness to women's voices' **Emma Stonex, author of** *The Lamplighters*

'It is a breathtaking feat of historical fiction, and an utterly astounding novel. It is wise, urgent and entirely compelling. I was bereft when it ended' **Wyl Menmuir, author of** *The Draw of the Sea*

'A blistering tale of early 18th-century love, betrayal, murder and revenge, wrapped up in a novel of smuggling, piracy, shipbuilding and a girl who is not as she seems. The prose is superb' *Historical Novels Society*

ALSO BY KIM SHERWOOD

Testament

Double or Nothing

A WILD &
TRUE RELATION

KIM SHERWOOD

virago

VIRAGO

First published in Great Britain in 2023 by Virago Press
This paperback edition published in 2024 by Virago Press

1 3 5 7 9 10 8 6 4 2

A CIP catalogue record for this book
is available from the British Library.

ISBN 978-0-349-01539-2

Typeset in Baskerville by M Rules
Printed and bound in Great Britain by Clays Ltd, Elcograf S.p.A.

Papers used by Virago are from well-managed forests
and other responsible sources.

Virago Press
An imprint of
Little, Brown Book Group
Carmelite House
50 Victoria Embankment
London EC4Y 0DZ

An Hachette UK Company
www.hachette.co.uk

www.virago.co.uk

*For my mother, Ellie,
who planted Fuchsia 'Tom West'
and Viola 'Molly'
in her garden*

'poets make the best topographers'

W. G. Hoskins

'this most beautiful of English counties'

Charles Dickens, on Devon

'For we think back through our mothers if we are women'

Virginia Woolf

'Rage – Goddess sing the rage of Peleus' son
Achilles, murderous, doomed ... '

Homer, *The Iliad*

'I shall then tell you a tale that, God willing,
will save us.'

Shahrazad to her sister, in *The Arabian Nights*

'And I was going to sea myself; to sea in a
schooner, with a piping boatswain, and pig-
tailed singing seamen ... '

R. L. Stevenson, *Treasure Island*

Devon, 1703. On the night of the Great Storm, the infamous smuggler Tom West confronts his lover, Grace, convinced she's betrayed him to the authorities. After a violent encounter that leaves Grace dead and her cottage in flames, Tom flees, taking Grace's daughter Molly to join his renegade crew.

As the years pass, Molly – now disguised as the young man Orlando – rises through the ship's ranks, outshining the men around her. But Molly remains haunted by her mother's death and the mystery that surrounds it. Driven by her need for answers and a desire for revenge, Molly strikes out by herself, intent on forging a legacy all her own . . .

Woven into Molly's story are the writers – from Celia Fiennes and George Eliot to Daniel Defoe and Charles Dickens – who are transfixed by her myth and who, over three centuries, come together to solve the mystery of her life. With extraordinary verve, Sherwood remakes the eighteenth-century novel and illuminates women's writing and women's roles throughout history.

BOOK ONE

1703

BE A MAN

The Great Storm of 26 November

I

If there was anything more frightening than God's fury, it was Tom West, trying to hold his temper.

The skies rained salt water. The world turned upside down, waves lifted into clouds. High tide blanketed Bantham Beach and slammed against the cliffs. The Avon surged, breaking its banks. The tempest destroyed Grace Tucker's garden, ripping up tender buds and frostbitten roots, until finally forcing the front door of the cottage open, admitting the violence of the night.

Grace stood in the parlour, boxed between Tom West, Benedict and the struggling fire – the heart of her home, black from providing heat for food and light for the table, which was stained too, with ink spills and the scratches of a child's first pen strokes. Now, the flames were reduced to embers, just as the kitchen seemed to shrink with Benedict hovering in the cross-passage and Tom leaning against Molly's bedroom door. The column of Tom's body had collapsed, those huge shoulders dragging on a failing back. In one hand, he held her journal. In the other, a pistol.

'Please, Tom,' said Grace. 'Tell me what's happened.'

Tom raised the book. In the firelight, he could make out where Grace had pressed nib to leather: *A True Relation of My Life and Deeds.*

'You must have kept this little confessional somewhere safe when I came around. Strange, to find it out tonight, with all the fineries I bought you. As if you was packing. As if you was running, while Devon drowns. And with my name on nearly every page.'

'It has only my life,' said Grace. 'I write it for Molly. And – for myself. There is nothing harmful in that. Please, tell me what is wrong – why have you brought this boy here?'

In the doorway, Benedict felt every bit the boy she called him. He had never met Tom's lover before. None of the crew had. Whenever they came ashore, ship burdened with barrels of brandy or chests of tea, Tom came here. The crew whispered about it: Tom West and his lover, a woman with a child begot by another man, Grace Tucker's dead husband, Kit. But never in front of Tom. No one told him he was a lucky devil, having a lady of quality to lie with whenever he wished, the likes of her reduced to a cottage like this, and only him for company; no one said how strange it was, Tom caring for a bairn with nothing of his blood in its veins. Yet this was more than a warm bed and pottage in the morning. Benedict understood that now, but not why Tom had raced here, tonight, as cattle drowned and church bells clamoured, rung by the gale. What did Grace Tucker mean to the men they'd dragged from the river, smugglers and Revenue bleeding alike?

He shuffled back. 'We should go,' he said. 'The horses—'

'No *harm* in it?' Tom said, cutting through him. 'Then I take it there is none of my movements in this masterpiece of yours?'

'What do you mean?' said Grace.

'A little late to play the fool, my love.'

4

'I play at nothing.'

'No?' said Tom. 'Then it weren't your words in the ears of Dick English that got me and my men ambushed tonight?'

'Ambushed?' Grace edged back, the heat of the fire against her calves.

'Captain Dick English and his Revenue was waiting by the tidal road at Aveton Gifford,' said Tom. 'The wind has been up all week. Only you knew I'd venture it anyway. Only you knew the profit at stake, and the satisfaction I'd get, seeing a storm in view and riding it. Only you knew where I'd bring the goods in. Nero and Daniel are dead. Shot while rowing. No warning, no chance.'

Grace paled. 'Are you hurt?'

Tom laughed. He squeezed the pistol's walnut grip, his fist swelling like a joint of pork strung too tight. 'Would it matter?'

'How can you ask such a thing?'

'Someone told them the Yeovil crew had let me down, and the wagons would have no batmen. Someone told them I'd land at Burgh and carry up the Avon myself. Someone didn't care if I was lain down to die tonight.'

'That boy you told me about – Frank Abbot. He was seen talking to the Revenue,' said Grace, 'before he ... left, for Barnstaple. He must have told Captain English.'

Benedict noticed Grace picking at a loose strand from her skirt. Everyone knew what had happened to Frank Abbot, but no one spoke of that, either. The villagers praised Tom's name as they always had, sprinkling the salt he carried from France on their food.

Tom licked his lips. 'What makes you think Frank left for Barnstaple?'

Grace glanced at the pistol. It was shaking in his hand. It was years since she'd asked how many of the rumours were true: if that pistol acted as just a warning, remaining in his belt, or if he was free with it. She knew how gently he could hold a child. She also knew how anger could change his face.

Now, she said, 'I heard some fishermen talking. Frank Abbot gave the Revenue information about you and was found dead on Burgh Island. I know you ordered it, or did it yourself.'

Tom's grip went slack on the gun and then tightened quickly before he dropped it. 'And haven't you got a whole load of docity, coming out with it. Or maybe that's just what you do best.'

'Whatever you think I have done,' said Grace, 'you are wrong.'

Tom fought for air. He was burning: nerve endings seared from diving into freezing water to haul his men out; thigh grazed by a bullet; bruised ribs. He was swaying on his feet. He was falling into Grace's green eyes. *Green like the land I love*, that's what he'd told her. *But not blue, like the sea you love more.* Her words. *One foot on land, one leg in water.* He had mounted a dead officer's horse and left his crew by the tidal road, driving the animal here as fast as he could against the hail. Benedict followed – at Hellard's command, no doubt – arriving minutes later. Tom would not tell Benedict to leave; he could keep his temper in check as long as the boy was there to witness him, with that lamblike worship.

'I've been good to you,' he said. 'Better than your precious husband ever was, or would have been. I've loved your daughter, when any other man would have scorned your bed for having a child crawling into it. I've – you know, Grace. You know what I feel. I've trusted you with my life, and the life of my crew. I thought I had cause.'

'Please, Tom, step away from Molly's door.'

'You think I'd hurt her?' Tom snapped, making both Grace and Benedict jump.

'No,' said Grace, her hands up. 'Please, just sit with me. Please.'

'Captain, we've got to go,' said Benedict. 'The storm will bring this house down.'

Tom breathed through his nose. There was the pile of lace and linen he had bought Grace, folded on the table, ready for a bag.

She was going to leave him. She had betrayed him, and now she was going to leave him.

'I'll sit with you, if that's what you want,' he said, gaze locked with hers. 'Benedict, get out. Go.'

'But—'

'*Now.*'

Benedict wormed on the spot, and then twisted away, back down the cross-passage and out the front door. The world was black, water and hills and sky merging, solid. He couldn't find the horses. He hung on to a damson tree, unable to escape.

In the kitchen, Grace and Tom sat across from each other at the table, as they had for the past three years. Tom's legs barely fitted. Grace perched on the edge of her chair. He set her journal down. His dark curls hung wet and filthy in his eyes. Grace reached for him, fingers skirting his swollen knuckles. Tom hunched, gripping the pistol closer.

'There's blood on your hands,' she said.

'Yours aren't looking all that clean, either, sweetheart.'

Seconds passed. From the other room came the sound of Molly crying. Grace rose. Tom's hand shot out, holding her where she was.

'Molly needs me,' she said.

'I need you,' said Tom. 'I need you to tell me. Did you talk?'

Grace looked over his face and then down to his fingers tightening on her arm.

'I can explain.'

Tom leapt up, his chair falling. Grace jerked away, but he held on. They were bound up with each other, flailing and

7

catching. One of them knocked the cutlery and pewter plates, and the last of Grace's ink shattered. Tom shoved Grace into the bookshelf. He grabbed a fistful of her hair, smashing her face into the wood.

'How could you do this? How could you?'

Grace cried for him to stop. Tom threw her away from him. She fell to the floor, landing in a nest of broken leather spines and torn fleshy parchment. Her lips were split and her chin glistened with blood. Tom stood above her. He watched Grace turn her head towards Molly's door. Then she was still.

Tom dropped to the floor. 'Grace?' He pawed her chest, burying his face into her hair. 'Grace? Why did you do it?'

His snot felt warm on her scalp. Grace tried to speak, forcing her lips to shape the words she needed. 'I never intended . . . '

'Tell me it was a mistake, you wrote it down and someone read your journal without your leave.' Tom stroked her cheek, her neck. His fingers dug into the hollows of her tendons. 'Tell me it was a mistake. Grace, tell me, now. Please . . . '

'I had to do it—' He was squeezing too hard.

Benedict stood in the threshold of the cross-passage watching. His feet would not take him any further than he'd already travelled, nor retreat to the storm. Bile clogged his throat. Tom was going to kill her. Benedict gripped his knife. She was to blame. Benedict had watched his friends die and she was the reason. Sweat melted the ice clinging to his clothes. Tom was going to kill her.

He had to do something. In the name of God, he had to do something. A cry outside. It could be a villager, come to check on Grace in the storm, or a Revenue man – or one of Tom's crew, come to help.

A shaky orb of light slipped down the hill. It was Hellard, carrying a lantern.

'I'm here!' Benedict shouted from the estuary bank. 'Help!'

'Benedict?' Hellard's voice was whipped by the wind. Lightning slapped the garden white. Hellard fell next to Benedict, seizing his arm. 'Where's Tom?'

'Inside, with that woman.'

'*Why?*'

'She told the Revenue. Tom's lost his mind—'

Hellard pulled his pistol free.

'Hellard, what are you doing?'

Hellard shoved past Benedict. Benedict remembered the blood beneath Hellard's fingernails after his talk with Frank Abbot. He hurried after him.

At the kitchen door, Hellard clambered over the building dam of branches and silt washed in from the Avon. The dancing beam of the lantern spilt into the parlour. Tom sat slumped on the floor, holding his head. Grace lay next to him. She was peering up at the wooden beams, breathing heavily. Her neck was red. A door opposite rattled: small hands on the other side beating the wood.

'Did she talk?' said Hellard.

Grace shifted on the floor. Glass grated her scalp. She lifted herself on one elbow, looking from Hellard to Molly's door.

'What have you come here for?' said Tom. 'Get out.'

Hellard, louder: 'Is it true?'

Tom picked his pistol up, shaking off the dust. He rose until he had to duck his head to avoid hitting the beams, and looked down at Hellard. 'Be on your way, brother.'

'Tom, you can't let her off. If it was anybody else, you'd kill 'em. That's *law*. If you don't be able, I swear to the devil I will. Oliver was bleeding out when I made my way here. I'll do it, if you won't.'

'Not while I'm standing,' said Tom.

Hellard lunged for Grace, but Tom barred the way.

'You gutless bastard!' Hellard wriggled in Tom's fist, pistol waving, the butt striking Tom's chin. Tom tossed Hellard back. 'Do it!' screamed Hellard, raising his pistol, not quite at Tom, but inching closer. 'Or get out of my way.'

A bang shook the walls. Benedict's heart lurched. Ears clouded. He couldn't hear anything. But there was no smoke. There was no gunshot.

Someone was kicking at the door.

Benedict stumbled down the passage, praying for Nathan or Kingston, anyone whose word of calm or humour might douse the fury of the Wests. The front door swung back.

'Aside, boy! Where is she?'

Benedict's flesh pricked. He knew that bark: Captain Dick English, who tonight had cut them down. Benedict raised the knife. The Book of Common Prayer came to him then, the succour of childhood, sealing him in time: *From lightning and tempest; from plague, pestilence, and famine; from battle and murder, and from sudden death, Good Lord, deliver us.* He tackled the oncoming body, but Dick was a bull to his billy goat and Benedict was cast aside, head bouncing against the wall.

In the parlour, Grace seized the mantel and heaved. She leant against the wall. Hail clattered down the chimney like dice from trembling hands. Sparks spattered on the rug. The room was dim and the voices muffled. She knew she was still in the kitchen, yet was certain she could smell spring garlic, whole shafts crushed underfoot in the wood where she walked with Molly, showing her daughter the flowers, lifting her on to the fallen oak. The tree had been struck by lightning and the roots were sooty. If Grace stroked them, her fingertips came away black and she could write Molly's name on the pale strips of bark. Tom had written his name, too, next to Molly's and Grace's, the first time he came with them. His name was the only word he knew how to spell, once.

'Tom,' she said. 'I have never seen you a coward. Don't be a coward now.'

Tom slowly turned his back on Hellard's gun, and faced her. He stared into her eyes. *Green like the land I love.* He could hear Molly screaming. He had lifted her, mottled red and brown and crying to know the world, into Grace's arms in her first minute.

The pistol in his hand twitched. Turn and shoot Hellard – break every oath he'd sworn to their mother. The gun twitched higher. He could shoot Benedict too, that sweet young boy, if it came to that. A little higher. He could leave this life, its power, its wealth, and take Grace and Molly away. He could lie beside Grace's betrayal every night. Give it all up for a woman who would see him die alone in a ditch. His arm was fully stretched now, the pistol accusing her.

'Be a man,' she said.

Tom raised a hand to cover his eyes, but faltered midway. He took all of her in.

Grace looked at him with love.

He clicked the hammer back. Fired.

Hellard flinched, stepping back and knocking into Dick English, who barrelled into the room with his pistol and sword drawn. Hellard swung with his gun, catching Dick in the temple. The lawman dropped to the floor. Hellard laughed, using the tip of his boot to tilt Dick's head this way and then that. Out cold, a scarlet ribbon threading through his golden locks. Pathetic.

Benedict stood in the doorway to the parlour, his eyes shut. The last thing he'd seen was Dick English cocking his pistol and kicking his way through the ruins into the room. Then a flash, and Grace's short cry and the thud of muscle and bone hitting the floor.

The child's wails were deafening. Benedict hugged his ears. It would not stop. It would not—

'*Benedict.*' Hellard was shaking him. The man righted a chair and pushed him into it.

Benedict looked around. 'Where's Tom?'

'In there,' said Hellard, nodding at the closed door.

Benedict could hear little soothing sounds coming from the child's room, broken up by sobs. Deep, male sobs. He said, 'I've never seen a woman killed before.'

'Don't be looking, then. Fifteen years to your name and wet as a babe.'

Benedict was aware of Grace's outstretched hand, her fingers curled like the opening head of a crocus. Her gown had come open, revealing faded freckles and pale breasts. A canker worm twisted deep in him. Next to her, Dick English lay in the wreckage. His pistol remained in his hand, just as Hellard's did. 'What are you doing?' said Benedict.

'Helping the storm along,' said Hellard. 'What she want with a beaufet fine as this in a damn hovel, anyway?' He knocked the glass-fronted cupboard over. To Benedict, the boom of smashed crockery was as loud as the ship's bow slamming on to a wave. 'First time anyone's been happy to see Dick English, I'll warrant – even his mother, on the day she spat him out.'

'She thought he'd save her?' said Benedict.

Hellard laughed. 'If she did, she was disappointed. He shot her.'

Benedict breathed: 'Why ... ?'

'Aiming at Tom. Whore got in the way. Ain't it tragic? Still, saved me and Tom some unpleasantness.' Hellard kicked the bookshelf. 'Here, look at this.' He picked up Grace's journal.

Benedict glanced at Grace. 'It's hers,' he said. '*A True* ... something.' Benedict looked again at the pistol in Hellard's fist. 'It was Dick, then, who shot her?'

'As much as I'd like to take the credit ... ' Hellard crossed to the fireplace. He stooped to the dying flames.

Tom stepped over Grace's body without looking down. He held Molly in his arms, pressing her face gently into his shoulder. She was six years old and fitted perfectly into his torso. She had lain along Grace's forearm when she was born, her head cradled in the crook of her mother's arm, her wet buttocks and squirming legs held steady in Grace's sure hand.

The child's blonde ringlets were touched by rust, Benedict saw – Grace's blood – and her toes recoiled from the pistol in Tom's belt.

Tom said, 'Don't.'

Hellard: 'Tom, if someone found this—'

'*Don't.*'

Hellard held the book by its tired spine, pages swinging loose. The last page to be written had already turned brown. He sighed, offering it up. Hugging Molly closer, Tom slipped the journal into his coat.

'What are you going to do with the boy?' said Hellard. 'Now Dick English has killed his mother?'

Tom paused, reading Hellard's face: the weighted glance at Benedict, the question posed. *Why not be the hero, and cast Dick as villain? It'll be our little secret.*

Benedict was looking at the child. Molly, Grace had called her. But she did wear breeches and a woollen waistcoat – cut down, Benedict realised, from one of Tom's. He waited for Tom to correct Hellard, but, after a slow silence, he just said:

'Boy's mine.'

'Stray shot of yours?' said Hellard. 'I always thought you were niggling her, 'neath Kit's nose.'

'I don't know about your shots, Hellard, but I hit what I aim at.'

Hellard blazed redder than the fire. A scene opened before Benedict: it was Hellard whose shot had gone wide; wretched power-starved Hellard who had fired at Tom, and Grace stood

13

in the way. No, it couldn't be – for Tom wouldn't allow the curtain to fall on a scene such as that with no answer. Hellard's cheeks must be reddening because Hellard himself was a stray shot: Tom's bastard half-brother, a cuckoo who lived under big brother's wing.

Tom wasn't paying any mind. He was looking down at Grace, seeming to Benedict like a man trying to solve some point that would always defy him. He spoke distantly: 'Grace would have none of me, while that bond still existed. But the boy's mine now.'

'What do you want with an orphan?' said Hellard.

Tom looked to Benedict, whose face was blotted with tears; he stood under the weight of the boy's stare a long moment, his fingers twitching. Then Molly whimpered and Tom looked down, kissing her head, tasting copper.

'Let the house burn,' he said, and turned his back on both of them, stopping just for a moment to consider English, who lay motionless in his own blood. 'And let the devil burn with it.'

As Tom walked out, Benedict could hear him whispering, deep and gentle: 'I'm here, child, I'm here. You're safe.'

II

This was no top-sail gale. No fret of wind. No simple storm. Ships within five hundred leagues of Devon hurried afore the wind, leaving the Channel curiously blank, as if God had removed from men the desire to go to sea. Those ships that tried to come into harbour were smashed across the docks, and the gusts blew so fierce, villagers and townspeople dared not collect the spoils. For two se'en nights, the wind had knocked chimneys from rooftops. Tiles were stripped from roofs like scales from a fish. In the house of the Justice of the Peace, the quicksilver in the barometer sank so low, the Justice followed it, praying on his knees for deliverance. Trees were robbed barren and fields shorn of corn. Elm and oak crashed into grand houses. Long grass was lifted from the earth, and caught in bare and breaking branches, so that the trees seemed to grow feathers. Lead cast from churches. Windmills span so furiously they caught alight and became blazing fists in the night. Rising salt water spoilt hogsheads of sugars and the tobacco waiting in Plymouth warehouses. Eddystone Lighthouse was wrenched from its foundations. The crew of the *Escape* gripped ropes and box-and-tackles and each other in the hold, listening to Frogmore Creek come apart around them. They prayed that the anchor would hold, prayed that the timbers weren't rotten, prayed that she would prove safer than the surrounding cottages thicketed by falling trees, but most of all they prayed for Tom's safe return.

Tom wished for the harvest moon. Forcing his horse up the mud track, the clatter and smack of branches almost threw him from the saddle. He hugged Molly to him. He could hear her teeth chattering. She wore no cloak or shoes. Benedict and Hellard rode on a single horse behind him. Tom knew the unofficial paths hacked out by badgers and wild men well enough, but, tonight, rains streamed down the lane with him, his horse sliding to Frogmore Creek, where the cottages had caved in and the water churned with debris. But the *Escape* was still afloat, naked masts swaying madly.

'Tom?' A lantern disclosed a calloused hand, then a fine face. Tom felt Molly flinch. Nathan climbed out of the creek. 'Thanks be to God, you're all right.'

'Not all of us,' said Hellard, jumping from the saddle.

'Revenue knew where we'd be,' said Tom. 'They might know where we planned to lay anchor, too.'

'Surely not even Dick English is so mad as to pursue us in this.'

'He won't be pursuing us anywhere. Not any more.'

As Tom spoke, a pistol crack swallowed the roar of wind and rain, followed by a cry from the ship: *'Revenue!'*

Lightning flooded the creek, painting a Revenue officer hiding behind a tree just a few paces away white with terror, a musket in his shaking arms. Tom locked eyes with the man, who seemed to be stuck on the sight of Tom West with a child in his arms, a child directly in his line of fire – the man pulled the trigger. Tom twisted, putting his back between Molly and the bullet, almost dropping her as the shot took a slice from his shoulder, and she screamed.

Tom floundered, just for a moment, lost in Molly's green eyes. He smiled. 'No need to be afeared.'

Tom hurled Molly over his other shoulder just as Nathan caught his arm and urged him into the water. He tried to keep Molly still while gripping his belt, saving pistol and powder. The night sky was studded with red embers that died as quickly as they came alive. Grabbing the ladder, he thought Molly weighed more than any barrel of brandy he'd ever hefted overside. Hands reached for him.

'Get the boy below! My cabin!' He passed Molly to Shaun.

'But, Cap'n—'

Tom shoved Shaun towards the hatch, turning back to the gunwale.

'What are you doing?' screamed Nathan.

'All hands fire upon them!'

Gunfire leapt over the estuary, the lustre of new blood. Tom jumped into the river. Chips of blazing wood rained down on him. He heard two officers on the bank arguing as they tried to reload. Tom waded from the shallows, found the collar of one man and slammed him against a tree, kicking the other in the chest, stamping on the fingers that clawed at him.

At first, she couldn't think: explosions rocked the ship, each shot showing her a red blanket threaded with gold, dark panels scored with knife marks, a desk cluttered with paper. The smell of salt and rotting sacks. Someone shouted in pain nearby, and the violence of it sent her scrambling under the desk. A flash at the porthole illuminated the open chest next to her: clothes, boots, and something sharp that cut her. Molly seized the bone-handled knife.

The door crashed open. Splinters sprayed Molly. Two men fell into the room. One of them was the angry man who'd ridden with them here. Hellard. Metal glinted. Hellard fell on top of the other man. There was the sound of flesh hitting flesh, and then a groan, and harsh breaths.

'Please. Please don't—'

And then there was a bang. A man in a red uniform without a face, just a hole, which Hellard continued to stamp with his boot.

Voices. The cabin filled weak yellow. Molly saw Tom in the doorway and wanted to run to him, but the dead man and Hellard were in the way.

'For the love of God, Hellard – he's done!' Tom stepped over the dead man's still-twitching boots. Hellard followed Tom's movement. His eyes landed on her. More sailors clustered in the doorway, a tall man with sandy hair, and the younger boy with dark curls and wide eyes, the boy who'd ridden with them here. Benedict.

'We've got more dead Revenue on the deck,' said Benedict. He was looking directly at Molly. 'We've got to flee.'

'Just set sail, shall we?' said Hellard.

'I don't know,' said Benedict. 'I don't know.'

'Who's the boy?' asked the tall man.

'Can't let him go, least not now,' said Hellard. 'He saw me shoot the bugger you're standing in, besides anything else.'

Tom's frown made her shrink further under the desk. But then he smiled, just a little, what Mama called his crams smile: pressed on to his face. He reached for her, opening his hand.

Molly gave him the knife.

'That's my boy,' he said.

III

The storm becalmed before the girl. Tom battled to coax her to stillness, to a fixity that left the child staring at the ceiling of the cabin, rigid, almost choking on the warm cider he held to her lips. He rocked her in the bed Nathan had built for him, nailed into the cabin, the only bed in Tom's life ever to fit him. *One leg in the water.* The wind exhausted itself. She turned into his body, foot bumping against his gun. The love token he'd given Grace when Molly was born hung on a leather thong around her neck, gleaming with her sweat. It was only when she stopped shaking that Tom realised he was shaking too.

'I'll take care of you,' he said. 'I couldn't stop Dick English killing your mother. But I saw him dead for it. I know I'm not your father, but I swore the day you were born. You're mine, you understand? And you always will be. I'll live up to my word.'

Molly met his gaze, looked for those eyes that held her as if she were the most important thing in the world. As if – as he once whispered into her hair, lying in bed with Mama – the green eyes of the Tucker girls would be what he missed most, should the Lord see fit to take his sight. Why God would do this, Molly did not know, but she seized those words now: He would miss me the most.

'We are going to tell a story,' said Tom. Grace had told Molly stories from the cradle, and the child developed them, play-acting for him when he visited. She was a wildego, this girl. Proper riptackle. Though, when he called her that, Grace told him to consider why a girl child who took after boys in manner was commonly compared to a riptackle: a badly broken horse, ripping its harness to pieces. Grace let her wear her hair short, wear breeches, when the fancy took her. *Let her play-act*, she said. Pretend to be a king, pretend to be a knight, pretend to be a smuggler. Pretend to be a queen, Joan of Arc, an actress. *Let her play-act freedom. Maybe it'll come into being.* Let her throw off the harness Grace had always bucked against.

Tom stroked her shorn curls. He hadn't intended to pass her as a boy – wasn't sure why, when Hellard called her one, he grabbed it. Just as he wasn't sure why he had accepted Hellard's account – to save himself from Benedict's judgement, or Molly's? She would never have to know the truth of what he'd done. She would be hidden as a boy from anyone looking for a missing girl. It would keep her safe, too, from the men on the ship, who'd take advantage of a girl, as she grew older. Though, of course, he'd find a home for her before then.

'You and I,' he said now, 'we're going to play-act that you're a boy, like you did with Mama, sometimes. And you're going to stay with me, on the ship.'

'Women curse ships,' she said. 'That's what you told Mama.'

Grace had replied, lightly: *Maybe ships curse women.*

'You're not going to be a woman,' he said. 'You're going to be a boy. For now. Until I can find somewhere safer.'

She jerked from him. 'You won't leave me?'

Tom pulled her back, afraid she'd convulse again. 'I won't, I won't. As long as you're a boy, you can stay here, with me. You like our games, don't you? Our duels and battles? Here –' he offered her the bone-handled knife – 'you can play with this.'

Molly carefully took it. She sat up, and pointed the blade at him, as she had in a thousand games.

Tom opened his hands. He smelt salt – but it wasn't the sea, it was his own fear. 'Surrender. I'm yours.'

She slept, resting on his chest, where Grace's journal waited inside his coat.

Tom listened to the men chasing water from the ship, listened to the laments from the cob cottages of Frogmore Creek, from the battered fruit trees and lean-tos, between which the men would string up the sails to dry. All of it – the five fingers of the Avon, blue twists shaping the hills, the wet soil and dog roses, the sunken lanes and tunnels formed from trees – pressed in on the ship, on him, telling him: *Escape.* Escape. But the tide was against him.

He eased the journal free. The pages were wet, moved in waves, collapsing with his sense of order. He found a conversation early in their courtship, if it had been that.

Grace: 'Please, leave the money, if it will ease your heart.'

Tom: 'My heart? I'm not your husband.'

Grace: 'No. But you are here.'

Tom: 'Perhaps I miss you.'

Grace: 'I doubt it.'

Tom: 'What else draws me to you, then?'

20

Tom still remembered Grace's arched eyebrows as she said, *I doubt it*, and the way he replied, like he really wanted an answer, an explanation: *What draws me to you, then?*

What drew me to it?

Tom's eyes, swollen and gritted, moved over his desk, bolted to the boards and overflowing with curling papers. Beneath it, his sea chest stood open. It was a tradition to paint the inside of the lid. His crew painted hills, farms, fences. Tom's was blank.

That was what had drawn him to her.

Tom had met Kit in the Pilchard Inn. Tom was eighteen then and Kit the same, although seeming so much younger. Tom's body had already suffered over a decade of hard work and hard blows. The worst blow Kit had received was his father's spiteful tongue. Tom remembered Kit slipping into the inn, looking for all the world like a prince come among his people in what he thought was a good disguise, to ask if he could buy Tom a drink.

It was beginning to get that way, even then: men offering him things, men shaking his hand. Ezekiel Day, Tom's first captain, had died before custom duties were raised on imported goods. Tom never had the chance to see what Ezekiel would have made of the opportunity, but he had learnt well enough to make of it anything he himself wanted. By the time Kit appeared in the Pilchard Inn, Tom and Hellard had raised investors and were taking their first cutter out to France, a fore-and-aft rig. Tom needed money, so he welcomed the new prince, who would turn out to be a pauper.

Kit bought him cloudy ale and sat down. He talked of nothing but his beautiful prize: Grace. Talked of wooing: the petticoat cloth he had bought her; the silk scarf; the brass candlestick. Even a chamber pot. All before her father cut off his advances. He talked of the gimmel ring he had borrowed money to purchase. Two bands of metal, one worn by him and

21

one by her while they were betrothed, and then joined together on her finger after they eloped. He described it in such detail, Tom felt he himself had slipped the ring over her small knuckle. Soft gold and silver, with two clasping hands at each end.

'Have you seen much Dryden?' Kit asked. Tom remembered Hellard's rasp of laughter – was Hellard laughing at such prattle, or the idea that Tom might know what gentry knew? 'In "Don Sebastian",' Kit said, 'he describes a ring just as I have given my lady wife.'

Joins so close to not be perceived, yet each other's counterpart. Something like that. Kit claimed he was Grace's counterpart; he made her whole, and only him. He described their wedding night with all the detail a drunken young man could muster to impress Tom West. He divided Grace into portions for Tom, offering a little more and a little more – thighs, breasts, lips – as if he were selling her virtues to a new buyer, as if this was a seduction. It was Kit's only currency, and he wanted to buy a new life from Tom. He described the sounds she made when he first entered her. Such words as would never be uttered if Kit were in a parlour, sipping Tom's tea, instead of in an inn, gulping Tom's Florence wine.

Here, in her journal, Grace recorded the night with shrinking letters: *When it came to it, I felt my body close, and, as Christopher pushed to enter, the muscles therein resisted only further, with no help but Christopher's spittle – added with what seemed a smile of embarrassment – and the pain was the greatest I have ever felt. I wanted to tell him to stop, but* . . . Now, Tom blotted the words, printing blood over Grace's shaking imagery – an axe cleaving a tree, a needle pushed into her body – and the hour she spent in the kitchen afterwards, with Christopher asleep, her bare feet numb on the stones and her white-knuckled hands clenched in her lap, breathing through the remaining throbs.

As he listened to Kit in the Pilchard Inn, Tom had felt

something – but it could not have been envy. He did not even know the woman. And such wooing was for fools. A chamber pot, God's blood.

Kit told Tom he found pauper wooing *truer*.

'What truth do you find in it?'

'The expressions of love: the poor require no precious gifts, they are ... simple, like you.'

The table hushed.

'Simple? Am I so easy, then? You know what I will do next?'

Kit laughed. 'You are more base, Tom: you act on what you want. Your wooing is from the earth.'

Tom remembered forcing his fists to relax, thinking: You are lucky. Usually what I do next is punch a man to the floor. But the word 'base' stopped him. It made him smile and say instead, 'Mine is from the sea, my friend, not the earth, and if you find you're having trouble wooing your young and eager wife, I'm happy to step in.'

Kit blushed at the crew's whooping. And then explained: he wanted to carve Grace a stool or a spoon, like pauper men did their wives, but he could not carve.

'You say she reads a strange amount,' said Tom. 'Why not a bookshelf? I'll take it in hand.'

And he had. He'd intended to ask Nathan. But, walking in the tawny woods along Wonwell Beach, he'd begun to collect soft driftwood and hard oak. He imagined the bookshelf he would make such a lady.

As he carved and nailed, he told himself it was only that: imagining. He would not give it to Kit, of course. But making it – where could the harm be in that? As he joined the wood, he thought about the books that would sit on those shelves, and realised he did not know what they could be, beyond the Bible. He had never niggled a woman who could read or write. What sorts of books were there in the world? When deciding on the engravings, he gently scraped two hawks, his eyes entirely focused on the blade, refusing to see what he was doing. Or feeling. It couldn't be envy, not for a spit of a boy who thought he was something. Nor for a lady with a mind, who knew the world and still chose Kit. Tom had never even met her.

He sent the bookshelf to Bantham on the back of a cart. Kit gave it to Grace. And Tom never mentioned to anyone that he had built a bookshelf with wood taken from land and sea.

The next time Kit visited the Pilchard Inn, he asked to join Tom's crew. He said he was after an adventure. Tom refused. He established a supply base on Guernsey to hold tobacco for him. Ran a race with Dartmouth's new Revenue cutter, and somehow won. Everyone shook his hand, and when he turned away they whispered a rumour that would not die: as the two boats kissed keels, Tom had lifted his pistol and shot the captain in the head. Kit kept coming back to the Pilchard, drunk and self-pitying, asking to be taken on an adventure. And eventually Tom said yes. Why? Did he know it would lead him to her doorstep?

Perhaps it was because I missed you, he had said to her, on just their third or fourth meeting after so many years of imagining.

Tom turned her journal to the first page.

I left home today. I shall never be allowed back. I shall never be received in society. I have defied the laws of King and God. I am eighteen years of age.

I rely on Christopher now. Can we create the home we whispered of in those breathless moments hidden by the harpsichord's song, or the careful wilderness of the garden?

We have come to Bantham. The coast is strange to me, and the people who live along it even stranger. My home

on the moor is now thirty miles away. I feel like Drake,
standing on the beach of a new world. What life we could
have here, if our fancies were made real. Christopher talks
of building a grand establishment once he has received
his estates. What manner of husband will Christopher be?
And what wife I? What kind of mother shall I make? Now
I look upon it, I am visited by how truly little we know of
men before we marry, and how little I know of myself.

Myself. I am a postscript to a story not of my writing.
Now is the time. Now is the time for my own story.

The book was trembling in his hands. He had hurled the
bookshelf across the kitchen, breaking the joins, destroying
her Aphra Behn and Duchess of Newcastle, her Shakespeare,
her Bible. Molly had asked him once, *Do you ever cry, when you
leave us?* He'd lied, telling her he couldn't cry. He had tears on
his face now.

Grace never cried, even in those years when Kit spent most
days from home while waiting for what he called 'the great
patriarch to finally draw his stinking last'. Grace spent her
days reading and writing: 'I have found a spot upon the rocks
to write with all the sea in my view. My stories should be as
wide as that view; the confines of the cottage scare me.' And
when Kit did return home: the pain of their lovemaking, and
Kit's promise she would soon be great-bellied, for what would
be the first of her labours. Rumours plagued her: that she wore
a gown fit for a royal ball to be wed in; that she pleasured the
priest before the ceremony as payment. When Tom heard the
last in the Pilchard, he looked to Kit, expecting the boy to whip
the fool who uttered it, but he only flushed uselessly. It was Tom
who knocked the man down.

Grace's accent seemed to make the local villagers step backwards: 'So I am growing used to the gradual fill of the estuary,

the smell of seaweed being covered, the sound of eddies and rock pools filling, the slap of waves against the rocks, the startled egrets, and then its draining once more – nature's theatre for my company. Buried here in the hills, the avenue of escape an ocean-mouth: endless horizon.'

Then Kit's father died, and no money followed. 'Christopher returned in such temper, three dishes smashed and myself feared he would strike me. The will has left him out. He says we should have waited to marry, that I was rash and foolish to believe that our parents would soften to our marrying when it was irreversible. It is now "you" and "your plan" – his doings are nowhere near it. There will be no money, and no immediate way from this shore.'

That's when Tom's name first appeared in Grace's journal: 'Christopher says he will turn our luck with Tom West. He is a smuggler or free-trader in these parts, held in such high esteem you could mistake him for Sir Gawain leapt from the ballad pages. I have never seen him, but whisperings create an image of a man seven feet tall, versed equally in swordplay, gunplay and heart-play. Christopher says he has invested what we have left in the man's runs to France. So now I must hope that this Tom West really is worth a tuppenny ballad.'

Grace lost the first child. She was pregnant with the second when Tom finally met her. Confined, until Tom broke her confinement.

Morning: too early for fishermen or lime boats. Kneeling over her vegetables, Grace had not raised her head to watch the breeze fan the gold-white light across the estuary, or to listen to the birds greet the ocean, hidden from view by the sweep of sandbank and cliff – all of which watched Tom as he approached. She was the last to see him coming, and even then she didn't know what she saw.

'Christopher,' she said, not moving.

'Tom West.'

Grace looked up into the sun. Her first impression, she wrote, was that a tall, dark oak had taken root in front of her damson tree, and then, suddenly rootless, the tree moved and light poured around it, drawing the outline of a man with something – someone – hanging from one shoulder. The legendary Tom West, with her husband on his back.

'Pleasure to meet you, Mrs Tucker.'

Grace blinked. 'Is he . . . ?'

'A little heavy,' said Tom. 'Could you point me to the bedroom?'

'Sir?'

'Unless you want him to sleep it off in the bushes?'

Grace flushed an even deeper red. She stood up. Soil showered from her lap. 'This way, Mr West.'

The hallway was narrow and there was a strained moment when both gestured for the other to go first, and they became stuck, Christopher's boot almost catching Grace in the face. She pressed herself against the wall, eyes on the floor. Tom went on, stopped, turned right.

When Grace came to stand in the doorway, Tom was bowing over the bed. Christopher toppled on to the mattress with a bounce. Tom followed, forehead coming to rest at Christopher's legs.

'Mr West?'

Tom rose quickly, but instead of looking straight at her he glanced about the bedroom, lingering on a miniature of a country squire, another of a woman with disappointment etched into her face. A pendant dangled above the bed; at first, he took it for a glass bauble. When he recognised it for crystal from a chandelier, he turned to make a study of Grace.

'How did Kit come to possess a pretty thing like you?'

'I am no thing, sir, and he does not possess me.' She never could back down.

27

'How unfortunate for him.'

'Mr West, I think you may have had more drink than is proper. Please—'

'Not yet, but another would help me on my way.'

'Mr Tucker does not keep alcohol.'

'How unfortunate for him,' Tom repeated, and Grace felt he was laughing at her. He was. Then: 'You have nothing for a thirsty man?'

'Mr West, I must ask—'

'I've carried your husband on my back from Burgh Island, Mrs Tucker.'

Grace breathed. 'I will give you water.'

She turned, crossing into the kitchen. Tom West did not follow her. She found him on one knee in the vegetable patch, the last carrot in his hand.

'You pulled up the bunch instead of thinning out,' he said, rising to accept the cup.

'I was . . . ' Grace began, and then stopped as he sat down on the wall.

Legs swinging, he looked up at the loose thatching. She watched the breeze play with his open collar. In years to come, she'd dip her fingers beneath his collar, probing the muscles there, the scar tissue. She noted in her journal that people called Tom a handsome devil, with the devil's own luck – as for herself, did she see anything handsome in his giant's frame, these broad shoulders and strong arms that hauled barrels up cliffs? In his slender waist and long legs, which would mount a horse well, she imagined, or his cropped hair, so against the fashion, and as dark as his eyes? Or his face, which mapped the fights of his youth, recalling White Hart Passage in Kingsbridge, though she didn't know that, where the mason had forgone cobbles for sheep knuckles, packing row on row of glistening white bone with damp earth – when a man got knocked down and struck his cheekbone on the ground, the ground struck right back. Much of his face had been shaped that way, like metal in a smith. Grace described what she saw, but declined to comment on what she took from it. As for the devil – well, all men were devils, Tom's mother used to say.

'The King over the water,' he said, raising his cup as his eyes dropped down her body. 'Congratulations.'

'Pardon?'

'The baby.'

Grace's hand went to her stomach.

'Kit didn't say nothing,' he said.

A wren landed on the bucket and jumped in and out, wings twitching.

'I have not told him,' said Grace. 'Yet.'

Tom's gaze settled on the hand still holding the slight bump. 'You can trust me. Though, I understand you don't hold me in the high esteem your neighbours do.'

'Understand this, sir: I have not asked Mr Tucker to stop free-trading because of your reputation.'

Tom's smile stretched to show his teeth. 'I understand entirely, Mrs Tucker. But, may I ask: how *do* you like your heroes?'

'Hero?'

'What I am to most.'

Grace looked past his smug smile to his stone eyes. 'With a little more soap, and a little less murder, Mr West.'

That almost knocked him down. 'Heroes have always slain the dragon. That's what makes them heroes.'

'Stories do that.'

'I hate to disagree with a lady,' he said, setting the cup down, 'but I've never murdered a man, and I'm not made by tales – I make 'em. It's been a pleasure, Mrs Tucker, and I apologise for misspeaking.'

'Which instance, sir?'

Tom laughed. 'I don't believe a man could ever possess a woman like you. But it's a lucky son of a bitch who comes close.'

Grace stopped her gasp, but thought she saw him smirk all the same. 'Thank you for bringing Mr Tucker home.'

Tom bowed, arm sweeping.

'And –' Grace began, tripping as his eyes flicked up – 'for your silence.'

Tom remembered her gaze locked on to his – remembered her trust.

He opened the journal to its last pages. When the account of her last week came together, Tom dropped the book.

Molly flinched awake, reaching for the knife – and found Tom retching over the side of the bed. She put her arms around him.

The Day After the Great Storm

I

Overnight, Bayards Cove had ceased being a dock. It was a graveyard now for broken sloops and ailing yachts and snapped rowboats. The river churned with tubs and crates. Sails ballooned with water, like the swollen cattle drowned upstream. Richard English leant over the cobbled bank, ready to take the next armful of nets and rope and shoes from the man in the dinghy, one of many trying to clear the wreckage. Down the quay, Bayards Cove Fort was brought to life again, long since replaced by the castle, but now a safe haven, some catching their breath there, others saved by its walls and refusing to come out. The chain slung across the rivermouth between Dartmouth and Kingswear, which kept French boats from the harbour, had snapped before the men had a chance to take it down, ripped clean free of its rock bed. The whole town had come apart – the army, the Revenue, the fishermen, the church – all in one night of God's wrath. What had they done to deserve it? That's what Richard's wife had asked him that morning; what his riding officers had asked him; what even the priest had asked him. What did we do to deserve this?

Richard knew the answer – saw the answer, in fact, coming

towards him now, around the corner on to the quay. Richard rose, straightened his jacket. He bowed. 'Collector Blackoller, sir. A terrible day.'

'Most, most terrible,' sighed Blackoller, looking down at this pent-up little man. It simply couldn't be more tiresome to have to put Richard English in his place after last night's losses. 'You are helping in the recovery, I see. Good man.'

'It's my duty, sir,' said Richard, watching the twitch at Blackoller's right eye.

'Not really,' said Blackoller, 'but it's good to see you in the spirit of things – to a point.'

Richard took off his hat, touched his bandaged wound, and replaced it. 'Sir?'

'I've just seen one of your men being tended for injuries. He tells me you led a raid last night on Tom West.'

'My duty, sir.'

Blackoller managed a tight smile. 'To a point.'

Richard kept his face passive. Around them, men and women shouted to each other – 'Grab that!' 'Hold this!' 'Someone help me!' – all hard at work, putting back together what should never have broken in the first place. He knew Blackoller's sloop had gone down last night, and its contents with it. The collector – the Revenue's highest father, who took all of the money gathered from Customs – had been given a sloop by the crown in 1700 to help stem the tide of smuggled goods into Dartmouth. Instead, he used it to start his own small operation. His brandy was salt water now, and that alone restrained Richard when the collector laid a gloved hand on his arm.

Surprising strength there, Blackoller thought, for a boy who arrived too early into the world; a boy whose mother almost gave him up for dead; a son whose father, even today, spoke of him as limp, weak, unable to stand up for himself. 'Listen to me, Richard,' said Blackoller. 'There's duty, and there's zeal. I've told you this before. It's important to respect economies. Tom West is part of our economy. I've given you a loose leash, hmm? But time to rein it in now, boy.'

Richard imagined himself the knight entombed in stone in the church, forced to endure the fondling of inferior men for eternity. 'Yes, sir.'

Blackoller smiled. 'There we go. Take the world as we find it, hmm? I know you've always had a pure cut to you. Well, look at you, here in the Revenue, instead of your father's trading company! One son set to inherit, one son high up in the Navy and you – runt of the litter, your father calls you, not that I say it's kind of him. But you wouldn't have scraps from his table, hmm? Set out to straighten the world up! Just keep to your limits, boy, keep to your limits.'

Richard dragged salt air into his lungs. 'Are you telling me to desist in my pursuit of Tom West, sir?'

'Dear me, no. How could I? Just don't go about it with such *vigour*. After all, what point is there to it? His ship is twice as fast as any Customs cutter or sloop – faster even than the Navy boys – and bigger than any regular smuggling vessel, well armed as she is.'

'We could build faster ships. We could buy the design from Tom's shipwright, Nathan de Bosco.'

'With what money?'

Richard fingered his hat again. 'What if a witness swore against him? Would you bring him down then?'

'Swore he's a free-trader? No chance of that, my boy, while Devon profits. And, if you want to catch him at it, you have to bring him *and* the goods in. If you couldn't manage it last night, when the man was trapped, what hope is there for us mere mortals? And, besides, Devon loves a scoundrel.'

'What if a witness swore he's a murderer?'

'Did you see him personally kill anyone last night? And do you have witnesses to corroborate your statement?'

'Not exactly, sir.'

'No. The men under *your* employ died by the storm, because *you* ordered them into it. You're lucky you keep your commission at all, sir, and it is only because we do not wish to shame your father.'

'What if he and his brother murdered a woman and her child?'

'Lord defend us!' A shadow drew Blackoller's attention to the circle of a buzzard. 'You do tell the most lurid tales. Can you produce the bodies?'

'The fire, the flood – everything was destroyed.'

'And did you witness these heinous murders?'

Through gritted teeth this time: 'Not exactly, sir.'

'But you were there?'

'Yes.'

'On your own?'

'Yes.'

'Why?'

'He assaulted me. Hellard West struck an officer of the law. They left me to burn.'

'Do you have a witness to this?'

'Is my word not enough?'

'How about a witness to say it was the brothers West who killed the lady and child, and not yourself?'

'Myself?'

'Between you and Tom West, Richard, who do you think more likely to win a contest of popularity? Between the two of you, who profits Devon? Whom does Devon *need*? Whom does she *love*?'

'I am speaking of justice.'

The collector sighed, a shrug rippling through his body. To

Richard, the man looked like jelly waiting to be flicked. 'Do promise me you'll be less zealous in your desire to ... to –' he looked about the ruined quay – 'to *clean up*. Yes?'

'Sir.'

'There's a good boy.'

Richard bowed as the collector bustled away. Then he swore, and the fisherman near him jumped. He raised a hand in apology and, with his other, drew out his flask. He was trembling when he took the first sip.

Boy. That's what Mrs Tucker had called him in her cottage, last week: *You come here like a conquering hero, sir, but I know better. Leave me out of your boys' games.*

He'd gripped her arm then, pinned her to the seat, spitting: 'Heed me.'

She was unyielding in his grip, but also non-resistant. 'Yes, sir.'

'Is that what you say to Tom West?' he asked, so close he could press his mouth to hers. '"Yes, sir"?'

'No, sir.'

He brushed the hair from her face. The child looked on from the fireplace, crouched, silent, watching. 'No?'

'He does not require it of me.'

'Require *what?*'

'Submission,' said Mrs Tucker.

Richard had laughed. 'You really think Tom West, of all men, is not desirous of mastering this cottage, and everything in it, every time he mounts you?'

'You don't know him.'

'If you think that, girl, you're even more a fool than you appear. And you will realise it only when it is too late.'

And she had, trusting Tom West to the last. Richard tried to regain mastery of his lungs now: emptied grain sacks. He sat down on a crate and told himself, as Mother used to,

Breathe, angel, breathe. But it was his father's voice that finally made his lungs kick open: *For fuck's sake, pygmy, how long must we suffer you?*

He would have Tom West. The monster that had pushed him to last night's events, to driving Grace and his men into the storm of Tom West's murderousness. It was Tom West who had left Richard to wake in hellfire, forced to flee from the oven before he could carry the whore's body out for Christian burial, or save the child – a torment that would haunt him for ever, that he'd left an innocent soul to burn to death. It was Tom West who had brought that stain on Richard's soul. He would have him hung in chains. He would see the whole Revenue purified. He would see that they all suffered him.

II

An ache stretched inside Benedict's skull, pushing at his eyeballs, kicking as he knocked on Tom's cabin door. A grunt from inside. Benedict pushed, hit by the reek of grief. The child slept beneath Tom's blanket. The huge man sat on the chair beside the bed, studying her face in the reluctant morning light.

'What do you want?'

'Captain. Tom. What are you going to do with her?'

Tom did not look up, just drew something from his boot – a clasp knife, which flicked opened as he gestured: *Get out.* Benedict tripped back, through the hold, ducking beneath waterlogged hammocks and clambering over spilt barrels, to the stern, which the men called Tom's Court. Benedict only knew Tom was following when a heavy hand closed around his neck, steering him into the table. He turned to face Tom, but leant back as far as he could when he saw the knife was still in Tom's hand. The corner of the table needled his spine.

'What did you say?'

'Only that – what do you mean to do with her?'

Tom swivelled the knife this way and that. '"Her"?'

'Molly.'

Tom closed the gap between them. 'That *boy* in there is going to be with us for a few days, and then disappear.'

Benedict couldn't force enough saliva into his dry mouth to talk.

'And, until then, you're going to keep an eye on him.'

'I can't—'

'If I tell you to look after him, that's what you'll damn well do.'

'None of this is my fault!'

'*Excuse me?*'

'I'm not a part of this,' said Benedict. 'I'm not guilty of anything.'

Tom seized Benedict's collar. The shirt tightened around his neck like a noose.

'And I am?' hissed Tom.

Benedict gripped Tom's hand. 'Sir, it's me. Please.'

'We're all guilty. Got it? She's dead.' His voice rusted. 'That child has no mother. I have no— We're all guilty. You'll lie, as long as you want those eyes to stay in your head. It's the only way to keep her safe.'

'But you said it's just for a few days.'

Tom drew his hand over his mouth, and then cast about, finding a bottle of brandy. He urged Benedict to sit, to drink. 'You took a few knocks last night.' Tom smiled, tugging a smile from Benedict. 'Son, you know I'd never let anything happen to you. I need you. I need your eyes. If I could trade Hellard and have you for a little brother instead . . .'

But Benedict didn't laugh. He was studying the brandy. 'Tom, sir, last night, Hellard . . . '

'What about him?'

'He stood against you. Can you trust him?'

There was a curse, someone tripping on the loose shots, and Tom turned to see Hellard blundering in the hold. Hellard picked up a broken bottle, threw it into a heap of sails. Tom called to him.

'Brother,' said Hellard, righting a toppled chair. 'Benedict, you look set to piss yourself. Sorting out our story, are we?'

'There is no story,' said Tom.

'Oho. That's it? You don't want your crew knowing you beat your women? You followed the law, Tom, and if Dick hadn't taken the shot, well – you'd have nothing to fear from your men on that score.'

'I suppose you're going to tell me what I should fear.'

Hellard shrugged. 'No need for the crew to know it was your loose tongue that nearly ended us all. Nor your mercy that will threaten us again.'

'Mercy.' From anyone else, this might have been a question, or a plea. From Tom, it was a lead weight.

'A little bird flew up the estuary to whisper in my ear. Turns out even a pity-hole can't keep Dick English. Should've shot the bastard. So many items to keep mumchance – wonder if I'll manage.'

The ship lurched, another gust. Benedict grabbed the table to keep from sliding. Hellard hung on to the door. Tom reached for nothing, held up by nothing, his balance the ship's balance, and, as Hellard tried to find his footing, Tom picked him up by the neck.

Tom's whisper at Hellard's ear was the murmur of low tide. 'No one is going to know – that I hurt her, or anything beyond that. It was English, and I left him to burn because that's what he deserves. That child is *never* going to know what I did to his mother. You started this story. You want to keep breathing, keep telling it, Hellard.'

Benedict couldn't hear the words, but watched Hellard try to conceal the punch of shock in his gut, and fail. The dirty halo wasn't blinding Tom today.

'That's right,' he croaked. 'That's right.'

Tom dropped him. 'Then we all know where we stand.'

'Yes,' said Hellard, hand to his throat. 'On your ship.' A snake grin. 'By your grace.'

Benedict waited for Tom to slash Hellard's throat. But he held himself, as the ship shuddered about him.

Hellard was the son of Josias West and a whore, thrust into the arms of the Navy as a powder monkey as soon as he could black a boot. Tom learnt of his half-brother through taproom gossip. He got him out of service. When he brought him home to his mother, Hellard was a bag of broken bones. Hellard rose with Tom in Ezekiel Day's crew, was there when Tom got his first ship, was there when ... Hellard was always there. Benedict had the sense Hellard was Tom's shadow. Sometimes, Tom enjoyed dancing with his shadow. Other times, he wanted to burn it away.

And Hellard – Hellard had been cast out before he was even born. He would tell a priest that Tom was the only soul who had ever chosen him. He would tell a bartender Tom was their father incarnate – that all Hellard's rejections were seeded in Tom, the strongest son, the most beloved, the most feared, the son who finally beat their father, when Hellard never could. It was never clear which confessor Hellard was more disposed to lie to, and which he saw as sacrosanct.

And Tom – did he tolerate Hellard because he was hell-bent on being a better man than his father? Or was he simply hell-bent, and Hellard the devil in his ear?

Either way, Tom squeezed Hellard's shoulder now, and Hellard chuckled.

'No fret, Tom. You and me, we've got a future to build, ain't that right? Always been us together. Never let you down. Right?'

'That's right,' said Tom.

'So, what's the boy's name?' said Hellard.

'Orlando,' said Tom. It was the name Grace had intended during her first two pregnancies, believing them – rightly – to be boys. They'd died with their names. 'Orlando West.'

Leaf

To INTERLEA/VE. v. a. [*inter* and *leave*]

To chequer a book by the insertion of blank leaves.

In *A Room of One's Own*, Virginia Woolf writes, 'For most of history, Anonymous was a woman.' How we remember history determines history. Women did not play a marginal role in our national story; it is the marginal remembrance of women that marginalises us.

Take Daniel Defoe. Studying eighteenth-century English litera-ture at university, I was told that Daniel Defoe invented the novel, and Daniel Defoe invented the travelogue. Aphra Behn, who was writing novels decades before Defoe, didn't get a look-in. Neither did Celia Fiennes, who wrote her tour of Britain before Defoe wrote his. There is good form for this elision. Celia Fiennes' first entry into what Sir Walter Scott called 'the kingdom of fiction' was unannounced and uncredited. In 1812, the poet Robert Southey published a miscellany titled *Omniana; or, Horae Otiosiores*; trans-lated literally, the title means *Notes or Scraps of Information About All Kinds of Things; or, Idler Hours*. One of Southey's scraps was an account of a long-distance race in Windsor Park between an Englishman and a Scot, and a description of the funeral of Queen Mary II. Southey had taken these passages from a travelogue written by Celia Fiennes around 1710, titled *Through England on a Side Saddle in the time of William and Mary*. Southey said he found the passages in 'the manuscript journal of a lady who was one of the spectators'. He did not give her name, although he knew it. His friend Charles Danvers, the grandson of Celia Fiennes' cousin William Danvers, had provided Southey with the manuscript.

(A brief detour: by the time Robert Southey became poet laureate, he was giving advice to Charlotte Brontë, who sent him her poetry. He advised her that, though 'it showed talent', she should 'give up thoughts of becoming a poet': 'Literature cannot be the business of a woman's life and ought not to be. The more she engages in her proper duties, the less leisure she will have for it, even as ... recreation.'

Oh, do fuck off, Robert Southey.

Brontë assured him: 'I have endeavoured not only attentively to observe the duties a woman ought to fulfill but to feel deeply interested in them. I don't always succeed, for sometimes when I'm teaching or sewing I would rather be reading or writing; but I try to deny myself.'

I try to deny myself.)

Celia's manuscript appeared next as an anonymous quarto, for seven guineas, in 1856. Her name would not appear on the cover until the twentieth century.

Daniel Defoe wrote what is generally regarded as the first modern travel narrative of Great Britain about ten years after Celia wrote her account. His *Tour through the Whole Island of Great Britain* was published 1724–6. Whenever Fiennes and Defoe are mentioned together, critics are sure to point out that she cannot have influenced him, given the delayed emergence of her manuscript. They add that the two did not even know each other.

Both Fiennes and Defoe write about Devon in their travelogues, and the legend of Captain Tom West, smuggler, hero – and murderer.

Daniel Defoe died in 1731, a fugitive from old and possibly false debts. Celia Fiennes died a decade later.

Daniel Defoe's eldest son, also called Daniel, witnessed her will.

(Notes for a lecture on women and writing, to be given at Girton College, Cambridge, on the anniversary of Virginia Woolf's lecture series, 'A Room of One's Own'.)

Such an Idea of England

1724

Celia & Daniel

'Mr Defoe to see you, ma'am.'

Defoe heard a cough from the parlour. Winter had sunk his chest too. In the delay, the maid studied him as if worried he might be off with the family plate.

'Please, show him in.'

Tweaking the satin bow around the manuscript in his arms, he sidled through the door.

Struggling light, tangled in Miss Fiennes' fruit trees outside, made Defoe's curiosity wait. First, he had measure of a pair of Japan tortoiseshell cabinets and a Japan tea chest, then a Dutch lamp, a cloister of empty chairs, and finally Miss Fiennes, seated on an ebony couch by the fire, now rising to greet him. Yes, the face of a woman whose father plotted regicide; a woman who rode to the peak of the Malvern Hills in order to have nothing limit her eyes but distance – rode all England, side-saddle on a donkey, to have nothing limit her eyes but distance.

'Would that we had met younger, ma'am.' He raised her manuscript. 'We could have shared some adventures.'

'I, sir, am as young as I ever was.'

'I have no trouble believing it,' he said.

Celia watched him pick at the Irish stitch of his chair, most likely estimating its cost. The news that Mr Defoe would soon publish his *Tour thro' the Whole Island of Great Britain* had sent her, three nights in a row, to her own manuscript, left to moulder in a drawer these twenty-four years. She packaged it in strong garden-er's twine for Mr Review, for Defoe the Hosier. She told him she desired to meet him, and, more, if he had the patience for irregular spelling, to exchange journeys. It did not matter if he had only undertaken half the journeys he claimed. It was the *idea*, as much for him as for her, she felt. Such an idea of England.

'I compliment you on your home, Miss Fiennes.'

'You are kind, sir. I think you are at Newington?'

'As far from the stench of sin and sea coal as I dare.' Mr Defoe placed the manuscript – which had looked at breaking point in his hands – on the table between them. 'Thank you for the opportu-nity of reading your travels, ma'am.'

Mrs Whithall eased in, carrying the silver tea set, as she'd asked. Celia didn't want Mr Defoe to know quite how far her nephew had ventured in the South Sea Bubble.

The door closed.

'You enjoyed the county of Devon most on your journeys, sir, it seemed?'

'I do not remember the like in any one place in England,' he said.

'Yes – those lanes going up hill and down, riding higher and higher 'til you see a great valley full of lesser hills and enclosures, quick-set hedges and trees, red earth and no roads. More than once, I found myself stuck behind horses, unable to turn around, those lanes are so narrow, even with the goods piled high on the horses' backs in panniers, so as not to take up another inch.'

'And the *goods* they transport,' he said. 'If I could write on one topic my whole life, it would be trade.'

'And that says nothing of the free trade.'

'Ah, yes – I see from your *Journeys* you enjoy a good French wine,' he said.

'And I see from your books that, as much as you might enjoy writing of serge and tin, you enjoy writing romance more, however *improper.*'

A grin, as quick to vanish as a goldfinch in spring blossom. 'Have you been reading things you shouldn't, Miss Fiennes?'

'Whenever I can, Mr Defoe. How you frown. You write your adventures without shame for Mrs Whithall, but would not recommend *Moll Flanders* or *Roxana* to me?'

'Miss Fiennes, the rhyme goes,

Down in the kitchen, honest Dick and Doll
Are studying Colonel Jack and Flanders Moll.

'And down in the kitchen it should stay.'

'Then it's a happy thing your characters recommend themselves.'

'I will take the compliment. I don't suppose you'll let me escape it.'

Celia felt old courage at her back. 'Here is a romance for you.'

'Oh?'

'The legend of Tom West.'

He thrust his shoulders back. 'Now, there's a name deserving of the word *legend.*'

'You know it, sir?'

'I was in Devon nearly twenty years ago when I first heard his name. Here was a man to inspire lesser men. Most master smugglers fetch their dry goods abroad, whether tea or brandy, and then fix a time and place where they design to land, and pay a lander to take the goods on from there. It's landers who earn most fame, or infamy, for operating beneath the nose of the law, where the captain of the cutter is free to escape out to sea as soon as the goods are set down. The lander hires sometimes two hundred

46

men or more to transport the tubs and bales inland, and more still – batsmen, standing armed with cudgels and pistols for any unfortunate Revenue officers. A lander, in essence, is general of a moderate militia. Tom West is a master smuggler who does it all. Seaman *and* lander. Captained the cutter, fetched the goods, brought them back, dodged the Revenue's ships, landed – and led men in unloading his goods, and batsmen to stand guard. Coast and county held in one fist.' He smacked knuckles into his open palm. 'King of land and sea, displaying such *raw nerve*, such *disdain* for those who might shift to stop him, that, even though it is *improper*, a man can't help but applaud.'

'Do you not normally find that such a legend is most likely the result of embroidery?' she asked.

'That only makes it a better story. And that's what counts. Though I might add that *who* tells it, and *who* reads it, counts *just* as much. One must think only of Aphra Behn's licentious writing.'

'Then Mr West's adventures could not be the adventure of a Miss West?'

He sat forward. 'You remind me, ma'am – I had my agents across the country – my friends – send me any news from their corners when I compiled my *Tour*. To make it as up to date as possible, you understand, after my own extensive circuits.'

Celia imagined a dog sniffing at his clothes for evidence of distant roads and slinking away disappointed. She remained composed. 'Of course.'

'I received a letter from Plymouth that piqued my curiosity. Rumours of a lady's journal, Miss Fiennes, and *murder*. The book is titled *A True Relation of My* ... The full name escapes me.'

'Murder, sir?'

'Yes – Captain West had murdered a woman. His mistress, or his daughter, my friend was not sure.'

'Did you discover the lady's journal?'

47

'I lacked the time. I suppose it lies in some drawer, as your manuscript did, if I judge the paper fairly.'

A blush like violent sunburn. 'If you had made out the lady's true relation, you would perhaps have known how she came to be trapped in that drawer; whether he was villain, not hero.'

'Not a villain,' he said. 'Only a rogue. Why spoil what sells?'

'I see. Yes.' Celia averted her gaze, fixing on the sideboard, where a box made of coal masqueraded as marble, a con she had submitted to when travelling through Wigan. 'You're quite right, I suppose.'

Defoe coughed. 'You'll permit me?' He rose and thrust the poker into the fire, a clang and scuffle that sent up a brief spark. 'An ancient beauty, Exeter Cathedral.' The grey smell of cooling embers was all that remained. He laid his hand on her manuscript. 'I hope you will take my words of encouragement for *this* story seriously, ma'am. A most informative account of our country. Do you mean to print it for private circulation?'

'Perhaps, sir.'

'Your family would, I am sure, be grateful. I know my son is already grateful to you, ma'am, for your kindnesses.'

'A good businessman,' said Celia, her words flatter than she meant them. 'That must make you happy.'

'Hmm. Yes. I have always been bred like a man, I would say a gentleman, if circumstances did not of late alter that denomination. And I am afraid my son inherits my circumstances.' He spoke lightly, but a sneer tugged at his face, which now struck her as stiff with exhaustion. She knew that his son was forced to mortgage and remortgage his father's homes in order to save them from those who would have the father honour old promises. Defoe seized a mole by his mouth and tugged, returning movement to his face. Gaiety flooded his brown complexion. 'My daughters could learn much from you. I am in favour of educating women. One wonders, indeed, how it should happen that women are conversable at all – let alone as engaging as you are in print, and in person, if you will permit me – since they are beholden only to what comes natural for their knowledge. I cannot believe God would make women so agreeable, and with souls capable of the same accomplishments as men, and all to be only stewards of our houses, to be our cooks and slaves. Though I see you have avoided the trouble of catering to a husband.'

'The price one pays for a far-ranging sentence.'

'Ha. Indeed. Yes, I say teach women not only music and dancing, but modern languages.'

'You are too kind, sir.'

He flashed a grin. 'I would venture the injury of giving a woman more tongues than one. I hope you know, ma'am, that the men and women of Great Britain are impoverished for not sharing your *Journeys* – and in not knowing Miss Fiennes a little better than they do now.'

Celia laughed. 'The world does not know me at all, sir.'

'But you know the world.' His hooked nose jabbed in the direction of her sideboard: the treasures collected on her journeys, inert. Shells from Seacombe; a gum of wall and plaster rubbed white and smooth by time and prised by her from the ruins of Yeovil; petrified moss, crisped and perfect as stone, clipped at Knaresborough. Marble knocked from the hills of Bakewell; lustre broken from the glistering stalactites of Poole's Hole. Seaweed from Lake Windermere. A gnarl of glass she spun at Nottingham; the half-crown she stamped at York Mint; paper made from plants at Shrewsbury. A cluster of Bristol diamonds, still bright.

'I know it a little,' she said. 'Travelling was beneficial to my health.'

His nod was a single downward stroke, sharp chin pressed to his chest. 'The road has often been my only relief.'

Celia softened her voice to meet the constriction of his – the

49

result, she wondered, of his recent afflictions. 'You have been sent many trials. You must be very tired.'

'I'll never drown while I can swim. Never fall while I can stand. Never die while I can print.'

The light fell off the spun glass. 'Yes. And it's taken you very far.' She poured him another cup. 'You have been counsel to kings and queens.'

'Something that comforts me now. Especially the memory of King William. I hope, in a future state, to have the honour of being reunited with him.'

Celia turned her cup in her hands. 'Do you fear it, sir? The future state.'

The repeating clock filled his silence, speaking for him: how time passes.

'I am more afraid of what may occur between now and the time I embark on my last journey. What I will leave my daughters, especially. Sophia, my dearest and best beloved, and still so young.'

'If she has her mother's capacity to endure and your capacity to invent, I am sure she will thrive, sir.'

He moved in his chair. 'And you, ma'am? Are you alarmed?'

'What scares me is immobility, and silence.'

'Ma'am?'

'There is a hospital for the widows of seamen in Hull. A canoe hangs from the rafters, and in this canoe sits the effigy of a man who was taken with it, wearing his cloth cap and with his bag beside him, both made from the skin of fishes. All is original, apart from his face, which they have moulded to resemble the Wildman – that's what the inscription calls him. The Wildman. He was taken by Captain Baker. You can see his oars and his spear. Captain Baker reports that the Wildman would not speak a word to him, and would not eat, so that, in a few days, he died of hunger. I think of him often, suspended there, still unable to speak, unable to row to freedom.'

'But you are not a savage. You are welcome in every great home of England – and even into the homes of poor cottagers. You will always be a lady.'

'Yes,' she said, and no more.

'You are no cook or slave, ma'am. You are probably as close to free as is possible.'

'In Exeter Cathedral Library, I was shown an illustration of the female anatomy done on their press. I did not recognise her. Either I cannot see myself, or men of learning cannot see me.'

'Then I shall buy you a looking glass.'

She laughed, but the doubt on her face did not pass.

Mr Defoe glanced at the clock. 'I must take my leave of you, ma'am.'

'How time passes.'

'Indeed. How time passes.' He bowed over her hand. 'It has been a pleasure, Miss Fiennes.'

'Yes.'

He held on to her hand. 'You are not going to claim the pleasure was all yours?'

She roused. 'I would not leave you so deprived. I would be delighted to know your daughters, and recommend them to travel. Next to reading, nothing can surpass travel for the improvement of our minds, the betterment of our lives. If nothing else, it would give young women more to do than dress fine and entertain soldiers. But so much more than that besides.'

'I hope to meet you on the road, then.'

Celia gave a brief curtsy, meeting his eyes, which were red-veined but courteous, and felt her own body lurch for his when he turned into the corridor and groped a moment for purchase on the opposite wall.

'Sir?' she called. 'Would you tell me, if you find that Devon lady's journal?'

A watery smile. 'You wish to see a rogue, where others see

an honest man. Give me leave to say, men are made knaves by breaking. Poverty makes thieves, distress makes highwaymen, just as bare walls make giddy housewives. Not that I suggest distress makes violence lawful, but I say it is a trial beyond the ordinary power of human nature to withstand. Men rob for bread, women whore for it. Ask the worst smuggler in the nation or the lewdest strumpet in town. Trade is down, tax is up, Tom West is led into temptation, that may be easily granted – tricking, sharping, shuffling. I daresay, if he could leave off the free trade, if he could live handsomely without it, he would.'

'And if he murdered a woman for his handsome life?'

A sigh. 'Let the honest man in this town tell me when he is sinking, when he sees his family's destruction, when he sees arrest and seizure, and tell me he refuses to lay hold of his neighbour who is in the same condition, for fear the neighbour may drown with him. Nay, he will pull him down by the hair of his head, tread on his neighbour with his feet and sink him to the bottom to get himself out. If Tom West were violent, I would wage such violence held him afloat.'

'You see Tom West in every possible flattering light, sir.'

He leant his head against the coolness of the wall. 'Perhaps I do. Perhaps I see my own drowning. Where is the wrong in that?'

'You must see –' Celia turned to the windows – 'that you do not see *her*, in any light at all. Only his shadow. If we could but hear the story from her own mouth …'

'There is a life to come after this, and a just God, who will retribute to everyone according to the deeds done in the body. Whether the romance of Tom West is nulled or quashed – I leave that to God also. Until then, I am your true and intimate friend …'

And then he was gone.

Her manuscript waited on the tea table, tired. She stood over it, feeling a pressure building in her chest, the kind of pressure swinging an axe might relieve. Her hands were empty. The light failed. She touched the edge of the satin ribbon.

Does a special word, some dictionary-maker's term, exist for a narrative never delivered? What word for a story that died in the womb?

She carried the manuscript back to the sideboard, slid the drawer open and placed her *Journey* inside. The drawer felt no heavier when she closed it.

BOOK TWO

1709

BORN TO FIRE

March Comes in Like a Lion

I

Tom's arms folded around her, and Molly knew she was safe. Most of the crew couldn't swim, but Tom insisted Molly learn. The *Escape* was anchored in the Channel. Kingston and Nathan looked on, tension in them, Molly sensed, afraid of the water, or afraid of Tom, who'd demanded she swim, though she cried at the thought of such cold depths. Tom dived off the back of the ship. Benedict threw out the lifeline, a coil that cut the sky, quickly drawn taut by the pull of the tide. Tom took hold of it, and called for Molly to jump. Her heart slammed against her ribs, but Tom was looking at her with such belief, she didn't want that look to fade. So she hurled herself into the air, hitting water, which threatened to yank her bones right out – but there were Tom's arms, grabbing her; there was Tom's hand, guiding her own to the lifeline; there was the calm steadiness of Tom treading water, and so Molly rested in the shelter of his chest and followed his movements. Pride warmed her as Benedict whooped from the deck, and, in her ear, Tom whispered, 'That's my boy. That's my boy.'

*

The *Escape* slipped through the dawn haze, running down wind, fore-and-aft sails taut. The striped wall of red rock and green roots between Scabbacombe Head and Outer Froward Point was still; no candlelight winked from the fishermen's cottages or flashed from the rocks, no warnings to the free-traders that Revenue were about; no lures for ships in a storm, inviting them on to the rock.

Tom stood at the bow with his head back a little, listening to the ship's song. Murmuring wind, the slosh of breaking waves; no whistle from loose caulking or groan from rotting timbers. Just Hellard, running his mouth to Nathan. Prell, Kingston and van Meijer up the riggings. Pascal at the whip-staff, a Frenchman who had sailed for the Sun King before free-trading from the cold Norfolk coast, across the marshes of Kent, to the golden sands of Devon. Laskey the Pole and One-Eyed Jarvis, old hands both; Shaun, once a press-ganged gunner for King William; and, of course, Benedict. Most free-traders changed crews as often as they patched their sails, but Tom's crew was fixed. They were his men. Though, listening to Hellard peddling blindmares, a man might come under the illusion that the *Escape* had a different master.

Tom leant over the gunwale, let the spray drown out Hellard. The sea's cold fingers got inside his shirt. He stroked the wet timber – the tar flaking from his nights spent picking at it. Below, the hold was filled with oilskin bundles, citrus tea clouding the usual stench of unwashed men, reminding Tom of Spanish lemon trees in the rain. He took a breath, dragging the sea to the depths of his body, and then ducked beneath the throat halyard and swung around the main mast to the whipstaff. Pascal tipped his hat and moved to the peak halyard.

'Coming about!'

'Ready!'

Tom seized the tiller as the men let out the gib until they were even-keeled. No pressure, no wind, a sudden peace, bearing away from Dartmouth. Tom watched the quay, the stacked houses and shops, the castle over the mouth of the river. The *Escape* was larger than most smuggling vessels, a danger if a Revenue cruiser came looking, but there was strength in size: strength that meant he could, and would, turn and fight. He searched for temptation from the hilltops, for a plume over Dick English's chimneys.

The night he told Molly that English survived the fire, she had grown lost in her reflection, warped by the blade of the knife she played with. She pressed the tip into the boards. 'That's how I'd kill Dick English,' she said, and she sounded, suddenly, so much older.

Tom had wiped his face, promising her, 'If it's justice you want ... ' Then he hesitated, as she tilted the knife, catching something of his shade. 'If it's justice you want – we'll have it, you and I.'

But today he saw no sign of life from the home of Dick English. His eyesight dated him every month of his two and thirty years. But he still had the youth of others. Where was Benedict?

Tom called for his spotsman. Quick steps below, the clunk of the hatch opening, and then Benedict slid towards him, the *Escape* pitching into squally water.

'Give your eyes unto the Lord, my lad,' said Tom.

Benedict forced the telescope open, steadying himself against Tom's shoulder like a child learning to skate – still so like a child, though now one and twenty. Tom had given him the telescope when he first came aboard, fresh from Kingsbridge Grammar School. His eyes were as good at deciphering close-set scripture as they proved to be spotting hidden rocks and eddies. The crew said he carried a constant

59

look of shock with him now, like a virgin after his first good niggle, eyes swollen enough to take in all of the coast's secrets.

'Nought following,' said Benedict. He turned to line up his transit, Dancing Beggars rocks with the spire at Stoke Fleming. 'Bearing sou' sou'west.'

Tom looked down the line of Benedict's arm, following the boy's pointing finger with the tiller.

'Sheet in!'

The sail slapped to starboard, and the *Escape* tacked through Start Bay, Benedict muttering to himself – 'Matthew's Point to Strete Church, Limpet Rocks to Tinsey Head, Start Point to Black Stone' – the great jut of land rearing over them, and then round to Ravens Cove, Sleaden Rocks, Two Stones, and Tom called, 'Heave to!' The sails faced each other, the jet of wind between them a sigh of relief, and the *Escape* drifted to a stop.

Benedict realised he was still holding on to Tom's shoulder, and looked up at the captain with a shy smile.

Tom winked at him.

Tom's father had told him, *When in danger, run to sea.* He meant it plainly, of course: that it's better to turn from the coast and head back out to sea if you don't know the rocks, even if there's a storm set to drown you. The most dangerous part of the run was landing, and if it weren't for Benedict they'd have run aground more than once. A spotsman needed local lore, but, more than that, a gift for memory, a gift for sight.

When Tom had first set out to sea, his mother begged him, *You're in no danger, there's no need to run. The danger awaits you out there.* He'd told her, *I know. I'm looking for it.* And she wept.

Shaun and Molly – Orlando to the crew, or, more often, Boy, the best powder monkey they'd known, filling the cannon balls and keeping 'em ready as if his hands were made for it – counted time with each other at the windlass, sending the anchor to the seabed, and the ship lurched to a halt. Then the clank of rowboats lowered into the oily black.

Lannacombe Bay was a half-moon bite from the land's outline, quiet but for the wind in the trees, a finger-to-lips *shhh*. Jumping from the rowboat, Tom took hold and pulled. Next to him, Molly pulled too, bearing her share. Waves, soft now, scrolled past his legs. With one last heave, he set the boat down and drew his pistol. Smoke whispered from the single cottage nestled at the apex of the beach, and Tom waved his men on, remaining in the open – inviting fire, his old captain Ezekiel would have said, who always stayed on board.

Untamed forest swallowed the noise of their boots on the wet sand. The cottage was served by a mud track, and Tom watched as a man slipped from the cover of trees, leading his donkey. Tom raised his arm, and the batsman responded, sniffing and spitting as other men appeared from the woods, urging their donkeys into line, for the track was wide enough for single file only. The beasts would carry the tubs inland to South Allington, where the next crew would take over.

When a bird chattered, Tom's grip tightened on the pistol, but all he could hear was the grunt of tired men with tired backs. By noon, the South Pool blacksmith and his sons would have the tea hidden in their trap among scrap metals bound for melting at Exeter. The tax on steel was high, and they'd take their payment in Spanish steel smuggled in by Tom next month. In the meantime, the ladies of Exeter would sip Tom West's tea from china cups.

'That's all of it,' said Kingston, mopping his brow.

Tom looked to the sweep of cliff above. He used to walk there, on the very edge, with her.

Molly returned to his side with the grin of wickedness she always wore in these moments. A born free-trader, this girl.

She did not look up at the cliff. Did not remember the steps her mother took over this land. There was mercy in that.

'You ready, Captain?' she said.

Tom nodded. Time to go home.

The dawn sun played shadow games on the sails of the *Escape* as she passed into Salcombe estuary. Here, the wind changed, no longer the buffet of open sea, and the *Escape* glided past sheltered beaches: Moor Sand Cliffs, Gara Rock Beach, South Sands, North Sands. Charles Fort perched on the outlying rocks. Soldiers had patrolled the turrets, alert and sleepless, in the last days of the Civil War. Now, half the night watch was lying in bed and the other half missing from their posts, as Tom had paid them to be. Sitting on a barrel on the deck, Tom watched smoke rising from one of the castle's slit windows, where he pictured a soldier warming his breakfast with back turned.

Past Salcombe's clasp of fishermen's houses in the hillside, the early fires of the shipwright and blacksmith, the rakish tilt of masts, and then it was gone, lost in the folds of Snape Point as they spilled into the calm of Kingsbridge Estuary, Widegates ahead, where seven inlets of the ocean collided, conspiring to bring a man on to the rocks just as he thought ahead to the Old Tavern and its pale ale. Starlings puffed overhead, followed by a cormorant disturbed from its perch. Tom twisted to watch bony wings heave the bird's weight into the air, trailing a fractured reflection along the water. When he looked back, the ship had nosed into Frogmore Creek, and the rest of the estuary closed behind them. This arm of the waterway was narrow and quiet, only limekilns at work, shimmering sighs of heat rising from the stone huts. Men shunting coal through the top of the kiln waved their shovels in salute.

Molly touched his elbow, smelling of sweat and powder. 'Set fair, then.'

He ruffled her hair. 'That right?'

She pointed to the spread sail of black-headed gulls. 'Birds fly high, clear blue sky.'

'March comes in like a lion, remember.'

'Don't I bring you luck?'

He looked down into her salt-flecked face, seeing his own madness, the madness of her presence here on the ship, still, the madness of this pretence, running out of time. He could have sent her away at any point in the last six years. Should have sent her away. But he couldn't. 'Yes. Yes, you do.'

II

Benedict waited in the window seat of the Pilchard Inn, only half paying attention to the game of chance with Boy, who was winning, as he – she – always did. This was how he had first met Tom. Another taproom – the Church House Inn – full because service had let out and the monks gave free stew and ale to anyone who attended. Benedict and his friends had walked from Kingsbridge for the promise of dinner, and Benedict's stomach was squirming by the end of the sermon. The same age as Molly now, he'd just been dropped from school, his sponsorship dried up, and he had no ear for God's words, but the stew came with a chunk of bread, and the ale comforted his aching head.

They had sat in a settle near the fireplace. Shouting to hear each other over the clang of the nearby kitchen, the volume soon made their disagreement about Captain Tom West an argument. Mark was insisting that Benedict's idolatry for the smuggler was mere fantasy, that the man Benedict saw as Robin Hood was a crook. Benedict banged the table to get Mark to cease prattling for just one minute, wanting to explain what Tom West meant to poor people, but only managing, 'The man is a hero—' before Edward stamped on his foot. Benedict turned sharply, and froze.

Tom West stood in the door. He was the biggest man Benedict had ever seen. He wore a serge coat, but no hat, and his hands rested lightly on a sword pommel and pistol. He wore his hair short, no wig or powder, no pretensions. He was looking straight at Benedict with a smile that spliced amusement and mockery. Benedict's upper lip grew damp with sweat. Then Tom stepped up to the bar, where the monk pointed across the room to a settle in the corner. Tom passed through the crowd, shaking hands, stooping to receive private words in his ear. Benedict only noticed the men following Tom then, one with a face like a rude Pagan carving – Hellard, he'd later discover – and one with his hair swept in a ponytail, as if he were a man of fashion – Pascal.

Tom passed right by Benedict's table. Mark stared into his soup; Tom seemed to consider him for a moment, and then glanced across at Benedict. He winked.

The free-traders set up a card game, and a few of the drinkers joined them. Benedict sat rigidly, watching. Stories of Tom had been whispered around the dormitory, many of them by Benedict. He realised now that the Church closing its books on him was not an ill turn – it would lead him to where he should have been, where he would have been if his father had lived and he could have kept fishing with him. Back to the sea, learning at the feet of Tom West. Benedict chewed on some way to introduce himself – until Kate came to serve Tom his drink.

Kate was older than Benedict, but he worshipped her with vain hope all the same, dreaming of the day he'd get beyond saying, *Good e'en*. Now, Tom caught her attention without any words. He occupied one whole side of the settle, and straightened as Kate approached, sliding his arm around her waist. And that was all it took.

'I'm in need of your help,' Benedict heard him say. 'Hellard, here, has just laid down blunt enough for a horse race. Would you raise him?'

Benedict's elbows became sharp pressure points on his knees as Kate moved closer to see the cards.

'I'm not too smart on games of luck, Cap'n West,' she said.

'I'll teach you.'

'I couldn't do that, sir ... '

'Of course you could,' said Tom, 'at least until we've thrashed Hellard, here. Then we'll have to be off, you and I.'

Kate laughed. 'Where would we be going?'

'Anywhere you like,' said Tom. It was then that Tom's hand rested on her back. 'But, for now, rest your feet for a minute, lest my heart break.'

Kate snorted, but still folded into the seat next to Tom, his arm resting loosely over her shoulders now, and his head bent to her ear. After a minute of whispering, Kate put forward a scatter of coins.

Tom won the hand and gave all the money to Kate, who went back to work with a smile Benedict had never seen on a woman. Mark and Edward tried to convince Benedict to leave with them, but he was determined to stay and talk to Tom once all the patrons cleared off. He ordered another drink, and another, until his money was gone and the room seemed unbearably hot, though the monks doused the fire. Hellard and Pascal left, but Tom remained spread out at the settle, his feet up. He must be waiting to talk to me, Benedict thought, must have overheard me and want me for his crew. Benedict got to his feet, but knocked the remaining ale on his table over. Kate slipped by him, ignoring the dripping liquid. Tom rose, bowing over her hand. The monk behind the bar was gone.

'May I be permitted a glance, now?' he said.

Kate laughed, and then twitched her skirts up, revealing small feet encased in ribboned and buckled shoes, and white silk stockings. Benedict felt himself stiffen, but Tom's voice remained steady:

'I take it the lady is satisfied?'

'The lady is satisfied if the gentleman is.' There was joy in her voice, joy at this coquetry and the appreciation in Tom's face.

'I live in hope.'

'I've got the key to the cheese room,' said Kate.

'What about him?' said Tom, nodding to Benedict.

'He's not invited.'

Tom laughed, and Benedict's ears blazed.

'Just a local boy,' said Kate. 'He won't say nought.'

'Then lead the way, m'lady. But if I smell of cheddar tomorrow ...'

Benedict kept his head down as Tom followed Kate, who was giggling, but then Tom's boots stopped on the boards and the smuggler called, 'Lad? Don't go to sleep in that.' A rag landed on the sopping table, and then the boots continued up the stairs.

He did go to sleep, and stirred only once in the night, with his face stuck to the rag and a rhythmic scrape of iron on stone in his ears: the frame of a cot shunting against the wall. The next time he woke up, a man was standing over him.

'Father?' he said, eyes still half-closed.

'Could be,' said the man. 'Though you look too slight to be mine. How old are you?'

Benedict sat up. Tom West, with his shirt half undone and his pistol belt hanging over one arm. Benedict wiped his face with his sleeve. 'Where's Kate?'

'Washing. I hope she's no sweetheart of yours?'

'What did she . . . ?'

Tom laughed. 'If you're asking that, then she definitely ain't a sweetheart of yours.'

Benedict flushed. 'Did you promise her marriage?'

'Not that I recall. But if I did, I'm not looking over my shoulder for some patriarch to hold me to my word. Unless you'd like to give it a go, son?'

'No patriarch but you,' Benedict whispered, ''round here.'

A chuckle. 'Low praise, sir. You can't sleep here all night. Where are you apprenticed?'

Benedict got to his feet. 'I don't have a home, sir, and there's no trade I want but yours. I want to be like you.'

'You don't need my trade to get a girl like Kate to the cheese room. You're not a bad-looking boy. Now, you'd better come on out of here—'

'No, please, you don't understand. I want to be a free-trader.'

'You got experience on a ship?'

'Fishing, sir.'

'Fishing. Lad, you don't know what you want. Find a hedgerow and sleep it off.'

'I could be the best spotsman you ever had,' Benedict rushed, as Tom turned away. The smuggler paused. 'I've known the rocks and cliffs round here since I was a boy. And I can read maps, and write, too. They taught me the Bible at the Grammar School, and more besides.'

'With that kind of schooling, you could be a clerk.'

'I want to be more than that. I want what you can teach me. Please.'

Tom bent at the knees to look Benedict in the face. 'What's your name?'

'Benedict White.'

Seconds passed, then a minute. He squeezed Benedict's shoulder. 'All right. Keep those eyes open for me, as you did for the Lord, and I'll make something of you. But, you ought to know, there's something in you that's more'n fine already.'

Now, in the Pilchard Inn, Benedict rubbed his shoulder where Tom's fingers had gripped him so certainly. He could hear the waves on the beach below, peeling from each other to widen the strip of sand to Burgh Island. Benedict peered out at Bigbury Bay, his eyes dragged onwards, to Bantham Beach, where Grace Tucker's cottage was hidden by the hill. What remained of Grace Tucker's cottage. The crew knew not to speak of it – how Dick English had murdered Grace and cast Boy into their midst – even to those close to their circle, like Charles Savage, their financial agent, who would arrive soon. If it was Dick English.

'You want to try and win it back?' said Boy.

'Win what back?' said Benedict.

'Well, everything.'

The table laughed at Benedict's shock. His earnings sat beneath Boy's palm. He smiled, despite the lurch in his stomach. 'You keep it.'

'That's probably for the best.'

He pulled her closer, messing up her curls. She shoved him. It was so easy to forget she was a girl. It was not in her eyes, which had the gleam of a knife-fighter, nor her smile, a grin flecked with blood from wind-cracked lips and diseased gums, nor the skinny body supporting broad shoulders. It was not in the ease with which she scampered up the rigging or helped Nathan smooth the wood of a new rowboat. As if she was born to this life. Did Boy – *Molly* – even know what being a girl meant? The key in Benedict's pocket felt heavier at the thought. He was the only man who knew her secret and the only man Tom had provided with a key to the house on Île de Batz. He meant for Benedict to protect her. And he would – this time.

The door opened. Tom ducked inside and crossed to the innkeeper, nodding as Nathan told him Charlie was still not here. Hellard and Shaun were arguing across the table, Kingston laughing at them. Kingston drew glances from the fishermen around, his skin darker than the smoke-stained oak beams. If he noticed, he gave no sign of it. He was only a few years older than Benedict, but wore another lifetime. He'd been set upon more than once by strangers believing he was an escaped slave, meaning to drag him to the local Justice. Whether he was or wasn't, Benedict didn't know. Since joining Tom, no one had set upon Kingston again. Next to him, Nathan was a slight but tall figure, a tree bent into a new shape by the wind. Pascal, Prell, van Meijer, Jarvis, Laskey – they all lounged across the bar, brandy for blood.

Drink did its worst to Hellard, who grew braying and mean, and sought bait, loving nothing more than making Benedict squirm, and holding his eye as he did so. He was contemplating such a thing now, Benedict could tell, and the spotsman drew a sigh of relief when the door opened again, bringing with it a strong wind, and then Charles Savage, pulling his hat down. He was a slender man of five and twenty years, with well-turned legs, a pistol stuck in his belt and a waistcoat of fine green cloth that showed no repair work. Something twitchy about his shoulders, as if he had his own destination, and found it hard to constrain himself to this place and time. Short curls hidden by a wig. A sharp nose, but soft, green eyes. Some of Tom's charm and Nathan's refinement, but nothing of Hellard's brutality, and enough learning and wit to fox them all, Benedict thought privately.

'You're late, Charlie Savage,' said Tom.

Charles bowed, keeping his irritation at being called Charlie to himself. 'A thousand pities.'

'Tell Nathan a band of dragoons didn't hold you up. He's been fretting so.'

Charles put a hand to his heart. 'Bless you. Not dragoons – Reverend Shapwick. He wants in.'

'You're forgiven,' said Tom, 'as long as you've got more than a parson's pennies on you.'

Charles dropped a leather bag on to the table. It chimed.

'Good man,' said Tom, sitting at the head of the table and drawing it to him. 'By the by, if you want to make it as a gentleman, you'd better improve your bow.'

'If you're giving etiquette lessons, Tom, sign me up.' Charles sat down. 'Until then, I'm tired off my legs with trotting from Brixham to Bigbury and beyond, chasing down purses. Mrs Potter, she who sells all sorts of private affairs to the ladies, she tells me these are hard times, in which neighbours are more ready to buy her merchandise than they are to pay for it – and it's not just ladies making off with false teeth and pots of paint. Farmers fear their crop might as well die in the field afore it dies at market, butcher boys are blowing air into meat, and the fishermen's wives say let the sea keep the fish, and keep their husbands too, for all the use they are.'

Tom rubbed his face. 'I suppose you're going to tell me how you turned hay to gold?'

Charles shook his head mournfully. 'My city ladies, in times past, were as punctual in their payments as they were in their prayers, but now there is not a goldsmith's wife to be found in town but is as hard-hearted as an ancient judge to a financial agent, such as myself, after her debts, or her promises. And the town gentleman: he might like to be seen tossing his purse of gold from one hand to t'other as if it were no more than an orange. But, when his financial agent asks him what he *keeps* in his purse, our young gentleman cocks his saucy hat, turns an ungracious heel, and invites said financial agent to kiss his swordknot.'

Hellard snorted. 'And do you?'

Charles tossed his head. 'A man has his pride.'

Tom landed his fist on the purse. 'Then I suppose this is but pulped orange?'

'Oh, ye of little faith. I humbly submit to the court a full grocery list. The usual, mainly – brandy, tobacco and tea – with a few smaller requests. The Justice is suffering from an empty wine cellar, and Reverend Shapwick is in need of tallow. He can't read his Bible.'

'Can't have that,' said Tom, opening the bag. The gentle clicks of sifting coins could be heard.

'How can folks invest, if they be so down?' asked Benedict.

'The wind might change, but folks won't sheer off Tom West. Not while I'm here to whisper sweet nothings. A mistress might be up to her ears in love and contemplation, but it's salt and lace she wants, and it's that I bring. If Mrs Lisle has lost her purse, or Lord Pearce his club, to whom do they come to keep them from tumbling and tossing with worry? Your very own servant. Flesh, wipe that frown from your pretty face. Thou shalt be firing coal and burning billets. Your pockets will be full of the rhino. You'll have coin enough to make birds swim and sturdy oaks bend like switches.'

Tom muttered, 'All the better to beat you into silence. Tea and tobacco at five pence a pound in France, brandy a pound a tub. That will be enough to supply the villages and send some to Plymouth and Exeter. We sell the tea on here at seven pence, tobacco at twelve and brandy at four pounds, we'll make enough to bring back double next time.'

'I've got the demand to meet it. More and more of these local orders. I'd have never hazarded inviting folk to hold shares in a free-trader's venture, but it works. If you don't succeed, their stomachs pay instead.'

'That's why the Revenue will never stop us,' said Hellard, splaying his legs. 'They can't stop wars or crowns, and wars and crowns leave people hungry.'

'And thirsty,' said Charles, raising his tankard.

'You've done well, Charlie,' said Tom, and put his hand into the bag. His fist came out full of gold coins. He let them fall, one clinking over the other, into a small purse, which he chucked back to Charles.

'Two other orders of business, Tom,' said Charles, slipping it into his jacket. 'A letter for you to carry to France, if you're interested, worth twice the brandy.'

'Letter from whom?' asked Nathan.

'Who cares?' said Charles. 'A love letter, fleet preparations, Queen Anne's measurements – what difference does it make?'

'It might make a difference to Anne,' said Nathan.

Benedict sat forward. 'Buying French brandy is one thing. Delivering notes for spies to the enemy is another, isn't it?'

'You're right,' said Charles. 'It's a lot more profitable.'

'We're free-traders, not spies,' said Tom. 'Free-traders they'll let pass, for a penny and a pinch of snuff. Traitors they kill, no matter how deep your pockets are.'

'Where's your sense of adventure?' said Charles.

'You're awfully eager,' said Tom. 'I trust it's only that the man who asked you for this *favour* has a pretty and obliging wife, and not that you're working for two masters.'

Charles raised his hands. 'Exceedingly pretty.'

'You'll have to introduce me.'

'Bored of your French girls?'

'You should have seen the pair Shaun and I had in Roscoff,' said Hellard. 'A whole night, they couldn't get enough – and no more'n fourteen. Pretty as the Virgin Mary, devil fetch me, and tongues that could suck a man to his last drop.'

'A whole night?' said Charles, glancing at the powder monkey; around twelve, he'd guess, and listening to this with a look of boredom. 'What a disappointment you must have been.'

'God's blood—'

'Curse me again and it'll be yours.'

'Boys,' said Tom.

Sitting back, Charles gave a laugh. 'You share in this party, Captain?'

'I don't share.'

Benedict flushed red. He had only made it to a bedroom in le palais de putain once. When the girl raised her petticoats, her beckoning hand became a desperate gesture – became Grace's hand, reaching for the child's bedroom door – and her breasts, dusky with freckles, were Grace's chest as the breath left her. Benedict lost his desire, throat closing until he choked, and the whore laughed at him.

'And the other business, Charlie?' said Tom.

'Captain Dick English.'

'Again?' said Hellard.

Benedict felt Molly stiffen next to him.

'His frustration isn't making him any sweeter. And it looks like your Justice is losing his balls. Dick English won't be shaken from Tom West or any of his boys. So, being one of your boys, Tom, I beg you to have done with this maidenly refusal and put a bullet in the man's brain.'

Benedict edged back. He folded Molly's sleeve in his cold fingers and tugged, urging her from the table by a few inches, waiting for Tom to tip it up.

'Maidenly refusal?' said Tom.

'You don't want to get your hands dirty, I understand—'

Tom rose, fists landing on the table. The tankards jumped. 'Stand up.'

'What? Tom—'

'*Stand up.*'

No one moved. No one spoke. Charles was going red, as if those two words had belted him across the face.

Tom snorted. His fists relaxed. 'Go home and practise that bow, Charlie. It'll give your spine something to do.'

Charles couldn't bear the blush of his face. He knew himself to be a coward. He didn't want to be a coward. He stood up. 'I am not your court jester, Tom.'

Tom sneered. 'An easy mistake to make.'

'You have been gone these last weeks.'

'And?'

'And I'm the steward, when the king is gone.'

'Flattery will get you no more than three inches o'er the knee.'

The table laughed. Charles didn't. 'I keep an eye on things for you.'

'*And?*'

Charles sought the reins. If he knew himself to be a coward, he also knew himself to be a smart man. Smarter than this rabble. Smarter than this rakehell, too, for all Tom might be cunning. Little had ever been expected of Charles, born to a small home of small hopes and small imagination. Well, he could imagine a lot. So, wait, Charles Savage. Just wait. And, in the meantime, hold the reins. 'And I'm grateful,' he said, 'for the opportunity.'

Tom sat down. 'Gratitude will get you further, but you're still shy of the prize, Charlie boy. It's love or nothing, for me.'

Amid the table's howls, Benedict glanced at Molly. She was watching Charles with an expression Benedict didn't like. Curiosity. Intent.

Mothering Sunday

I

'Il est arrivé!' The town of Roscoff acknowledged Tom West's return with fervour: deals to be made with the big Englishman, goods to sell and goods to buy. Tom had been using Roscoff as his French base for a year, and the pockets of each sailor and fisherman had deepened since. Word spread quickly down the main street, from chandler to ostler, from shipwright to brandy merchant, from the front doors of sandstone houses to the cathedral doors in the square. 'Tom est arrivé.' Inside, work was underway to restore the roof, whose timbers stretched like the naked ribs of a ship. Sebastian Gautier was in the nave, discussing funds with the bishop, when a young man stamped with his livery tugged on his ermine sleeve.

'Capitaine West est arrivé, Colonel Gautier.'

Pascal heaved the tiller and the *Escape* made for port, a huge wall jutting out into the water. Small sailboats cradled by its arm bobbed up and down, lifted by the swell of water that announced the *Escape*. On deck, tobacco smoke drifted over the heads of the crew. They formed a circle around Tom, listening to his orders. Molly walked its perimeter to the port side. Through the spray, Roscoff looked like it was made of gold. Grand houses built on soft granite slabs hugged close, their tall rooflines a gleaming hill of slate. In the centre, a spire clamoured for the heavens: the stack of domes pointing ever upwards, the arched window framing a waterfall of bells.

Behind Molly, the anchor dropped in a clank of chains.

'Do I have to stay with Boy, Tom?'

Benedict's hushed voice still caught Molly's ear.

'I need some relief,' said Tom, turning away to mind the unloading. 'And Hocktide is too far off.'

Shaun laughed. 'You'll never have your first niggle at this rate.'

'What do you know about it?' said Benedict.

Shaun leant closer. 'I know that we're going *a-mothering*, while you spend the day mothering Tom's pet.'

Molly pushed between them. 'This pet bites, dullard.'

The gangplank fell with a bounce. The port was a T-shape, running into Roscoff's main street. Benedict put his hand on Molly's shoulder and she followed, studying the churning black below. The houses at each corner of the port were bigger than any she'd seen in Devon, save maybe Plymouth. One was twice as long as the ship. Another had a tower like a castle.

'They say Marie Stuart stayed there,' said Benedict.

'Who?'

Benedict did not answer. They reached the High Street. It was like walking into thunder. People everywhere: tugging on goats, wrestling chickens, carrying great rings of rope that looked like slow-worms slithering over the shoulders of the crowd. The rich walked arm in arm in strange colours.

Gargoyles and gabled windows hugger-muggered overhead. The street was cobbled, and wide as a river. Horses and carts splashed through the gutter down the middle. And, everywhere, the smell and stamp of the sea. Ships carved over the doors, into shutters, on weathered faces.

A man bumped into Molly and she fell into Benedict, righting herself in time to jump out of the way of a carriage. The wheel was taller than her. Benedict tugged her on.

Molly studied his worried face. 'Tom said he wanted relief. I know you do, too.'

'No, Boy. That's not ... He meant a different kind of relief. He meant ... I can't explain it. But it's not to do with you. And *I* don't want relief from you. I promise.'

Molly stopped. 'Yes, you do. You're my guard. And you hate it.'

'Guard?' Benedict was going red.

'You know our game, don't you?'

'What are you talking about?'

Molly looked up into his bright blue eyes. They were empty: no sign that Benedict guessed which side of Hocktide Molly would be on, if the world knew the shape of her body. Molly would join those women who set out from cottages and houses in great fits of laughter, hauling cords between them, whether rope from their husbands' fishing boats, or tassled cords from their curtains. Finding a passing man, they would detain him with a pretty smile and a promise, and then bind his arms and hands until the man bought his freedom with whatever coin was in his pocket – or, if the man were daring, a kiss. Molly would be so daring to free herself with a kiss – felt so daring, as a man. As a woman ... As a woman, she would want none of men pretending to be powerless, would want no patronising favours. There were times she felt sure Benedict knew all this – Benedict, with his pinched, worried glances – but now the naivety on his face made her doubt.

Benedict steered her into the square. Alleys ran between the terraced rows to the sea. A couple of fishermen burst from one, net full of sliding silver fins. Eglise Notre-Dame de Croas-Batz was gunmetal grey, with a great roof that swept low to the floor and vestries crowding its sides, crawling with stone spirits. When they got closer, Molly counted mermaids and ships. Half the building was still timber.

'Merchants and seamen paid for it, every brick,' said Benedict.

'Did Tom?' asked Molly.

'You could say that,' said Benedict. 'First free-trader to land here. Making money for the town.'

'Then is it God's house or ours?'

'Don't ask things like that.'

Smoked meats, honey, cream cheese, fish baking in the sun. Stronger than anything else were the onions overflowing from every stall. It all lay on Molly's tongue, salty and perfumed, making her stomach cramp. Benedict bought some bread and sausage and led Molly to a stall glistening with trinkets.

'What do you think of these?' she asked, lingering by a tray of medallions and picking up a small silver oval. It showed a man standing in a boat, surrounded by children.

'You're a sailor at heart. That's St Nicholas – he protects seamen, and lost children.'

Molly turned the coin over. She had been born on St Nicholas's Day, twelve years ago last December. On the back of the coin read *Priez Pour Nous*. 'What does this mean?'

'We can ask Pascal. You want it? Tom gave me some money.'

'Can I have the money instead?'

'Ha. Put it back and we'll eat.'

*

79

They sat on a damp wall in the shadow of the cathedral. Benedict broke the baguette in half.

'Do you want a apple?' Molly asked.

'*An* apple,' said Benedict.

'Why do you always say I'm wrong?'

'I don't.'

'You do,' said Molly, pulling an apple from her coat.

'Is that from the ship?'

'It's from the market.'

'You mean you stole it?'

'I took it.'

'That's stealing.'

'Ain't that telling me I'm talking wrong?'

'Stop being smart and listen. You don't steal from here, just as you wouldn't from the ship. Do you understand? You don't commit a crime in your own home.'

'We do that all the time.'

'We're not criminals, Boy.'

But Molly was looking past his shoulder. 'That man's staring at you.'

Benedict turned. A figure stood inside the church doors, polished high-heeled boot crossing into the light. Benedict stiffened as a hand emerged, trailing a gaping sleeve, and beckoned.

'He must know I'm Tom's.'

'Don't go.'

Molly folded inwards as a frown changed Benedict's face. When he told her to stay put, she nodded, watching him crunch over the gravel to the cathedral door and drown in the square of black.

Molly finished her baguette, and then, after a few minutes, ate the rest of Benedict's. The church bells began to ring. It was growing cold – not just the air, but the cold that came over her when left alone. When lonely. She was always lonely on Mothering Sunday – always left alone by Tom, who couldn't meet her eye on this day. She watched a spindle-shanked dog skirt the market. Seagulls wheeled overhead. Molly closed her eyes, listening to their starving laugh. *You know our game, don't you?* Breathe. Mama's hand on her cheek. Tom's warmth around her. Breathe.

Molly opened her eyes, heart steady as a gun. A line of figures walked up the passage closest to her, carrying boxes. The first man had dark skin, almost as dark as Kingston's, but he wore a turban. His clothes shimmered. A few people turned their heads as he passed; others nodded recognition. He cut through to the back stall, where a merchant shook his hand. Molly jumped off the wall and squeezed into the crowd.

A few of the boxes had been dropped behind the shimmering man, who was speaking with the merchant. Molly found one with an open lid. It was filled with painted beads. She slid her hand in.

A fist seized her wrist. Molly looked up the muscled arm, into the foreign face.

'I wasn't stealing,' she blurted.

'Whose boy are you?'

'Tom West's.'

The grip relaxed.

Molly glanced at the chests. 'You're a Barbary pirate.'

The man turned and addressed the merchant, who chuckled. 'Do you know what Barbary pirates do to children?' he asked.

'Eat them, Shaun says.'

'I'd like to meet this Shaun.'

'I don't think you would,' said Molly.

There was an old woman hunched among the men. She seemed cold: in her cupped hands, clipped bones shivered, as it seemed the very bones beneath her flesh shivered. But her luminous green eyes were steady.

'Fortune teller,' said the pirate. 'Wise woman.'

'She can tell you the future?'

'For four deniers she can. Six deniers and she can change it. Future is only cheap to those can afford it.'

'Boy!' Benedict hauled him around. 'I told you to stay still!'

Molly's hand went to the knife in her belt.

Benedict let go, slowly. 'Listen: that man in the church had something very important he wanted me to tell Tom; it can't wait. Make your way back to the ship.'

Molly looked like she was about to argue, but for once she didn't, just shoved her hands in her pockets, fingers turning something there, as if smoothing a stone or a coin. The medal, Benedict thought as he hurried off. She'd stolen it.

The palais de putain – that's what Hellard called it – was set in the mud streets criss-crossing the hills surrounding Roscoff. The stairs seemed to slip away from Benedict as he climbed, the smell of the cheese room in his nostrils, out of place, out of time. Tom was in the last attic room, the girl at the door had said.

'Sir?' Benedict called. 'There's a man wants to see you; he's coming right behind me. Tom?'

The sound of a creaking bed, then bare feet shuffling on the boards. The door opened. A girl about Benedict's age smiled at him. Her hair was tangled, and she smelt of warm sheets and shared breath. She wore Tom's shirt and no stockings.

'Oui?'

'Tom?'

The girl shrugged, walking back into the room, the door still open. She bent over Tom's sleeping form, a gentle hand on his bare shoulder, then her lips on his cheek. Tom shifted, an arm pulling her closer, and she laughed, speaking in soft French that Benedict did not understand. She gestured to him as Tom began to argue, and then Tom grunted agreement and she moved away. Tom sat up, the sheet falling. The moment seemed to last longer than it could have, every detail of this world Benedict still did not know sinking into his mind to be picked over later. It was a narrow bed and, as with everything, too small for Tom. In the candlelight, his tanned skin and heavy muscles were red and the scars that cabled his body danced. His hands rested on the slab of his stomach and his legs, thick with hair, were crossed over tangled blankets. Benedict blushed when he realised where his eyes had ended up.

'Seen your fill?'

'Sorry,' Benedict blurted.

'You know, sometimes I wonder if Shaun is right. Perhaps you are a sodomite.'

'He said that?'

'Well, there *is* a half-naked girl in the corner.' Tom laughed, reaching for his trousers. 'Message?'

'It's a colonel, wants to talk to you, said he'd meet you in the alley.'

Tom nodded, looking around for his shirt. From the corner, the girl laughed. Tom gave her a crooked smile.

'I'll be needing me shirt back.'

'Take it, then.'

Tom inched closer, the smile growing. Benedict turned his back, listening to the girl's quick feet on the floor, her squeal, the bounce of the mattress, then silence. He looked back over his shoulder just as Tom undid the last button, pulling the shirt over her head. She wore nothing underneath. She had a dark mole on one breast. Bile plugged Benedict's throat.

'Merci, my love,' said Tom.

'Amour,' she corrected, tapping him with her foot.

'Amour,' he agreed, reaching into his pocket for his purse.

Molly paid the witch with coins that had been in Benedict's pockets. 'Change my future. Stop me from becoming a woman.'

The witch snorted, but devised a potion. Hystericals, medicines for the womb: tormentil and bistort to stop menses, asafoetida to shrink the womb in revulsion; medicines to harden: rosemary and nutmeg to strengthen the brain, angelica seeds to strengthen the heart; and French female dog mercury, to cure the disease of womanhood. Molly swallowed the vile thing, and the witch laughed, but promised all the same: 'You will never be a woman.'

Molly remembered Mama's laugh, how full it was, as if with just her laugh she dared everything, gave everything. It was nothing like the witch's laugh. Mama was a woman like no other Molly had met since, and yet she had still been stamped out. Molly would never be that. It was final, the deed done, signed away. Orlando West would stay. But, still, she thought of herself as Molly. For she could never stop being her mother's Molly.

The back door of the brothel spilt light into the alley, where a carriage waited, the door open, revealing a pale hand. Tom cocked his pistol in his belt and climbed into the gilt thing.

'Good evening, Capitaine. I am sorry to disturb your rest.'

Tom settled in a corner of the carriage. Opposite, a man with a cobweb-grey periwig and egg-white face smiled at him. Tom could make out no other details. He kept a hand on his pistol.

'I am Colonel Gautier. You perhaps know of me?'

'Sir.'

The colonel fixed his eyes on Tom from beneath drooping lids. 'Most men of your birth now make me their bow.'

'There aren't any men of my birth.'

Gautier laughed: a high-pitched trill. 'Quite right, Mr West. I must thank you for meeting with me. I have heard so much about you. Yet, even the tales of Tom West the giant did not quite capture you! Have you ever met a man your own size?'

'Not yet.'

The colonel gave a short hum. 'I have come to you, Mr West, with an idea that will make us both very rich.'

'And why have I been singled out for this kindness?'

'Most Devon smugglers land at Saint-Malo or Le Havre. You do not. They command small barques, even twelve-man rowboats with single sails, if they command anything at all. Even more are simply ... *chancers*, paid by someone else. So little leadership, so little loyalty. A sad fact, yes? You, however, are different. You own your ship, and it sails faster than any on the seas. You land in Roscoff, a town of wealth and ship-wrights who stand in no fear of the law. All whom you come across owe something to you or can profit by you. You have bought a French town, Mr West.'

'You *have* heard so much about me.'

'I am even told you are close to holding all of Devon in your palm.'

'Someone's been lying to you, Colonel. I already do.'

'Good man, good man. I am self-made, just like yourself. You will know the East Indiamen have a monopoly on tea. Colbert failed to charter French companies. We would not invest. He did not see the obvious: why raise a ship, when one can simply put money into a ship already going? And so what if it is English? We have had enough of endless wars. I have many friends on the East India Board, after years of London life. As you will know, the import taxes to England are going up every day to pay for our countries' little skirmishes. Yet England is the main audience for any tea my friends and I do not sell in France. And, in France – bah, you will have heard of this lunatic new scheme, put forward by Vauban – ten per cent tax on *all* forms of income, to replace the taille paid by the peasants – as if we do not have enough to worry about, with the fall of Lille, the capture of Minorca, and still Louis invites war! Between Versailles and London, we are all suffering. It is time – how do you say? – to read the waters. If a great king does not appear, a great revolution will.'

Tom nodded, following Gautier's gaze as he turned to stare out the window at the brothel.

'Mr West, I see a society in which all people can eat and drink and grow quite as fat as they like. In which everything you could desire is coming on the next tide.'

'Sounds like paradise.'

'Doesn't it? But for this paradise to exist there must be trade. Slaves. Labourers. Bankers. Merchants. More than any of this, however, there must be *ships*. I already have Normandy. Now, I want the south-west of England. There must be a man to take my tea from the legal ports of France and carry it, not just to the English coast, but into Plymouth, Exeter, Bristol – even London itself – without giving a single bit away in tax. Not a ramshackle fleet of beggars and vagabonds, but one man who can control the entire passage from start to finish. A sea king. I envision a great world, Mr West, with you at the helm.'

'Good for the world. But becoming too well known and

too successful for commanding those vagabonds gets a man deported.'

Gautier brushed his periwig as if it were a captured creature flopping over his shoulder. 'How old are you?'

'More'n thirty.'

'Then isn't it time you made something of yourself?'

Tom went rigid. Gautier watched him coolly.

'By becoming the man they hunt down when you boast to the wrong society lady about how you play Tom West? How you give him a paper crown while anointing yourself king of the tax-free trade?'

'That's more like it,' Gautier smiled.

'Excuse me?'

'I believe you are haggling with me, sir.'

Tom smiled. 'You wish to take advantage of the loyalties of upwards of three hundred men between the French coast and the English capital, men who are loyal to *me*. So, if you were getting ready to suggest that, in our arrangement, I give you ninety per cent of the profit and receive ten, you are missing your mark.'

'I was going to suggest five. But I submit. Would twenty suit your needs?'

'Forty would suit 'em just fine.'

'I am bringing the tea all the way from India, my good man.'

'No, the East Indiamen are. Then selling it to you, who'll re-stamp it, in case I get caught. I smuggle it in and then give it back to the East Indiamen, who change the stamps over and sell on their duty-free goods, after giving you a percentage for cutting the deal and running the risk. But I am running a bigger risk in this vision of yours, Colonel. My neck. The crown doesn't take lightly to a man who makes deals with Anne's enemies.'

'I am surprised you have not asked for fifty.'

'A man of my birth?'

Gautier clapped. 'Can you have your ship ready for my cargo next month?'

'I have to go back to Devon first and unload the hold, but I can be back in time.'

'Be sure you are. There are always more ships.'

Tom smiled. 'But none so beautiful.'

II

A man of my birth.

Tom lounged in his chair in the ship's court, two glasses too many. The men were singing his name. Molly slept in the corner.

A man of my birth.

His mother had nearly died, delivering him.

As had Grace, twice, before Molly. But she hadn't feared death – had feared, rather, dying alone. In her journal – which Tom had learnt, as Benedict would call it, by heart – she wrote of seeking out the midwife, and hearing there about Tom West's first minutes in the world. She was a born storyteller, Grace. He could see her climbing the hill, with one hand on the taut bump of her stomach. The splintered stays of her gown pinched her ribs and made each breath painful. Behind her, red and green fields sloped towards the ocean, where the thatched roofs of Inner Hope Cove hid behind the trees. A single coil of smoke escaped the tangle of branches, perhaps from the fire she had lit in Widow Harding's bleak parlour that morning, earning pennies. Cloud shadows chased each other across the water, and Thurlestone Rock jutted up through the high tide. Further out, fishing boats skimmed the horizon, some slipping over its border. It would be calm sailing.

Grace's stomach pulsed. The baby's arm or leg moving, or her muscles loosening too far, her body opening on to the ground, like before. She folded her arms around her waist in a tight hug. Each stir of her womb made her scalp itch in the confines of her cap. She glanced around. The earth here told the story of men's movements: cartwheel tracks overgrown with grass, and boot prints alive with weeds. No one had been up here for a while. Grace pulled her cap off, feeling the damp rim left by her fear. She tried to pick out the church steeple at South Milton, but the village folded into the valley. Widow Harding had described the midwife there with the superstitious faith of the old, swearing the instruments and herbs kept by this Constance Weatheridge could cure even blind babies. She must be able to ease these cramps, if nothing else. Grace set off down the hill with the matted curls of her hair bouncing against her nape. In years to come, Tom would always make sure to linger, when sweeping the hair from the back of her neck – the heat there like holding hands to a fire – but it would only last a second, before cold air pimpled her flesh.

She hadn't been sure what to expect from Mrs Weatheridge, she wrote. If the midwife was in her girlhood when Widow Harding was first having children, she might be knotted with age now, just as the oaks lining Grace's way were tired where once they stood firm, or were even struck down, like this one at the foot of the hill, cleaved by lightning. And what if Mrs Weatheridge knew about Grace? Folks were not hiding their gossip from her now: their whispers at church and market

were those of minstrels play-acting at cunning, hisses loud
enough for even those at the back to hear.

Shouts for lunch in the hay fields – 'Bread and ham! Cider!
Hurry, now!' – and Grace tugged her cap back on. Following
paths worn by quick-flowing foxes and soft-footed deer, she
found the deep, unbound centre of the wood. Late garlic
spilt over the roots below, and birds threaded through the
branches above. That was how Grace talked about the landscape: she gave it words that introduced Tom to his birthplace
as if for the first time. She brushed dirt from her skirts. She
had walked over five miles that day and knew that, between
the earth, wind and sun, she must look every bit as slovenly as
people said she was. Would Mrs Weatheridge take one look at
her and close the door? Her own family most certainly would.

South Milton was built around the church, which looked
over a main street of cob cottages and two branching lanes.
The midwife's house was one of three set into the hillside.
Grace climbed the steps. Rose bushes growing beneath the
porch eaves embraced her in their damp sweetness. She
remembered a line of a folk song: 'roses around the door
mean you love your mother more.'

'Was you looking for me, lass?'

Grace turned to find an old woman with a face like a rotten
apple. 'Mrs Weatheridge?'

'That be me.' She gripped a bucket of water with swollen knuckles.

'I beg your pardon – I was informed by Mrs Harding that
you bring children.'

'I haven't been about the midnight industry for going on
two years now. What did you say your name was?'

'Mrs Tucker.'

The bucket dropped by an inch, sloshing water down Mrs
Weatheridge's skirt. 'Oh, for heaven ... '

Grace realised the midwife was going about with no shoes. 'I'm sorry,' she said. 'I should go.'

'No, no, follow me inside, dear. Not that way; front door is so stiff, I'm not sure it even opens any more.'

Grace trailed Mrs Weatheridge to the garden. The midwife's broad beans were looking much finer than her own and there was a full sack of lettuce heads by the back door.

'Bring those in with you,' said Mrs Weatheridge.

Grace bowed down, the muscles in her lower back grinding, and gathered up the sack. As she straightened, she saw gravestones just beyond the garden wall.

'Coming?'

The kitchen was dark, crowded with oak. Mrs Weatheridge set her bucket down on the sideboard.

'Well, you hold that sack like a bairn well enough,' she said.

Grace almost dropped the misshapen lump in her arms. She blushed as Mrs Weatheridge took it from her with a laugh.

'Maybe a little more practice needed,' she said. 'Sit you down through there and have some tea.'

'Mrs Weatheridge, I do not wish to importune.'

'Sit.'

Grace passed beneath the beam into the parlour, where the smell of hot sugar struck her. There was a great fireplace with a pot that summoned rumours of witching. Two armchairs waited by the fire and Grace crossed to them, peering inside the pot at a dark bubbling liquid.

'I call it hedgerow preserve,' said Mrs Weatheridge. 'I used to take that pot on the back of my pony all over, from Start Point to the River Erme. I used it for pork joints when no bairns were on their way, and bairns when there were no pork joints. But now no one knocks at my door saying I must go with them and help, and Arthur ... Well, I don't have much need for pork joints no more.' She smiled at Grace. 'I'll set the water boiling.'

Grace sat down. The armchair's stuffing was sunk in a dip too broad for her or Mrs Weatheridge to fill. Grace thought of the graves outside as she watched Mrs Weatheridge heave the pot aside. Her hands were bigger than most women's, joints glistening like wild pearls. Grace's grandmother on the moors had been in her fifties when Grace left, but her skin was kid leather, never put to use and stretched.

'You must be thirsty, walking all the way from Bantham.'

Grace sat up. 'How do you know I live in Bantham?'

Mrs Weatheridge paused over the fire, the copper pan for the water trembling in her hand – these shakes never left her now, Tom knew. She would be able to see Grace's anxious face in its burnished side. Tom imagined the run of her thinking. The girl was pretty enough to spark all this talk, for sure, and the bump of her stomach stretched her mantua. The lass must have taken the dress out herself, and was not much of a seamstress. Surely, if what people were tattling had any truth to it, Tom West would at least give the girl enough money to keep her looking nice – and so she would tell him, when he next brought Mrs Weatheridge tea and tobacco. Setting the pan down over the embers, Mrs Weatheridge smiled over her shoulder at Grace.

'It's an old woman's pleasure, knowing the business of others when she has none her own,' she said. The splash of water from the pitcher and scrape of the poker filled Grace's silence. 'Have you eaten today?'

'Pardon?'

'I baked biscuit bread just last week.'

Mrs Weatheridge shuffled out. The kindling warmth of the fire made Grace unfurl. The parlour was boxed in – a dresser, a captain's desk – and cluttered with surprising objects: a clock, a balance, Delft china. Grace looked over her shoulder and saw a bookshelf.

Rising, she squeezed through the furniture and drew the first volume down. The soft calfskin cover and peeling vellum told her it had been read many times and for many hours. The title was faded, but Grace could still make it out: Nicholas Culpeper's *Directory for Midwives*. She turned the pages. Handwritten notes crowded the margins, growing even busier around the diagrams.

Tilting the book towards the firelight, Grace studied a picture of the womb. No woman was attached: the stomach floated on the page, peeled open like a spring flower, or a corpse spread for examination. A baby curled inside, fully formed hands hugging his stomach. Grace snapped the book shut and took another down. More drawings: wombs like inverted vases, each containing a boy with a small penis jutting from between his legs, and even, here, a fully grown man hunched over, waiting for his release. There were no girls. Sentences glared up at her: 'God did not make imperfect instruments'; 'Laughing, crying if it be immoderate, is extremely hurtful, as also immoderate anger, causing oft times abortion'. Had one of these many faults pushed her sons too soon from her womb?

In the doorway, Mrs Weatheridge held the biscuit tin pinned to her body so it would not rattle and disturb Grace; she would say later it was like watching a creature see its own reflection for the first time, watching its embarrassment. After another minute, the back of Grace's neck reddened and she put the book back clumsily, forcing it into a far too narrow space. Mrs Weatheridge stepped forward; Grace turned at the floor's creak.

'I was just . . . '

'You're welcome to read all you like,' said Mrs Weatheridge. 'Mind, some of it's not true. One of those books says that, if you're vain, your bairn will be born with ruffs around its neck. Another says, if you crave rabbits but are denied, the bairn will have long floppy ears. The stage lost some great imaginations in those man-midwives.'

Grace returned to the fireplace. 'Why would you employ books that mislead you?'

'Sometimes the truth of things is only seen clear against what's false.' Mrs Weatheridge lowered herself into the chair, inch by inch. 'Now, open that box.'

Grace worked the lid off and took the white paper from on top. The biscuits reminded her of the churchyard outside: they were the same shape as coffins, and would have been baked in a moulded tin plate like the one she'd used in her first pregnancy, trying her hand at sweet treats. After, the biscuits became associated with the small box in which they buried their son, and she never tried again. Grace wondered if Mrs Weatheridge could guess her thoughts; something in the midwife's eyes seemed to recognise what she held tightest inside herself. But Mrs Weatheridge just pointed at the boiling water.

'I suppose you can brew tea like proper gentry.'

Grace took the boiling water from the flames. A stained teapot stood ready, and soon the smoky leaves expanded into the room.

'We had a tea set imported from China,' said Grace, after a minute of stirring. 'After a dinner party, my mother would take the women aside to brew the tea and discuss all the things not said in front of men. Then we'd take it into the salon and the men would follow us, smelling of brandy.'

'Did you not ever stay back and eavesdrop on the men?' asked Mrs Weatheridge. 'I would never have resisted.'

That made Grace laugh. 'More than once. But it was never anything as mysterious as I wanted it to be – the tin works, the hunt.'

'Pour yourself a cup. If you came all this way, I suppose whoever brought your babes before now cannot help this time.'

'Reverend Shapwick recommended a man, but he has nothing else to offer. And I do not want to ask the Reverend for another recommendation.'

'Wronged you, has he?'

Grace shifted under the woman's level gaze. 'I have reason to believe he keeps brandy and tobacco for the smugglers in the church rafters.'

'You don't need reasons and suspicions, girl – that's a known fact. But it don't bother most folks. Some, it even encourages, having a priest who knows how they keep in food and comforts and doesn't condemn them for it. You don't have such gratitude for free-traders?'

'Ought I?' asked Grace, clutching the cup, even though the heat burnt her fingertips.

Mrs Weatheridge clicked her tongue. From the defiance on the girl's face, either she was having a dalliance with Tom West and was ready to defend it with all the anger she could muster, or she hated his very guts. Something Tom would laugh at, when Mrs Weatheridge asked him which it was.

'I heard tell your husband hasn't been around much of late.'

Grace gripped the cup harder. 'No. He had to go away, for ...'

'Left you to face it alone, has he?'

Grace drank quickly, the tea burning her throat.

'You're not the first,' said Mrs Weatheridge, 'and you won't be the last. But it don't make his running any less than shameful cowardice, for that's what it is, and I hope you know it.'

Grace put the cup down, her hands shaking too hard now. 'That's not what other people say. They say I must have done something to drive Mr Tucker away. They say—'

'They say Tom West visits your house an awful lot.'

A beat. Then, 'You have heard that?'

'Yes. How many months along are you? Five?'

'I am not sure. It was hard to tell, at first. I did not think I would take with another child. Captain West brings me Mr Tucker's pay sometimes. I have – I have buried two sons. There is something wrong with my body.'

'Who told you that?'

Grace sat back. She only knew herbs for women's diseases, cures for women's wombs.

'Did your mother not talk to you about having a bairn of your own?'

'There was a book of prayers to be passed down to me. But I forgot to take it when I left. I mean, when I . . . '

'Flight of love, was it?'

Grace thought of Christopher's hand on hers during hidden moments in the garden. Of her father's hand wrapping around her wrist and squeezing. 'I only came here because—'

'Because you are alone,' said Mrs Weatheridge. She watched Grace struggle with a reply, the girl's too-thin cheeks twitching. She knew the pain of admitting to the silence that grew around you when all else had gone. It had taken a year, after Arthur passing and their daughter marrying in Totnes, to prepare just enough pottage for herself. 'I ask because, if you haven't been great-bellied for more than five months before now, you might not realise: within six weeks, it will be clear for all to see. You must know you can be taken to the courts if someone says your child was not from your marriage?'

Grace pulled her cap from her head. She twisted it between her hands. 'I know I cannot trust the parish. When my last son died, there were rumours that I would be charged with causing his death. I have never been much liked here. I am too different. I know the dangers if Mr Tucker does not return.'

'There is a greater danger than that, lass.'

'Ma'am?'

'Tom West. The bigger your stomach swells, and the longer your husband is gone and Tom delivering his pay, the more folks will look to Tom as the child's father. They won't speak against him. But he is not always here, and will come to a bad end, more than like. Give a man such as him enough rope and he'll hang himself. It will go hard with you, if your neighbours turn spiteful. Especially if he has no real reason to protect you . . . ?'

'None,' said Grace through pursed lips.

Mrs Weatheridge raised her eyebrows. 'Yet he has always gone for beauties out of the common sort.'

Tom would thank her for this compliment, but she would see through him.

'You seem to know him better than I.'

'I brought him into this world.'

Grace tried to squash the surge of interest as quick as it came, not wanting to show any curiosity about his life, or even feel it.

'He was one of my first,' said Mrs Weatheridge, 'but I'd remember it anyway, such a near disaster as it was. The West family lived in Inner Hope Cove, in one of the fishermen's cottages. Josias West was a crab man. A sight to see, those thirty-foot boats heading out into the bay with every man in the village heaving at the oars. And, the winter months, the families out in the square, weaving crab pots. The young boys weave the bottoms, that's how they get their learning in the trade. Had things been different, Tom would be there now, teaching lads to do what he learnt his self.'

Grace knew Hope Cove well: the sprawl of tangled nets, the aroma of salting pots, women's washing criss-crossing the narrow lanes. But she could not imagine Tom there, the heft of his shoulders narrowed to that small space. 'What happened the day he was born?' she asked. 'What disaster?'

'Josias was a fierce man,' said Mrs Weatheridge. 'The crabs weren't enough for his thirst. No doubt you know how wreckers light false beacons and lure ships on to the rocks to pick dead men's pockets. Josias was one of the worst. It always kept Tom one foot out, I reckoned. He was so tall and big, at so young an age, he took charge of the other bairns, and the men respected him for it. But he was on the outside too, for the secret fear they had of his father.'

Grace thought of the reverential nods Tom received when he passed by, and the lowered voices that followed him. King and exile, still.

'They just had one room for eating and sleeping, the Wests. I lay Anne by the fireplace. I remember the heat, and the two bairns she already had, crying no matter how I bounced them. Josias was out on a wreck. He came home reeking of ale and sea. He was angry, something gone amiss, and I was too young to know what to do as he smashed his way about. Soon, black smoke began to fill the house. He'd knocked over a candle and set the kitchen on fire. Can you imagine how quick those flames ripped through the thatch, reaching the next-door houses? Soon, there were shouts outside and folk running for water. And then, among it all, too quick for us to get out, the baby came on. I was afraid he'd not be able to breathe, all that smoke and the flames coming in on us. But Tom arrived into the world roaring and kicking for his life. And he kept it up as he grew. I always kept an eye on him, for there seemed something more to a boy born to fire than the act of a violent man. Something fateful.'

'What happened to his family?'

'Josias left Anne with six bairns: Tom's two elder sisters, two younger girls, and of course the last little boy, James.

Tom was more like James's father than his brother. To his sisters, too. He was about twelve, by then, and earning for all of them. Anne became ... faded. A ghost. But it was a sweet sight, Tom playing with James. The boy didn't live past four, poor lad. A bad humour took him. Then – well, that's when Tom fell in with free-traders, and stopped going out with the crab men. Could all have been very different. But he's stretched himself where he couldn't in that cove, I suppose. The whole of the sea is his, now.' Mrs Weatheridge sat forward and squeezed Grace's arm. 'Lass, do you want this bairn?'

The question was only a murmur, but still Grace recoiled.

'Don't fret; I'm not offering to bring it on early,' said Mrs Weatheridge. 'But I'm asking you, do you want it?'

'I am frightened. What do I have to give this thing? I feel I am a merchant ship, hired out.'

Mrs Weatheridge put her sleeve to Grace's nose and wiped. 'It has all of you in it,' she said. 'Go to that bookshelf and fetch the last on the right.'

Grace did as she was told, checking the title as she passed the book to the midwife: *The Compleat Midwife's Companion: or, the Art of Midwifry Improv'd*, by Jane Sharp. The midwife thumbed through it and, lingering at her elbow, Grace caught scattered sentences – the importance of not hurrying the labour, how to help children turned in the womb – until Mrs Weatheridge said, 'Here. Look at that.'

Grace accepted the book slowly, as if it had the weight of a newborn. She looked at the full-page picture and her heart sped up. A woman with a secretive smile and hair that curled like seaweed stood with her arms held apart from her body, as if to say, *This is me*. Her breasts were as swollen as Grace's. Beneath was the same diagram of the open womb that she had seen in Culpeper's book, but here it was part of the woman, and there was the child inside, the umbilical cord moving from him to his mother's body. A flower lay between the woman's legs, each petal delicately drawn.

'You are growing life,' said Mrs Weatheridge. 'It needs the warmth and safety only you can give it, and will need you even more when it comes into this world. What that world is, now ... I'll allow you don't have any power over your husband's decisions, or the law of the land, but you can decide where your child believes the horizon lies. You feel trapped. Are you going to trap your child too?'

'I am imprisoned by gossip, by my empty purse, by my body. What choice do I have?'

'Stake a claim and say what's yours – and do it now, or you'll never own anything, least of all yourself.'

'Mine ... ' Grace rested her hand on her stomach, squeezing gently. Ink stained her nails, midnight-blue crescent moons. She imagined her baby's tiny hand meeting her fingertips. 'It's all just words,' she said.

'And?'

Grace covered her left hand with her right, replacing her child's imagined grip. She felt the ridge of her knuckles and the bump left by her quill on the inside of her index finger. All of this was her story.

Until it wasn't. Until she told her story to Richard English, and destroyed everything Tom had worked to give her.

'More, Tom?'

Tom sat up, finding van Meijer with the jug before him.

'Can you take more?'

Tom waved the man off, swayed upright and lifted Molly in his arms. Carried the girl to the deck, where the sea was pinking under the first blush of sun, luxuriating in the stretch of high tide. He sat down on a barrel, and Molly stirred, so small still.

100

'Happy Mothering Day,' he whispered, drawing biscuits wrapped in paper from his pocket. 'For you.'

'You left me,' she said, so quietly she was likely still in a dream.

'Never,' he said, stroking her cheek, the invisible map of salt water, her second skin. 'You're mine.'

The Butchers' Serenade

The piping of the butcher boys came from Fore Street, attending the Crabtree house, the youngest girl just married. Tom heard them as he waited for Charlie Savage in the garden of Kingsbridge Grammar School, Benedict a shade beside him, and Hellard playing at slicing a worm in two with the tip of his boot. Armed with marrowbones and cleavers sharpened to a special note each, the butcher boys were producing something like a peal of bells, and they'd keep at it until their clean blue sleeves, the white paper in their hats and their almost-complete octave was rewarded with a half-crown. Tom hoped it would be a long time coming. The clamour suited him. He'd wanted an out-of-the-way place to meet Charlie and tell him Gautier's proposal, away from interested ears. Charlie was late, as usual – either carelessness or a small act of defiance that made Tom chuckle. Molly lay on the grass in the tidy orchard, reading a book she'd pinched from the shelves of the school.

'Do you miss book learning?' Tom asked Benedict.

Benedict winced. 'No, sir.'

There was a harrowed look about him, and Tom believed it. Molly was intent on whatever she'd picked up. Grace had loved her books. She read with aching eyes, hunched over some dictionary, the shrunken candle beside her bed. As Molly grew inside her belly, Grace stopped sleeping, sinking into dreams only to struggle free and lie awake, clutching her stomach, checking her thighs for spilt blood.

Heroickal: 'noble, stately, excellent, the three Heroickal Vertues are: 1. Moderation of Anger; 2. Temperance in Covetousness; 3. The despising of Pleasures. The part of an Heroick Poem is to exhibit a venerable and amiable Image of Heroick Vertue.' Grace would consider Thomas Blount's *Glossographia*, the book left open on the kitchen table while she stood out in the rain, killing a chicken. The rain diluted the blood and it ran to her elbows a think pink-white. It was true, people did talk of Tom as such: their own Robin Hood, who risked the Revenue to bring them salt and brandy. But he did not despise pleasures, and Devon loved him for it. He had no moderation of anger or temperance in covetousness, and Devon turned an eye from it. Even admired him for it. Grace thought that Thomas Blount should meet Tom West.

He came to her then, as if summoned. A knock at the door, a call, which came through the house and reached Grace in the kitchen garden. The dust of feathers hung from her slick hands. For a moment, she considered wiping them on her quilted petticoat – *her petticoat*. She wore the linen with a hand-sewn silk jacket only, cambered by her belly. She could not fix her dress before—

'Here you are.' He stood on the path, half in shadow, the sun setting.

'Mr West. I thought you might be Mr Tucker.'

'You often do,' he said. 'Yet it seems to me we're not very much alike.'

'No. Well. Is my – is Mr Tucker with you?'

'Ill, aboard my ship. I've brought you more money – more, I am certain, than the local magistrate would give if you went

103

to complain that your husband had abandoned you for Tom West . . . unless that is something you have done already?'

'Without evidence that Mr Tucker never meant to come back, or that I did not deserve such – I believe the phrase is "reasonable correction" – I know it is hopeless to do so.'

Tom nodded. 'Good. Because I know you might intend it as a strike against Kit – but a pretty girl like yourself calling me a free-trader in some clerk's record . . . that could be a strike against me. And – trust me, sweetheart – I do strike back.'

Gulls squabbled overhead and Grace followed them, neck twisting. She kept her eyes averted until she could swallow her choke. 'I do not intend to make trouble, sir.'

'I am very grateful,' he said, and the deep calm of his voice made her turn to search his expression as he continued, 'because it would be a great trouble to me, you know, it being needful to strike at you. I do not think I could do it.'

Grace did not know how she was supposed to respond.

'Kit is seasick,' Tom said, in her silence. 'Some men just don't have the muscle for it. He is sorry for how he acted. This absence, it's all just regret.'

Grace's shoulders were too heavy; she was being pulled down to the earth. She was tired, she wrote in her journal. Too tired to be angry or afraid. 'I think it is easier for men. If you grieve, you can drink all the ale in the world and brawl and find new beds. When we do it, there are still children coming and homes to keep standing. But, please, leave the money, if it will ease your heart.'

'Me? I'm not your husband.'

'No. But you are here.'

'Perhaps I miss you,' he said.

'I doubt it.'

'What else draws me to you, then?'

'I think you like to laugh,' she said. 'You like this power. I tell him I am to have his child, and he flees to you. I seem to be embarrassing you, Mr West. Would you rather not discuss such delicate matters between a man and his wife?'

'I'm sure he didn't mean it. What he said, about not wanting the child. He'll change his mind.'

'It is not up to him. It is my child.'

'Save the outraged speech for Kit, there's a good lass. This is none of my doing.'

'Not your doing,' said Grace. 'No, I suppose not. You just gave him the ship to sail away on. I am busy, Mr West, and your presence gives me no pleasure.'

Tom took a step towards her and then checked. A wolf grin flashed across his face. Grace stood still as he balanced the small pouch of money on the wall and swung away. She could hear him whistling all the way to the ocean.

Individuum: 'one single thing ... a body, inseparable; a Moat.'

Matrice, or matrix: 'the place in the womb where the child was conceived. Matrices of Letters or Characters, are those Moulds or Forms, in which the Letters ... which Printers use, are formed.'

She could create life, the very thing that summoned words to being, but she could not print her words, not from here, nor trust that in their printing she would survive history. She knew she would not. She might not even survive her own time. From here – with no power and no way out – what could her words do?

Time's up. She would face her husband, come what may.

Benedict's hand on his sleeve. Charlie Savage was saying thank you to the mistress over his shoulder and crossing the green towards them.

'My apologies, sir,' he said.

Tom stood up. 'Fine sport to be had in making you sorrier, Charlie boy.'

Charles removed his hat and bowed. 'Satisfied?' He looked at the powder monkey in the trees, the boy looking right back.

Hellard said, 'How about a kiss a bit lower to make it better?'

'Tempting as that sounds,' said Charles, 'it looks like you dropped the essential component.'

Tom and Benedict followed Hellard's gaze down to the severed worm in the grass. Tom's laughter pealed with the butchers' serenade. 'God's truth. Now, listen, Charlie. We're about to make a lot of money.'

Molly watched the huddled conversation – except, it wasn't that. Benedict, Hellard and Charlie were on their tiptoes, for, though Tom whispered, he did not bend his head. Molly flexed her shoulders, made a jut with her chin, a mirror for Tom.

The deal done, Tom led Molly over the street to the Old Inn, the slap of rain and stench of the butcher chasing them upwind.

Grace had later told him of her resolve, lying in his arms before the fire, wearing nought but a fur he'd bought her. A fisher boy had called to her that Tom West's ship had come in, and that they all sat now in the Pilchard, enjoying their spoils – a jibe he delivered with a sneer. Christopher was just a short walk from his own house. He wasn't going to face her, not now, not ever, with the child soon to be upon the world – or to leave it.

Then she would go to the Pilchard Inn.

What did men do? Call him out. She would call him out.

Tom had laughed at that, and she clipped his ear for it. Sitting before the fire of the Old Inn now, Molly reading at his feet – she'd stolen the book – Tom remembered how tender Grace's touch was as she stroked his forearm, telling him how she had walked to Burgh Island at low tide, planning what she would say to Kit: *Now, you have to face me.* Let them ask what in God's name she thought she was doing there alone at night; let them ask what she meant by questioning her husband in public; let them be embarrassed, let them shuffle about. None of it mattered. She had to face him, once. Had to ask him: *Do you know what you're doing?* It was just that question; just that answer. Because, if he did understand and chose to act no differently, then she could forget him and bring up her child by herself, without regretting his absence.

Grace put her cold hand to the door. The taproom was small: low ceiling, thick walls, blotched wood. Silence fell. Grace caught the eye of a villager she knew, then others she didn't. Christopher was not here.

'Mrs Tucker, isn't it?'

Grace looked around. The blacksmith. 'I'm looking for Mr Tucker.'

'I don't think you ought be here, Mrs Tucker.'

Grace looked him in the eyes. 'Please.'

The blacksmith dropped his voice: 'In the back, with Cap'n West. But I don't—'

'Thank you,' she said, and walked through the taproom, hands clasped at her stomach.

A heavy door separated the front and back parlours, and Grace pushed slowly, giving more and more of herself to whatever waited behind. Tom West's crew occupied every table, some resting heads on crossed arms, others tossing cards across the stained surfaces. Tom West was not there. Grace felt the baby lurch and held herself tighter – Christopher was asleep by the fireplace. The light played along the slope of his neck, danced in his golden curls. It was him. He was right there.

Grace stepped forward – a fist curled about her arm and jerked her back.

'You shouldn't be here, Mrs Tucker.' A low rumble at her ear, the restraint in each word telling her to follow the tone he had set.

'Go to the devil,' she hissed.

A few of the men looked up; Tom pulled her out.

He steered her through the inn without mercy. Grace blazed red. She stumbled into the crisp air as he let go.

'How *dare* you?'

'How dare *I*?' He laughed. 'You walk into a tavern alone, in the middle of the night, with all the docity—'

'I have a right to see my husband, and you have no right to stop me. I am going to have my child and he ... he ... and *you*, every time *you* guard him as if ... Damn you, Tom West, you're a worse coward than he is, and, if I were a man, I'd knock you down flat.'

Tom stared at her. He shifted into the light of the window and she could see he was smiling. 'Go ahead.'

Grace swung as hard as she could. She did not slap him; her fist took him on the chin, Grace on her highest tiptoe. Tom stumbled one step, then another, surprise sending him into the wall.

'I didn't think you had it in you,' he said eventually. 'Should have known better, I suppose.'

'I have more in me than you'll ever feel in yourself, no matter how many people you bully into thinking you're something big.'

Tom stepped forward, the bulk of him filling her vision. 'Watch yourself, Mrs Tucker. I don't have to *wish* I could knock you down.'

Grace swallowed the words and brought them back to him calmly: 'Go ahead.'

Tom's chest heaved. His fingers wrapped around her arm, unbreakable. 'I'm taking you home.'

'Get *off* me—'

'Words can only achieve so much. They can't break my grip, and they can't stop me doing whatever the damn hell I please to you. So *move*. Don't you know what being here does to you?'

Grace felt the words sink inside her: *Do you not know I no longer care?*

Tom plucked her from the ground. Grace felt the moment of flight like a launch from her own skin. He carried her home across the sand, the swell of her stomach pressed between them. Grace studied him: caught the throbbing line of his jaw, felt his anger. The ocean roared along with him, reminding her that it was just the three of them, and the ocean had long ago chosen sides. At her garden, Tom finally looked down into her face. He was so close, Grace could feel his breath, feel the movement of his thoughts.

He put her down.

Grace pressed against the door.

He did not move.

'I don't want you here,' she said, quiet, almost kind.

The click of shells and stones beneath his boots. 'Nor should you.'

He still did not move. Grace's neck hurt, looking up into his eyes. He had never seemed larger than at this moment – and, somehow, never this bare.

When his back was turned, she nudged the door open and slipped inside, bolting it behind her.

He had asked, his fingertips spanning her stomach before the fire: 'Why did you say that? That you didn't want me?'

'To make you leave.'

'Why?'

'I was afraid of you.'

He bowed his head. 'Are you still?'

'No.'

Now, Tom stretched his legs out, and Molly leant her head against his knee. At the bar, the butcher boys carried on their serenade, their blue sleeves not so clean, after all, spotted with the rust of old blood.

As if delicate threads ran between them, and she felt them jerk now, Molly looked up at him, a question on her face.

He wanted to ask her: *Are you afraid of me?*

But he knew the answer.

It wasn't fear that bound her to him; it was love.

Two Nights Before Good Friday

Île de Batz hummed with wildflowers. The moon was high, salting the path to the beach. Late; no sound drifted to the island from Roscoff. Molly was running down to the water when she bumped into Hellard, who swore and raised his hand.

Tom snapped, '*Hellard.*'

Hellard retreated. Molly relaxed her grip on the knife. Nathan came up the path and joined them.

'We casting off?' Molly asked.

'No,' said Nathan. 'Not if we know what's good for us.'

'Coward,' spat Hellard.

Tom shook his head, looking over the sand dunes and then down to the crescent beach.

'East Indiamen say there's a line of Revenue cutters and Custom sloops from Dartmouth to Plymouth,' said Nathan. 'Out for us in force.'

'Why?' said Molly. 'They can't know our aim, can they?'

'Bad luck,' said Hellard, 'that's all. Or they're making a show. We can outrun 'em, anyway, if they fall prey of sudden zeal.'

'We should wait them out,' said Nathan. 'Sailing too close to the wind will get us killed.'

'And have Gautier give his trade to a crew with the guts to carry it?' said Hellard.

Molly waited for Tom's bite, but Tom's eyes were on her: on the knife in her hand.

'We sail tonight,' he said.

'Captain, that's madness,' said Nathan.

'And you'll stay here,' Tom said to Molly.

'You know I won't,' said Molly.

'Strange kind of powder monkey,' said Hellard, 'can't get his hands dirty.'

Tom shouldered through them. 'Enough talk,' he tossed back at their feet. 'Just get ready. All of you.'

The narrow sea was in the mood to fight. Tom gripped the riggings, swaying with them, Benedict next to him, his telescope out, and Molly too, glancing between Benedict and the horizon. Revenue ships lined the edge of the sea, sails puffed out like proud pigeon breasts, the sun kindling behind them.

'How many?' she asked.

'Captain – ready weapons?' Kingston, from above.

'No.'

'We can take the bastards—' An argument: van Meijer, Prell, Laskey.

Nathan called from behind: 'I told you this was madness! Captain, we've got to turn back to Roscoff.'

'We're not fighting, and we're not turning around,' said Tom. 'We're going to heave to, and cast off the dinghy, empty.'

'Then what?'

'The crawl space. Below deck. All of us.'

'We won't fit,' said Benedict. 'The false bottom was designed to hide tea and brandy, not men – and, even then, we don't use it for our stores.'

'We don't hide our goods because I don't hide,' said Tom.

Molly and Benedict looked at each other, deciding not to ask what this was, if not hiding.

Hellard called from the fore deck: 'Guns ready!'

'Well, fucking unready 'em and get in the crawls below the bilge,' said Tom.

Hellard slid towards him, the deck wet with spray. 'And let those parasites seize it all? God's blood—'

Tom grabbed him by the chin, the other hand going to Hellard's pistol and folding around it, stopping his draw. 'Now is not the time to try my brotherly love.'

For a moment, nobody moved, and then Tom shoved Hellard towards the foresail, and the men followed. Spray leapt over the side of the boat. Tom yelled to Molly to get a rope and lash it round the mast. When she brought him the end, he wrapped the rope around his waist and then hers. The crew careened across the deck – Tom stood fast, Molly with him – and together they hauled the tiller round as the boom crashed from port to starboard overhead.

Waves lunged – they were being tipped down towards the hungry water. Molly's fingernails dug into Tom's arm.

'Scared?' Tom called.

'Never!'

Tom laughed.

The boat dropped, the wind trapped between the two sails, and they were suddenly, violently, becalmed. Tom looked down into Molly's face, which glittered with sea salt and excitement.

'Now, get below,' he said.

With Molly gone ahead, Tom kicked open the door to his cabin, fought with the lock of his sea chest, hauled it open. The inside of the lid was painted, now: red earth, golden sand, blue waves mottled and thick. Molly had done it. He threw his shirts aside, jammed the silver pistol with the walnut grip – won from an old Cavalier at cards – into his belt, and seized the lead box that contained Grace's journal. He shoved it into his coat, buttoned his coat shut.

Tom's spine burnt, curled up like the fossils Molly collected. She curved into the shelter of his body, as if they'd died together. Above: boots beating the boards, the clatter of hatches, the pop of casks opened, chests forced.

'Dick English?' breathed Nathan.

Kingston, his hands cupped to the boards: 'I don't hear him.'

All of them huddled here, listening to the Revenue thump up and down between hold and cabins, listening to them laughing, to one man spitting on Tom West's crest.

Benedict: 'Why don't they cast off for Devon?'

Tom shifted his head, as much as he could, and put a finger to his lips. The sea swelled below, as if aware the crew were so close. This must be what it's like to drown. His father had carried a bracket of fire up to the top of Hope Cove on his donkey. The fire winked to ships at sea, telling them: *All's well.* Tom watched the ships go down from the window of the cottage, watched the men drown, watched his father pick the bones.

A finger brushed his hand. Molly was tracing the lines of his palm.

He raised his eyebrows.

She mouthed: 'Your future.'

Reading his future. His future was sitting above, now being counted by the Revenue, now drunk by the Revenue, and the numbers altered. Molly's touch was gentle, following his scars and calluses. He remembered Grace binding a prayer about her hand. Grace had chosen Bible verses for the birth of her sons. Great-bellied again, the Bible sat unused on the shelf. She tied cloth about her palm all the same, and stitched into it not a prayer, but a name, a summoning: *Molly.*

A week or more after the night at the Pilchard Inn, Tom had knocked at her door, then entered without permission. When his boots sounded, she dropped her book.

'No call to be afraid,' he said. 'It's just me.'

Grace blinked. No call to be afraid – just him. As if this were normal. But there was something comforting about him – about the strength of his arms, the rumble of his voice, the confidence in his eyes – something that made her want to lean on him, tell him her secrets. When he first read these confessions, deep in his cups, he picked a fight with Hellard over nothing and broke a bottle of brandy against the wall.

Grace stood up. The room was small: it was either retreat, or step towards him. She remained where she was. 'I was not expecting anyone, sir.'

'I thought you might need . . . ' His eyes drifted down her body. 'Where is he?'

Tom bit his lip. 'Kit stayed in Guernsey.'

Grace felt it like a punch in the chest: winded, dizzy, sick. 'I am sure Guernsey is very pleasant at this time of year,' she said.

'I should have said – he's stayed behind,' said Tom. 'Guernsey is . . . No one need hear about Guernsey. I'm sure you have more sense than that, anyway, an intelligent girl like you. Smartest I've ever met.'

'You flatter me, sir. I hope the girls on Guernsey are clean.' She watched Tom's mouth open in shock, with a hard feeling of victory. 'Or perhaps he is not staying there for such pleasantries. Perhaps he is taking the waters. Is it that kind of place?'

'He'll come back on my next trip,' said Tom quickly. 'In the meantime, you can use this to buy yourself some silk gloves. I think green would suit you. Like your eyes.'

Grace looked at him, her head tilted. 'Why do you come here?'

The bag sagged. 'I told you—'

115

'You could send anyone to bring me that pouch, to pay for my silence or your absolution, whichever it is. But instead you come here yourself, the great Tom West, setting every tongue wagging. Why?'

Tom sniffed, rubbed his nose with a thick knuckle. 'Maybe I like talking to you.'

'Why would I want to talk to *you*?'

'Who else have you got?'

The tears came without warning. Grace covered her mouth. She sat down, her skirts folding wrongly about her, catching on something. And then Tom West was on one knee before her. She stiffened as he reached for her cheek.

'I don't have a kerchief,' he said.

Grace felt the same flight from her body, like none of this was truly happening. 'Then you are no gentleman, sir.'

'We already know that,' he said, making her laugh. 'Here.' He tucked his great fist inside his shirtsleeve. She held her breath as he dabbed the tears away with the stiff cuff. It smelt salty; he carried the sea on every part of him. 'I didn't mean . . . I would never want to upset you,' he said. 'Unless it was to hear what you'd say next.' His voice became rougher, as if the words were so unfamiliar they were painful to form. 'I *do* want to talk to you. I'm—'

'Enchanted?' Grace felt herself go cold.

Tom was silent for a long moment, and then: 'I don't rightly know what that means. But it sounds like something I'd enjoy.'

Grace knew her smile showed.

'You'd laugh at a lesser learned creature?'

Grace shook her head. 'What would you like to talk about?'

Tom made himself comfortable on the floor, crossing his arms over his bent knee. 'What was it like, where you were born?'

Grace drew the sleeves of her faded mantua over her fingers.

'I grew up on the moor. My father is a squire.' She tried to think how to describe her world to him.

Tom leant over to her fallen book. He closed it gently, returning the volume to the bookshelf – the parlour so small, his span so great, he hardly had to stir to reach the wood he'd laboured over, which he stroked gently, only looking back when she continued.

'I was intended for three boys, all born the same year as me. They died before we reached seven or eight. Then, when I was a little older, my father decided we would not be placed out.'

'I don't know what . . . '

'Sent away, to nunneries, or the boarding schools city merchants send their children to. I learnt French, and how to paint and sing, at home. Beyond that, the limit of my experience was bound between Monks Cross and Clapper's Bridge. That was as far as I was allowed to walk alone. I loved standing up there, watching the wide universe around me. I dreaded going home, returning to needlework.'

'You did your own sewing?' said Tom. 'I always imagined you with silk stockings and jewelled garters.'

Grace arched an eyebrow at him. He shifted slightly, but his smile remained. 'Samplers, or cloth frames for mirrors,' she said. 'If you could master the alphabet in stitching, if you could move between blackwork and whitework, cut and draw . . . it meant you were no longer a child. You had grown up, you were ready to . . . '

'Darn the alphabet into your husband's sleeves?'

This time, she did nothing to hide her laughter.

Tom stretched his legs, boot resting near her feet. Her skirts had snagged, and he could see that her stockings were brown with dirt, but still his body tightened with want.

'I was never good at it,' said Grace. 'I always pricked my thumbs.'

'Does that mean you're not yet a woman?'

'What do you think?'

Tom's gaze dropped to her stomach. He moved as if to reach for her, but then stopped. In her journal, Grace wondered if he had been going to touch the roundness of her body, the proof, if it was that.

Yes, it had been his intent to touch her, but he'd feared her reaction.

'I think you can be anything you want to be,' he said. 'You've made it this far.'

'This far,' she repeated, gazing about her. 'I am not sure it is much to celebrate. I only wish, if I had *your* power ...' She saw his growing frown, and fell quiet.

After a minute, he said, 'Does your father still live? Perhaps he could help you.'

'Did Mr Tucker never tell you how he and I came to be wed?'

'Not that, exactly.'

Grace thought of drunken nights – of the sort of things men might tell other men about their wives, *exactly*.

'Kit told me it was marriage for love,' said Tom. 'He talked about you constantly, so that eventually I could imagine you as if I knew you. He told me you were the most beautiful creature on earth.'

'Marriage is different, where I am from. If one marries for love, it is the greatest sin. Mr Tucker imagined his father would forgive him. Perhaps he would have. But he died owing so much, it hardly mattered. There was no estate to inherit.'

'Then you eloped because you loved him?'

'Yes. No. I had to escape. I will not tell stories. Only, I had to escape.'

'I know that feeling.'

'You ran away to sea?'

'In a manner. I was helping owlers before I was a man.'

'Owlers?'

'We smuggled wool out.'

'What did your father think? Would he have accepted you back, if you needed his help?'

'I've never needed any man's aid,' he said. 'I aid my people. I could help you, if you'd accept it. Money, housing, food, clothes – they're yours, if you want them.'

'Yes, you could help me. You could talk to Mr Tucker. You could tell him . . . You could bring him home.'

A violent savagery came over Tom's face. 'Why would you want him?'

Grace's fingers gripped and pulled apart. 'He's my husband.'

Tom pushed up from the floor abruptly, putting his hand out to say, *Stay where you are.* Grace rose anyway, almost brushing his body. She wrote later that his anger – unexplained, quick – was like a cloak of thorns cast about his frame. She stood in its snare, not backing away.

'You're welcome to each other then,' he said.

Tom held Molly closer now, as dust and loose caulking fell over them. A group of men above, making a report:

'Looks like five hundred pounds of tea, sir.'

'And the crew?'

'The boat is gone, sir.'

'Gone *where*?'

'They must have abandoned ship near Jersey.'

'And we're sure it's this scoundrel, West?'

'That's his name carved in the cabin door, up there.'

Molly had carved the crest in the door of Tom's Court. It was her own design: a compass whose southern point split into an anchor; two cutlasses crossed behind the midpoint of the compass, and two pistols crossed behind the tip of the anchor.

A crown topped the northern point. The W of the compass was scored deepest.

'Well, English's face will be priceless. After all these years, it's us who bring in West's cargo.'

'But no West.'

A sniff. 'No need to complicate matters. A tip-off against Tom West is a rare enough chance. Have to be seen to chase it down. But, by God, can you imagine if we actually brought the man *in*? Get the anchor up. We'll escort her into Dartmouth.'

A shiver across his palm. Tom looked down: Molly weighing his future.

The lead box was cold against his heart.

The Night Before Good Friday

I

The *Escape* was shouldered by a cutter and two luggers into the Dartmouth Customs yard, where her sails were let down, her ropes tied and her hold left empty.

Tom kept them in the crawl until each cask was off, until the officers went home, drunk and rewarded, and the dock was returned to the slap of waves. Then he closed his hand around Molly's and said: 'Time to take what's ours.'

Molly shuffled after Benedict, and stumbled out into the hold. The cannon balls were rolling loose. Molly darted to them as Tom unfolded, looking about his spoiled kingdom.

'Get out there, get anything you can carry on deck, ours or otherwise, and get us out of here.'

'This scheme beats even our Start Bay run, under Ezekiel,' said Hellard. 'Why not just tell me, back on de Batz?'

'I don't answer to you.'

'Or trust me?'

Tom laughed. 'Now, why would I do that?'

Hellard salvaged brandy from the mess, took a swig, and then offered the bottle to Tom with a soft jab in the chest. 'Ain't I shown myself to be trustworthy, all these years? Never let my tongue wag, have I?'

The smile drained from Tom's face. He glanced at Molly. 'That's right, brother.'

Another jab, harder now. 'A rare thing, ain't it, for men like us, men who've done what we've done, to have someone to trust? Rare enough to be treasured, I'd say.'

Tom's hand folded around the brandy. 'Let's see what they've got in this place.'

From the door to Tom's Court, now hanging on one hinge, Benedict watched Hellard chuckle and Tom urge him on ahead. But, as soon as Hellard's back was turned, a look of exhaustion struck Tom, and he put a hand to his breast pocket, as if trying to soothe his own heart – or perhaps convince himself of something, despite the hurt of it. Watching Molly, now, as she righted the weapons store, Benedict wanted to ask Tom, *How could you forgive Hellard for killing her mother, whatever promises you once made?* For he was certain, now, that it was not Dick – the conviction born that night and rising every year – but Hellard who had killed Grace.

The *Escape* was moored at a slip that led to three Customs warehouses. Inside, crates and barrels were stacked taller than the most overgrown hedgerow.

Next to Tom, Nathan said, 'Nice of them to leave it all neat for us.'

'Gentlemanly, you could say.'

'You planning on selling this stuff back to the other free-traders who lost it?'

Tom scratched his chin, watching as the men went about their work quietly, efficiently: the concentration of victory about to be had. 'What free-traders?'

Nathan shrugged. 'Could be Bale in North Devon what had these confiscated, could be Coxe. Might even be Collector Blackoller. That would be a fine joke.'

'There are no other free-traders in Devon.'

'Ah. Yes. I see your point.' Nathan was shaking his head, about to turn away and help the others, when Tom seized his arm. He followed the captain's fixed stare. Through the warren of salt, copper, iron, there was the light of a small office, and the shadows of moving men. 'Dick English?'

'They didn't have every tidesman, coast waiter and dragoon on duty for nothing. Someone told them I was expected back tonight.'

'Captain, what are you intending on?' Nathan said.

'It's not intent if another man sets events in motion,' said Tom, drawing his pistol.

Nathan followed him.

They came up on the offices: wood panels and bare windows. Inside, a desk, cabinets, sea charts. Around the desk, three men. The captain who had boarded the *Escape*, glowing from Tom's brandy, unable to control his glory now because Richard English was at the desk, white with fury, trying to reassume command. Tom knew the captain by reputation: a bittle-headed assistant collector, only shifting himself when he was sure he wouldn't be roasted. He would have waited to see the rowboats were off the *Escape* before boarding. He and Dick were equals, the captain the assistant collector at sea, and English the assistant collector on the coast, but it was Dick in charge now, haranguing the Justice for more leeway and more men. The Justice was demurring, placating, refusing.

Nathan looked a question at him: *I thought the Justice was in your pocket?*

More than that. The Justice was his venturer, though Nathan didn't know that. He had just as much to lose by Tom's fall. It wasn't him that talked.

Tom clicked the hammer back.

Nathan grabbed his wrist, mouthed, 'You can't.'

Tom seized Nathan's hand and squeezed, close to breaking the carpenter's fingers.

'Murder a Justice and you'll be hanged for sure,' Nathan hissed. 'God's truth, *you can't.*'

Dick swept ink and pens from the table. 'What gives you the right to draw *air*, let alone a salary? I give you a traitor in Tom's Court, I give you time and tide, I give you Tom West, and you give me tapped casks!'

A crash made Tom release Nathan: the fall and bounce of barrels. The argument in the office stopped. Tom turned and ran back towards Molly, keeping his head down, a shot firing somewhere from behind – Dick English splashing through pouring brandy. Hellard was trying to control chaos, half the men not wanting to leave the rest of the bounty, the other half loosing the ship from her ties, and Molly on deck, hoisting the main sail, shouting at Hellard, 'Get it together, for fuck's sake!'

That made Tom laugh, in the middle of it all. Another shot. Tom looked back. It was Dick English, at last within spitting distance, his blond hair and blue eyes the devil's own, caught in a flash from the sky.

So shoot the devil down.

Tom tried to squeeze the trigger, but his finger wouldn't move, seized at the joints.

Dick was patting his belt – his powder was wet. He was a small man, with a small man's anger, but affected unconcern now. He looked at Tom as his father used to, as if he could see right through him, measure his worth – and English didn't think it much.

Tom struck the flint in his holster, once, twice, and then hurled the little blue flame into the lake of brandy. Fire like hell denied sprang up between them.

*

They made it out with more than twice what Gautier had given them. The ship settled into Frogmore Creek, shivering with strain. The men were in Tom's Court, drunk, thrilled, mad, out. Kingston led the board in knife throwing, the blades quivering against the door. Molly waited her turn, beer half drained, spinning her medallion on the table. When Tom ducked into the court, she slammed her palm flat over it.

'Where's Hellard? And Shaun?'

'Gone,' said Kingston. 'Didn't say where.'

Benedict was asleep with his head on the table. Tom pulled at his collar and let go – Benedict hit the table with a thud, and did not wake up.

'What's wrong?' asked Molly.

'Some eyes that lad keeps!' said Jarvis.

'Some eyes the lot of you,' said Tom, kicking Nathan in the shin. He sat up with a start. 'Nathan – you tell Hellard what we heard?'

'What did you hear?' asked Kingston, needling the knife free.

Nathan glanced around. 'I . . . I don't think I told him—'

Tom slammed a bottle down in front of the carpenter. 'You're supposed to be the one with smarts. Here was me thinking you cared for the Justice's good health.'

'I'll come with you—'

'You've got in my way enough for one night.'

Molly jumped up. 'What's happening?'

'Just a reckoning. Nothing more. Stay here.'

Molly wanted to argue, but knew better. She watched him go. Her hands itched.

Kingston tapped the wall: three bullseyes. 'Someone's blood spilling tonight.'

Nathan put his head in his hands. Gold winked at him. Boy, spinning a coin. 'What is that?'

Molly opened her palm. Nathan closed one eye. Everything was moving too fast.

'Don't tell Benedict. It's St Nicholas.'

Nathan turned it over. He squinted until the words on the medal came into focus. Priez pour nous. Pray for us.

II

The moon spilt over the chapel, pierced by the steeple and left to bleed: a stuck pig. The family graveyard tumbled down the hill, as if seeking to climb into the Justice's garden. Among the stones, a gaping black wound. A fresh grave, yet to be filled. A death in the family. The litany of Tom's childhood: if a grave was open on Sunday, if a thread of melting wax curled your way, if a dog howled under the window of a sickroom – it all meant death. All those superstitious fools, hoarding signs until they garlanded themselves with death writs, shouting: *I'm weak! Come and take me!*

Tom had been weak, cracked himself open for Hellard, showing him every softness, every leniency. So, he shouldn't be surprised if Hellard now sought to shove him in the open grave. Nathan had presumed the traitor was the Justice himself; Hellard would hope to use that supposition to cover his own tracks: kill the Justice tonight and say, *Here, a gift for you from your loyal servant – the neck of a traitor done up in a bow.* But Hellard didn't know the Justice funded Tom and used the return to maintain this double-piled house in jolly red brick and white cornice, and that he wouldn't risk his new sash windows on something as trifling as morals. What had Hellard betrayed Tom's love for?

Power, envy, greed, or simply the bitterness of the unwanted and unloved whoreson? Tom had wanted him. Tom had loved him better than their father would have. Hellard was spared their father's blows, at least.

He'd be spared nothing tonight.

This thought chased around Tom's skull as he circled the house, but he knew it lacked conviction. His mother's voice was stronger. *Promise to care for him, no matter what. Do not inherit the sins of your father.*

The servants' entrance was ajar. Tom primed his pistol and stalked the stone-flagged corridor, past the pantry, to the kitchen. He stepped into the quivering shaft of a candle, by which he saw Shaun helping himself to a tin of white cakes wrapped in crisp paper, and Hellard helping himself to a cleaver from the marble block.

'Hellard West, wanted for petty housebreaking.'

Shaun coughed up sugar, powdering his lips.

Hellard weighed the cleaver, and with each swipe at the air his grin grew. 'Justice of the Peace butchered in his bed after accepting some cruel tidy bribes from Tom West and then peddling captain and crew to the law – now, that's a ballad worth its paper.'

Tom rolled his shoulders. 'Quite the story.'

'You never did know what to do with those who break the code.'

'Maybe I'm learning.'

Shaun was trying to close the lid on the tin and dropped it now, a rattle that bounced off the walls. Both Tom and Hellard looked to the kitchen door. No scrape of furniture, no footsteps.

Tom jerked his head. Shaun tugged at his hat and scurried into the service corridor. His retreating steps marked seconds between Tom and Hellard, as they approached opposite ends of the table and laid their weapons down.

'The Justice didn't know my intentions.'

Hellard licked his upper lip. A sheen of sweat there. 'Then it must've been Benedict or Charlie Savage what betrayed you.'

'Or you.'

Hellard was mottling Devon red. 'I've lived by your word and your name since I was a lad. Ain't I been called a hangallus and worse because I do your dirty work and never complain? Ain't I sat peaceably for scraps while you heap Orlando's plate high? I kept my vow and never breathed a word to your new foundling of what you did, nor what you almost didn't do, which in my books was worse, you standing here now so mighty, as if the code means ought to you—'

Tom reached across the expanse and seized Hellard by the back of his head and slammed his face into the cleaver lying on the table: once, twice, three times. Then held him there, forearm pressing into Hellard's neck, another hand catching Hellard's wrist – his brother going for his pistol – and pinning his arm down, all of Tom's body over Hellard's now, a man caging a horse he planned to break. Hellard yelled out. Tom pressed his face into the cleaver all the harder. A trickle of blood wound from Hellard's cheek.

Tom bowed down, his lips to Hellard's ear, and whispered something. Silence. Tom pushed. The thread of blood unspooled. A nod.

'Say it,' hissed Tom.

'I ain't nothing –' a groan – 'I ain't got nothing without you.'

'That's not what I said.'

Blood dripped on to the flagstones.

Then, Hellard's voice like it was killing him: '*I* ain't nothing without you.'

Tom let go. 'Remember it.'

Hellard slid to the floor. Tom stood over him. He picked up the cleaver. Hellard caught him by the leg. 'Then why d'you keep

me around? You don't want to be Josias, that it? You've already
outdone him.'

Tom was ready to stamp on Hellard's hand when sea sickness
tipped him. He was a child, watching from the floor as his father
prepared to stamp him out, as his father screamed, *You're nothing
without me.* Hellard's laughter righted him. Hellard was crying
with laughter. A chuckle got stuck in Tom's throat. He dropped
the cleaver on to the table. Squatted down. Dabbed at Hellard's
cut with his sleeve.

Hellard gripped his hand. 'You and me to the end. That's
what we told your ma when she was in her last.'

'I know.'

'Who should we fear judgement from?'

Tom got to his feet. 'I'm not waiting for judgement.'

Hellard rubbed his neck. 'That's right. She broke the code.
In her nature. Did what you had to. And you'll do it again.
Benedict, or Charlie.'

A board creaked above them. Tom's gaze dropped to his
bloodied sleeve. 'Wait for me outside.'

Hellard slipped away. Tom drew a chair closer and sat down
with a sigh. He was unwrapping a cake when the door opened.
The Justice in his nightrobe, a quilted luxury. Tom could have
charged tickets for the look of horror on the man's face as he took
in Tom's bulk, the blade on the table, the box of sweet treats.

'Captain West, I performed everything in my power to call
Richard English off – the man is sick for you.' His words were
thick, either from sleep, or dread. 'A villain on your ship had
him salivating over titbits.'

'He used those words – a villain on my ship?'

A hesitant smile. 'He calls you all villains. But he did seem
quite certain it was a seafaring villain, not one on land.'

Tom cracked his knuckles. 'I like a gentleman who hears a
noise late at night and ventures downstairs himself.'

The Justice seemed to be waiting for Tom to rise. Finally, he closed the door behind him. 'I was expecting Mrs Rowe. Our cook. Your presence here is highly irregular, sir, highly irregular.'

Tom's eye was drawn back to the cleaver, the line of blood. His own blood was racing. He'd been moments from killing his brother. 'The name.'

'Captain English never identified the wretch, sir.'

'He doesn't trust you.'

'I am aware how much Devon benefits from your ventures, sir. I assure you, such ventures can continue.'

Tom bit into the cake. 'Devon will enjoy whatever she's worth. But, if Dick English continues to get in my way ...' He picked a lump of uncooked flour from his teeth. 'Usually, a parson brings these cakes round to local people, after church on Good Friday. He takes his gratuity from the lord of the manor. Some give their thanks – that being all they can afford – others tip royally. But you don't wait on the church. Mrs Rowe bakes 'em for you special. Wonder how you thank her. How you'd like to be thanked, for your efforts.'

'I will compel Captain English to consider his position, sir.'

Tom wiped sugar from his stubble. His palm came away damp with sweat. He was burning with it. 'You have an open grave in the yard.'

The Justice tugged the knot of his nightgown tighter. 'My eldest son.'

A clock sang somewhere deep in the house. 'I'm sorry.'

'His brother is healthy.'

It wasn't clear to Tom, from the tone of the Justice, whether this made it more or less grieving.

Good Friday

Molly watched from the stern as Tom came up the creek, unsteady on his feet. The crew were still asleep. The dawn chorus celebrated from the treetops. Tom seemed oblivious to the birds – oblivious to the ship, even – as he slumped on to the bank, his head hanging, a relief to it, as if holding himself up was a daily punishment. Molly swung overboard.

'Tom?' He did not stir. Silt sucked at Molly's bare feet. 'Tom?'

He jerked up. 'There you are.'

Molly laughed. 'I've come to finish the job.'

'The job?' He was hoarse. Pale.

'The metaphysical art of palmistry.'

Nothing.

'Your future,' Molly said. 'Give me your hand.'

Tom's fist uncurled so slowly, she expected a pearl to be waiting there, some secret. But there were just the black lines of sweat. Fire and earth.

'Go on, then,' he said.

'It won't come cheap.'

'What?'

'Your future. It'll cost you.'

He looked scared.

'A shilling. I just meant a shilling. I don't want your soul.'

He took his hand back, wiping his face. 'Too late,' he said.

Molly squared her feet in the earth. 'You saw Dick English in the warehouse, didn't you? I saw him, too. I thought you were going to shoot him.'

'I was.'

'Why didn't you?'

Tom bowed his head.

'He killed my mother.'

Tom raised red eyes. 'That's right.'

'And that's why you set fire to the warehouse. That's why you make a mockery of him. That's why you drive the varmint mad.'

'That's right.'

'But you won't kill him.'

'Killing him would be a mercy.'

Molly touched his hand. 'You know I'd do it, don't you?'

Tom's gaze was fixed on the knife in Molly's belt. 'I know it.'

The mill poured with water, like rain sheeting from rooftops after a storm. The churn was so fast and so loud, Tom could hardly hear Mr Cook telling him about his plans for expansion, telling him how much flour Tom's investment could grind, how much coin that flour could make, as the Avon hurried along besides.

'Sounds like the kicking of a drowning man,' said Tom.

Mr Cook looked at the wheel in surprise. 'S'pose it does. Get used to it. Mind, my wife says I shout so loud for my tea, it's as if the wheel is turning in my head. I says to her, I been hoping Cap'n West would have time to see me for weeks now, and here he sends word he's got to thinking about legacy, about the future – expanding, like – and wants to invest some of his coin in my labour. But does she listen? No, sir. You know how women are.'

Tom cleared his throat. 'Yes. I do.' He looked up at the mill, three storeys in grey stone and fired brick against blue sky, and, beyond, the cresting hills. 'Reckon we can turn a profit together, Mr Cook.'

Cook licked his lips, asking with a fool's grin, 'Drink to that, Cap'n West?'

The cider settled sweetly in Tom's stomach as he set off into Loddiswell Woods, the afternoon sun on his face. Benedict and Molly said they'd be down at what they called the beach, the gentle curve of the Avon, where a horseshoe of mud and sand invited waders. It was strange weather: snow a fortnight ago, and now so warm he slung his coat over his shoulder.

The beaten track, which was brightened by copper leaves trod into the black and purple earth, sank into the high hedgerows, from whose banks ivy and ferns lolled among wavering daffodils, and above them trees craned for the sky, luminous green lichen shivering on the branches. White run-off cascaded down the hillside, and to his left the ground fell away, a deep drop to the Avon, churning brown. It soothed Tom's heart, which had been beating like lead shot bounced in a man's pocket since last night. He had asked Molly, as they rowed up the Avon this morning, 'What if we were to leave Devon?'

'You mean go to Île de Batz for a while?'

'I mean leave. For good.'

A look like he'd used a word she didn't comprehend. 'Devon's our home. We *are* Devon. This is where we belong. It's in our blood.' A pause. 'My blood.'

As if blood didn't join them.

He'd heard land like this called *the waste* – unbroken woodland, moors high and dark, wet lowlands, sandy heaths where nothing grew, salt marshes flooded by the estuary twice a day. A man was proud of his ploughland, of making earth that touched sky or sea turn towards him instead. Tom understood the desire to dominate, to tame – but there was a part of him that wanted to turn wild in the wastes, and be forgotten. To rest here, where the power of man did not know him. The power of mercy, the power of deliberation and justice – which he'd managed to deliver to his brother, a rein on his temper, but not—

A laugh.

Molly, ahead, laughing at Benedict.

Tom pulled at his neckerchief, the sweat there like a fever, and followed the sound on to the river beach. He stood high on the lane, looking down the drop to where a tree had recently fallen; Benedict sat entwined in its naked roots, his feet in the water. Molly was braver. She'd rolled her breeches up and taken her shirt off, hanging it from a branch, where it stirred in the breeze like a flag. She was floating in the water, fearless of the strong eddies circling this sheltered dip, fearless of the cold. That's my boy.

Tom looked at her again. Ribs that stuck out like culverts. Skinny chest, strong arms. Nothing of the woman about her. Except. Could he see more flesh on her hips? Was her chest as flat as always? He moved so that he could see Benedict's expression: listening attentively to some story Molly was telling. Very attentively.

'Then the men would charge their guns with powder, fill a pitcher with cider and gather under the best tree in the orchard,' Molly was saying, kicking with one foot, drifting in a circle. 'And one time I dressed in boy's clothes – I mean, in my best suit.'

Grace had told Tom about this, finding mirth in it: how Molly had dressed as a boy and gone among the local ciderists and been taken for a young hand – just five, then – presumed for somebody's son and allowed to join them in the orchard to drink to the best tree.

'I see,' said Benedict, nothing in his expression changing, no sign he knew what she was really telling him, as Tom knew he did; no sign he understood she was confessing: *I dressed as a boy before the ship.* That it was in her nature, somehow, to flee a woman's life; that he, Tom, had given her what she always wanted.

'It was custom for the women to bolt every door and window, whatever the weather, and the men weren't allowed back in until they could guess what was on the spit. Wives always made sure it was a rarity, sometimes not even edible. Old boot, once.'

Grace had told Tom about this, too: how Molly knew from Grace's work at the farm as a carder what the women planned to roast. How Molly had come among the ciderists dressed as a boy, but with the knowledge of a girl.

'But I knew what was on the spit. Sea bass, biggest you've ever seen. When they realised it was me, they found it so funny, I was given the best fillet. Mama said I was just like Tom: cunning enough to pull it off, charming enough to escape punishment.'

'I'm sorry,' said Benedict.

Tom took a step down the bank, Benedict's tone a fish hook in his gut.

Molly was considering Benedict. She said, 'Nothing to be sorry for.'

'I just meant . . . your mother.'

Molly looked up at Tom, no surprise on her face. She'd known he was there the whole time. 'We'll have justice. Ain't that right, Tom?'

Benedict turned around, and Tom noted the look of panic and guilt on the boy's face before Benedict could conceal it.

'That's right,' said Tom. 'Man determines his own fate, one way or another.'

Benedict bowed his head, as if praying – for what, Tom didn't know. Forgiveness, maybe. Mercy. Or grace.

Molly walked ahead, twining a snapped snowdrop. Tom let her escape earshot. Rising winds made Loddiswell moan and sway. Next to him, Benedict was quiet, fidgeting with hat and scarf, on and off, tied and loose. The sun slicked the mud, gilding the clear water running over the track.

'I've a problem to solve,' said Tom. 'After some interesting talk.'

'She brought it up.'

Tom sniffed. 'Seems Dick English has made a new friend.'

Benedict winced.

'Only you and Charlie boy knew about the deal with Gautier. And the Justice tells me English fingered a man on the ship. So, Charlie's out.'

Benedict stopped walking. He glanced ahead at Molly – thinking that her presence would save him, Tom guessed. But she had turned the corner, her mind on buzzards overhead or the first bluebells: the curiosity enjoyed by those who feel safe.

'And Hellard,' said Benedict. 'Hellard knew, too.'

'And Hellard. That leaves two questions. Who, and why.'

'Tom, I'd never betray you. I swear it.'

Tom stood in the track, looking into the blue of Benedict's eyes. So very much like his little brother, before he'd died. 'On what do you swear?'

'God. As my soul be saved, I swear it on God's name.'

A woodpecker made Benedict jump so hard, it may as well have been his executioner's pistol.

Tom laughed. He cupped Benedict's cheek. 'My lad.'

'You know I'd never do anything to harm you or Boy. You've got to know that.'

Tom could smell the boy's desperation. He seized Benedict's chin. 'I know you want your soul saved.'

Benedict wrapped his fingers around Tom's wrist. 'The Lord knows me innocent. Just as he knows you innocent.'

'Of what?'

Benedict tugged at Tom's grip, but it wouldn't give way.

Tom murmured, 'You looked very much a boy caught in a lie, when Molly promised justice for Grace's murder.'

Benedict shook his head. 'I know you'll get justice.'

A horrible smile. 'Have faith, do you?'

A nod.

Tom steered Benedict back one step, then another, to the edge of the path. 'Then you weren't thinking of telling her anything she doesn't need to know?'

Benedict couldn't feel the ground beneath his heel. The earth was tumbling away to the river below; time was tumbling away. This was it: the moment Tom's favours and virtues snapped. The moment Tom's care for him was forgotten, and he was crushed in the man's fist. The moment he'd prayed against.

O Lord, grant that this day I fall into no sin, neither run into any kind of danger; but that all my doings may be ordered by thy governance, to do always that is righteous in thy sight.

Do what is righteous, in your last moment.

Benedict gathered his voice. 'What might I tell her? That the nightmare she suffers is you? *You* are the demon behind the door, beating her mother. It was *your* roars she could hear, not the bark of Richard English. Is that what worries you at night, Tom?'

A slow sneer. 'What worries me is the long drop behind you.'

Lord, may it please thee to strengthen such as do stand, and to raise up them that fall; and finally to beat down Satan under our feet.

'I'll tell you what keeps me up at night,' said Benedict. 'A sequence. I heard a shot, and a punch. English fired at you, but hit Mrs Tucker instead, then Hellard struck him. That's what Hellard says. But, when I hear those sounds at night, Tom, they are in the wrong sequence. A punch. Then a shot. Hellard swore to do the deed if you wouldn't, I heard him. So, what if Hellard struck English, and then fired his pistol. Hellard killed her, and you forgave him. Because he's your brother, because Mrs Tucker broke the code – and you needed Hellard to be the villain.'

Words unsaid, almost unthought: *You still do.*

Canopy creaked overhead. Snowmelt shivered.

Benedict pushed on: 'I didn't betray you. It was Hellard. It's always been Hellard.'

A gradual smile flickered on Tom's face. It made Benedict's stomach clamp, pinching all his courage. The wind separated them. Benedict's scarf spooled to the ground.

Tom bent and picked it up. 'You will redeem me by any means, won't you?'

'Only the Lord can redeem us. If you want absolution, you must expose Hellard, and deliver justice to Molly. She lives with her mother's killer and does not know it.'

Tom hung the scarf around Benedict's neck. 'Dick English is the villain, here. Not me, not you, not even Hellard. We're her home. You're both my home, you and Molly. Remember that. And if it was Hellard who whispered in Dick's ear – he knows better now.' *I'm nothing without you.*

You can't believe that. Benedict intended to say this, but only the racket of the river sounded. He watched Tom walk on, rubbing at the burn where Tom had jerked the scarf in place. He couldn't breathe. He tugged the noose free.

April Fool's Day

'Paint it Devon red, he tells me. Paint the whole hull red. With the Navy all around us, and half of Plymouth up in arms at the new Dock that serves us and takes their waters and fills their town with foreign labourers, and Cornish giants just over the Tamar – paint the new ship Devon red, he tells me.'

Molly leant over to the bucket and flicked paint at Nathan's back. 'There, now you'll blend right in, and Dick English won't trouble you.'

'*You* trouble me.'

'I aim to.'

Molly looked out over the Tamar to Cornwall, the cottages and fringe of trees on the opposite bank made grey by the afternoon light. The curve of Dock kept the sea from sight, holding Eddystone Reef from her, where the lighthouse used to stand, the lighthouse Tom had taken her and Mama to visit because he said it was a miracle, that his ladies ought to see this one hundred feet of stone rise up further than any lighthouse ever before it. 'Here's Devon for you,' he'd said, carrying Molly on his shoulders all the way up to the top, so high Molly was certain they'd be able to touch the clouds – and almost could, when they emerged into the open gallery. Mr Winstanley himself had shown them around. Mama asked so many questions, Mr Winstanley called her a lady of great learning. Molly remembered the rush of pride.

The lighthouse was struck down the night English ambushed them, the night Molly came on board the *Escape*, the night Mama ... The only trace of the lighthouse now was a length of chain wrapped around a rock. A ship from Virginia struck the reef right after, they said, all souls gone, leaving a lace of tobacco over the wrecks and cobbles, like tinder damming the streets. After the Great Storm, the dead – cattle and swine, sailors and fishermen, clergy and clerks, dead mothers looking for dead children – were said to outnumber the living. But not Molly. Just Mama.

Now, she was learning how to steam and bend the futtocks into ribs, how to drive in the knighthead, how to attune the keel to the currents. Nathan introduced her to shipwrights and caulkers and yard sailmakers. She watched every move he made, becoming his shadow, until she could feel Nathan's movements in her own body.

'You adding a bullseye next?'

Molly looked around. Isaac, from Cornwall side.

'On my back, more like,' said Nathan.

Isaac came by more and more, these days, idling with Nathan. Nathan wiped sweat from his lip with the back of his wrist, trailing paint there. Molly caught Isaac's eye and grinned. Isaac nodded: 'All right, Orlando?'

'Reg'lar, like.'

'Reckon so – been at this painting long enough.'

'Damn you, Isaac Whaler,' said Nathan.

Isaac just laughed, putting one foot on Nathan's ladder, craning his neck to see the ship, its masts waiting for sails, its boards waiting for polish, but still more glory to it than any church. Molly watched as Isaac fingered the turn-up of

Nathan's trouser leg, just briefly touching Nathan's pale skin. 'Can I tempt you to the beer shop?'

'See that?' Nathan pointed beyond the wet dock to the yard at Cattewater. A seventy-gun listed against the rolling wind. 'That ship belongs to Sir Morice himself, and she's waiting to use this slip, because Tom wanted it.'

'So?'

'So, it might be fine for *Tom* to ask the man who owns Dock to wait on his pleasure, but *I'd* like to keep working around here, and if his pleasure has to wait too long ...'

Molly watched Isaac pinch Nathan's trousers and tug a little. Then the man said, his voice tossed on a gust, 'What about *my* pleasure?'

Molly turned away – catching the warmth on Nathan's face as he peered down at Isaac – to study the busy stores. Benedict said it was a crime that the shipwrights and sailmakers and canvas contractors all worked on fast days. They would curse Dock, bring the lighthouse down again. Nathan said the only crime he was interested in was the bad material the storekeepers supplied for bolt ropes.

'Wish 'ee well, Cornishman,' called Tom, so loud the yard boys working nearby all looked up.

Molly saw Isaac's hand move, not drop, just drift to the ladder, as if he'd been clutching it all along. *Wish 'ee well* meant the same thing in Cornwall as it did in Devon: goodbye.

'Are you the Lord of Plymouth now, telling me where to go?' said Isaac.

Tom laughed, following the deep grooves in the earth down to the water's edge, grooves made by dragging oak to sea. 'I'm lord from the lick of the Severn Sea, north of this shire, to the moors in the east; from the south wholly washed with the British Sea, right here, to the west, where the Tamar serves as a bound between me and Cornwall – any compass point you care to look, son, it's mine. And you can use any exit you like.'

'Pretty speech,' said Isaac. 'You must like me an awful lot, spend all those words on me.'

Nathan dropped the paintbrush, slopping red down his shirt. 'Damn it! I'm trying to work, here.'

Molly slipped between them, picking it up.

Isaac shrugged. 'Wish 'ee well, Lord of Dev'nshire. Nathan, come see me when you're not so red-handed.'

Tom watched him until he was out of sight. Molly saw worry jab at him. Then: 'You wanted to show me something?'

Molly wiped her hands on her jacket. 'Up top.' She led the way, boarding the new ship, with Tom following, Nathan behind.

Rain was coming on, fat cold drops getting down the back of Molly's shirt. She took Tom to the aft deck.

'There it is.'

Where the whipstaff should have been, there was a ship's wheel. Tom looked at Nathan. 'Sure on this?'

'The Navy's rigging her vessels with wheels, fast as she can.'

Tom took hold of the wheel.

Molly said, 'Feel that?'

'What?'

Molly grinned. 'Adventure. This is the king pin,' she said, taking the corded spoke. 'Lets you know when you're running straight.'

They called the ship the *Venture*. Nathan built a roundhouse at the stern. It stood seven feet high, with a skylight that gleamed pewter in the storm light. Inside were a table and bench, two berths, and store cupboards for the best of the weapons, meat and drink. Wind shivered the glass in the roof and rattled the

BORN TO FIRE

door, but it was bolted shut. Molly forced a shoulder against the
jamb as she needled the tip of her knife into the wood, digging
out the anchor points of Tom's crest.

'Got you setting his praises in stone, has he?'

The knife jerked. Molly looked over her shoulder. Hellard,
filling the window of the roundhouse – he'd opened it from the
outside. That would have to be fixed. But it was too small for
him to squeeze through. The only way in was the door, which
Molly now locked, saying over the drop of the bolt: 'In oak.'

Hellard sniffed. 'What a good little powder monkey you are.
Sleeping in his cabin, foot of his bed, all these years. Listening
to his woes. And maybe more besides. I started off as a powder
monkey in the Navy. Got me the scars. You ain't got none from
him that I seen. Your body is pure as snow. Ain't beating you
with no strap. What I wonder is, maybe he's beating you with
something else. That the slap of his balls swinging free I hear
at night?'

'How do I know what you dream about?' said Molly. Her
throat was full, suddenly, choking on something.

Hellard laughed. 'Question is, do you know what you are
to him? You're the heir fucking apparent, after all I've given
him – and why?' Hellard tapped his nose, where a white stripe
gleamed. 'Know why he gave me this cut?'

Molly concentrated on gouging fine peelings from the wood:
the sharp line of a cutlass.

'You show your back to me, son, I'll swing free on you without hesitation.'

Molly didn't look around. 'Do that, Tom kills you.'

'You're forgetting his tender soul. Came at me no warning,
no provocation, and for what? Reckons someone betrayed him
to the Revenue, but he knows it weren't me. Blood binds us,
always will. Wonder what's in your blood – some canker of
treachery, I'd warrant . . . '

Molly worked the knife back in. 'You don't like Tom's rule, leave.'

'Tom's rule, Tom's rule. Who was it by his side under Ezekiel Day, hauling the biggest barrels, backing him up against rival owlers? Who saved his life more'n a dozen times, when the tide was up and luck was out? What man was it to bury the bodies? What didn't we promise each other? No. Big brother and me, we're not done yet. Someone's got to inherit the earth. Best to wait around.'

Molly turned, now. She was smiling pleasantly. 'Wait for what?'

'This tenderness of his. It's a short fuse. And one day it'll blow up in his face. He weren't mad at me. He was afeared.'

'Why would Tom be scared of you?'

Hellard ran his tongue over his teeth, and it seemed to get stuck, bulging there in his cheek. Then he shrugged. 'Ask Benedict.'

Molly tightened her grip on the knife. 'How do you know if I got scars on me or not? You looking?'

Hellard drummed a beat on the wall of the roundhouse. 'Maybe I'm looking to brand you myself.' He winked.

Molly was carving the *W* for *West* in the compass point when a gentle tap made her lift her head, which throbbed with blood.

'Benedict?'

'Tom.'

Molly unlocked the door. Tom ducked inside. Glanced at the crest. 'You could be a sign painter, you wanted to be.'

'I want to be a shipwright.'

Tom sat down at the head of the table. 'Not captain?'

'You're the captain.'

He smiled, and Molly tried to return it, but worms turned in her stomach.

'What's wrong?' asked Tom.

Molly put her knife down on the table. 'Why do you keep Hellard in the crew? He's nothing but trouble.'

Tom picked something from the corner of his eye, inspected it. 'Better a wolf in the fold than a fine February.'

Molly sat down. 'Birds of a feather flock together.'

'Listen to me, son. You're young, but you're smart as paint. When you're captain of a crew like this, you are father to gentlemen of fortune, who live rough, live for the gamble, even in the shadow of the hangman's noose. That's a special breed. They love you and they fear you in equal measure, and they enjoy both in equal measure. They never had fathers themselves and they like the feeling. That's what you must cultivate for their loyalty, and loyalty you need when you set about building an empire.'

'That what you're doing?'

Tom lifted his head. 'I ain't doing anything less.'

'And Hellard? He's afeared of you, but he don't love you and that's for sure.'

'Better Hellard in front o' me than behind.'

Molly squared her shoulders. 'I'd rather him six feet below me.'

Tom laughed. Scratched the back of his head. The laughter faded. 'Just needs some sense beating into him.'

'You might regret your mercy.'

He cleared his throat. 'I haven't yet.'

Leaf

To INTERLEA/VE. v. a. [*inter* and *leave*]

To chequer a book by the insertion of blank leaves.

In late August 1762, a discordant group of fellow travellers arrived at Efford Manor, the Plymouth home of Dr John Mudge. Sir Joshua Reynolds, the first President of the Royal Academy, and (Joshua would say) the first painter in Britain to achieve modern celebrity, led the holidaymakers. With him was Dr Samuel Johnson, otherwise known as Dictionary Sam, and Dr Johnson's servant, Frank Barber, born into slavery and freed as a child. Frank lived with Dr Johnson for thirty-two years, the longest relationship either would have. Dr Johnson made Frank his heir. The men were joined by Frances Reynolds: painter, poet, critic, and Joshua's sister and housekeeper.

The writer Hester Thrale, later Dr Johnson's confidante, deliciously compared Joshua and Frances' relationship with that of the novelist Fielding and his sister:

> When she only read English books, and made English verse, it seems he fondles her fancy and encouraged her genius, but as soon as he perceived she once read Virgil, farewell to fondness, the author's jealousy was become stronger than brother's

affection ... I have fancied lately that there was something of this nature between Sir Joshua and Miss Reynolds; he certainly does not love her as one should expect a man to love a sister he has so much reason to be proud of; perhaps she paints too well, or has learned too much Latin, and is a better scholar than her brother; and upon more reflection I fancy it must be so, for if he only did not like her as intimate why should not he give her a genteel annuity, and let her live where and how she likes: the poor lady is always miserable, always fretful; yet she seems resolved nobly enough – not to keep her post by flattery if she cannot get it by kindness: – this is a flight so far beyond my power that I respect her for it, and do love dearly to hear her criticise Sir Joshua's painting, or indeed his connoisseurship, which I think she always does with justice and judgement – mingled now and then with a bitterness that diverts one.

Johnson was close with many female writers and artists. 'It is a paltry trick indeed', he wrote, 'to deny women the cultivation of their mental powers, and I think it is partly a proof we are afraid of them, if we endeavour to keep them unarmed.' While in Devon, Johnson met a female shipwright who had educated herself, and written a book.

(Notes for a lecture on women and writing to be given at Girton College, Cambridge, on the anniversary of Virginia Woolf's lecture series, 'A Room of One's Own'.)

Unnatural Incidents
Mixed Up with True History

1762

Frances, Sam & Frank

Here is a quandary: how to tell Dr Johnson that what she can never forgive her brother for, of everything, is the carriage.

Not simply that Joshua had bid her sit so high up that she had nowhere to hide. Nor that he'd instructed the driver to make it a slow crawl about town, so all could stop and admire the fine trimmings until her ears matched her cheeks, the former red with cold, the latter ablaze with embarrassment. One by one, Mr Burney, Mrs Montagu, Mr Garrick, even Goldsmith had stopped and gawked. *Look at that for a carriage! How well Joshua Reynolds must be doing!*

Nor even that the carriage was in reality second-hand: that he may as well have sent her out in paste diamonds, an actress whoring away their childhood reared in Christ on Devon's red earth. Not all of that, though it was bad enough. But this: that he had turned her into a travelling advertisement for the success of his portraits, when he would not teach her how to paint.

She must find some way of telling Dr Johnson – to beg his

advice, he who called her *my Renny*. She cannot remain with her brother any longer. Joshua was famous for mixing paints that combined alchemically for disaster. His answer, a shrug: 'All paint cracks.' He could afford nonchalance. Men went to him for immortality. She was cracking now. And there was nothing that would preserve her.

'Sir, in your dictionary—'

'Oh, pray, let us talk on other matters,' said Dr Johnson. 'Yesterday, an old woman accosted me over *pastern*, of all things. "Why, sir, did you define *pastern* as the knee of a horse?" I could only tell her, "Ignorance, madam, pure ignorance."'

'One word.'

A sigh. 'Well, then?'

'What of *freedom*?'

Johnson snapped off the head of a hollyhock. 'What of it?'

'Liberty,' she said. 'Exemption from servitude. Independence.'

His fist closed around the gaudy and unmeaning petals. 'Ah! That puts me in mind of a story I heard at the Otter Club, in Plymouth, last night. About a girl who ran away to sea, like our Frank, and became a smuggler.'

'Ran away?' she said.

'Yes, refused the woman's life, dressed as a boy, and grew up on a ship, under a tyrant, until her sex was discovered. She is now a shipwright – the manager of a great enterprise, and quite Queen of the Dockers, the neighbouring enterprise that steals Plymouth's water. Rogues! I am a Plymouth man. Let the Dockers die of thirst! Dr Mudge says this lady is now to author the book of her life. An adventure reminiscent of the fictions of the last age, when the romance would crumble if you deprived it of a hermit and a wood, a battle and a shipwreck, and men so splendidly wicked their endowments threw a brightness on their crimes, for whom scarce any villainy could make them perfectly detestable, because they never could be wholly divested of their excellences. But such have been in all ages the great corrupters of the world, and their resemblance ought no more to be preserved than the art of murdering without pain.'

Fanny paused in her step, keeping time with Dr Johnson's twitch. So, first this shipwright refused a woman's life, and now she was writing a life. Fanny had refused to be a governess while Joshua was away studying, taking on a job as a milliner instead. Her mother had cried. Stitching velvet ribbons designed to catch a man's attention was only one rank above prostitution. Fanny tried to recall what she had refused since. 'Sir, does she intend to publish such a book?'

'I've dispatched Frank to secure us the story – think how Miss Charlotte Lennox would appreciate it! We might call it another *Female Quixote*!'

'You do not place stock in this lady's veracity, then, sir?'

He was thumping his ear, the world swallowed, she knew, in cloud. He pushed on: 'What value veracity? A sad reflection: with what hope can we endeavour to persuade you ladies that time spent at toilet is lost in vanity, if you are more effectually promoted by a well-disposed ribbon than by goodness or knowledge?'

She patted her hat. 'You would give Miss Lennox an even greater gift than your patronage if you encouraged her away from romance. These wild stories of hers that argue for the power of a woman's, um, mortal body – this *insistence* on dismissing Miss Carter's emphasis on a woman's mind – the Bluestocking ladies say it is an assault on all they've worked for. To be considered as minds, not bodies – minds free of a woman's intemperance and hysteria, minds of virtue. Transcendence, until we are as men.'

'Ha – and is that to be so desired?'

'So we are told.'

'So you believe?'

A shade of a smile. 'I believe that the highest degree of feminine excellence, in exterior grace and interior virtue, constitutes the most perfect existing object of taste in creation. Men seek the sublime, wavering between security and destruction in a point of terror, wanting to control power outside of your power. But it is to women I give true beauty.'

He leant on her arm. 'You must write thus.'

The smile fled. 'Mrs Montagu, of all women, contends she spent the first half of her life counting pennyworths of figs and weighing sugar candy, before she dared to write.'

'Oh, lamentable luxury.'

'She would tell you, sir, that there is nothing sadder. And you know it. A sad waste of genius. And that is how Miss Carter and all the others see Miss Lennox.'

'You ladies playing gaoler to each other.'

'Perhaps we hope to persuade you gentlemen to give up the key.'

His fingers twirled. His feet danced. He chewed at his lips, his body a minute hand, ticking back and forth, waiting for the tremor to pass before marching on. 'Miss Carter wrote to me that Miss Hester Mulso gave her an upbraiding for enjoying romance! Called such tales a strange heap of improbable, unnatural incidents mixed up with true history and fastened upon some of the great names of antiquity. Taking up Mr Richardson's side, of course. Keep them smiling. That's the rule, eh, my dear Renny? Keep them smiling.'

Fanny took his wild elbow, feeling the weight of sorrow, knowing he classed himself with his ladies in his lifelong bid to escape penury, suffering and misery. Dr Johnson set a higher value upon female friendship than most men. Perhaps because, in his own words, he awoke every day to *find myself still fettered to myself*.

He thinks he understands. Maybe he would understand.

But now Johnson was worrying about whether he'd been rude that afternoon to Mrs Mudge, after he asked for an eighteenth cup of tea and she cried, 'What? Another, Dr Johnson?'

'I did not count Dr Mudge's glasses of wine last night,' he

complained, as they turned the corner in the yew garden. 'Why should *my* tea be counted today?'

'I heard your glasses would have taken quite the counting.'

'My dear Renny, you are as naughty as can be; do not rebuke me for the occasional dip, when most men of my acquaintance are sopped around the clock.'

'I do not rebuke you.'

'Then neither should Mrs Mudge for my tea.'

'You know she doesn't really care how much tea you consume.'

'Then what, madam, is the problem?'

'Women pour the tea, sir. Pour it eighteen times, if you request it eighteen times. Do you realise how difficult it is to contribute to conversation with any intelligence while popping up and down like a spaniel?'

That look on his face, of realising offence – that look of fear.

'But that's not why Dr Mudge was scowling so,' she continued, 'if that's what worries you. He thought you were being rude to her because of her station.'

'Station? Mrs Mudge?'

Fanny laughed. 'She was his housekeeper, before his wife.'

'What should I care for that? My work is of my own hands. I tell you, Renny, I am one of the few left who can print and bind a book. You know that maid of the Cotterells thought I was a robber. I look the common man. I *was* the common man.'

'Never common, sir.'

He batted his ear, as if knocking her words in or out. 'I never courted the great; they sent for me. But Dr Mudge, marrying his housekeeper. Now, there *is* something out of the common.'

'Mr Sterne says it proves Dr Mudge is a genius.'

A snort. 'I didn't realise the bar was set so low. They should have given me my freedom years ago.'

His freedom – his pension. If not hard sought, hard won. How to win it for herself? As her brother's keeper, she could not marry her way to freedom, as Mrs Mudge had, and nor would she earn a pension from the crown, as Dr Johnson had for the service of his dictionary. As a child, Joshua had copied his sisters' drawings, had followed their charcoal lines on the limewashed walls of the long schoolroom passageways, followed in games across the moors. As soon as he reached age, he was apprenticed to Thomas Hudson as an artist. While Joshua was on the Continent – seeing first-hand Grecian art she could only imagine to be preferable to that of the whole world, because the Grecian form terminated every enquiry after beauty she'd ever read – she was stuck in Plymouth, attempting miniatures. She kept them hidden in her bedroom, for, when Joshua saw her oil paintings, he said they made other people laugh and him cry.

Fanny looked back at the gentle curve of Efford Manor, the cluster of copper beech and oak tree, and then to the line of elms, the forest ploughing the steep drop, the river olive and drab in shadow, dappling as the breeze picked up. The diamond-dust glitter of it.

'Sam,' she said, the hand of a new wind at her throat, 'I must beg your advice. About Joshua.'

'My dearest dear – he is almost the only man whom I call a friend. He knows the rules of being a gentleman. He will follow them.'

She let her hand be squeezed and flung about in the sudden contractions of his own. Sam knew her next words, knew them without her voicing them: *The rules of gentlemen will kill me.* But they were his rules too.

Sam risked a look at her. Those lips clasped like a purse, the manner she used when working hard to remain the sweet girl he had always known, but her eyes, the blue of childhood, were heavy with disappointment. This sight of hers, this vision; when she painted his portrait, she captured him peering at books, trapped in darkness and grubbing the pages with his insistence, a man

154

struggling to see his way out. For she believed grace was half celestial, and a body would charm no matter its deformity if the soul could be seen; she believed the beauty in his breast was a source from which an endless stream of fair ideas flowed. Her brother, however, painted Sam at ease, one crabbed hand the only indication of – of him. She had overheard Sam once, he knew, saying portraiture was indelicate in a female: so many hours sitting so close to a man, staring into his face. His self.

'Perhaps the lady shipwright can teach you to be as bold as she, give you a man's raiments and a ship on which to wear them as you sail away from us all,' he said, his rally tripped up by a rasp in his chest.

'Must I dress like Joshua to paint better than Joshua?' She flushed. 'My desire to paint does not proceed from a cast of mind inconsistent with the delicacy of the female character, whose true excellence consists in not endeavouring to excel out of the domestic sphere. I paint only because – because I must. But it all comes to the same. Nothing.'

'Madam,' he said, rocking back. Tears, stupid and insensible. 'Pray, do not call my love nothing. I have known but one mind that would bear microscopic examination, and that is yours. I am very willing to wait on you at all times, and will sit for a picture whenever you desire it, for, whenever I sit, I shall be with you.'

She almost dropped a curtsy. 'For which I know myself honoured.'

Presenting him now with the naivety she was known for, the timidity that charmed or infuriated, and certainly maddened Joshua, who called on her to at least *ape* wit and good humour in return for the success he had brought into their lives – wit that might mask the great blank of history, art, anatomy, chemistry, which Sam knew she begged from Joshua. *Seneca*, she wrote, *said that had he been debarred from the study of physiologica, it would not have been worth coming into the world.*

A lady had asked Sam once, *What would you give for an education?* He told her he would give all he had. (And, in fact, he had.)

'My dear Renny, do not make any decisions you may later regret. For, without Sir Joshua's influence, his protection, his welcome – there will be nothing in my power to keep you housed.'

There it was. Fanny swallowed down the tears. No, nothing rash, for though she pasted advertisements into her journal for lessons in Greek and Latin, the next day she almost always tore them out – and though, when they battled the waves for Eddystone Lighthouse yesterday, she resolved she would beg Dr Johnson for his help in her flight to freedom, she knew now there never was a greater fool than Frances Reynolds.

'There goes your black,' she said, pointing, so that Dr Johnson would turn away from her tears. 'Do you fear he'll run back to the Navy, so close to the margin of the sea?'

'Not Frank. For he knows I am very unwilling to lose him. I have made amends for fetching him home again from the Navy. I told him, "If you serve on those ships, you will be stolen back to that place of great wealth and dreadful wickedness, a den of tyrants and dungeon of slaves, and lose your natural right to liberty and independence." No – he is off on our quest . . .'

Following the road down from Efford Manor to Plymouth, Frank was thinking about Dr Johnson's bid to make amends, his bid to see the ocean through Frank's own eyes as they took the Admiral's yacht out to Eddystone – Dr Johnson's new understanding that, in running away to sea, a man must be content to leave everything behind but himself, to whom he must trust. The imaginations excited by such an unknown and untravelled expanse as this coast were not those that would arise from the artificial solitude of parks and gardens, Johnson had said. Here, man was made unwillingly acquainted with his own weakness.

Frank prayed with Johnson last night. He heard him tell God that, when he surveyed his past life, he discovered nothing but

a barren waste of time, with some disorders of body and distur-
bances of the mind very near to total madness, which he hoped
He that made him would suffer to extenuate. *Spare me that I might
commit myself to use the faculties which thou hast given me with honest
diligence, and to overcome the insensibility and heaviness I perceive.*
Frank had placed his hand on the centre of Johnson's back.

This melancholia skinned Johnson raw, leaving him naked to
pain, pain that had gripped Johnson since Frank first met him.
Only a boy, Frank had scratched the words *Antigua/Antiguan* on
the back of Johnson's scrap drafts for the dictionary, while the
great bear see-sawed over his work, insensible to his own tears.

I am very unwilling to lose you, Johnson had told him. What about
what Frank was unwilling to lose? Would love and loyalty chain
him to the melancholia and madness of Johnson's house for ever?
Would the labour of Johnson's sorrow always fall to him?

Over his shoulder, the proud red brick of Efford, the hedgerows
yellow and pink, the bushes and ivy, the lawn, Sir Joshua and his
box of colours, Miss Frances and her own smaller box, and Dr
Johnson in his drab brown coat and burnt wig, always the same, no
matter Frank's protestations – it was all now swallowed in forest
clinging to sheer earth. Colour was important to these people. For,
though Miss Frances said all colours resolved into one light, he
knew she believed him defective in form and complexion, and held
to the idea that, as a total want of cultivation precluded external
beauty, so a total want of external beauty precluded the power of
cultivation – believed the Negro race to be a lower order of human
being than the Europeans.

Sir Joshua said he wanted to paint Frank. He had never said
this before, but wanted to now, here at the edge, where England
turned into colour. Miss Frances had painted Anna Williams, the
blind poet Johnson housed, whom Frank battled daily for some
measure of order. Miss Frances rendered Mrs Williams grey,
inward, boxed. Washed of world. Stuck. How would Sir Joshua

render Frank? What colour did the doctor's friends see, when they looked at him? What colour did Frances see, she who feared him with every glance, and now sought the example of freedom? What did freedom mean, he heard Miss Frances ask. Well, what did it mean? Johnson's love, or the taste of air on the admiral's yacht?

China House jutted out on the harbour edge, its fires silent, now a seamen's hospital, the cook had told Frank, funded by the lady shipwright. It was said she was nursing a dying man there. Her carpenter. Her banker. Her old pursuer from the Revenue. Her father. Her husband. Nobody knew, only that she visited every afternoon, and brought with her a book from which she read quietly, calmly, as if it was a ritual decided on long ago – no longer the words that mattered, but the compact of the pages.

The door of the hospital stood open, inviting the sea air, which itself would invite the men back to their feet, back to their ships, back to that horizon. Frank lingered there. There were twenty cots in the first room, all occupied by shadow, though sun silver-plated the city. Here, men picked their souls and spines free of each other, letting pain burst its banks, men who did not seem to be waiting for solace. Men dying alone, without conversation.

He felt cold, there at the door.

He stepped back, into pearly day. Then stopped, catching sight of another Negro man inside, a man missing both legs from above the knee, yellowed eyes fixed on him.

Frank bowed.

The man grinned. His teeth were perfect painted wood. He raised a hand in a gracious wave. 'You Navy?'

Frank nodded.

'Here for a shipmate?'

Frank scratched at the back of his neck. 'No. Just to see the place.'

'Our ferry woman paying the river man in the next room. She pays all our ways. River man demands his tax.'

'I know it.'

The man nodded. 'You know it.' He closed his eyes.

Frank edged through a cloud of flies, brittle bumps, to a low door and three steps.

A private room, a large bed. A large man, grey with time mis-used, and a savage manner about him that reminded Frank of a white man he'd known on the Orange River estate. He wondered if this man hoped to be forgiven for comparable instances of brutal-ity, for a priest was leaning in the corner, as if trying to disappear before his task. A woman sat by the man's bedside, a journal in her lap, the woman wearing deep purples and scarlets, outrageous colours in this church of death, and a grey wig covering grey hair, wisps Frank could see, the woman in her sixties, but her cheeks still smooth.

Frank was stuck on the bottom step.

She sat up, rolling her shoulder, as if to make any grab for her pistol an easy motion. But there was no pistol. She raised an eye-brow at him, asking lightly: 'You've come for me?'

As if he were the river man.

'A message, ma'am. Dr Johnson asks the pleasure of your company.'

The old woman glanced at the man in the bed. His eyes were closed. A smile playing at his mouth. When he spoke, the voice put Frank in mind of turned coals.

'The dictionary-maker calls the ship-maker.'

'What for?' asked the woman, with a roll of the eyes at her companion.

'He wants to write your story,' said Frank.

The woman raised the book, as if in salute. 'It's already written.'

BOOK THREE

1710

WOMEN ARE THE
WILDLIFE OF
A COUNTRY –

AND MEN SET
THE GAME LAWS

In April
The cuckoo shows his bill;
In May
He is singing all day

I

Tom tied the rowboat to an iron hook in the bricks and
jumped on to the steps, the boat knocking in relief against the
back of the house, like a dancing bear thumping for freedom.
He paused to polish the buckles on his shoes with his sleeve
before lifting the rusted iron knocker – the front door to
Gautier's house had a brass lion head, he knew – and letting
it fall gently. Climbing up behind him, Nathan told Tom he
looked pretty as anything, before making room for Hellard,
who was running a palmful of spit through his hair.

The door opened, revealing a servant with a stare like
a lobster too close to a boiling pot. 'M'sieur West?' The
man said it like all Frenchmen, *Ou-est*, two syllables. Mister,
not Captain.

Tom stepped inside, forcing the man to shuffle backwards.
Hellard closed the door behind them. Tom examined the

kitchen. He took the man in front of him to be some kind of second footman. Music reached him. Gautier had invited Tom and his men to his house in celebration – ostensibly of the completion of the new altar in the cathedral. *What are you taking Nathan and Hellard for?* Benedict had asked. *They won't watch out for you.* Tom said Benedict should apply his gaze to watching Molly.

'Vous avez manqué le diner, M'sieur West.'

He'd missed dinner. 'But not the brandy, I hope?'

The man's lips twitched. Tom couldn't tell if it was a smile or blanch. 'Je dois vous diriger vers le salon. Mais d'abord, M'sieur West, votre ... '

Tom followed the man's gesture to the sword and pistol strapped to his waist. 'None of the fine gentlemen in there are ready for a duel?'

'Épées ornementales, M'sieur.'

Tom bit back his reply, unbuckling the sheath, nodding at Nathan and Hellard to do the same. 'This ain't so ornamental,' he agreed, offering the sword. His smile returned when the man's arms dropped by a few inches.

'Not so,' the servant murmured.

Undoing the strap of his holster, Tom pulled the pistol free. He handed the man the empty strap and stuffed the pistol into his belt at the small of his back, pulling his waistcoat and jacket over the butt. He shrugged free of his damp great coat and chucked it over a wooden chair.

'Pretty enough?' he said.

The man seemed about to say something, but pointed Tom onwards.

Tom went towards the music with his fingers itching. If he were Dick English or any other Customs man, English or French, the way he'd trap Tom West would be to bait his self-consequence and his coin purse. Invite him to a party full of gentry and their bored, perfumed wives. Ask him to cast off his arms first – société civile – and then draw every stage sword in the room on him. He kept his hand by his side, ready to move to the pistol, but, when the footman opened the salon doors, the harpsichord in the corner played on. The women fixed their eyes on Tom, curious and not hiding it. The men looked away, powdered wigs a-twitching. Tom brushed his fringe back, and saw Gautier coming towards him.

'Captain West, so good of you to come. Gentlemen.'

'Sorry to be late. Business.'

Gautier shook his hand. 'An excuse to which I can never object. All well, I trust?'

'No cause to think otherwise,' said Tom, sweeping the room, distracted by a woman in burgundy satin who laughed without minding her surrounds, unlike the careful simper of the other ladies.

'Relax,' said Gautier. 'You are a hero to these men.'

There was a commotion behind Gautier: a spaniel darting through the room, the woman with the laugh lifting her skirts to let the silky thing race between her legs, turning towards him as she did it. Tom saw her stockings – calculating how much he could sell them for in England – and tracked upwards, lingering on the tightly drawn stays. When he looked up, she was grinning, unembarrassed. She had dark curls, which she wore with no powder, and she shook them a little now, as if to lock his attention. He wanted to tell her she didn't have to try so hard – she'd got it before she lifted her skirts.

'Ah, M'sieur West. This is Madame Rhys. She is from your wretched island – I thought you might like the company.'

'I do already.'

She bit her bottom lip as she smiled, a practised excitement that still bedevilled him for all that. She curved her hand into the crook of his arm. 'Let me introduce you to the assembly ... We'll have the bishop first, hmm?'

Madame Rhys led him to each man in the room, and Tom stood through brandies and smoke, and talked of fishing ventures in the North Sea and the Sun King's poor health and the Battle of Oudenarde. With each conversation, he was steered towards the town's expanding port, the danger posed by Barbary pirates, and, most of all, England's high import taxes, and Louis' madness. When a captain from the same militia regiment Gautier pretended to command asked Tom what could be done to keep the wealth of the town's traders *inside* the town, Tom glanced at Madame Rhys, but she only looked at him with detached curiosity. Gautier was on the other side of the room, whispering to a serving girl. She looked about Molly's age. Tom met the retired captain's bloodshot eyes.

'I'd suggest building a taller town wall,' he said, 'but it would only bottle up that expanding port of yours. Other than that, gentlemen, I'm not certain how I can be of assistance ...'

The captain sniffed, his flared nostrils revealing a white line of snuff. 'How you can be of *service*, Captain, is to keep your money inside the town wall we already have.'

Another man – a local shipwright, Tom thought – placed his arm on the French captain's shoulder. 'What our friend, here, is trying to say, sir, is that we are all aware of how important your business could be for Roscoff. We are expanding: more buildings, more ships. I hear you run your business in England by *shares* – so do we. If you were to invest in our expansion, what fruit we enjoy, you would enjoy also.'

Next to him, Hellard thrust his hands in his pockets. 'You all know an awful lot about our business.'

'Only what Colonel Gautier tells us – he speaks of you with high praise, be assured.'

Gautier's back remained turned. He was holding the serving girl's arm, and her ears were going red.

Nathan, who was stroking the dog on the edge of the circle, asked gently, 'So who's telling Gautier?'

Madame Rhys squeezed Tom's arm firmly enough to make her nails felt through the wool.

He smiled at the men before him. 'I think we understand each other, gentlemen. I have an agent who deals in money. I'm sure he and the colonel's business agent can put something together.'

'You say a man who *deals in money*,' said the shipwright. 'May I ask what *you* deal in, if not money?'

'Salt water,' said Tom. Everyone laughed. Tom could feel Madame Rhys's fingers crawling up his arm. The serving girl had left the room so quickly, she tripped on her bustled skirts.

The close of the evening – windows cracked by servants to vent the smoke, sea air stiffening men's backs as they shook hands and exchanged promises – and Tom alone with Madame Rhys in a corridor panelled with violet silk. The embroidered cloth blurred with her mantua in his vision. He pressed her body against the padded wall, close enough to see where she had dabbed rouge on to the high points of her cheekbones.

'Aren't you going to tell me to stop?' he asked.

'Do you want me to?'

Tom leant against the wall with one arm.

The other remained tight around her waist. 'I've been thinking about you all evening, *Madame* Rhys. What is Madame Rhys doing in Roscoff? Perhaps she is running from a scandal. An affair. Perhaps Madame Rhys decided she would not suffer the judgement of fat, northern speculators, so she fled to France with her lover, but soon found herself lonely again. Are you lonely, madame?'

'Terribly. I suppose, sir, *you* cannot be lonely with such colourful companions.'

Tom looked over his shoulder. Nathan was taking a pinch of snuff from a man who had all the self-satisfaction of a turnpike trust manager spying a coach and four coming down the road, now brushing Nathan's upper lip with his knuckle, and lingering there. A blush crept over Nathan's cheeks. Not the first time Tom had seen Nathan cloistered in some man's company; he had told him to think on his sin and its punishment. If the full deed could be proven, it would be death, and that a mercy. If it could not, he'd be exhibited through the borough, and finish in the pillory. *I won't have one of my crew well-mobbed and pelted through the streets. Last time a sodomite was caught, the butcher boys severed his penis and half-suffocated him in the muck of the beast pen before he was even examined by a magistrate. Some other trade, you might lie with a man and hope for luck. Not on my crew. Some sins I don't want for company.* Now, Nathan wiped his mouth and leant out of the toll-taker's orbit.

'Where did you find him?' asked Madame Rhys. 'A molly-house?'

Tom's grip on her tightened. 'What did you say?'

'A meeting place for men of ... flexible tastes. Don't tell me I shock, Captain. Fear not. Prosecution doesn't trouble houses with more than one footman. At least your carpenter has *charm* about him. Your first mate, however, is the kind of gentleman a lady locks her doors for.'

Hellard was demonstrating a magic trick using coins from the purses of two particularly round-eyed young gentlemen, who, Tom was sure, only exercised their minds in hearing and reporting gossip, great and little, over a day-long breakfast. He and Hellard used to play that same con on plough boys.

When they were rumbled, they'd stand back-to-back and fight it out.

'Suppose I ought to rescue your nobles,' said Tom.

'And leave me? If they can't recognise a crook, he's doing them a favour.'

'That's my brother you're talking about.'

'I thought I saw a resemblance. What good looks you both share.'

Tom gave her a fierce scowl. 'Half-brother.'

She shrugged, moving under his weight. 'Brothers. Useful, until they aren't.'

'Ate yours, did you?'

'He sided with my husband and his fat, northern industrialists. Can you believe it?'

'Depends what you did,' said Tom.

Her fingers flirted with the button of his shirt. 'Does it?'

Tom released his breath, long, low, forgetting Hellard, forgetting Nathan. 'Whatever it was, I'm certain I'd enjoy it. And you, too.'

'Of course you are. You're all certain you can save me from boredom, from the weeks spent shut up in the country while my lord and master shuts up another lady in the city. So you whisk me away, and abandon me to survive on my wits in Venice because you lost a card game.'

'These Roscoff merchants to whom you are now ... confidante, a salve to the ego? Are they not exciting company?'

'Not as exciting as some.'

'So, when Gautier directed you to brighten my evening, you thought I might be a bit of excitement?'

'Does all this questioning mean I've failed?' she asked.

'Failed to what?'

'Brighten your evening.'

'So bright, I'm blind,' he said, smiling when she laughed.

'You are a terrible seducer,' she said.

'*You* are supposed to be seducing *me*,' he countered. 'Tell me – why is he so anxious to get my attention?'

'Gautier is greedy. He wants to take over your empire. Cut out the middle man.'

'*He's* the middle man.'

'That you'll have to settle between you.'

'And how does he know so much about my empire?'

'The maid who is his current amusement. She is the younger sister of the servant girl you are taking to your bed in your cottage on Île de Batz.'

Tom cleared his throat. 'And it doesn't bother you, this amusement of his?'

'It's a warning, that is all. Soon, he will be bored with me.'

Tom felt her shift in his grip, and then her warm hips pressed against his. He heard the clink of coins in his pockets, disturbed by her movement. 'Then this is a proposition of your own?'

'Yes. Run away with me. An adventure, Captain.'

'I wonder if I can afford you.'

She shrugged. 'Gowns, a house, a box at the theatre – what are such things to a man like you?'

He laughed. 'Expensive.'

'All the better, sir. You have no notion of how it fatigues me to be eternally making myself agreeable to a set of men who might be buried tomorrow, and nobody would miss them.' She slipped a hand inside his jacket. 'The only thing to do is dress as a boy and stow away on your ship.'

Tom released her, and dug in his pocket for the purse he kept there. 'I wish I could say yes, but I don't think my ship would be a fitting place for a lady. Please, take this for your pains.'

'Should I be offended?'

'You're a free woman. Be whatever you like. I'll be back next month. It would be a great pleasure to see you again – and hear any new whisperings, if you aren't too offended by the notion?'

Her hand closed around the purse as she kissed him, grazing the stubble by his mouth, as Grace used to. 'Only disappointed, Captain.'

'You want to stay away from her,' said Hellard.

'Staying close sounds more fun,' said Tom, leading the way up the path to the cottage, the tick of want not exorcised by the brief row from the mainland.

'Remember what happened when you stayed close to Mary de Bosco? You itched for going on a se'en night. I warned you off her, too.'

Tom put his arm around Hellard's shoulders. 'We're a long way from Hope, now, brother. And I'm not convinced you didn't give little Mary that itch in the first place.'

'You don't want a French compliment of any kind from that Rhys bitch. I could see it in her eyes. Trust me.'

Nathan shouldered past them. 'An adder's more trustworthy'n you, Hellard.'

Rich smoke beckoned them to the garden, where Molly and Kingston were practising swordplay and Benedict was baking fish over a fire that flickered against the stars, a candle in the vaulted walls of a salt mine. Nathan clapped Kingston on the arm and collapsed on to the grass. Hellard sat beside Benedict, stealing the food from his hand.

Kingston smiled at Tom. 'How were your slavers?'

'Don't start preaching,' said Hellard, 'or we'll sell you to 'em. Besides, they're not slavers. They're merchants. Gullible merchants, too.' Coins winked in his hands.

Kingston's expression seemed suddenly embalmed. Tom remembered the first time he saw Kingston shirtless. The narrow sea. August sun aiming to poach them in their own sweat. Kingston's back was alive with snakes, great coils that slipped over each other in the glare. The kind of scars that could kill a man.

'Town opened its arms to us,' said Nathan. 'That's for sure.'

Tom edged his hands over the flames. 'For now. Hellard's right.'

'First time for everything,' muttered Molly. Hellard pushed past Benedict to grab the fish from her hand, too, but she jerked away too quickly.

'There's some French compliments from these people we'd do well to be wary of,' said Tom, keeping his eyes on Nathan. 'Some sins we don't want for company. Remember that.'

Nathan's voice was constricted. 'I do.'

Molly fed the withered branch of their last Christmas tree into the flames. 'What sins do we want for company, then?'

Tom was about to answer before Benedict or Hellard could say anything, when fear gripped him, cold fingers pulling at his gut. Sparks surrounded Molly, painting her silhouette in gold and white.

She looked like Grace.

Women curse ships.

A young woman on a ship full of men. How could the others not see it? What would happen when they did?

And Gautier's spies – what if that young, blushing maid repeated what his own cleaning girl had seen: the presents he bought Molly, filling her room, or the morning she'd found them practising with swords, and he'd swept Molly over his shoulder, kissing her stomach until she squealed with laughter. What if Hellard walked in on her changing? She went every day to the shipyard with Nathan, talking to the chandlers and canvas contractors in French better than Tom's, learning their trade. She was better than the work-boys her own age. What if there was an accident at the yards, and some town doctor had to tend her?

'Pride,' said Tom, the word drifting in on the tide.

Molly smiled, as if his pride were a great present.

He hadn't asked the cleaning girl how old she was. He presumed around sixteen, but she could be fifteen ... could even be close to thirteen, Molly's age. If he'd given Molly over to the Church, as he'd imagined, she would be in service by now, too, sweeping and polishing for some bent-over miser with a frigid wife, who would make it his business to take the virginity of any maid.

A man a little like himself.

He had saved her from a life of cramped walls, sewing and cleaning and cooking for some man, the small servitudes Grace hated. He'd given Molly what Grace wanted – freedom. Not the kind Madame Rhys had, which was still servitude, only in better clothes. Real freedom.

He could have given it to Grace. The thought circled him. He could have given Grace enough money to set herself up somewhere in France, to write and read, if that's what she wished ... but he'd wanted her there, waiting for him, in those cramped walls.

'Where's my money gone?' said Hellard, patting the earth. 'Come on, you bastards. I earnt that money.'

The coins flashed between Kingston's fingers. 'Did you?' he said.

II

Woods were the free-trader's friend. Poacher, fox, cuckoo, spirits, lawless and unto no man. Molly's favourite wood, Gallants Bower, where she walked now, perched over Dead Man's Cove, rocks like pulped slate and hard sand and shingle. The woods hid Dartmouth Castle from view, kept the Navy and the Revenue from looking too closely at the network of caves connecting beach below and woods above. The caves allowed Tom's men to leave salt and tea in the hollow tree for collection. Molly hoisted the bag over her shoulder. Too few bundles for the landsmen, and Benedict busy with something else: Molly's first landing alone.

The green offerings of garlic and the close conference of ferns – Molly breathed them in, ambling now, the dig of the pistol at her hip growing less bothersome, more familiar, like the knife at her other side. Tom's father, Josias West, had left on a fishing boat bound for Newfoundland, on the promise of blubber and chipped bone. Tom had told Molly this in Totnes, once, as they passed a shop selling whalebone stays; told her, when Molly asked, that, yes, a woman's body grew to fit such a contraption, and more besides, that the cords were not actually bone, but cartilage from the mouth of a whale, porous enough to filter krill from sea. Tom had seen baleen whales, appearing as snow-capped hilltops rupturing the ocean's surface. Ripped from the whale's bleeding jaws, the stays would breathe as the woman breathed, would grow with her, until it was not known if the woman was contained by the stays, or the stays kept from breaking by the woman. A second skin.

'Bone grows with bone,' he had said.

'But wouldn't it hurt?' asked Molly. 'Being confined so?'

Tom said: 'Reckon it depends how you're built. Most women, they adapt to confinement.'

But not me. Bone grows with bone. Molly's pelvis grew to pistol and blade.

The hollow tree occupied a clearing, the roots of the oak pushing all else aside, such was its age, the weight of its crown. How it came to be hollow, none knew – some said lightning, others that a ghost burrowed there. Tom had encouraged stories of its haunting to keep away unwanted patrols, and, though Molly knew they were just stories, she still stopped a few feet off, giving the tree time.

But fancy is just fancy, and the only thing she heard was birds, crabbed at being disturbed. Molly stepped among the roots – raised like the veins threading Tom's forearms – and got purchase on the trunk, climbing up the one, two, three steps to the hollow. She heaved the bag over her head and dropped it inside.

The hollow distorted the sound of boys laughing. Molly froze for a moment, attention caught uselessly on the dewy spittle of a spider's web just in front of her face, and then shook to life. She twisted, one hand gripping the lip of the hollow and one drawing her pistol. Aimed straight.

Four boys, all a bit older than her, and a girl, red-faced and frizzed, her cap pulled back and her shawl hanging from one shoulder.

Molly jumped to the ground. Kept the pistol raised.

'Help you, gentlemen?' she asked.

The four boys looked like they were trying to hold a tableau: one had his hand on the girl's arm, but his grip was going slack; one was chewing on something, and had left his mouth open in shock.

Tom would say: *Fire before they recover. Take the bit between your teeth.*

175

Benedict would say: *Take the bit between your teeth only if you wish to fly headlong the steps of anarchy.* But Molly didn't know what that meant.

The girl had hair as red as the hull of the *Venture*. She was crying – tears of frustration, looked like, tears of torment. One of the boys was carrying a basket, and he threw it down now.

Too late. They'd gathered their wits.

'You must be a demon, come out of there,' said the boy, nodding at the tree. 'Though I ain't ever seen a demon so slight.'

'You escorting this girl home, are you?' asked Molly. 'Carrying her basket for her?'

'We're gentlemen, like you said. Point that somewhere else.'

Molly cocked the thing. 'This tree don't want you here. Neither do I.'

He picked up a branch. 'Don't see how you got much of a say in it. Four of us, one o' you. This don't concern you. Just a game we play with Annie. You were going to shoot, you'd have done it already. You're nothing but a little boy.'

Take the bit between your God damn teeth.

Molly fired. A clap of birds expanded into the bower, blackening the sky. A wail: the bullet had gone through the boy's sleeve, leaving a coin-sized hole, without taking any flesh with it. That hadn't been her intent, but it would do. The boy dropped the branch and it hit the basket of eggs with a crack. He turned and ran. The others followed. Annie was left swaying, pale, her sweat on the air.

Molly holstered the pistol.

'You didn't have to shoot,' whispered the girl. 'They were just ... They're just ... '

Molly shrugged. 'Don't draw if you don't intend on firing.' That was Tom.

'Thank you. Thank you.'

Molly cleared her throat. 'No odds. Walk you home, shall I?'

Annie wiped her nose on the back of her wrist. 'Please.'

'Where you live?'

'In town.'

Molly picked up the basket. 'These are broken, mostly. Still want 'em?'

Annie stared at the basket for a long time. Then: 'No.'

Molly turned it upside down. The eggs fell, congealed, like the glistening spider sac, and broke across the mud, coward's blood.

'What's your name?' asked Annie.

'Orlando West. They call me Boy.'

'Who?'

'I'm a shipwright apprentice.'

'I'm a kitchen maid in the castle.'

'That so?' Molly stiffened as Annie held on to her arm over a ditch. She didn't let go. 'You know a man named Richard English?'

'The Revenue captain? I've seen him.'

'To talk to?'

'No, sir. He visits the gunners and the priest more often than his own men, they say.'

'Why's that?'

'He pays 'em to watch for free-traders. His own army, like. The dragoons won't stay loyal to him for more'n a day.'

Molly twisted the empty basket this way and that. 'How's he strike you?'

Annie looked up. Molly followed her gaze. A cool blue, up there, calm. 'Proud. A proud man, him. Bent on God's work.'

'How's that?'

'Ridding Devon of murderers and thieves.'

'That's how you see free-traders?'

177

Annie laughed. 'No. Of course not. But that's what they are.'

Castle Cove, they called it, all of Queen Anne's men bristling to defend her by parking themselves in one spot, where they might polish their pikes and cutlasses and muskets, away from any opportunity to use them. Castle *Kevie*, Molly heard a Flemish free-trader call it once: Castle Hen-Coop, only men instead of hens, if you can distinguish them. But, up close – walking from the fringe of woodland with her arm around Annie's waist, the hill so steep they slid unstoppably down to the town's defences – Dartmouth Castle was impressive: the sprawl of its ramparts, the fortalice striking to the sky, the gun tower almost wading in the water, and the church with its three great steepled roofs. A whole town existed in these walls, a town of armed men who would shoot Molly down where she stood, if they knew to whom she swore loyalty. And, over the glittering water, the bountiful green of Kingswear, and another castle.

'Why do you smile so, sir?'

'Don't it make you grin?'

'It makes me tired,' laughed Annie. They fell into the shadow of the first wall. The guardsman nodded hello, and opened the doors.

Molly followed, keeping one hand driven in her pocket, hiding the pistol beneath.

'And it makes me afeared,' said Annie.

'Afeared of what?'

'Our coop ain't producing as they should.'

'So, it's true what they say,' laughed Molly.

Annie didn't smile. 'I was sent to fetch those eggs, and I come back empty-handed.'

'You come back with me,' she said, following Annie across

the courtyard. Above: men on the ramparts, winter sun winking on their armour.

'And what good is that when it comes to today's breakfast?'

Molly stood aside, letting Annie go first through the next
door, then kept on with her to the end of a passageway that
smelt of pig shit. 'I tells you what,' she said. 'I'll tell your
master you was robbed on the road, and I scared 'em gone,
but not before the basket fell.'

'What matters that?'

'I'll tell him, he'll have the finest chickens and ducks he
ever laid his eyes on here by the end of the day.'

Annie had stopped walking. They stood together in the
cool grey stone, footsteps above and shouts below, but no one
yet around. The stamped earth shifted beneath Molly's feet,
eating her boots. Molly waited for Annie to say something.

When Annie kissed her, Molly's hand went to the knife in
her belt, but she didn't draw, just stood there stiff as Shaun's
pecker tenting a blanket in the morning, sweat slicking her
upper lip and red building behind her eyes. Then, finally, she
put an arm around Annie and squeezed her waist. Pushed
into her kiss, seeing Tom stooping down to kiss the maid in
the passageway of the house on Île de Batz, seeing the way
his hand caught at the folds of her blouse, tenderly, and doing
the same herself now; seeing the way Tom buried his head
in the girl's neck, dropping kisses there, and the way the girl
gripped Tom's forearm, pulling him closer, a sound of pleasure coming from her.

Annie laughed, pulling back. 'You've got gumption,'
she said.

Molly caught her breath. 'That and more besides.'

'You mean it about those hens?'

Molly nodded.

Annie took her hand. 'Come and see my master.'

Molly hesitated, tugging Annie back without meaning to. 'Will you do me a service, in return?'

'I already kissed you.'

'No, I mean – will you tell me where Dick English most likely is?'

A frown. 'Why? Do you have a tip for him, about the free-traders?'

'I've got that all right.'

Excitement in her eyes. 'What is it?'

'We're a lot closer than he thinks.'

Dick English was the only parishioner in the Church of St Petroc. Molly stood in the doorway, one hand on her pistol. The church was all stone, the gently curved roof the belly of a petrified whale. Dick sat at the front, gazing up at the stained glass, which wavered blue and red. His head was uncovered, so blond he looked a haloed saint himself, the brace of candles at his elbow sputtering. A godly man, Annie had said. He looked it from here: at peace with himself.

Molly felt for the hammer on the pistol. Her hands weren't working properly.

'You, there!' English called.

Molly jumped.

'If you're in, get in; if you're out, make your way. You make me colder than the saint's bones.'

Molly's heart was a rabbit near death. What would Tom say, if he could see her here, now? What would he say, when Molly told him of the deed?

Take the bit between your teeth.

Molly closed the door, shutting out the calls of the castle. The hinges gave a long groan, making Dick English look around.

'Do I know you, boy?'

Somewhere, pigeons fussed. 'They told me the church was a sight not to be missed, sir.'

'Who told you?'

'The kitchen, sir. A chance not to be missed.'

Dick English nodded. 'So it isn't.' He turned back to God's light, seemingly studying the altar, the priest's door, the windows, but without, Molly thought, taking any of it in.

Molly followed her feet up the nave. Stopped on a flagstone marking the dearly departed. Dearly loved. The departure had been dear, and the cost had been great, leaving Molly with memories so sparse they were spare change, easily lost: holding Grace's hand, wading out to the doorway of Thurlestone Rock; falling in bluebells and being lifted from the purple crush; running to the tide, water gleaming like spilt coins, laughing as she ran, Grace there with her, laughing too, and Tom, Tom's laughter without any weight to it. So few moments, hoarded, squeezed, until rinsed pale. Molly tightened her hold on the pistol. Looked down on Dick English's head.

'Do you know the story?'

'What?' A whisper, Molly's.

'The kitchen boys tell you the story? How the monks stole those sacred bones?'

'No. No, sir.'

'Petroc was a Welsh lord. He gave up all his worldly possessions, fame, power, fortune – relinquished them in order to go to Ireland and study piety.'

'Easy things to give up, when you're born to them,' said Molly. 'Harder if you've earnt them, sir.'

Dick English smiled: Molly could see the corner of his mouth twitch, could see the slip of his Adam's apple as he continued.

'He travelled to Cornwall with the good Word. Turned the mad king there to its glory. Then Italy, where he had audience with the Pope. He travelled to India, to lands without names. He tamed wolves. When he died, his bones were venerated and lain to rest in Bodmin, only to be stolen by monks from Brittany, who wished to vaunt them for money. King Henry II ordered the bones won back and returned to England, which they were, landing here, before going on to be paraded at Whitehall. Thence they returned to Bodmin, where they lie still.'

Molly eased the pistol from the holster, just an inch, feeling the leather stick. 'What do you take from this, sir?'

Dick English scratched his check. There was no dirt beneath his fingernails. 'Just a good story.' He turned and smiled.

Molly's hand burnt, as if the pistol were hot from use. She could neither let it fall, nor draw it. Dick English's eyes were the blue of shallow water over warm sand.

'And your story, sir?' Molly asked. 'I'm told you have risked your life more than once in the hope of catching free-traders.'

'I've risked enough. But my bones won't be venerated for my fight against these wretches.'

'No, sir?'

'I study their ways, but I am not yet wise.'

'How is that, sir?'

'I might still give Tom West too much credit – to believe he'd not send a boy to do his murdering.'

'I am sent by a dead woman whom you killed.' The words caught in Molly's throat. She drew.

Dick English was faster.

Molly watched the snout of the gun come up, knew she was beaten – and swung her pistol into the candles, knocking them into Dick English's lap. Molly ran, Dick English screaming behind her as she hauled open the priest's door, stumbling on to a grass track between church and castle wall. She scrambled up the brick, the sea bottle-green on the other side, a long drop guarded by rocks. She heard Dick English yell for the guards and ran, pitching herself at the tower, gaining height now – an arrow clattered above – she heard English mount the wall, and ducked as a bullet passed overhead – climbed higher still, until below there was only deep blue. Molly threw herself from the tower.

In June
He changes his tune

Molly tried to keep the pain from her face as Nathan drew the sling tighter. The stateroom was silent. Benedict was paler than limewash. Tom stood, fists on the table, face taut. Molly tried to stop the shaking in her hands, left bloodless by the sea. The *Venture* pitched and rocked around them, bound for Roscoff, the sails straining to outpace Tom's anger. She'd broken her promise to Annie. On deck, Hellard, Kingston, Pascal, all of them kept their peace.

Benedict: 'Captain, I'm sorry, I didn't think—'

Tom lashed out, arm swinging, catching an open bottle and sending whisky spraying over Benedict. The bottle fell, but didn't smash. Benedict cowered where he sat.

'I don't need you to tell me what's God damn evident!'

Nathan cleared his throat. 'It ain't Benedict's fault, Cap'n.'

'It ain't nobody's fault,' said Molly, standing up. 'Nobody but Dick English.'

A snarl: 'He invite you in, did he?'

'He invited my judgement on his head the day he killed my mother, and you know it.'

Benedict's back was already against the wall when Tom tipped the table over and shoved Nathan aside.

'*What do I know?*'

Benedict covered his eyes. He felt his stomach go, for it was happening again, and he couldn't move.

'You know what you swore to me,' said Molly. Her voice shook. 'I've waited long enough. I'll have justice, or let the whole world burn.'

Silence.

A terrible rumble from Tom's chest. He was chuckling.

Benedict opened his eyes.

'And you know what?' said Molly. 'I got wax all over his nice red coat.'

Laughter like bells from a ruined tower.

The *Venture* at night was a well-worn conversation: the shipping lines crossed and recrossed, the fug of whisky and sweat, the murmur of card games, the creak of the keel, the sudden cry of some creature intent on being heard. Tom sat at the desk Nathan had bolted to the floor of his cabin. Molly was asleep in his bed, every blanket they could find on top of her – for the child had swum deep. She could have smashed her skull against the rocks – could have drowned, the fist of shock reaching down her throat and binding the cords there until she couldn't even scream. And then he would have been stripped of them both, such as those souls he sometimes saw haunting the docks, no ship to catch, no home to return to, those men who had failed in any duty they'd ever been granted.

He'd sworn to protect Molly the night she was born. It had taken a lot of his own brandy for Tom to summon the nerve, he remembered. Walking across Bantham Beach, he had felt the heat of drunkenness, despite the frigid surf seeping through his boots. The frost melted in his chest, dropping between his legs, a pit of fear, a pit of want. He knew his desires had no place in Grace's cottage, especially now. He looked from the bloody scrawl of the sun setting on the water to the moon, crimson and swollen, waiting to take its place. The sky seemed too full, just as he felt. He wanted to be empty. If he could be taken apart, she would do it tonight.

Grace was nudging the mackerel with her fork. A yellow rind of butter unfurled from the fish's mouth like a diseased tongue. She was about to push the plate away when she heard the crunch of footsteps over the shingled estuary bed. She stood up. A single pound on the door told her it was not Christopher, but Tom.

She did not want to see him, she wrote, especially not feeling like this. He knocked twice more, and then there was a silence in which Grace thought he'd gone away, before she heard the door sweep back leaves she had allowed to gather in the cross-passage.

'Mrs Tucker?'

Grace stood at the head of the table. He stopped in the doorway, squeezed by the frame.

'You're here,' he said. His gaze fixed on her face. 'Are you ill?'

'I am well, thank you,' said Grace. She wanted to say she'd also thank him not to barge into her home as if it belonged to him, but instead continued, 'I've been having short pains all day, but they are only small.'

Tom ducked through the door, noting how she took a step back. She was not wearing a cap, and her curls – which would shine like Devon sand in summer, if she revealed them to the sun – gave her a free look, wild even, that matched the feverish glow to her eyes. Her whole body carried it.

'Have you felt them before?' he asked.

Grace recalled Mrs Weatheridge's story of Tom's birth – fire and sea – and wondered if he was thinking of the pains he'd witnessed gripping his mother before each younger sibling arrived into the world. But she had experienced early pains with her second lost child, and read about such paroxysms in the midwifery book Mrs Weatheridge lent her. These pains were mild, comparatively.

'It is nothing for you to concern yourself over,' she said.

'I just arrived back,' he said, and scratched his chin.

'Yes?'

He couldn't keep his hands still. He put them in his pockets. 'Are you eating that?'

'Is that what you came here for?' she asked. 'Dinner?'

'Can you blame—?' Tom broke off as Grace pitched forward and clutched the mantelpiece.

'Oh, God,' she breathed, and then water sloshed from between her legs on to the flagstones. Tom took her arm, but she shrugged him off. 'Mrs Weatheridge,' she said.

'What?'

'The midwife. Get her, now, *please.*'

'I can't leave you.'

'I need her.'

Tom looked down at the pool seeping around his boots, like the sea, minutes earlier. 'If you wish,' he said. 'But I'm putting you in bed first.'

Before Grace could argue, he bent down and picked her up. Such weightlessness made her want to sob. He went into her bedroom backwards, kicking the door with the heel of his boot, and laid her down on the mattress, pulling his hands out from under her body slowly.

'There,' he said. 'I'll be back with Mrs Weatheridge, quick as I can.'

Grace began to speak, but then went rigid, her jaw clamping.

Tom could see the whites circling her eyes. 'It's coming *now*,' he said. 'I can't go.'

'You have to; I can't – with you – I can't.'

187

Tom covered her hand with his.

Grace looked at his fist: the knuckles like stones packed beneath the skin, the fingers that were rumoured to have once choked a Revenue man until he was so frightened of death he soiled his trousers.

'Boil water, and clean your hands. It's important – the book says so.'

Tom looked at the black lines of his palm. 'If you wish. I'll be back; don't be pushing.'

The bedroom door closed and Grace sagged. She wanted to cry and never stop. The drop of crystal from her mother's chandelier was swaying – wind gathering outside. She breathed to its beat and felt the sweat on her face cool. A strange calm seemed to lift her until she could no longer feel the sheets beneath her; instead, she was lying in purple bell-heather on the moor, with the hoof beats of ponies reverberating through the ground and into her body. Then, her whole self shifted downwards, as if trying to evacuate. She scrabbled at her stockings, yanking them off. She needed to spread her legs, but her shift kept them pinned; she was dragging it up, scratching her thighs, as Tom walked in.

He checked in the doorway, and then carried on. Placing the tub by the bed, he pulled his bone-handled knife from his belt and dropped it in the boiling water. He hoped the ocean's fingerprints would come clean. He'd brought her candles from France, and set them on the dresser. His hands were shaking as he struck a spark from the lock of his pistol; the first wick came weakly into life, outshone by the red-earth moon that he saw now through the window. The beeswax smoke carried him to cathedrals. He turned to Grace and imagined for a second taking her across the sea. She was studying him through the sweet haze. He knelt down at the foot of her marriage bed, the scar tissue of too many fights pulling at him, as if warning him that offering his hands to first hold her baby would be one step too far. Then she arched from the bed and it began.

The bedroom throbbed with body heat and salt water. In between her cries – lonely, angry, pained – Tom thought he could hear snatches of prayer: 'St Margaret, let me see my child ... Lord Jesus, if it be your will that I ... let my child ...' The words ran on, smoke-bound nothings that became trapped, a grey underbelly beneath the ceiling. He kept his head bowed from her open knees.

Grace was desperate to escape and maintain her body, refusing to leave, refusing to give up. She raised herself to her elbows, head hanging, eyebrows dripping with upside-down tears. She wanted her mother with a need that threw her into childhood. But she would not see her mother again and, no matter how she pushed, the child would not come.

'I can't.'

'But, Grace – you're managing fine ...'

'I can't do it. I can't get it out.'

Tom opened his mouth, shut it again. Fought his fear. 'Take the bit between your teeth and push, girl.'

Grace closed her eyes. Breathed. Once, twice. 'I must get up. Help me, please.'

Tom lifted her, his sweat-soaked skin rubbing with hers. Grace knelt with her legs wide open. He knelt with her. She leant into Tom's body, her head on his shoulders – so broad, so unshakeable – and felt his arms come around her. In that moment, she loved him.

Tom breathed in the smell of her and it was too close and too much. He needed the sea, brandy, the splash of oars. He leant back, and her head slipped from the crook of his neck, but then he saw something cresting between her legs. He put his hands down there and felt the child's head, curls slick with mucus and blood.

189

'I've got her, I've got her.'

Those words filled him as the baby slipped free and filled his hands; Grace cried out in relief as her body emptied, and then her cries were joined by the baby's. Grace looked down at the life cradled between their bodies, and then dug her nails into Tom's arm as another pain seized her. The idea of forcing her body open again was too much. She felt Tom's lips on the back of her neck and pushed. The placenta came free after two more paroxysms, and Grace's final groan was swallowed by the baby's wails.

Tom lifted Grace with the squalling, squirming thing on to the bed. She sank into the sheets, and Tom passed the baby into her waiting arms.

Grace shifted her daughter along her forearm, cradling her head in the crook of her elbow and containing her kicking legs with her hand. She gazed down into her black eyes.

'This may hurt,' said Tom.

'What?'

'I have to cut the cord.'

'No, I don't . . . I want to do it.'

Tom fished his knife from the now tepid water. He made two ties in the cord, then, putting one arm around the baby, he placed the knife in Grace's hand and covered it with his own. They cut together. Grace felt that somehow her daughter knew, her small fists fighting, once the link was severed. She gritted her teeth at the strange discomfort, and then tied the cord at her baby's navel, whispering words of encouragement, although whether it was to the child or herself, she did not know.

There were linens folded in the dresser, and Tom shredded a sheet, his back half-turned as Grace held her daughter to her breast. But still he glanced over, and his throat was swollen when he finally sat down next to her with the swaddling ready.

'Before we wrap her up,' he said, 'she should have this.'

Grace looked at the gold coin in his hand. A love token, the doubloon bent, with just one letter scored into the metal: *T.* He'd brought her a love token.

'You have to wrap it in cloth and place it over her navel.'

'Why?'

Tom smiled. 'Luck. Tradition.'

Grace laughed. 'If you insist.'

Tom caught the little girl's eyes once more as he wrapped the coin in his necktie and balanced it on her stomach, holding it there with his fingertip, as if tying a bow. Grace wound swaddling over her, her hands brushing his.

'Beautiful,' he said. 'What name shall we have?'

'Molly.'

'Molly Tucker,' said Tom, and then sat back an inch.

'What is it?'

'Nought.'

'Tom? Tom . . . where's Christopher?'

Tom retreated to the edge of the bed. 'Kit's not coming back. That's what I came to—'

'What do you mean?'

'There was an accident.'

Grace stared at him. Molly squirmed in her grip and she looked down. 'She's hungry. You need to go.'

'Grace, listen to me—'

'Go, now. I don't ever want to see you again. I don't want your money, I don't want your influence, I don't want *you*. Go.'

Tom stood up. The ground seemed to shift under him and he had to grab on to the wall. 'I'll fetch Mrs Weatheridge.'

He'd vowed, as he bound the coin to Molly's stomach, that he'd look after her as if she was his own. Tom put his hand to his chest – nails digging into the skin – his heart, a bruising pain. Yes, he had given Kit the escape he wanted. Yes, her home became empty of the man that belonged in it. Yes, he had made sure all of Devon saw him at her door. Yes, he had loved her. Yes, he missed her still.

All of this he would confess.

But there it ended. He had left her bereft, and then she bereaved him in return. He'd warned her: *Women are bad luck at sea.* Her reply: *Are men bad luck on land?* He had told her the honest truth. *Yes, we are.* And she'd turned against him anyway.

His heart faltered over its beat. He pounded his chest.

Molly sat up. 'Tom?'

'It's all right.'

'What was that?'

'Nought but Davy Jones knocking.'

She lay down. He found the trunk with the heel of his boot, and urged it under the desk. He knew he should throw the journal into the sea. Burn it. Bury it. Forget it. Had tried, more than once. But this was all he ever managed. Lock it away. Lock it away and keep the key.

That's what Benedict had said, about hiding Molly, early on. *It ain't natural, sir. Locking her away with no key to her nature.*

Tom eased on to the bed. She held his hand. He squeezed. This: this was her nature. Nothing else mattered.

Molly smiled, rubbing her eyes. 'I had that dream again.'

Tom tried to relax. The devil banging at her door, someone screaming ... Tom unbuckled his sword sheath and set it against the wall. 'Move up,' he said, and Molly obeyed. He put one arm around her, and she laid her head on his chest. 'If a demon comes knocking, I'll blow his head off. How's that?'

He felt her smile against the bare skin of his neck, and then the soft brush of her eyelids closing.

A soft question: 'What are we going to do?'

'About what?'

'Dick English. It's got to end.'

'You don't need to worry about that.'

'He thinks he's righteous.'

'All men think they're righteous.'

'How do you know the righteous from the villain, when the villain seems so sure of his convictions?'

'The man left standing – that's the man in the right.'

She looked up at him. 'That doesn't sound like justice.'

Tom wiped his forehead. 'It is, if it's you.'

A Week Before St Margaret's Day

I

A leg of mutton. Oysters, capers, salted fish. Boiled rabbit, a sirloin of beef. To be followed by plum pudding, and all of it served on ceramic, the pewter platters put away. Molly tugged at her neckcloth, feeling a fool in this German serge, bought at market in Roscoff yesterday.

'Trying to make a gentleman of me?' she'd asked Benedict.

Benedict just shrugged. 'Tom's design.'

And now it was clear why Tom had paid for chairs made of walnut and a table of mahogany, why he'd replaced the lock on the front door with brass fittings. Colonel Gautier ate his food unthinkingly, ate so much Molly felt sick watching, and, next to Gautier, Madame Rhys ate almost nothing at all, hiding her smile behind a glass of sweet brandy. It was the first time all summer this strange couple had visited the house on Île de Batz, and Tom had sent the crew into town for the night, keeping only Molly and Benedict to entertain their guests.

'I am told you are turning quite the profit in mills, Captain?' said Gautier. It wasn't really a question. 'And salt mines.'

'Man's got to put his money somewhere.' Tom looked different. He wasn't armed, and it showed, Molly thought. He looked

194

almost gentle, his smile flickering between her and Madame Rhys. Almost.

'Quite right. I imagine you do not require a venturer at all, any more. Your Justice must be quite put out.'

'What he don't know can't hurt him.'

'You take his money, still? But what do you do with it, if you no longer need him to fund your operations?'

Molly tried to catch Benedict's eye, but he was jamming his finger into a pickled oyster determinedly. Molly had never known Tom to talk so openly. Why now, with these people? And why like this?

Tom answered: 'The Justice's money? You're eating it.'

Madame Rhys laughed, then covered her mouth with the back of her hand.

'Very good, Captain,' said Gautier. 'Very good.'

'When are you due to leave us, Captain?' asked Madame Rhys.

Molly rubbed her shoulder. They'd been staying in Roscoff while she healed, Tom insisting they would wait until she was healthy again, regarding her increasingly as if she were made of china.

'Next week.'

Benedict dropped his oyster.

'We'll be going back for St Margaret's Day,' said Tom. 'Kingsbridge Fair.'

'St Margaret,' said Madame Rhys. 'Is she the one born of a dragon?'

Tom pointed his knife at Benedict. 'Ask my scholar.'

Benedict blushed. 'St Margaret is the patron saint of expectant mothers.'

Madame Rhys smiled at him – such a smile, it was as if she smiled for him alone. Benedict turned the colour of the plum pudding waiting to be served.

'I'm *certain*,' she said, 'that she was *something* to do with dragons.'

'Yes, ma'am. That is, you're right, ma'am. But she wasn't the daughter of a dragon. The dragon was male.'

Rhys leant in, as if sharing a conspiracy. 'Men have children too, you know, Mr White.'

The colonel laughed. 'Not if we can help it, hmm, Captain?'

Tom glanced at Molly – it was almost imperceptible, but she felt it. 'Ain't really a choice, in my experience.'

'But the woman has all the choice in the world?' asked Madame Rhys.

Tom wiped his fingers on the table linen. 'That kind of talk, you're going to scandalise my young spotsman.'

Rhys sipped at her brandy, winking over the rim at Benedict. 'He could do with some scandalising.'

Gautier roared at that. The man was a pig drunk. Molly would bet he was a pig sober, too.

'I m-meant,' stammered Benedict, 'meant a dragon did not give birth to her.'

'Regale me, sir,' said Madame Rhys, now contrite.

'St Margaret was the daughter of a pagan priest. She converted to Christianity and swore a vow of chastity.'

'Poor woman.'

'Her godmother took her to Turkey, where she caught the eye of a Roman prefect,' continued Benedict. 'He proposed to her. She said no.'

'I suppose *that's* the choice you were referring to?' said Madame Rhys, casting a sidelong look at Tom.

'Suppose what you like,' he said. He was near drunk too.

'So, what happened when she spurned the Roman's advances?'

'He threw her in a dungeon and ordered that she be tortured.'

'But of course.'

'She still refused. Satan arrived, in the form of a dragon, to eat her.' Benedict took a hasty sip of his drink. 'She was swallowed whole, with just a cross and a dagger. She stabbed her way out of the dragon, climbing from his side, just as Eve grew from Adam's rib.'

Madame Rhys raised her glass. 'Hear, hear!'

'And then the prefect had her beheaded.'

The colonel slapped his thigh, he was so amused.

Rhys raised her glass to Tom. 'To choices.'

'She had a knife,' said Molly, before Tom could return the toast. 'She can slay a dragon, but she can't slay a man?' A shrug. 'Deserved to lose her head.'

Rhys's smile was tilting in her direction, now. 'If only men were mere dragons. But I suppose you're not a *real* man, are you?'

Tom dropped his oyster: a clatter.

Molly gripped her knife under the table.

'How old are you?' asked Rhys.

'Thirteen.'

'Man enough, then, perhaps.'

Tom pushed his plate away. 'Time for pudding.'

Rhys's attention moved back to him – was always on him, Molly thought. 'That's something I don't miss about our dear country. *You've come in pudding time!* Do people still say that? As if baked apples were something to live for.'

'If you don't like it,' said Tom, and Molly expected him to tell this woman she could leave, 'we have exotic fruits even a woman of *your* experience might not yet have tasted.'

'You have a *lot* I haven't yet tasted, Captain West,' she said.

The chair scraped as Molly stood up. She said, 'I've had my fill.'

II

Gautier had given Madame Rhys clear orders: 'He has invited us to his home. You will find a way to remain after dinner. You will seduce him in his own bed. Any man would reveal his weakness to a woman as lovely as you. You will report back to me his secrets, whatever they may be.'

'Why must you know his weakness?'

'Would you have me lose to his strengths?'

'Must there be a fight?' she asked. 'He has proved trustworthy.'

He laughed, then. 'There is always a fight, in games of gold sovereigns. Crowns, after all, do not come cheap.'

So, after dinner, Madame Rhys said she felt too delicate to face the choppy seas back to Roscoff. She begged Captain West to sit with her awhile, while she regained her strength, and Gautier took his leave. Rhys saw the look Tom gave Benedict, who said he would check on Orlando. A strange house, this one, where a free-trader was kept company by a spotsman so wide-eyed, so petrified, he must have seen more than a few dragons in his time, and a sullen powder monkey. Weaknesses? Yes, here were at least two.

Tom asked if she'd like tea, and she assented, following him into a room where the paint on the wainscoting was still fresh. He drew back a chair for her.

'You're not afraid,' he said, lingering by the fire, where a brass fender, tongs and poker all hung without a dent on them, 'for your reputation, without a protector?' A mirror over the fire reinforced his shadow. On the mantelpiece was a black mask, a cowl with a hooked nose and slits for eyes, leaving the mouth free to snarl and bite – and other things. The mask was made from raven feathers. Rhys had bought it for Tom some weeks ago, inviting him to a masked ball which he'd never attended, telling her, *I don't wear masks.* True to his word, the feathers looked dusty.

She said, now, 'I haven't had a protector for a long time, sir.'

A smile, but a distracted one. 'What must society think of you?'

'I doubt they think of me at all, any more,' she said. She could hear the rattle of tea being prepared in the kitchen. 'But it's the opinion of *your* society I care for.'

Tom pulled his neckerchief free, tossing the silk to the hearthstone. 'You know this is only a simulacrum of society, hollow as cheap plaster.'

The door opened, and Rhys let the girl put the tray down, taking the opportunity to consider what allure was to be found in this plaything. Here was an artless innocent, to be sure, a girl who could be seduced by mere flattery – if she was told she was the rising sun, she'd believe it.

'*Merci,*' said Tom, and the girl gave him a look of question and confusion. *Why have you this woman here?* she was asking. *Aren't I enough?* Pathetic, how women could so easily make a man their whole reality.

When the door shut, Rhys set about pouring. 'Sir?' He shook his head. She'd never seen him so rigid. 'Simulacrum, was it?' She nodded to the bookshelf. 'Somebody's been reading.'

'The boy.'

'Mr White?'

'Orlando.'

Rhys stood up, taking the cup of tea with her to the shelf. She ran her finger along Aphra Behn. Honoré d'Urfé's *L'Astrée*. Three novels by Madeleine de Scudéry, each so big that, between them, they took up one shelf. Here was Scudéry's *Les Femmes Illustres*, the only one she'd ever made it through.

She drew the first volume from the shelf. 'Have you read much Scudéry?'

Nothing.

'Rather persuasive. Cleopatra arguing for female liberty and education.' She thumbed the pages. She felt a change in him, his attention drawing taut. She lingered over an illustration, taking a sip from her cup. 'Seems a strange thing to find a powder monkey reading. Then again, I'm surprised a powder monkey can read at all, let alone in French. I suppose you taught him?'

'Taught himself,' said Tom.

'Smart boy. Take after his father?'

A snort. 'No.'

That gave her nothing.

'He's spent the whole summer reading,' said Tom, sounding like his throat was closing. 'Anything he can find in the bookshop.'

'I'd be happy to lend him some volumes from my collection.'

He bowed. 'Obliged.' His head didn't come back up. He gripped the mantelpiece.

'Mm.' She put the book back, coming to stand by him, where he was nudging the grate with his shoe. She set her cup down on the mantel. The mask stared up at her. 'You don't look terribly obliged, sir. In fact, you look very much like you're wishing me to the devil.'

He stopped twitching. She let her finger brush his, there on the coldness of the mantel. The cords in his neck were standing out. She couldn't tell if he wanted to kick the tiles clean off the fireplace, or turn and take her.

'Should I be afraid – to be alone with you? Are you such a dangerous animal?'

He looked at her. 'Yes.' She knew that look: a man so wound up with longing and frustration, he'd kill for relief.

'Funny,' she said. 'I don't feel it.'

'How much is Gautier paying you?' he asked. 'To overcome that fear?'

Rhys shrugged. 'He pays for my way of life.'

'I don't think this can be called a way of life. Just a way of surviving.'

Rhys linked one finger with his thumb. With her free hand, she picked up the mask, holding it to her face, then lowering it. "Tis pity she's a whore – is that it?'

Tom seized her hand, pulling her into him. The mask fell to the floor. Rhys felt the strain at his breeches against her stomach.

'You know what they call prostitutes, back home?'

'What's that, sir?'

'Free-traders.'

She smiled as his arm slipped around her waist. 'It strikes me we've been here before, but nothing came of it. Perhaps you don't want to trade with me, after all.'

'I would, if it were free.'

Rhys slipped a hand between their bodies. She ran her finger over the shivering head, finding the linen there damp.

'Has anybody ever given you anything in your life,' she asked, 'for free? They haven't me.'

Tom kicked the tongs and contraptions aside, lifting her up and pressing her to the wall. She closed her legs about his waist. His hand, rough and dirty, swept past her stockings and shoved her shift up. The whores in town wore nothing underneath, she imagined. But she knew the men she danced with, knew they wanted a feeling of quality – knew drawing mewls of lowdown pleasure from quality was what made them flush. She gasped when he brushed her where so few men bothered to seek.

'Do you want me?' he asked.

She gasped again – involuntary. 'Yes. Yes.'

His thumb kept moving against her. 'Do you want me, or Gautier's protection?'

'You – I want you. Your protection.'

His hand stilled for a moment. That shadow again.

She dragged him down to her, kissed him, a real kiss. Whispered against his ear, 'Baise-moi, Capitaine.'

A smile. 'You sound like the girls at the palais de putain.'

She drew out his belt. This man didn't want quality. He didn't want innocence. He didn't want the maid, with her loving eyes. But he didn't want the girls at the whorehouse, with their histories, either. He wanted oblivion.

She bit his neck, a jolt that went straight to his member, now pressing against her.

'Baise-moi,' she said again, 'jusqu'à ce que nous oublions qui nous sommes.'

He pushed inside her.

Tom locked the door behind them, finding its new fittings too smooth, almost breaking the damn thing with his hard wrench. Rhys was quiet, a swift look over the house. He followed her attention to the four windows, the newly painted shutters, the sky a dusty blue, no birds singing yet. Somebody's dream home. His, maybe. She remained silent on the row to Roscoff, only thanking him when he lifted her from boat to jetty, but she held on to his arm as they climbed to the centre of town. He thought she'd steer him to Gautier's house, but the tug on his arm took him past the cathedral and up into the hills. Her house was on a new street: three storeys, eight windows, two balconies, two chimneys. A way of life, leagues from his own. She hesitated by the gate, as if she couldn't open it with him there. The sleeping smell of lavender irritated him.

202

'Merci,' she breathed, and for a moment he thought she was asking for mercy – asking that he spare her.

He bowed over her hand. 'My pleasure.'

She came close, so close he lost the smell of lavender. There was just her, smelling of him. 'Not just yours.'

Tom watched the front door close behind her. He scrubbed at his face, looking out to sea. Quiet, but unfixing. He dug fingers into his chest – his heart was violent – and tried to choose a direction. Left, down the hill, back to the cathedral he was helping Gautier fund. Right, up to the whorehouse where the men would be sleeping. Or back to the island, back to Molly.

He followed the hill up, birds beginning to sound their alarm at him now. Rue Laënnec was steeper than he remembered. He was sweating. His heart pounding. This night had not followed his design at all – though what he'd hoped to achieve was now vague to him. Molly's injury had made Tom consider keeping her safe in Roscoff, where she'd need a woman to mind her, especially as her body changed more evidently every day, time tumbling on – she would only keep changing. He stopped, looked around. He'd reached the corner of Rue Brizeux, and across the road was Chapelle Saint-Nicholas. The sailors' church, before the cathedral. A plain building, its tower adorned with a bell only. No gargoyles, no ships, no cannons. He crossed to the front door, stepping over a man sleeping there, a man who reeked of brandy and piss, and found the door unlocked.

Inside, the church was just as plain. Tom had never set foot in here before. He knew it was where Benedict came to pray. The walls were painted white, the ceiling bowed wood. He sat down in a pew, fingering the carving of flowers.

A single spermaceti candle shuddered in the walls, the priest or the sweeper forgetting to blow it out. Cheaper than wax – which blazed in the cathedral – but better than the sputtering of tallow, which had filled Grace's cottage with the crackle of cooked meat when Tom returned there for the first time after the birth. Her front door was open, trying to draw the last light in and bottle it, he imagined, before realising she'd filled glass globes and bowls with salt water in a constellation around candle stubs on the doorstep, the light spooling around the water in gold threads, a glowing bramble. His mother had done the same, and sat with her neighbours, old women bent over their bobbins, pricking card for Honiton lace. It never turned much of a profit, as far as Tom understood, but the mothers and widows and spinsters spent the evenings laughing. Grace sat in the doorway, cloaked in wool, with Molly in one arm, gangly now at three years old, and a cushion and pricking card in the other, working alone. She was telling a story, a soft murmur to Molly, and she didn't notice Tom until he cleared his throat.

She spent a long minute regarding him. Tom wanted to get at her thoughts, but she'd learnt to hide them. Later, he found only one line in her diary for that night. *I missed him.*

'This ain't no way to spend your nights,' he said. 'You should be at an assembly, with all the gentlemen waiting to dance with you.'

'You speak from experience, sir?'

Tom shrugged. 'I don't wait.'

'You've waited three years. Even after I solicited your help.'

'It's a new century. Maybe I hope it will make you merciful. Something amusing in that?'

Grace was grinning. 'Only imagining you making up to dowagers at an assembly.'

Tom sat down, and she didn't resist as he eased the cushion off her lap and cradled it for her. Molly sighed, on the edge of sleep. Grace leant into him. He kept the card straight as she pricked it with a delicate hand. He tried to make out the design for the lace, but his attention kept returning to her bare neck, so near his lips.

'Do you miss that world?' he asked.

'In this moment?' she said, glancing at him. 'No.'

He'd only have to dip his head, and he could brush a kiss over her skin. Time passed, filled with the tick of the bobbin, and their breathing. He'd obeyed her command – *I don't want your money, I don't want your influence, I don't want you* – until she came to the Pilchard, a year past, her gown as empty as her stomach, her cheekbones flint, and still the most beautiful woman he'd ever met, wilful, knowing, afeared but not intimidated. She said she'd come to beg him – for what, he never knew, because he offered her the world before she had the chance to ask for pennies. Her question, then: *And what do you require in return, sir?* He was tempted to ask what she'd give, if only to hear her rejoinder, to hear her say he'd be getting a bargain – most courtesans asked for a house with a view and a gilt carriage, not bones for stock – but the bitterness lodged in her eyes pushed him off balance. Nothing, he'd told her. He had Frank Abbott deliver the money, wanting to prove to her that he meant it.

But now, waiting for her to bid him to leave, he wondered if she wanted more than nothing from him.

'Tell me something, sir?'

He didn't trust his voice.

'If you're not a man to wait, what are you waiting for now?'

'Waiting and hoping,' he said, 'are entirely different matters.'

She kissed him, then: gently, happily, hopefully.

When he left, he emptied a bowl of water and dropped in coins for wax candles.

Tom linked his hands now, the way he would to give Molly a lift into her saddle, back when she needed his help. He hadn't prayed for years, nor asked God to hear him. He wondered if God watched him all the same; if God heard Rhys urging him to fuck her, heard her promising she'd make him forget; if God watched him drive himself into Rhys with such force a painting fell from its hook, the frame probably broken, with Rhys urging him to go harder, to give her everything – forget everything.

How did she know there was something – someone – to forget?

If God had watched, then he would have seen Tom cry, known his tears made Rhys's neck damp, known she either believed or pretended they were tears of relief, as he pulled out and shot his seed on to the hearthstone.

He almost said Grace's name, at the end.

Of all his blasphemies, that would be unforgivable.

The first time they lay together, it was Grace who cried. He asked if he should stop. 'No,' she said. 'I'm happy.' He'd never seen a person cry from happiness before. She gave him something for free, expecting nothing – perhaps less than nothing – in return. She gave him her love.

Tom looked down at his empty hands. What had he done with it?

III

The mask looked up at her. *Not a real man, are you?* Molly raised the candle, stepping into the debris: a smashed frame, a broken teacup, the black dust of coal. The mask waited among them, black eyes glittering with promise. Beneath her bare feet, the boards were cold: it stretched up her body,

206

wrapping itself around thighs, vagina, stomach, the chest that remained bare – both of breasts and hair – getting in between the gaps of her nightshirt. It was a shirt of Tom's, really, a grey thing made soft with time, which she had tied with beads and feathers over the summer, bored, Benedict said, not understanding the transformation Molly prayed for, summoned, calling on gods and saints and devils. Molly played the shaman, Molly played the witch. Molly played Orlando, Molly played Molly. Molly wasn't playing. *Not a real man, are you?* God, change me. Make me – me. Grant me the capacity to be a shape-shifter, changeling, man, woman. Grant me this: me.

Molly picked up the mask. Fastened the black satin ribbons among her short curls. Fixed the mask in place, breathing in the smell of a gamekeeper's hut, of a milliner's workshop, snapped ligaments and glue. She set the candle on the mantel and squared up to the mirror. Her reflection shuddered there, the beaked creature staring back, the loose arms of the shirt distorted, growing wings. Molly moved her head this way and that, watching the creature follow, its movements inquisitive, seeking, querying her body: the hips where a man's hand would grip, the back he'd seek to arch, the gaps he'd want to fill.

You're a problem, the mask said. A puzzle, you are. Don't know the answer, neither. Problem without an answer. Pity poor Tom's boy, the mask laughed. You ain't got no place waiting for you.

Hellard ate the last of the pudding before seizing the decanter and draining the remaining wine, the pastry and liquid gumming his throat. Sniffed, spat. His bladder sloshed. Hellard looked about Tom's dining room, deciding where to piss. He stumbled towards the door, gripping the frame when he saw a

light across the hall in the parlour. Tom up? Come on, then –
I'll piss on you. Knock you down, prise your arrogant mouth
open with my boot, and piss right into your gullet, make you
swallow with my pistol to your fore'ead. Hellard steadied himself, watching shadows swing over the floor. And then a figure
stepped into his line of sight.

Hellard's bladder almost gave. It was a demon. But then he
saw it turn in the light and realised it was just the boy admir-
ing himself in the mirror in some mask. The prodigal fucking
son, the undeserving heir, refused nothing, fucking his own
reflection.

Hellard's testicles weighed heavily in his trousers,
everything itching. The boy turning this way and that, bare
legs slender, ankles like a whore. Dressed in a man's shirt –
like a whore there, too – the way Tom's girl at the brothel
would parade about in his shirt after, as if she enjoyed being
owned. As if being Tom West's bitch was a matter of pride.
Hellard scratched at the scar on his nose. Spat again. The
boy hesitated, then turned quickly – and, in that movement,
the shirt came apart, and Hellard saw a neat little cunt and
pure white flesh.

A hot pool of rage for a moment had him lose all control,
had him clawing at the door jamb, taking off fresh paint, as
the boy – the *girl*, the *girl* on their ship, the *girl* set to inherit –
stared, unmoving.

And then the candle went out – the girl blew it out. Hellard
drew his knife from his belt – undid his belt, too, wrapping it
around his fist – as he pushed blindly into the parlour. Bumped
into a chair and kicked it. Knocked a lamp on to the floor.
Span about, dizzy as he'd been on his first ever sea voyage,
that young unspoilt cunt in his vision, asking for it – but the
room was empty.

*

The sea was glassy, small boats gliding on its surface, towing their reflections with them. She'd run the boat aground, and then fell back into the waves, bounced about, the beach at her back blinking with sunlight, the noise of Roscoff waking up. The mask stroked her blazing cheeks. She couldn't breathe. She stripped off the shirt, the ridiculous beads and talismans, giving the slick coolness of the water her burning flesh, but nothing helped.

'Molly!'

A name that sent panic lancing through her. She turned: Tom on the beach, calling her name for the entire world to hear. Molly sank deeper into the water, watching Tom stride down the sand towards her. She couldn't read Tom's expression from here, but could read his walk: somewhere between anger and fear. He was always somewhere between anger and fear. That's where love existed, Molly thought now, as Tom ran down the beach – between anger and fear.

It was the mask that made Tom run: seeing Molly's small figure in the sea, her bronzed body. Seeing her turn, and seeing that black mask on her face, a child demon with its eyes on him, a changeling devil from the sea.

'I thought that was you,' he called, running into the surf.

'You just called me – that name,' said Molly, treading water.

'What?'

'Molly. Somebody could have heard.'

'A slip,' he said.

'If I made that slip, you'd kill me.'

He paused, and then kicked off his shoes and kept coming, walking into the water. 'Speaking of slips, those French books you read . . .'

'What about them?' asked Molly, stilling. Tom didn't know. She was safe. Cut out Hellard's eyes, and she'd be safe.

'You said they were adventure stories,' said Tom.

'They are.'

'Cleopatra learning to write counts as an adventure?'

'You been reading them?' Molly asked.

'No need to sound so surprised.'

Molly shrugged, trying to find a level voice. 'I didn't know you could read French. Madame Rhys, on the other hand . . . '

'Take that mask off,' he said, waist deep now, almost level with her.

She obeyed, hands trembling, knowing her face was tear-stained, a map of distress.

'My boy.' Tom waded forward, hand extended. 'What happened?'

Molly hesitated. 'My shirt's in the boat.'

He shrugged from his jacket, finery bought for yesterday's folly, threw it about her shoulders and then picked her up. He kept his eyes from her body, as if she offended him. He carried her to the shore's edge and sat down, legs stretched into the fringe of white. She moved from his lap and copied him.

'That's what the two of you did after dinner?' she asked. 'Late-night reading?'

Tom put his arm around her. 'You sound like a jealous wife.'

I'll send you away.

Molly punched him in the knee.

Seagulls looped above them, a contest of cries. 'I thought you ought to have a woman, as you get older. A companion. See what a woman is.'

'If that's what a woman is,' said Molly, 'I'd rather drown today.'

'I didn't hear her complaining,' said Tom – a reflex, his stare fixed on the ships shimmering in and out of nothingness on the horizon.

'I don't want her to be my companion. I don't want her to be *your* companion.'

'You know you're the only girl for me.'

Molly held her breath. 'Am I?'

'You doubt my word?'

'No, I mean – am I your girl?'

The smile dropped. 'My daughter? No.' His voice like there were hands at his neck. 'You're not my daughter. You know that.'

'Son, daughter, it – it don't matter,' said Molly. 'Them's just words.'

'What are you asking me, then?'

'I'm asking – what I am. What I'm to become. I'm asking, am I yours?'

A crack: 'Yes.' Tom cleared his throat. 'Always.'

St Margaret's Day

Fore Street rose from the estuary like the crest of a helmet.
The houses lining the hill had gone up since Queen Anne
came to the throne, and their tiled fronts and sashed windows gleamed, their gardens and orchards sweetening the
air – when the cattle and horses gathered for sale didn't command the wind. To the east and west, where the ground fell
away, two brooks eased their way to the town mills; there'd
been no rain for weeks. Molly breathed it in deep – she'd
missed Devon.

Kingsbridge was busy for the fair, but the men and women
carrying their goods and setting up tables got out of Tom's
way, calling, 'Welcome back!' – some patting him on the back
or shaking his hand as he passed. The reek of the butchery
in the middle of the street caught Molly: hot blood and bone,
death peeling its secrets for the midday sun. She hurried after
Tom's broad shoulders, past the church, to the corn market and
shambles at the crown of the helmet. There were stalls selling
cloths, crockery, sweetmeats. Music played somewhere. Tom
had said Molly could buy anything she wanted – but no stealing. The flagpole was raised, and in its slender shadow Shaun
and Benedict laid out their stall of tea and brandy and glass and
lace and tapestries. Hellard would be nearby. He'd said nothing when Molly saw him the next day. He'd not lingered near

her cabin on the ship, either. Perhaps he hadn't seen anything. Yes, that was it, Molly told herself for the thousandth time. He hadn't seen anything. She was safe.

Tom hailed a councilman beneath the flagpole, which was ready for the glove raising, the leather thing stuffed and garlanded, waiting on a fishing line to be pulled up.

'Now you are here, Captain,' said the councilman, 'we can start proceedings?'

Tom nodded, and Molly followed his gaze down to the estuary, the verdant snake. You would be able to see all the way to Salcombe, were it not for the estuary turning from south to south-west. The parish church and the chequered hills of Portlemouth drew their line over the horizon instead. Molly looked up at Tom. He was happy.

'Perhaps you'll permit me something,' he said to the councilman. Sweet talk.

The man wiped his brow. 'Anything, sir.'

'Let my powder monkey, here, raise the glove.'

The councilman peered at Molly, regaining his composure with admirable speed. 'Honoured, sir.'

Molly was about to back off, to say she didn't want all these eyes looking at her, when Tom shook her by the shoulder. She straightened her neckerchief, and followed the councilman to the flagpole.

Drums brought the crowd to silence, people so thick in the street its sixty-foot breadth seemed nothing, and everyone stared her way.

The councilman was unfurling his scroll, and around him the other great men of Kingsbridge stood in their gold chains, each one of them bowing their heads in Molly's direction. The councilman began reading the Latin declaration, which, Molly knew, promised there could be a fair here for ever and for ever, that all free trade could commence, and that all clemencies would be granted for the nine days the glove hung. In other words: free-traders go free.

Molly took hold of the pulley, and the glove sped up the flag-pole, swinging this way and that, and Fore Street cheered. She could see Nathan and Benedict, both applauding, and Hellard, a blank look on his face, in the doors of the Old Tavern, and Tom, smiling on. Molly met his eyes, and Tom winked.

Hellard watched, tracing the outline of the girl's body as he had every time he'd been near her in the last week, following the womanly turn of her hips, the stripe of soft skin across her pelvis, visible when she reached for the riggings or hauled up a cannon ball, and now, as she stretched to watch the glove rise. All grown up. He remembered Tom cradling the crying thing in his arms as he fled Grace Tucker's cottage. And all the time, she'd been twitching her tail at him, asking to be sniffed out. A ripe girl, this one, sharing Tom's cabin – Tom plucking her – while she flaunted it before the rest of them, making merry fools of them. But not Hellard, not any more. A joke, that was what it was. Tom's joke on him. Crowning a cunt to inherit what Tom owed his brother. It was unnatural. Well, Hellard would correct what was unnatural, just like he'd made sure Grace Tucker's docity was corrected. As soon as Tom was out of his way. It had to be soon. It had to be now. This throb inside him was unbearable.

Richard English stood inside the butchers'. The stench would carry in his clothes for days to come. He watched the boy raise the glove, and watched Tom West laugh without care. He beck-oned one of his dragoons to him.

'That boy,' he said. 'Do we know his name?'

'I cannot say, sir.'

'That's the diddyman who tried to shoot me.'

The boy was flushed with happiness, the glove swaying over his head. Richard remembered his own loss of equilibrium as the boy whispered: *I am sent by a dead woman, whom you killed.*

He watched as Tom folded the boy into his arms, ruffling his hair.

They had never found a body.

Then he hadn't left a child to burn. Relief squeezed Richard's chest. But Tom had let him think just that; so many years, so many supplications for God's forgiveness. So many nightmares.

'We call the powder monkey Orlando.'

Hellard was skulking in the shadow, the hungry coward who had given him time and tide on Tom and then done nothing to see through his capture. The dragoon's hand went to the pommel of his sword, but Richard seized his wrist.

Hellard drummed his fingers on the chopping block. 'I'm Orlando's doting uncle, as it were, and Tom the doting cuckold. He booted Kit Tucker out of bed and off the ship, and won himself the bitch and her pup. What happened next is a story for the ages. It ends with Tom swinging and me and the pup setting sail as free men.'

'Your tongue is loose today, sir.'

'For a price.'

Tom sat on a barrel, resting his head against the outstretched arms of the pillory in the centre of Fore Street. Kingston, Nathan and Charlie Savage lounged with him, the two men arguing over where the name Love Lane came – the hollow that ran by the estuary. Both swore they knew which amorous couple had the honour, and the descriptions were only getting more graphic. Tom drank his cider, looking about for Molly, finding her perched on top of a water conduit, having climbed its twelve feet, with a group of boys. She was tossing something up in the air that flashed each time she caught it. Her knife. The boys looked to be hanging on her words.

'I don't suppose I could trouble you to get to your feet and bow over that pillory, could I? It won't take a minute to lock you in.'

Tom brought himself back slowly, refusing to hurry. He smiled up at Dick English. Crossed his legs at the ankles. He could see, in the corner of his vision, that Nathan's hand was on his pistol and Charlie Savage had hold of his sword. Kingston folded his arms over his chest.

'You know you ain't no trouble to me, Dick. Besides, I don't think I'd fit.'

Only one dragoon with Dick English, and him not drawing his weapons. Tom was aware of the queer chatter around him, yeoman farmers pretending to go about their business, cattle owners buying and selling, housewives sniffing new soaps and examining Exeter serge, parsons and schoolmistresses debating a finer point, shoe makers, bakers, saddlers, wheelwrights, miners, labourers and small farmers comparing woes and blessings, but all of them waiting, just waiting.

'Not today, maybe,' said Dick. 'But give me time. I can cut you down to size.'

'Not for nine days,' said Charlie Savage. 'Free-traders get passage at the fair. Seems like a waste of our taxes, you patrolling. Who should I complain to about that?'

Dick glanced at him. 'Are you a free-trader, then, Mr Savage?'

Charlie laughed. 'I am today.'

'What about attempted murder of a Revenue officer?' said Dick. 'Are you party to that, too?'

Charlie choked on his pasty.

Tom relaxed against the pillory, feeling its smooth wood on his nape. A flash of metal in the corner of his eye – Molly watching on, knife in hand. She'd said to him, on the way home, 'Do you think Dick English will pursue me?' He told her, 'We *are* Devon, remember?' And the crowd was bearing him out, for here was an innkeeper who he supplied, standing by for action, and the mill owners, and the farmers.

'Attempted murder?' said Tom. 'Did one of your Revenue boys fall out of bed and hurt his head?' The men around them laughed. Dick English wasn't blushing, but Tom could see it in his ice-blue eyes. He brushed crumbs from his fingers. 'Besides, ain't the pillory meant to shame moral miscreants?'

'You could do with some shame, sir.'

Tom shrugged. 'Don't see as I can help you with any attempted murders, Dick –' and he knew the man understood his meaning – 'but, if you want to carry me off to the town gaol, I reckon the consequences would be amusing enough to let you try.'

Another laugh.

Dick sniffed. 'You are a *stain* on this community.'

A shuffle of anger from the men around them.

Tom looked about him, at the colourful stalls, at the girls with flowers in their hair, at the musicians, whose instruments were silent now. 'Don't look stained to me, Dick.'

Dick leant in, a whisper that only Tom and his crew could hear: 'Then I will stain it with your blood.' He straightened, a smile on his face, and doffed his cap to the crowd. 'Enjoy the festivities.'

The Day After St Margaret's Day

I

Charles Savage is in trouble. Word went around, from Richard English's neighbours – merchants, Navy men, women pausing in the business of ordering the morning to consider the stunted fury of the man and pity his wife – who watched him slam the door of number fourteen behind him and march down the narrow hill which dropped into Dartmouth, to the traders on Smith Street, who shared knowing looks – *Charlie Savage is in for a spanking* – as English stomped down the steps past Charity House, intent on Charles Savage's shop.

Charles rented the ground floor of Merchant's House, a mortgage that cut a hole in his purse each month, but worth it for all that it made people imagine his purse was limitless. His shop – the front of his house – overlooked Church Close. St Saviour's was hammering its bells, the endless practice of the terminally purposeless. Sitting in the window, Charles rolled the cup of hot chocolate across his pounding forehead. *Zealots* – was there anything worse? Perhaps only the clatter and filmy brown of Mill Pool, beyond the church, the stench of it this morning prompting Charles to add his sums up again. There was talk of reclaiming Mill Pool, turning the waste to flatland, the Holdsworths and Seales taking even more inches from the sea. Charles's grandfather had been swallowed by the sea on some foolish trade gamble, his father reduced to a clothes shop. That wouldn't be his fate.

If Mill Pool were reclaimed, Merchant's House would be worth all the more and rent would go up; finally, the money Charles made in Dartmouth from Spanish oranges and dried fruit, from port wine and Biscay salt, from serge and Newfoundland fish, it wouldn't be enough to hold him here, beneath the gaze of the Navy and the Revenue. There would be better horizons. He'd invest in Dock at Plymouth and get away from Dick English and Tom West and the whole cursed lot of them. Charles leant against the coolness of the glass, attention wandering over the old ducking stool to the pillory. The cobbles were slick with rotting fruit. God, Tom West was an unnatural cove, sitting there so calmly as Dick English measured him for the stocks yesterday. It had seemed funny, then. Waking up with a wasps' nest in his skull, Charles cursed himself for a greater fool than the bell ringers.

His own bell rang. He thought he'd locked the door. Charles twisted, too trapped behind his desk to reach the door before a red coat, blurred in the glass, told him who was coming.

God's flesh. You've done it now. Gone and told the man: *Yes, I'm a free-trader.* Might as well have hung a sign up outside: *Come and take your itch for Tom West out on my backside.*

He smiled at Dick English, who closed the door behind him, saying pleasantly, 'Good morning, Mr Savage.'

'I wouldn't oversell it.'

Dick English looked about the room, lingering on the bird-cage with the yellowhammer Tom had brought Charles from France, saying, *You missed out on some fine birds, Charlie, but none of them wanted to come back with me once I'd described you. Here's a substitute.*

'Are you alone here, sir?' asked Richard.

'Are you?' returned Charles.

Dick smiled, just the corner of his mouth. It looked like a new experience. 'I am never alone when in sight of St Saviour's. Neither are you, Mr Savage. One imagines that's why you positioned yourself here, looking out on to the instruments of God and man's law, with equal impudence for both. Perhaps they will help you mend your character, one of these days. We can only pray, of course.'

'Pray for yourself. I don't need any help.'

'Yes,' said Dick, getting something from his coat – Charles felt his stomach fist. It was just a piece of paper. He dropped it on to the desk. 'I think you do.'

Charles looked down his nose at it. The curtain of a cloud passed before he nudged the scroll all the way open. The blood was draining from his face, and he knew Dick would notice it.

'Well, ain't this quite the tale,' he managed. 'You make this up yourself, did you? Grammar ain't quite there, sir, if you don't mind me saying so.'

'You are most amusing, Mr Savage. As you were yesterday.'

'Now, look, that was just boys being boys.'

'And what do you call this? Boys being boys?'

'You expect me to believe Tom West murdered a woman, on the say-so of a piece of paper with no signature? Not even an *X*?'

Dick sniffed. 'Come for a walk with me, sir. You look in need of fresh air.'

'Air is not my friend today, sir. My head aches consumedly, all of a sudden.'

'And yet I insist.'

Slowly, Charles got to his feet.

The tower of St Saviour's threw its shadow over them, but it wasn't enough to keep the sight of Captain Richard

English and Charles Savage walking side by side from the notice of the men in the window of the Seven Stars. 'Oh-ho,' they said. 'Tom West's not going to like this.' The curtains in Rose Cottage twitched. The washerwoman carrying her load from Pilot House drew up short before them, a small gasp. Richard strolled alongside Charles unconcerned, a bow for the men squeezing from the slanted door on the crooked Tudor House at Fairfax Place, who returned his bow with their own exchanged looks: *English is at it again.*

'The night of the Great Storm,' said Richard. 'I suppose you recollect that night?'

'Like I said, your company does ought for my head.'

'There was an ambush on the tidal road at Aveton Gifford.'

'I weren't a financial agent to any parties in that area, in 1703,' said Charles, looking out to the water between houses, anything to avoid the looks of those around him. 'But I've got some notion of what you mean. Idle talk only, you understand, but idle talk that has me to understand you ambushed men with no warning, and laid three of them to rest for ever in the earth, and them only boys.'

'You make it sound like they were taking their elderly mothers to church at the time. I can assure you, sir – they were not.'

Charles pulled his hat down as they dipped on to Lower Street. He hadn't recognised the hand on the paper. But, of course, it would have been dictated, very few of Tom's men having penmanship. 'Let me have this straight,' he said. 'You, and the author of this tale, if you're not one and the same, claim that Tom West's location was betrayed to the Revenue by a woman that night, who he then killed for the deed. And what do you hope to gain by showing me this?'

'Would it be too much to expect you to be shocked that a man regarded as a hero would *murder* innocents in cold blood?'

'There's a code – as I hear it, you understand,' said Charles.

'If you cross a free-trader, you invite death. This woman, it's a pity she opened the door when death first came knocking. Not that I blame her. Who hasn't had hope enough to believe in the promise of security and comfort, enough to put off consequences down the line?' A white cat crossed from the shadows. 'But I'd wager – and here I hope I do you justice, Dick – I'd wager that's not the whole story. I'd guess it was *you* who came knocking. Maybe she saw that red coat and thought she could trust a man in a uniform. I'd guess – if you'll permit me, sir – that *you* made her betray Tom West.'

'Do you expect remorse?' said English.

Charles drew to a stop and looked English in the eye. 'You coward. All of Devon applauds Tom West, the free-trader who has everyone from Exmouth to fucking Elburton calling you Limp Dick English, and you can't stand it. So you invent a tale you think will send 'em brustling. Tom West the woman-murderer. You have too high an estimation of their souls, Dick.'

English narrowed his eyes. 'And what about your soul?'

'I sleep fine at night, thanks for asking. I know the only way to have good of this beast is to take his coin until I no longer need him. But you – you don't *want* rid of the beast. You want to saddle him up and ride him straight to hell, just to prove to us all how hot the flames burn. So you invent little tales.'

Richard smiled. 'Profit will blind a man. That, and fear.'

'I ain't scared of you.'

Richard shrugged. 'This is what I need of you, Mr Savage. You will invite Tom to meet you on Salt-Stone tomorrow night at low tide. Confidential matters to discuss. You will of course find yourself otherwise disposed. I will keep the appointment for you.'

'And why would I do that?'

'Follow me.'

Charles felt like a condemned man being led to the gallows as Dick urged him around the corner on to Bayard's Cove. The river was busy. The door of the Customs House was ajar, men going to and from the docking traders. The castle sat over them all, as did its prison.

Richard smiled at him again. 'Do you understand, sir?' Charles couldn't keep his lip from curling, but Richard only laughed at him. 'Good.' He gripped Charles's arm. 'One more point. Tom West's powder monkey, the boy who raised the glove yesterday?'

'What about the squab?'

'Tell Tom you have vital information concerning a threat to the child's life.'

'Do I?'

Dick patted Charles on the arm. 'Good day, Mr Savage.'

II

When Tom broke into Charlie Savage's house, it was dark out, and no neighbours stirred at the sound of smashed glass. He swept the shards to one side with his shoe and ducked into Charlie's bedroom before the man had a chance to get out of bed. Tom closed the door behind him slowly, letting the click of the mechanism fill the room.

'Don't get up,' he said.

Charles drew his blanket higher. The sudden need to piss filled him like air shot into a pig's bladder for play. 'What are you . . . ? It's not safe for you here, in Dartmouth.'

Tom glanced at the window, where curtains muffled the

sounds of the Seven Stars. 'Funny,' he said. 'Dartmouth's in Devon, ain't it?'

'Yes—'

'Then I'm safe.' Tom crossed to the fire: glowing coals, a poker resting in the grate. He stabbed the poker into the bed of ash, sending sparks into the air. 'Seen Hellard lately, Charlie?'

'Hellard?'

Tom waited.

Charles placed bare feet on the boards, covering his legs with the blanket. 'Hellard never comes to Dartmouth. Doesn't have your courage.'

'Ever ready with a pretty word, ain't you?' Tom looked about at the wallpaper, the mirror, the heeled riding boots, polished to a gleam. He twisted the poker deeper into the coals. 'And look where it's got you. Not bad, Charlie boy.'

'Th-thank you.' Charles knew he'd stuttered, and hated himself for it.

'So, this is how you spend your nights. Reading. Alone.'

Charles blushed, moving the book under the blanket. 'Aphra Behn.' At Tom's raised eyebrow, he added – lamely, even to his own ears – 'A romance, sir.'

'You need to get yourself a woman, Charlie.' Tom watched the poker tip gather orange scales. 'But mayhap you can put this reading to good use. I've come to ask for your help with a mystery.'

'Anything, Tom.'

'I wonder if Dick found you so obliging this morning. You recall the assistant collector's haydigee last year, hauling us in to Customs. I swore blind it couldn't have been you to speak against me. Nothing to gain, everything to lose. Sweet Benedict was sure it was Hellard – so sure my brother would betray me, it leaves a bitter taste. Now, I hear you've enjoyed a good tell

224

with Dick. Here's my choice: either you are the viper in my nest, or Hellard.'

'It wasn't me!'

Tom smiled at him. 'But you see it *must* have been you, Charlie, because Hellard never comes to Dartmouth, so he can't have visited to whisper into Dick English's ear. You, however, live just streets from the man.'

'He knew anyway,' Charles rushed. 'He knew everything.'

Tom maintained his smile. 'That sounds awful ominous, Charlie.'

'Dick thinks he knows – Dick's making up tales. He asked me to arrange a meeting with you on Salt-Stone tomorrow night, where you'll find him set to trap you. Orlando's in danger, he says. Showed me a piece of paper. A witness report, unsigned.'

'And you agreed to be Dick's messenger boy?'

The need to piss stabbed at Charles. 'Sir, you've got believe me. He pressed me.'

'Pressed you?'

Charles stood up. He wore a shirt that fell to his thighs, and no breeches.

'Now, that's strange,' said Tom, pulling the poker from the fire. The metal spat. 'I don't see a mark on you.'

'Tom – wait – I didn't believe a word of what he was saying—'

Tom closed the gap between them, trying to keep the same calm curiosity on his face, keep this rage strapped down. He nudged the hem of Charlie's nightshirt with the poker. 'Maybe I'm looking in the wrong place, hmm? Where exactly did Dick *press* you?'

Sweat coated Charles's body, sudden and sweltering as the poker edged between his knees, and his bladder burnt, and a drop of piss hit the boards.

Tom took a step back. Looked at the spatter. He snorted, feeling suddenly sick, and tossed the poker back to the fire. He turned to the sideboard and found two glasses. Knocked twice on the wood with a knuckle, then made a fist.

Charles was ready to pick up the poker and swing for Tom with all of his strength. But, as Tom poured the brandy, Charles saw the pistol stuck in his belt, and the knife. He sat down, wiping the sweat from his face with his sleeve.

Tom passed him the glass and relaxed in the only chair. 'You know the price for talking behind a free-trader's back. Talking behind *my* back.'

Charles didn't dare drink.

'You know what I should do to you, by every code, by every rule that we hold to.'

'I also know what I'm worth to you.'

'You're not worth the piss on the floor, Charlie.'

'Without me, you're just a neck too thick to feel the noose around it.'

Tom narrowed his eyes. 'You'll have to talk me through that one, son.'

'What were you, before me? A dog sniffing at the butcher's door for bones. And what did you do with those bones, once you'd got 'em in your teeth? Dig a hole and bury 'em. If I hadn't offered you my services, you'd still be digging like a good boy. This grand plan of yours to compromise every fisherman and his wife, drag 'em into your schemes as venturers, it only works because *I* make it work. Your investments in mills, salts, inns – those are *my* books, and you don't know how to read 'em. You need me more than I need you.' Charles stood up, planted his feet and pissed into the fire. The coal hissed, and quieted. He turned to sneer down at Tom. 'So, go ahead. You need to hit someone to feel all manly – I know I can't stop you. I know what you are, Tom. But, after that, you'll have to count me out, and do the rest of the counting yourself. Those are some pretty big sums, Tom. I don't think you'll get very far.'

Tom studied his brandy, and then put it back in one gulp. 'Dick mention anything else?'

Charles rubbed his throat. 'Nothing worth repeating.'

Tom shrugged, as if shaking life into his arms. 'Indulge me.'

'Something – something about a murder he wants to pin on you.'

Tom looked again at that drop of piss, the size and shape of his thumbprint. Hellard had gone to Dick English and given a statement – *I witnessed Tom do murder* – but left his name off. He imagined Dick English insisting: *Why don't you just give me it all now?* Routes, times, signature. And Hellard's answer: *Because, if it goes wrong, I don't plan to be in the scummer for any of it.*

'I didn't believe him,' said Charles, 'about the murder.'

Tom stirred.

'You're Tom West. Am I to believe you'd follow some code, when it comes to your own woman? You'd just change the code.'

Tom got to his feet and dropped the stopper back into the brandy – brandy he'd given Charles. 'I'll leave you to your romance, Charlie.' He patted the red-faced man on the cheek. 'But, listen to these words, and take them as the words of God: you share a conversation with Dick English again, you repeat anything we've discussed here, the last thing you ever do in this life will be to lap up your own piss. You understand me?'

'I already told you,' said Charles. 'I know what you are. You follow the code, when it suits you.'

The fire spat. Tom swayed.

'You expect me to thank you for your mercy?' said Charles.

Laughter broke from Tom. 'Maybe there's hope for you, yet.' He shook his head and left by the back door.

Charles got to his feet, knowing for the first time in his life what it meant to be weak at the knees, and threw his brandy on the fire. White flame ate the stink of what he'd thought were his last moments.

Tom stood in the garden, boxed in by evergreen shrubs and potted plants. The bile in his throat was sour, and spitting on to the neat gravel path did nothing to alleviate it.

Two Days After St Margaret's Day

I

'I'm going with you.'

Molly blocked Tom's way, standing between him and the cabin door. The sea pitched under them. Tom's gaze was fixed on the floor. Molly could hear Nathan, Kingston and Benedict in anxious conference above them, in the stateroom. Tom had ordered them back to the ship, anchored beyond Salcombe – Benedict to look after Molly, and Kingston to take arms and lead the others, to find Hellard in whatever inn he was drinking at and keep him there, by force if necessary, until tomorrow morning.

A deep breath. 'Boy – Molly – get out of the way.' His silver pistol was stuck in his belt.

'I won't,' said Molly. 'I won't let you go alone. I can't lose you too.'

Tom started forward, his fist coming up as if to seize Molly's jacket. The pistol in his belt jammed against Molly's ribs as she put her arms around him, unable to make her hands meet, and she felt another in his pocket.

'Molly,' he whispered. 'My girl. This has to end.' He sounded desperate. 'You were right. It has to.'

'I should be there when it does. He killed my mother.'

Tom kissed Molly's curls, then picked her up and dropped her on to the bed. The door slammed, the key turned.

Salt-Stone was a hundred feet long and fifty feet wide, an island that only appeared in the middle of Widegates, the broadest sweep of Kingsbridge Estuary, at low tide. There was a contest that Tom had taken part in as a boy: who could swim out to Salt-Stone from Kingsbridge as high tide came on, and dive down to touch the rock first. They got up to other mischief there, too, the rock belonging to no man, lying between the parishes of Charleston, South Pool and Marlborough. Unclaimed, Salt-Stone was lawless. Dissenters met to pray when the rock was uncovered. As Tom grew up, as Ezekiel became his lord, Tom's mischief grew beyond drinking, gambling, fucking, fighting. Grew to more than boyhood's dissent. A man finally, he committed his first murder in the name of Ezekiel Day on Salt-Stone: a rival free-trader, a wrecker, and then nothing but a dead man at Tom's feet. And now he'd commit two more. First, Dick English. Then, his brother. The sins of the father would be his own.

Tom approached the estuary from Love Lane, where, in his youth, he'd kissed a different girl each day of the week, on a dare. Sheltered by trees, he pulled the mask Madame Rhys had given him from his coat, and hid his face from the moon's betrayal. He dropped towards Square Quay, skirted the lone house and jumped into the mud of the riverbank, which slurped at his boots. His mother used to pray for clouds, for it was then his father would go out and lure ships on to the rocks, and she would be spared him another night.

Seven channels bound for the ocean met here at high tide. The eddies had plunged more than one sailor into the water.

Their bodies would be found snagged on rocks, faces so smashed their wives didn't recognise them. Now, the estuary bed crunched and sank beneath him, inviting him to its depths. Tom turned his collar up, keeping his stride as quiet as possible, Salt-Stone ahead like a beached whale, and, beyond it, a ragged line of trees, unnaturally still, as if the whole estuary were holding its breath.

He moved one pistol to his back and covered it with his coat. Both were primed. Time for this to end.

His mother used to pray his father wouldn't return from wrecking – Tom hadn't thought about that for years, but saw her now, kneeling by the fire, muttering, 'God, take him.' She wouldn't even ask for forgiveness. Just: 'God, take him.'

When Tom first got into trouble big enough to make its way back to her, she told him, 'Things that are good and good alone, given the right conditions, can exist. Things that are *only* evil – well, there's no such thing, boy, for even those natures despoiled by an evil will still have their soul. Nothing can take that away. You must choose whose will you'll be listening to – yours, or the devil's.' He'd repeated this to Benedict once, who told him it was a hedgerow translation of St Augustine.

Tom twisted his sword in its scabbard, first left, then right. It was smooth, no rust to slow him down.

He remembered Charlie telling him to have done with this maidenly refusal and put a bullet in the man's brain. Asking if his reticence was a fear of getting his hands dirty.

He should have broken into Dick English's quarters, the day after the Great Storm, and slit the gutless bastard's throat. And then done the same to Hellard. So, why hadn't he? A promise to his mother? His hands were plenty dirty already.

Grace would say, *Perhaps you want to be punished for what you did, and hope one of them will have the will to do it.*

Tom tugged his pistol free.

And deprive that girl of her only guardian left? Without me, she's got no one to take care of her.

And whose fault is that?

Tom brushed the roots of a bedraggled tree at the edge of Salt-Stone, circling the rock. No one else hiding in its shadow. He couldn't tell if Dick English was up there already.

So, take the bit between your teeth.

He grabbed hold of the loose rocks and hauled himself up, drawing as he did.

Dick English was waiting, his pistol drawn too, a glint of steel, unable to pick Tom out from the gloom, the mask doing its job.

Fire. Fire, now. God, take him.

Too late.

Richard found him. Flinched, and then laughed. So, Charles Savage had prepared Tom for what he'd find. Richard kept his pistol level, trying to retain the same calm Tom had maintained, lolling against the pillory. The mask made Tom look like something a witch would summon, something that would suckle at her teat and eat of her insides.

'Good e'en,' he called. 'I take it Mr Savage's sense of self-preservation is even lower than I'd hoped?'

Tom walked towards him, glancing about for any other men, but they were alone. Unless Dick had someone watching from the shore with a bow, or long-range musket. He wouldn't bet on their marksmanship at this distance, though, even with the moon's assistance.

Fifteen feet apart now, and circling. 'I guess you're not as persuasive as you reckoned.'

'That's not what Mrs Tucker thought.'

Tom's trigger finger twitched, but the gun did not go off. 'How would you know?'

Twelve feet between them now. The rock was quiet, and they

could both hear the pop-pop-pop of the sand, worms burrowing down. Salt and the burn-off of lime laced the air.

'She kept a journal, as I recall,' said Richard. 'I didn't find it in the wreckage, afterwards, so I presume you have it.'

Tom said nothing.

'I would imagine she confided all there,' said Richard. 'My visits. The time we spent together.'

Tom glanced around him again. If Dick was baiting him, it was because he'd not expected Tom to come ready for a fight, and troops were waiting too far off in support. Buying time. A man didn't bait a bear by himself, without making sure the bear was tied to a stake beforehand. But he saw no one, heard no one.

'You should know: she didn't volunteer the information readily. I had to threaten the child to induce her. She didn't give me another option. You understand *that*, I'm sure.'

She didn't give me another option. Tom said nothing.

Richard kept his voice casual. 'I told her the child would be taken upon the parish, and she would be sent to an asylum for unstable mothers.'

'She was a good mother.'

Richard raised an eyebrow. 'Then why did she let you into her bed?'

Tom blinked sweat from his eyes, the mask blinking back at him, his eyelashes brushing feather.

Richard was praying the two men waiting on Dodbrooke Quay to take Tom into custody were even now stealing upon the island. Fool, not to have stationed them closer. 'I've always wondered – did you know what was at stake for Mrs Tucker *before* you killed her – or after? Perhaps she wrote it down in that journal, and you only bothered to open its pages once the deed was done.'

Tom said nothing. *Fire.*

Richard laughed. 'I see it, now,' he said. 'It was there for you, all written out in her neat hand, but you didn't take the time to read it, or perhaps you couldn't read. You never gave her the chance to speak for her actions, so you killed her without knowing the truth – a truth you could have borne, you believe now, flattering yourself with a magnanimous understanding of a mother's love for her child.'

Tom couldn't breathe.

'Oh, Tom,' said Richard. 'I'd pity you, if I didn't know you.'

'I don't need your pity.'

'No,' said Richard. 'You had hers. 'Tis an unending mystery, what a man may do, and a woman still love him. Here's one I've always wondered on: Christopher Tucker. Did you kill him, to empty her bed once and for all?'

Tom saw the shock on Kit's face as he fell overboard, the ship rolling and Kit drunk. The look of surprise – betrayal, even – in the slender moment in which Kit waited for Tom to lunge forward, while Tom did nothing, watching the princeling fall into darkness, the night and the narrow sea taking him, and Tom still rooted where he stood. *Did you kill him?* No. Yes.

'And now you harbour the son. Orlando must be a hard thing, to love the man who erased his father and beat and shot his mother. Unless, of course, he doesn't know.'

Tom's gun hand was shaking.

Dick was wringing a stray's neck, just a last satisfying wrench. 'I thought you'd left the child to burn, as you left me. That would have earnt you hell, if nothing else did. I should have known better. What I imagined your worst sin would have been a mercy compared to the truth. You raised the boy to look upon you with worship. What do you think he'd do, if someone told him the truth?'

'If you had any proof, Dick, you'd have had me in the gallows by now. Then again, what's proof without a circuit judge to sign the death warrant? And what's that testimony in your pocket without Hellard's name on it? My brother played you for a fool. Kept you from gunning for him, got your promise to leave him be should the axe fall on me, in return for something that ain't even worth the ink. And, if either of us is going to be charged with murder, Dick, it'll be you.'

'How's that, sir?'

'You pushed Grace to it. You made her turn on me. It's your fault she died. And I will have justice for that.'

'Is that a confession, Mr West?'

Tom said nothing.

'Strange, no guilt bothers me,' said Richard. 'I don't hear her voice in my ear. I don't dream of her. I don't see her form lingering at the door, or buried in blankets in my bed. I don't hear her laugh. She doesn't haunt me, sir, but I'd wager she has not left you alone for even a minute. Wouldn't you like some relief, Tom?'

Tom fired.

Richard fired.

II

Benedict closed the door to Tom's cabin, finding Molly hunched in the corner of Tom's bed. The look on her face was derision, asking him, *What good are you, while Tom goes to murder, and you sit still?*

'I don't need minding.'

'I might.'

She said nothing as he sat at the foot of the bed, drew out a deck of cards.

'I get this feeling, when I'm waiting. Up deck, spotting, or waiting for a landing. It's like something's watching me.'

'Watching you watch?' she asked.

Benedict's stomach sloshed. 'Yes.'

'And what does it think of you, while it watches you watch?'

'I don't know,' he lied. 'I don't like to muse on it too much. Reckoned you might distract me.'

Molly reached for the cards, thumbed the stained paper. 'What's the game?'

Benedict smiled. 'Cribbage.'

'There's only two of us.'

'I'll be dealer.'

Molly laughed. 'I bet you will.'

'What?' he said. 'You don't trust me?'

Molly rubbed her hands together, and Benedict saw that her wrist was red. Tom must have forced her aside. Benedict closed his eyes against a vision of Richard English dying in a puddle of his own blood, choking on it, his teeth loose.

He winced as Molly brushed his knee, drawing him back. 'I trust you.'

Benedict cleared his throat. 'Then I am a happy man.'

As they played, they listened for the sound of Tom returned, for the words Molly longed – without compunction – to hear, and the words Benedict longed – with the fear of God – to finally be freed by. *Dick English lives no more.* When they did hear a clatter above them in the stateroom, they both dropped their cards, face up, Molly saying it must be Tom and Benedict lifting a hand for quiet. They heard the man above crash into something and swear. Hellard.

Hellard – with Tom gone, and Nathan gone, and all the men gone. Molly edged into the corner of the cabin, hissing, 'Lock the door, Benedict!'

All the blood had drained from Benedict's face. This was it.

All these years, he'd sworn to protect her, and, now the moment was here, he felt so scared he couldn't think.

'*Benedict, the damn door!*'

He jumped. Looked at Molly, at the desperation and determination in her eyes. He dug the key from his pocket. 'I'll lock it behind me.'

'What?'

'I've got to –' he drew his sword – 'I've got to go.'

'No, wait—' Molly froze when he pulled her closer, kissing her awkwardly on the ear. And then he pushed her aside.

She heard the lock turn behind him. She listened to Hellard stumbling about above, the sound of glass smashing – the weapons cabinet – and to Benedict's running footsteps, like someone running from a fire – except, in this case, he was running towards it. She heard Benedict's voice now, greeting Hellard calmly, and then heard a strange laugh – Hellard was laughing at him. She listened to Benedict's strictures, suddenly strong; listened to Hellard's pacing demands. And she felt darkness close on her – felt herself in a shut room, and on the other side a man boxing a woman in; she heard that woman bargain for life with the kind of courage she knew the woman had always worn, an armour so heavy it must have been exhausting. God, how this woman would hate the word courage, and how she would pick it up once more, though donning it broke her.

A scream ripped from Molly, as above there came the sound of flesh on flesh, steel on steel, and Benedict crying out in shock.

She wheeled about the cabin – the knife, she couldn't find her knife. It wasn't in the bed, it wasn't in her coat. She had to save Benedict. Tom had to keep another pistol in here. Molly threw books from shelves, upended the mattress – then remembered the chest under the desk. She dragged it out, seized the weight Tom used to measure profits from the desk and brought it down on the lock.

Tom was dancing. He slipped his hands around Grace's waist, as instructed, and turned with her, following a song she hummed beneath her breath – turned as the bullet passed by, singing a line across his chest. He kept spinning, dropping the used pistol from his left hand as his right hand drew the pistol at his back, and came about to fire again.

Tom fell to one knee and squeezed the trigger, as Dick English fired his second pistol over Tom's head.

Two bullets: one in Dick English's chest, Tom thought, and one in the shoulder.

He jammed both pistols in his belt, and drew his sword. He walked the twelve paces to where Dick lay twitching, his breath stuttering on the air.

Tom used his boot to roll the man on to his back. He threw his mask on to the ground and looked Dick English in the eyes.

'I always knew you'd disappoint,' he said.

A bubble of blood popped on Richard's lips, seeping into his beard. For a moment, Tom was his father, telling him, *A Revenue captain? I never knew such a wasted investment as you.* Richard gripped hold of Tom's boot.

'What did you hope from me, Tom?'

Grace's voice in Tom's ear: *Salvation. You were hoping for salvation.*

'I was hoping you could shoot straight,' said Tom, 'at the very least.'

Richard moved his free hand, groping for his sword pommel. The moon glinted along Tom's blade, hanging above him.

'And I'd hoped ... ' said Richard, feeling along his belt, sticky with something – his own blood. 'I hoped you'd ... '

Tom bent down. 'Spit it out, Dick. I'm in a giving mood.'

'I hoped you'd be taken alive –'

A snapping branch brought Tom around in time to see two dragoons clambering on to Salt-Stone, twenty paces away.

'– so I could have you shamed in the pillory before I killed you.'

It happened in moments: the dragoons raised their muskets, Tom drew Molly's knife from his coat and flung it in their direction, hearing one go down as he glanced back to Dick, who had drawn his sword. Tom raised his own, but the block was too late, and Richard's blade slithered beneath his and into Tom's stomach.

III

Molly threw aside Tom's shirts, a finely tooled belt, spare buckles for his shoes, a lead case which landed with a thud, and found a pistol at the very bottom.

Powder. She needed powder.

God's blood, it was with the cannons, neatly stored by her own hand.

Trust to Tom West – and keep your powder dry. That's what Nathan said. But now all she had was an empty pistol, and no Tom, no Benedict, and no crew.

A step on the stair. Now, coming down the gang walk.

A thud at the cabin door.

Molly clutched the useless pistol. 'Benedict?'

A laugh. 'No, girl,' said Hellard. 'Just you and me, now. Why don't you open the door?'

*

Shouting himself hoarse at the effort, Richard dragged the sword three inches from the wound, then plunged it back in. Tom snarled. Richard scrabbled for a fistful of Tom's hair and dragged the man's head back, baring his throat to the night.

'Still disappointed?' he asked.

Tom felt Molly's gentle touch at his neck.

He felt Dick grip the sword tighter and seized the blade himself, keeping it buried inside, even as it cut through his palm. A brief tug of war, and then Tom pulled the blade even deeper, bringing Dick falling towards him. Tom elbowed him in the throat and pulled the sword free with a cry.

Richard fumbled among the rocks and roots. His hand landed on Tom's sword. He brought it up as Tom brought Richard's own sword down – the clash blinded him.

Tom swung again, the two blades skittering against each other, and then ducked beneath a slash for his throat.

'Captain!'

Tom looked around – it was one of the dragoons, done tending to his dying comrade, now trying to find a mark between the two fighting men.

'Fire!' screamed Richard.

Tom met Richard's sword in the air, feeling his arms going, just as Dick's were, feeling life worming free, just as Richard looked like a ghost. They'd kill each other. Nathan would keep Hellard from the ship, and Benedict would care for Molly. They'd kill each other, and Molly would think – would know – justice had been done.

'*Fire!*'

Tom heard the dragoon curse God's blood – heard him ready to fire, even if he might hit his captain: that's how much they wanted him dead. He twisted his sword so that Dick's met no resistance, the man stumbling into him. Now all he had to do was turn, so that his back was to the dragoon, rather than

Richard's, and the dragoon would finish him off. They'd bleed out together.

Turn. Finish it.

God, take me.

He heard that tune again. The song Grace murmured beneath her breath. He held Dick up, their blood intermingling now – and didn't turn with her music.

The dragoon fired.

Richard yelped, the bullet hitting him in the back, making it three for three.

Tom met his eyes, so close he could drop a loving kiss on to the man's forehead, if he chose. There was shock there, and hatred, and great grief.

He released him. Dick hit the stone and didn't move.

The dragoon dropped the pistol.

Tom stepped over Dick's body, towards the dragoon, who tripped. Standing over him, he licked his lips, the salt thick as a sea storm. Just a boy. He pulled Molly's knife from the other man's chest.

'You've killed your captain,' he said. 'If you speak of this, they'll hang you. And I'll be wearing the hangman's hood. Devon is *mine*. Flee.'

'I will, sir. Thank you, sir.'

Tom spat. Turned his back. Limped away, unstopped.

Why don't you open the door?

Hellard didn't know the key was in Benedict's pocket. He thought Molly had it. If she could just keep him thinking that – delay him, until Tom returned ... Panic shook Molly as the hinges clapped under Hellard's boot.

'Open the damn door, whore!'

Molly bumped into the desk, stepping on the lead case.

241

Hellard's expression that night on Île de Batz took up her whole self: the look of a man consumed. He knew. He knew.

'Call me that again,' Molly called, 'and see how you like the outcome.'

Another laugh. 'I suppose you'd prefer whoreson, but you're not his bastard, are you? Just his bitch – a bitch raised in vice you are, baneful and vicious.' Another kick. 'You know what you need, girl? Whipcord to the back. Dick English, he plans the pillory for Tom's whipping post, plans to lash him there for all the townsfolk to pelt with their rotten eggs before he mounts the gallows. Make a mockery of him with some overripe vegetables. Got a wholesome notion of justice, Dick does. Me? I'm more direct. I reckon I'll make Tom's bed your whipping post. Tie you down, take my time.'

Molly closed her eyes. Remembered the weight of Mama's courage. 'Plain dealing, Hellard,' she called. 'Here's a promise. I been long suffering. But you lay a hand on me – or Tom – and I will be baneful, and I will be vicious.'

'Oho, here's a pretty trick,' said Hellard. 'Ready to die for your pantomime daddy, and after what he did to your mother. That how you pay her respect, she what deserves your reverence and obedience, she what spat you out?'

The slim box beneath Molly's shoe rattled with the pitch of the ship.

'What are you talking about?' she said.

'Plain dealing?'

Molly swallowed. 'Yes. Plain dealing.'

'Open the door and I'll tell you.'

Tom's lap was warm with blood. The horse plunged down the hill to North Sands. Tom slipped off its back, crashing into the waves, where his rowboat was tethered. He should have urged the horse into Kingsbridge and found a doctor, he knew that. But something compelled his arms, handling the oars, as ruin seemed to rain down on him, seemed to ooze around his boots, seemed to want to drown him.

The *Venture* was lit up, lanterns ablaze on deck. Tom tried to shout, but no sound came. He tried to stand, but slipped, flailing – finding the ladder on the ribs of the ship. He heaved himself up, his sword left behind, shaking so hard he fainted as he toppled on to the deck.

'Molly!' Had he shouted that? 'Molly!' Stars swung above him, like snow skidding over ice.

When someone put a foot down on the deck, Tom was standing before the world righted in his vision, reaching for his pistol – which he had not reloaded – and his sword – which was missing. He sagged into the barrels behind him, tangling his fist into the netting.

'Just me, Tom.'

'Brother.'

Hellard brushed his hair back. Behind him, the stateroom swung with candlelight.

'Where's Orlando?' said Tom, glancing at the hatch down into the ship. He could hear no one.

Hellard smiled at him.

For the first time that night: here was fear.

IV

'Where's Benedict?'

'I'm not his mother, there to mop his brow. Left him in a

puddle of his ... well, sick or piss, I'm not sure. Boy can't take his drink. You know he's been living under an illusion, since the Great Storm? Told me himself. Believes it was *me* who killed the bitch. Been waiting, it seems, for you to deliver justice. Ain't that sweet? Had to set him right, o' course. Told him I'd *love* to take the credit, but, sadly, that credit belongs to someone else ... Reckon it's time he became a man. I'll give him chapter and verse afore I bury him.'

'Is that what we are?' asked Tom. 'Men?'

Hellard tapped the sword he carried against his leg. 'Got to say, Tom – and you'll pardon me – you don't look like much of a man, right now. Trouble standing, strikes me.'

'Now I'm a lad who can't take his liquor?' said Tom. The light from the lantern flickered closer, threatening to reveal his bloody collapse.

'Would I suggest such a thing?' said Hellard.

'Not if you want to keep your tongue.'

'Ha. Let me ask you something, then, while I still got my tongue. How long were you intending to keep this up?'

'What?'

'Playing daddy.'

'To Benedict?' asked Tom, looking again at the stateroom, at the hatch.

'To that girl in your cabin.'

Silence.

Tom straightened. Held his head up. 'I'm not her father.'

'I know you're not,' said Hellard. 'Which makes this all the more sodden witted. We more than like have a dozen bastards between us. They don't *mean* anything. And this one isn't even your shot. So, what's so special about her that you'd drag her on to a ship and give her everything you owe me? You had it all growing up; you had the house, the ma, Hope Cove. I had nothing. And now you're training her up to inherit the ship,

244

glove-raising queen of the fucking parade. Come on, brother, let's have the truth for once. Call it a confession, afore you meet your maker. Call it a sacrament. Girls do not belong at sea. They belong at their mothers' feet.' This, with a grin.

Tom tried to harness his voice. 'I recall you were eager enough to bury her mother at the time. Now, such concern. I'm moved.'

'You were going to forgive that *whore* for our boys' deaths.'

'Hellard, stop talking,' breathed Tom.

'You think I'm afeared o' you?'

'Yes, and I think you always have been, because you've got half a brain in you. Don't stop now.'

'The big Tom West.' Hellard laughed. 'I heard you, crying in that damned orphan's bedroom afterwards. The great man reduced to tears. They all think you're so tough. What would they think to see you braid a little girl's hair? Sing her to sleep?'

'I don't care what they think.'

'Yes, you do, or you wouldn't be keeping her a secret. And you're right to care. You're playing foot-licker to the ghost of a dead woman and her wretched baby. She wasn't your wife. She was just a body, there to yield. Like this ship, waiting to be filled – that's all women are. Law says so. Church says so. I've heard *you* say so.'

'No, you haven't.'

'And now you've taken on her child. What do you want a girl for?'

Tom pulled himself up slowly, holding a hand out, fingers spread: *Stop.*

Hellard stepped closer. 'I'll answer, if you won't. It's forgiveness. You've branded forgiveness into that cunt, and trained her to whisper sweet unconditionals into your ear while you take it. Nothing like laying a ghost's bitch to lay a ghost to rest, is there?'

Tom swung. Too slow, moving through space as if time had

245

stretched around him. Hellard ducked, then pressed in, seizing Tom's chin.

'Pretty, like her mother, that one,' he said, 'and locked in a room I'll have the key to. We're going to have some fun, that wench and I, while she lasts.'

'No.' Tom jerked free.

'Who's going to come to her rescue? She died with her mother, for all the world knows – I've made sure of that. Orlando took her place. My new ward.' He laughed. 'And now she'll die in your bed. This ship isn't yours any more, Tom.'

Tom's punch sent Hellard sprawling, and Tom after him. He caught the mast. Then the air smacked out of him. The pair went crashing over barrels and into the fishing nets. Hellard's knee found his groin, his ribs, and then Tom grabbed hold and sent him flying.

He heard a scrape of metal.

The sword rasped Tom's ribs. He gripped Hellard's wrist, twisting until he felt a snap. Hellard screamed. The sword clattered on the deck. Then the water swelled and the two men keeled, Tom's face an inch from Hellard's. He squeezed the wrist until it crackled. Hellard flopped and jerked, a fish without water. An elbow sent Tom sprawling. Hellard was bending to pick up his sword. He drew the tip along the deck, scarring Tom's ship. Tom watched it come closer. He couldn't move. Here, at last, he couldn't move. He couldn't stop it.

'Molly . . .'

'So that's her name,' said Hellard, pressing the sword point to Tom's chest.

'Step away from him.' Benedict, in the door of the state-room. Blood glistened on his head. He was holding a pistol, level at Hellard.

Hellard looked Benedict up and down, so much amusement in his face Benedict almost pulled the trigger right then.

Sleep took Tom, a feathered bed, but wet, wet with something. He sank into it. Fathoms. Death was fathoms deep.

'Well, look'ee here,' said Hellard. 'All grown up.'

'Step away from him,' said Benedict, 'and drop your weapon.'

'No,' said Hellard. Benedict blanched, and Hellard laughed out loud. 'Tom, you should've trained up a better watchman than this. Not even a watchdog. Without Tom at the leash, you're just a scared bitch, like the one below.'

Tom woke with a start to the needle of the blade, and saw the resolution on Benedict's face as the boy fired.

Tom grabbed Hellard's ankle and hauled, his brother going down before the bullet could find him.

'Tom, what are you doing?' shouted Benedict, but Tom didn't answer, just retched as Hellard's grip shifted for a stabbing blow.

Benedict grabbed a lantern and swung it through the air, the flames catching Hellard across the face. The scream was so terrible – the smell so terrible – Benedict dropped the thing.

Fire swirled from Hellard's coat, and his scream turned to shrieks as he picked the lantern up, lunging for Benedict, who scrambled back. Hellard howled, crashing towards Tom, his whole self burning now, burning to some point at which all that existed was hurt and anger.

Fire. Tom watched it come down towards him. I was born to fire.

Molly climbed the side of the ship, the broken glass of the porthole weeping in her palms. She dropped on to the quarterdeck. It was something from a nightmare. Hellard, ablaze, bringing a fiery club down on Tom, the flames making the pool of blood Tom lay in shine like pulped Spanish oranges in the sun. Benedict standing agape, watching.

Tom waiting.

Molly hurled herself at Hellard, catching him around the waist and pulling him overboard. She fell through the night, fire eating her, Hellard clutching her.

The sea accepted her.

Tom sat up. One knee. The other. Grace telling him, *You promised me.* He lurched to the side, grasped his belt – keeping powder dry that wasn't there, his fingers sinking into blood instead – and jumped, Benedict's shout above him. He hit the water and drove deep, arms outstretched now, light coming from somewhere – Benedict, waving the lantern above, or God – as his hand closed around a slender wrist. He pulled, gathering Molly in one arm, and turned, striking for the surface. Molly was limp, and, above, Benedict was yelling, 'The rope! Take the rope!'

She wasn't talking. He couldn't feel her breathing. Tom fed the noose around her waist. He tried to tread water, tried to lift her from the grip of the sea, but could feel himself losing.

'Pull!' he shouted. 'Get her up!'

He was sinking – he let go, and she rose above him, spinning like the crystal pendant hung above Grace's bed, scattering its light – and then all the light was gone. The sea rushed in. Tom felt Kit's hands on him – no, Hellard's – as he fought free and they both gasped for air.

Tom hugged Hellard, and wrestled him back under. He couldn't see him, could only feel him thrashing, as if Tom had grown another body, some possessed self, which he fought for survival now. There, in the dark, in the cold, it was only a dream, black swirling about as he beat himself into submission, and it was himself he pulled deeper and deeper, it was himself he squeezed until there was no air left, it was his own kicking desperation he endured, his own unbreakable thirst for body and stride and life, it was his own hunger and greed he broke, and left to fall into the wastes, left to die – God, die, please die – as he kicked for the surface, and rose – himself. Still himself. And still loved, a rope falling about his shoulders, and Benedict, above, begging him to take hold of it and be saved.

In July
He prepares to fly

Laskey and Shaun washed the red from the boards in silence. Nathan, holding a compress to his head – which was purple from where Hellard had cold-cocked him in the King's Arms – paced around them, crossing the threads of Kingston's prayers. The rest of the crew waited on the poop-deck steps, or hung from the riggings. Benedict squatted on the deck outside the stateroom door, crying, and all around pretended not to notice his tears. Crows formed an impatient gyre overhead, recognising a kingdom without a king.

Molly sat in Tom's chair in the stateroom, the grooves of Tom's crest at her back. On the table, Tom lay motionless, his insides open for all the world to see. The surgeon was the best the Navy had to offer, Nathan had promised. The man worked with sweat dripping from his brow. He'd been trembling when he applied the poultice to Molly's burnt arms, and he was shaking now, stitching Tom together, unbreaking a broken man.

Molly held Tom's silver pistol on the surgeon, resting the walnut grip on her knee. 'A fair deal,' she had told the surgeon. 'Save him and retire rich. Lose him and retire much faster.'

*

Grace wanted to show him the moors. She dared not approach Widecombe-in-the-Moor for fear of her family, a fear he could not coax her from, but still she wanted to show him the Devon that made her. So, they rode out from Bantham towards the line of black on the horizon, Tom losing the sea, but, with Grace on his saddle and Molly in his arms, not minding too much. The moor was heather and brush, great stones, scarred earth, gnarled trees; the moor was wild and open, the wastes as they once were; the moor was fog and rain; the moor was ore waiting to be tapped, but it was a brave man to do it. The moor didn't want to be tamed.

They rode towards Tavistock, where the hills became greener, a wood not yet hacked back for mining. She'd spent young days walking the world to reach this river, where trees dripped slowly at the bank and the bridge formed a gentle arch over the cascade of amber on granite.

He asked her, 'You've gone brought me to some magic place to have your way with me, ain't you?'

'Sleeping in the hedgerows,' she laughed. 'My mother told me I'd end up here.'

But she didn't look too upset by it.

It was the most peaceful Tom had ever felt.

When he woke, dawn turning the stream to a mirrored sheet, he was seized by fear – reflected in the water, there was a great horse, standing twenty paces along the bank, its head down, eyes fixed on him. Tom covered Molly with one arm and reached for his pistol with the other. Grace grabbed his wrist.

'Look,' she said.

Across the bank, a foal flinched under his gaze.

'Take the bairn,' he said, 'and get behind me.'

She squeezed his arm. '*Tom.* Trust me. Put the gun down.'

'But, Molly—'

'What is it, Tom?' said Molly. 'I'm right here.'

Tom jerked, dropping the gun as he turned to look at Grace – but it wasn't Grace, it was Molly, restraining him with that same gentle insistence, that same look of foolish trust.

'Molly?'

'I'm here.'

The mare wasn't there; instead, there was his desk standing in the river, and drifting in the water was the lead box with the journal locked inside.

Tom sat up. He was in bed, in his cabin. Molly sat on the mattress beside him, soothing his arm. She breathed a sigh of relief – such a sigh, it made her seem old. She grinned, and she was a child again.

'Long live the king,' she said.

Tom looked beyond her, to the lead box on the floor, which lay open and empty. Molly's face was black ice. Her arms were bandaged. Tears stung him, and Tom blinked them away.

'You saved me.'

'Someone had to,' she laughed. That laugh.

'Hellard – what did Hellard do to you?'

'Nothing,' said Molly. 'Benedict locked me in and went out to face him by himself. Benedict, you should know, is an idiot. But a noble one. All Hellard could do to me was sling insults, and they don't bruise, terribly.'

'What did he say to you?'

'Does it matter, now?'

Tom cleared his throat. 'Yes.'

'He called me a whore.'

'You're not that. You never will be.'

'I know,' said Molly. 'He said . . . He said you did something to my mother. That you hurt her.'

She was looking at him with confidence.

'I did,' he said. His heart lurched. 'It was my fault. That she

252

died.' The tide beat in his ears. 'Dick English only hurt her to get to me. I should have stopped him. But I was too slow.'

'Tom.' She took his hand. 'You have to forgive yourself.'

Vertigo. 'I can't.'

She kissed his bruised knuckles. 'I forgive you.' Her smile fell. 'Are you crying?'

Tom shook his head. 'Did Hellard say anything else?'

'Only that he'd tell me more if I let him in the door.'

'Did you?'

'I'm no fool.'

'No. No, you're not that. Where was the key?'

A shadow over her face. 'Benedict had it.'

Tom glanced at the case on the floor. 'So, you couldn't have let him in, even if you'd wanted to?'

'No,' she said. Her face unreadable. 'You're no fool, either.'

'Molly . . . ' He crooked his finger under her chin. 'You don't believe him, do you? Anything he told you – anything else he might have said about me – you've got to know—'

'Of course I don't believe him,' she said. 'I've trusted you all my life. Loved you all my life. And I will, to the end.'

Unconditionally.

Laudanum was carrying Tom on its tides when Benedict closed the cabin door behind him, but still Benedict raised his hands before Tom could reach for his pistol.

'Surrendering to me, son?' said Tom, coughing. Blood on the pillow.

'Molly's settling with the doctor.'

Tom nodded. Bunched his hands into fists. He could not make out Benedict's face properly, just the paleness of his skin and the crimson on his shirt. Hellard's last words stuck beneath his fingers, the small shift of skin and windpipe. He could feel the tremor of supple cords and veins, feel them break, like seaweed coming apart. He tried to shake the rupture from his mind.

It was then he saw Grace's journal in Benedict's hand.

Tom looked up into the boy's eyes. 'You were going to shoot him.'

'You didn't let me.'

'You're something better'n me. My witness . . . '

Tom was fading, but the sharpness of Benedict's reply jolted him: 'What did you call me?'

'"I can see in the dark," you told me. It seems you can. Kill me. It'll save your life.'

'My life?'

'Oh, Benedict . . . how many sins can I let you be party to? My saint of saints. Be God's avenger. You'll only get one chance.'

'Tom – I could never hurt you. You know that.'

'Somebody's got to stop me.'

'You're not yourself. You saved us. Hellard would've—'

'Yes,' said Tom, sinking. 'Yes, he would have. Didn't you ever wonder why I brought you on my ship?'

'My eyes.'

'Your blue eyes. Just like my little brother's. So like, it's uncanny. If I were a God-fearing man, I would think perhaps his soul had come back to me in yours. He was the brother I wanted. Instead, I got Hellard.'

Benedict reached for Tom's hand, but recoiled at the dried blood in the cracks. 'I found her journal, in the box . . . '

A rumble: 'And found the key on my body?'

Benedict forced light into his voice: 'Here was me thinking I had all your keys.'

Tom did not stir. His eyes were empty.

'I thought it was Hellard.' Benedict stroked the cover: *A True*

Relation ... He'd read, while Tom slept and Molly believed Benedict was minding him: read of Dick's visits to Grace's cottage, the way he mauled and harangued her, the terror he left behind as Grace found herself trapped between her love of Tom and her dread of English. Grace's words: *I die by inches.* 'But Hellard told me he didn't shoot her, so I ... I took another key from you. Begging your pardon, sir. Only – I had to know. She was scared of Dick. She foresaw it all. Dick English killed her. Like you always said. Didn't he?'

Tom seized his hand. 'My boy.' He squeezed the slender fingers. 'You know I love you.'

Benedict raised an arm to knock away his tears. 'You finally have justice, now. We can forget all of it.'

Benedict flinched as Molly, Nathan and Kingston came through the door without knocking, the surgeon on their heels. The journal tumbled from his hands.

'He's not dead,' Molly rushed, looking like she was going to be sick. 'This man saved him. Dick English lives.'

Tom tried to get up, sank back. His gaze settled on the surgeon, seemed to measure the man for a coffin. 'I understand I have you to thank for saving my life,' he said, and Benedict knew that tone – trying to talk himself down. He'd heard it in Grace Tucker's cottage.

Sweat shone from the surgeon's moustache. 'You were not so ready to leave it, sir, as required much skill to keep you here.'

'Then it was an unskilled job you did?'

The surgeon, glancing around now for a way out.

'Tell him,' said Molly. 'Tell him what you told me.'

'Tonight, I have also sewn another man. A man with three holes in his red jacket, sir.'

'And he lives?'

Silence, knotted, awful, and then: 'Yes, sir.'

Nathan swore.

Tom wasn't breathing. 'Then I take it you used all of your skill on him.'

The surgeon chewed his moustache. 'He was grievously injured, sir.'

'How much grieving it warrants, I don't know.'

'He cannot walk, sir.'

'Cannot walk at all?'

'No, sir. One of the bullets has damaged his spine.'

'Then he can't serve the law.'

'Not in his current condition, sir, no.'

In the doorway, Kingston laughed. 'Limp Dick English just got limper.'

The surgeon was struggling not to denounce them, Benedict realised, denounce them and their mirth. 'He is being removed to his parental home,' he said, 'where he shall have to be tended by his mother.' He said this to bring shame upon them, but it just made Kingston laugh all the harder, and, in bed, Tom smiled the smile of a contented man.

Benedict wondered: contented because he had removed Dick English from the board, without having to kill him? One less sin? Or contented to send the runt back to the litter he came from, where his father would tell him, again and again, *I should have drowned you before you drew your first breath*?

'Will he recover?' asked Molly.

'If God is with him,' said the surgeon.

'Give me odds,' said Molly, 'not superstition.'

Benedict was flushing for them now, but Tom only looked proud.

The surgeon sucked his belly in. 'In my opinion, as a man of science, Captain Richard English will spend the rest of his days bedridden, unable to stand up for himself. If such a man was worth killing before, he is not now – for there is no honour in besting a cripple.'

Tom waved. 'Behold, a man of God and science,' he said, 'trying to save his patient long after he has left the table. I hope you'll keep me in your prayers, too, doctor.'

The surgeon bowed. 'I am unlikely to forget you, sir.'

At that, Benedict thought Tom would struggle to his feet, would seize the man by his collar and press upon him the importance of forgetting.

But Tom only smiled. 'You and all of Devon, Doctor.'

Rain lashed the ship, spitting through the broken porthole, and with it a cry from on deck: 'Revenue spotted!'

Nathan crunched over the glass to the window and looked out. 'Time we were off to France, Captain. More than time, whether Hellard's coming back or no – and, from the red on the deck, I'd take it that's unlikely, though God as my witness I don't want to know more.'

This was it. Benedict felt feverish. No way a tame Justice would save them from arrest now, not after Tom crippled a Revenue officer, transforming the son of a powerful merchant into a lie-abed. They didn't even have the anchor up, and Tom was laid low. This was it.

'You've got to let me on to dry land,' said the surgeon. 'I won't be arrested with you.'

Tom tossed the blanket off – and folded, cursing God's eyes, God's teeth, God's blood.

'I can get us out,' said Molly.

Tom, hoarse: 'What?'

'You can't stand. The first mate is at the bottom of the sea. I can get us out.'

Benedict tried to read Tom's face, but couldn't. Eventually, the man said, 'Sail close to the land, you'll pick up warm winds. Mind Benedict's transits or we'll end up on the rocks. Make for the Channel Islands, you'll find support there. You're the faster ship. Don't let them think otherwise.'

'I know,' she said, crossing the room to hold his hand. 'Trust me.' She turned her glittering determination on Benedict. 'Lend me your eyes?'

In August
Fly he must

She led them on a merry chase. Tom listened from below – listened to her command the furling and unfurling of the topsail, listened to her shout at the men to pull harder on the sheets and the halyards as rain and waves came at them and the ship shook like a plaything in a bottle, listened as she outstripped the Revenue, as she tossed words at them through the wind – *Come any closer and we'll shoot you to pieces!* – as she ordered guns ready, as she coaxed the ship ever closer to the rocks, picking up speed. God, she was daring, this girl of his – and, yes, God, she was his.

He climbed from bed, though pain burst in black spots over his eyes, and picked up the journal from the floor. He staggered to the porthole. He wouldn't say he was sorry. He wouldn't beckon death or call on punishment. He wouldn't renounce evil and all its power, and all its treasures. For she was his. He'd been forged by fire, right from the start, and this ship, and these men, and that girl – they were what a man got, what he deserved, if he was birthed in the heat of a smithy, battered and dented, but tougher than any metal going. He had been tested, tempted justice, and he had passed. He would hold on to what he'd won. No more waiting to be punished. He was the one who'd decide on punishment.

Be a man, she had said.

He was father, king, God. And he needed no petty, desperate scribbling from a woman who – when every memory was turned over, every word examined – had betrayed him, in the last. For here was a girl who would never betray him. Here was love, and it was his. He hurled the journal through the porthole.

In the doorway, Benedict – out of breath from scrambling to tell Tom they'd made it – watched Tom hurl away his pain, ready, he thought, for absolution. Though, Tom hadn't wrought justice on the head of Grace's murderer. Hellard was dead, but Tom's brother was not the man to pull the trigger, as Benedict had believed. It was Dick English who fired the shot, Dick English who lived – yet Tom acted as if he were released, free from . . . what? And, if Tom were free, why did Benedict feel he was witnessing Tom's soul lose air by the porthole, cupped and shrinking, not a liberated flame, but a dying ember?

Leaf

To INTERLEA/VE. v. a. [*inter* and *leave*]

To chequer a book by the insertion of blank leaves.

I am thinking of breaking into the National Portrait Gallery. I took an online course in art crime during lockdown and I think I could do it. I wouldn't steal anything (well, probably not). I'd just do a little rehang, one room only. The room devoted to Dr Johnson's circle. Have you seen it?

Joshua Reynolds' portrait of Samuel Johnson shows him dressed in brown, as he always was, wearing a wig in better condition than it ever was. His hand, seized with pain, rests on papers. He smiles into the distance, eyebrow raised. Hanging on the wall beside him, the portrait of Biography Boswell has been arranged so that he looks upon Johnson's face, and Johnson upon him. Hanging at Johnson's other side is the woman known as 'Mrs Thrale, Dr Johnson's dear mistress'. Her face is open, her smile ready to share a joke, but Johnson is turning away from her.

Hester Thrale was also friends with Frances Reynolds, who did eventually leave her brother's home. Frances' unpublished art criticism was found among Hester's papers upon Hester's death. Hester's will also recorded a book she intended to leave to her daughter, Cecy: *A Wild & True Relation of A Lady Shipwright and Free-Trader*. But no one could find the volume among her property.

Dr Johnson came into Hester Thrale's life when she was a young woman and he an old man, ill and impoverished. Hester was married to Mr Thrale, a brewer with a grand house at Streatham, where Hester ran a revolutionary Bluestocking salon. It is hard to say what Sam and Hester first felt for each other, when Sam was brought for dinner at Streatham. From the early days of their friendship, there were rumours of a love affair, though there is no evidence of it. There is evidence of two minds falling in love. They sat up until dawn, talking. She wrote her *Thraliana*; he wrote his dictionaries and essays; they swapped dreams. They promised to burn the letters.

When Mr Thrale died, everybody expected Hester to marry Sam. Instead, she married Mr Piozzi, an Italian music teacher. Sam wrote her a letter of uncontained fury, rebuking her for marrying a Catholic. Society exiled her. Her elder daughters, Queeney, Susannah and Sophia, spurned her with the encouragement of the male guardians appointed by her late husband. Her youngest, Cecy, was caught between them. All her other children had died. Hester said that if Cecy were stolen away, that would be the end of her life: "tis so very comfortable to have *one* at least saved out of *twelve*.'

Sam and Hester would not speak again. He died in 1784. It had been a twenty-five-year relationship.

When Hester published Sam's letters in the form of a biography, she was hailed for discovering a new way to write a life: intimate, conversational, true. When I first read Boswell's famous biography of Dr Johnson, I was taken in by Boswell's great need to be loved, to be something like Johnson's son and claim Johnson as a father. And if he pushed all of the women in Johnson's life to the margins, I didn't know any better.

Boswell threw every insult he could at Hester, from her book to her choice of husband:

If Hesther had chosen to wed mighty sam
Who it seem, drove full at her his battering ram
A wonder indeed, then, the world would have found
A woman who truly prefer'd sense to sound.

Hester shrugged him and his allies off with a shrug: 'I am told *all* the vipers sting terribly this year.'

When Boswell published his *Life of Johnson*, he made sure to force Hester out of Sam's story. He won. For centuries, Boswell has been hailed as inventing a new form of biography: intimate, conversational, true. And there he hangs, under Johnson's loving gaze.

That's all I want to do. Swap James Boswell and Hester Thrale. I'd like Dictionary Sam and Hester Thrale to lock eyes. I'd like her to tell him what happened next, after he scorched the earth and left her standing on it.

In 1788, Hester returned from making the Grand Tour with Mr Piozzi. They picked up her daughter, Cecy, and travelled to Devonport, which had risen from Plymouth Dock in the name of one 'lady shipwright'.

(Notes for a lecture on women and writing to be given at Girton College, Cambridge, on the anniversary of Virginia Woolf's lecture series, 'A Room of One's Own'.)

A Thousand Pretty Tricks

1788

Hester & Cecy

It was the hottest April and May Hester had ever known in England; everybody was leaving London. She and Mr Piozzi and Cecy would try Devonshire, certainly the Italy of England, where she would work at her travel book. Her inflexible daughters continued their behaviour, and Cecy did not condemn her elder sisters; they had made some fruitless attempts to get her from Hester, but now she was setting out to a very distant province, where Goneril and Regan could not seize her.

So, then: a long and coasting journey of it to Exmouth, where they had got a very pretty house upon the Strand, with the water quite washing the wall on one side, and a smart little garden on the other. By September, it was very fine and very hot still. The Exe eased yesterday's remaining grey powder from her hair with all the tired love of a mother. Hester brought her hips up, inviting the meeting place of estuary and river, sea and moor, to lift her until she was floating – the pressure of tailbone and pelvis taking her back, briefly, to confinement, and the smell of the house when she lost or maintained another baby. A sum of pregnant parts, Boswell called her. Streatham always had the stench of a hospital about it, month in, month out, confinements coming on each other until it seemed she was running Mr Thrale's campaigns pregnant; minding Dr Johnson, from night to early morning, pregnant; touring Paris pregnant; burying children pregnant; writing pregnant; nursing Mr Thrale pregnant, whether her master suffered melancholy, or testicles swollen by a new love; and always: jesting, jousting, quizzing, quoting, laughing, outdoing, out-enduring – *ruling* – pregnant. Hester depressed the balloon of her bathing dress. Pregnant no more. Five years of marriage with Mr Piozzi, longing for his child, and pregnant no more. And only the wayward sisters survived, from all those confinements, and her Cecy – as long as she could keep Cecy hers.

A deep breath – hips, haws and blackberries on the air – easing shoulders, breastbone and knees into the shiver, even as the sun licked her. What a world it was – she, Hester, living among the Europeans in a social quarantine these last three years, and all for marrying her Catholic musician. There were days when she wanted the mists of Venice to close in and keep her. But now her letters of Sam were published, and Miss Hannah More said Hester had fashioned a novel biography. She had made her way back, and whatever society existed here to be had – the Staffords, Lord Huntingdon, Lady Betty Cobbe and her daughter – she *had* it.

Still, Exmouth was a private place, and she should enjoy some distance between herself and Boswell and Baretti – all these men, who, as they condemned the Bluestockings for being nothing more than gossiping spies, traded in haughty abuse, puffing and abetting each other to take aim at her in a manner they wouldn't have dared when Sam ... A stroke of cold came over Hester. She'd floated beyond the shallows.

From the parlour, Cecy let Defoe's *Journal of the Plague Year* droop in her hands as she watched her mother, so small and yet so strong, cut through the waves. Mama was reading Defoe, and insisted Cecy did too, telling her it was once a very well-known book. So, what did that signify? Mama always told her: *You wouldn't have survived my father*, at whose hands Grandmama had almost died so many times. Mama insisted Cecy learn to recite a sonnet, pick up some Greek and Latin, become a fine woman worth her fifty thousand pounds, telling her again and again: *I was taught to play a thousand pretty tricks, and tell a thousand pretty stories and repeat a thousand pretty verses to divert Papa*. On the mantelpiece, the portrait of Sam glowered at Cecy, next to his books.

Cecy faced into the wind, knowing she'd be crunching sand between her teeth for days – but still, it was better than being stuffed up in Lady Cobbe's parlour on a day so intolerably hot the violent red cliffs baked until they bled, and surrounded by all those strange instruments and paintings Lady Cobbe collected wherever she went, even here at the end of the country. The waves counted the pebbles of Budleigh Salterton like a greedy banker, click-clacking beneath Cecy's boots. She dropped her gaze, hoping to seem preoccupied in their hunt for fossils.

Mama was in full flow. Conversation, conversazione, gespräch – it didn't matter what language it took place in, or where, or with whom – her mother was known as the best wit in whatever country she occupied. Though Lady Montagu might be Queen of the Blues, Mama was Queen of Talk. Even Sam said so – king to her queen. At least, he was. Mama's beauty was unending self-expression. The beauty of Lady Eliza Tuite – their companion today, with her mother Lady Cobbe – was self-possession. Cecy's own beauty would be self-immolation.

'A play may be cancelled, a poem censured,' Hester was saying, 'but the first thing for a book is to be *read*, the second to be *praised*, the third to be *criticised* – the only irremediable misfortune is to be *forgotten*. You will feel this yourself, when your collection of poems is published, Lady Tuite.'

Eliza shrugged. 'The same unmeaning dance. You know I do not seek plays or balls or pleasure gardens. Only friendship, and shared sensibility. Give me those who value *me*, not those who like me in disguise.'

Cecy flushed, for she felt Eliza's attention on the back of her neck. Eliza knew – knew that, as Cecy sifted pebbles the colour of bruises, searching for the spiralling bones of an ammonite, she was play-acting a role. The role of simple ease. And, with that, simple loyalties.

'And what does Lord Tuite think of your desire for shared sensibilities?' said Mama.

The women shared a laugh. Cecy understood that Eliza avoided her husband, with a preference for the close company of her own sex.

'You will both be too young to remember,' said Lady Cobbe, 'but of course Lady Luxborough – she was a poet, quite like you two – was bound by law to the countryside, and quite forbidden to go within twenty miles of the Bath Road, where her friend Lady Hertford lived. For her husband was afraid of the *communications* Lady Luxborough and Lady Hertford shared.'

Cecy grimaced as her mother recited Mary Whateley with a theatrical flourish of her arm:

> 'And well has Shakespeare (ever honour'd name)
> To female friendship giv'n immortal fame.
> So dear was Rosalind to Celia's Breast,
> When, by her father's tyrant power oppress'd.'

'Shakespeare,' declared Lady Cobbe, 'will always be your best defence, for they cannot undo the great bard now Garrick has made him a saint. Remember that, my daughter.'

'I need no defence,' said Eliza.

'Of course not,' said Hester. 'Just as I would never experience such tyranny from Mr Piozzi.'

'Nor I Sir Henry,' said Eliza.

That, Cecy did understand. Hard for a man to tyrannise from another county. But her mother was not dissembling. Mr Piozzi was a good man, for all her sisters said otherwise. Still, Cecy felt that old disquiet, to hear her mother implying by contrast that her father had suited such terms.

'But, for all female sensibility is something to be most grateful for,' said Mama, 'and believe me I know it, for do I not spend every day here writing letters to Mrs Byron? But, for all that, the Wits and the Blues are a formidable body, and quite happy, I am reliably told, to have me safe out of their way. For, to be a respected Blue, a woman's female virtues must be as high as her intellect, if not higher, and I have sunken low in the estimates of all, in marrying my Piozzi.'

'That is not true friendship,' said Eliza.

Cecy was struck by Lady Tuite's certainty, and felt a sudden fist of shame at the memory of Mr Baretti's fury, the girls' old teacher. Baretti had annotated Mama's edition of Sam's letters. Three words of Mr Baretti's thumped in Cecy's skull now. *You lie, bitch.*

'What an honour you must hold it,' said Lady Cobbe carefully now, 'to have shared friendship with Dr Johnson.'

Mama laughed lightly. 'An honour indeed.' Cecy saw her face soften. 'Ours was a mutual regard founded on the truest principles: religion, virtue and community of ideas ... Saucy soul, I used to think when we first met – *community of ideas with Dr Johnson!* He insisted I wrote daily in my *Thraliana*. He always wanted to hear a new verse or translation. And all the time he fastened many of his own notions so on my mind, that I was never sure whether they grew originally there or no. Of this I was sure: that they were the best and wisest notions I possessed, and that I loved the author of them with firm affection.' Waves throbbed against the stone. 'Until my mind was swallowed up whole in his and lost.'

The Devonport ball was a rout, a racket, a hurricane with Mrs Piozzi at its eye.

'Madness is in itself no incurable disease; half one's acquaintances have been as mad as our poor King can be, and do vastly well again,' said Hester. 'So why must the King be precluded recovery? *Because he is King*, and has people about him ready to ease his shoulders of the trouble. Poor man! How distressful is his situation! And in how much danger his life ... For we all know the opposition people want an unlimited Regent. How *unconstitutional*. Pitt, I think, wants a republic. How unconstitutional is *that* too, but far less dangerous. Anything but despotism, for God's sake – let us not take up what France is beginning but now to lay down! I know, as naval gentlemen, you will agree with me.'

The captains and lieutenants gathered about her bowed their assent. The ball was enlivened, they all agreed, by the arrival of Mrs Piozzi and her pretty daughter, whose silence her mother more than made up for – so why not flirt with the mother, in an effort to enjoin the daughter? The Italian husband and stepfather, after all, simply looked bored.

'Tell us what to make of this Regent, my lady.'

Hester snapped her fan. 'Oh, we are turning into democrats here wholly from love of the King. Would to God the father were well, or the son honest – or both.'

'You have an uncommon understanding for a woman, my lady.'

Hester inclined her head. 'And you have the common misunderstanding of most gentlemen, sir.'

Beside her, Cecy was set to quite lose all the fluid in her

body, squeezed out in a sweat that left her a dried-up fruit as the assembly gasped and shrieked with laughter. She looked at Mr Piozzi. There was that faraway look in his eyes, as if hunting for clues, and she knew he was analysing what he understood of Hester's role as nurse to Sam, and Sam's fear of madness. Or perhaps he was counting up the number of men Mama had nursed, and knew himself to be one of them, hoping she could cut the roots of his melancholia.

'But that is quite enough of politics, for here is an irresistible tune. Which one of you young blades will win the first dance with my daughter?'

Cecy tried to grab Mr Piozzi's sleeve, but missed, and was soon led on to the dance floor by a man with sweaty hands whom she could not name.

In the gallery, the great old women of Plymouth looked down on them, redoubtable monuments of the last century who had probably poured Dr Johnson's tea. One of them, more tanned than all the others, stood out to Hester, for she wore no mourning dress, but instead a gown that almost matched the blues of the officers. A Blue, Hester thought, and smiled, and the old woman smiled down on her. Seated beside her was a woman Hester's own age, dressed in ox-blood red, which quite set off her curls, still golden, and uncovered.

Next to her, an officer said, 'That good lady is the patron saint of Devonport, and, with her, her daughter.'

'Oh? Why?'

'She built it.'

Hester nodded, thinking of the hours spent in Mr Thrale's brewery. 'How good you honour her, sir.'

'We all worship the lady and her daughter, Miss Grace. Our lady shipwright, and a writer of romance, too, though some say her book was not a novel, but true history.'

'What is its title, sir?'

'*A Wild & True Relation of A Lady Shipwright and Free-Trader.*
She tells a tale of a murderer, Tom West, who loved and killed
her mother, and a childhood spent on his ship, dressed as a
boy, and how she lived among knaves, and bested them to
rise to power. Quite the folk tale. Tom West was a legend in
Devonshire.'

Hester was going to ask, *Why doubt her story is true?* But then
she remembered what she pretended not to know: those three
words, *You lie, bitch.* 'Who is her husband, sir? Ought I know?'

The officer shrugged. 'Sir Orlando. A famous whip, in
these parts.'

An explosion of giggles disturbed him, as girls old enough to
know better raced through the ballroom, and officers bedecked
in enough campaign medals to know better still gave chase. The
officer begged her pardon, and pursued them.

Hester turned to Mr Piozzi with a smile she hoped to trans-
mit to him. 'Did I not tell you we'd receive every pleasure here,
and be most happy?'

'We'd be happier in Italy,' he murmured. 'We *were* happier
in Italy.'

Hester looked to mad-headed little Cecy, dancing sweetly.
'If I go with you, I am sure to lose her. I must not stir from my
post if I mean to defend it. No, we shall return to Bath, and
there I will finish my book and gather my reminiscences of
this country, and Cecy will dance at more balls, and attend the
library, and be mine—'

'How can something be yours, if you have to keep it from
escaping?'

Hester tried to catch her breath. She looked him in the
eye – those beautiful eyes, the same shade as his violin. But
she could not hold his gaze, so glanced up at the patron saint
of Devonport, who seemed to be regarding her with interest.
Hester had spent so long trying to make her own mother

271

stronger, and, after losing her, missed the strength she'd always possessed. And this woman sat laughing with her daughter, as if the two were agents of a great conspiracy, and enjoyed being so.

'*You* may come again to me,' she said, 'but if I let *her* go – she never will. I will lose her, for ever, as I have lost her sisters. I can try and please the public with my writing, I can overlook the spite of individuals – but there are only three critics out of them all I care for. The three cruel misses. And they hate me.'

Mr Piozzi held her hand, a gentle clasp, and Hester felt in his shaking grip a desire to shake sense into her, and his restraint from doing so – for he'd never speak what she already knew, what she'd already lost, in a whole life trying to talk her mother and father and tutor and uncle and husband and the Blues and Sam and her daughters – all society – round. Horror squeezed her heart. Something would happen, she was sure, that would separate her from Mr Piozzi, and she would lose it all.

'We had so many storms before we met,' she breathed. 'Are they not over now?'

'How can I convince you they are?'

A laugh so she would not cry. Hester hid her face with her fan, and, when she lowered it, there was her dazzling smile. She excused herself, trailing bons mots through the terrible squeeze.

Cecy hid from her mama's appalling tears, offering her best look of soft sweetness to the officer who held her.

'You're a delicate little thing,' he said. 'I am afraid of using you too roughly.'

'Oh, no, sir,' she said. 'I trust myself to your gentleness.'

In the gallery, the patron saint of Devonport and her daughter broke off their murmured communication to rise and curtsy to Hester, who set her eyes on the lady shipwright and found herself able to breathe at last. The lady shipwright seemed to sense this, for she let grateful silence lap between them, until Hester reached for her hand, and pressed.

'Ma'am,' she said, 'I may be foolish and wild, but I come to seek advice from you. I am told you have kept a book, recording your labours for freedom and fortune. Does the book survive?'

BOOK FOUR

1711

I AM ALL THE DAUGHTERS OF MY FATHER'S HOUSE

AND ALL THE BROTHERS TOO

Twelfth-Day Eve

This was a true stateroom. Molly stood behind Tom, trying to keep herself from fidgeting with the sleeves of her jacket. The scars on her forearms seemed to crawl, six months on. Tom's broad shoulders made the fine chair with its velvet and studs look like it was designed for a doll; the East Indiamen stared at him as if he were a creature in a zoo.

Molly had painted the flags they used to call the ship to them: one half-yellow, half-blue; one chequered red and white. *I wish to communicate with you. You are running into danger.* The great warship turned on them, eight nine-pounder guns and twenty-two six-pounders swinging about, the lion figurehead roaring into grey sea. Tom rowed over with Molly, Kingston and Nathan – the men aboard the warship wincing at the sight of Kingston. And now Tom relaxed in the ruby light of this cushioned room, and smiled at the ship's captain, who reminded Molly of a silver birch in winter.

'Well, Captain, how's tea?' said Tom.

'Sixteen pounds – to Colonel Gautier.'

Tom shook his head. 'That won't do at all. He's not paying you enough, sir.'

A weary look. 'And I suppose that is the danger you warned of?'

'Yes.' Tom cupped his chin in his hand. There was a

twinkling on his face, and it made Molly proud that he could play in this room, unshaven, clad in black, salt-stained and most likely bloodstained, while these cultivated men searched for how to pose, where to put their hands, where to look in the face of him. 'You're being robbed,' Tom said.

'If Gautier is to make a profit, he has to pay beneath the line – he has onward costs. I am a reasonable man, sir. We still earn more than we would if we paid duty. Everybody profits.'

'Hmm.' Tom looked about, as if striking on an idea. 'What if there weren't any onward costs?'

'Sir?'

'What if there was no man in the middle? No Colonel Gautier. What if, instead of delivering these goods to Gautier, and Gautier then delivering them to me, I took those sixty-odd chests off you now, for eighteen?'

The captain gave a delicate cough. 'Gautier would be ruined. He lives on borrowed gold.'

Tom shrugged. 'Ruins fade.'

The captain glanced at his officers. There was greed in their eyes, Molly thought, as well as a boyish thrill.

'So that mightier civilisations may rise,' suggested the captain, studying Tom's expression, waiting for an incline of the head, a bow, Molly realised.

'Long live the king,' said Tom.

Molly knew he didn't mean the Company. The captain did not.

'We would make the exchange now?' asked the captain.

'You'll have to haul off land another league or so first. If your men will be so kind to assist, we'll carry the cargo over to my ship by rowboat.'

'Why must we haul off?'

Tom looked to the panelled window, gleaming with rain. 'There's a custom-house schooner southward, at the very edge of English water. Right now, he could arrest us. A league off, all he can do is watch.'

The captain tittered. 'Surely he'll not be so blithe as to stand and watch, rules or no rules. You'd be waving it in his face, sir.'

Tom drummed a beat on the table with two fingers. 'There was a Revenue man with mettle once. But not any more.'

'What happened to him?' asked another officer, this one pink-cheeked with bravado.

Tom stood up. 'I did.' He gestured to Kingston. 'My first mate, here, can give your men orders.'

The pink-cheeked man seemed to choke, reminding Molly of bulbous fish in the monger. Tom looked at him with mild interest, and the officer dodged his gaze.

Twelfth Night

Fire, rosewater, nutmeg. The staff in the guildhall piled the hearth in the council chamber high with half-trunks hours before the guests arrived. In the kitchen, busy hands uncorked four-score bottles of perfumed water to pour tremulously into pierced eggshells. Beneath the pillared walkway, the artist put the finishing touches on the pasteboard stag, adding horror and defeat to its eyes. The Mayor paced the parlour, practising his speech. The staff hadn't known him do this for years, but tonight, of course, was different. Tonight, free-traders shared the Twelfth Night feast. Tonight, Tom West would sit at the table where Oliver Cromwell had plotted his battles, and he would eat under the gaze of justice, and equity, carved into the overmantel.

Tom brought the *Venture* up the Dart, past the castle, past Bayard's Cove Fort – where Charles Savage boarded, waving over the side at the Customs House – past St Saviour's, Tom at the wheel himself, despite his breath shivering on the air. The people cheered him on his way, through skeleton forests and raw hills, knocking ice from their path, the river holding vessels of great burden and great guns to her cold bosom. From the shivering mudflats, grey herons turned their heads to follow him, and, above, curlews formed a stormy cloud, whooping and screeching his return.

Benedict muttered his transits like prayers. Tom followed the boy's twitching eyes to Greenway Court, and then to Raleigh's quay and the locked doors of the provision store. From the riggings, Molly began to tell Kingston the story of Sir Humphrey Gilbert's battle with a lion of the sea, but Benedict interrupted, saying that was all nonsense.

'Look there to the Anchor Stone, where unmanageable wives were put to the ducking stool,' said Benedict. 'That's where women who lived by stories were bound, until the water of high tide looked set to drown them.'

Tom gripped the kingpin. There was a question on Molly's face, Tom knew, but he didn't meet it, reaching out instead to cuff Benedict around the head. The boy started. The sudden betrayal and bitterness on his face made Tom raise an eyebrow, waiting. But Benedict only paled into silence. Kingston looked off, humming.

These outbursts were becoming more frequent, as Molly's body changed, tempting fate, and Benedict waited for Tom to protect her by sending her away from the ship, as he'd promised. 'You know this can't last,' he'd whispered to Tom as Nathan set about building a separate bed for Orlando in Tom's cabin. 'You can't overturn nature.' Tom had told Benedict, 'You don't understand the girl, stick to transits' – which Tom followed now, pursuing Benedict's line from Dittisham church tower to the clump of plum trees and around to Sharpham, where a murmuration blackened the sky, dancing knife-points. The *Venture* eased into the generous waterway of Totnes, into the eyeline of the red sandstone tower of the church.

'Well,' called Pascal, 'somewhere, Dick English is weeping.'

A cheer from the men. A smile like the flick of a knife from Tom.

The crew of the *Venture* were greeted at the guildhall by the Mayor himself, who ushered them into the court room – to the right, the Mayor's throne and the pews for councillors and lawyers; to the left, the Dark House, a cell so small a man could not stand up, with no window and no air, at which some cold passed through Tom, but he laughed as Molly swished her shoes over the Purbeck marble, and they continued up the stairway, to the council chamber.

Molly's nerves stung as if spiked by a weever fish, and she knew the crew felt the same way – for what neater way to capture Tom West than to invite him to the house of justice? But the council chamber had been transformed into a dining hall, not a trap.

Enough food for the five and thirty guests – and a pack of hungry dogs too, Kingston whispered. Tom was ushered to the foot of the table, which to Molly took on the gravity of the head, for the Mayor looked very poor all the way at the end, by comparison. The leader of the fishermen and the leader of the blacksmiths and the leader of the silversmiths and the leader of the tailors, and all the councilmen and all the landed men, bowed and laughed and cried 'Happy Twelfth Night!' to the free-traders, and all of their wives and daughters did too. Tom had become one of the richest men in all of Devon.

'We'll have to start a guild of free-traders!' This was repeated among the guests, until the Mayor himself echoed it, and it no longer sounded such a joke.

At Tom's right hand, Molly fiddled with her green and yellow sleeves. She took in the scene in deep draughts: the delicate frieze of dancing horned horses, the plump pink petals of Henry-the-wife-killer's rose picked out in plaster in the corner, the precious lead and glass in the great window. Next to her, Miss Binnie, heiress to an orchard fortune, chattered happily. The girl mirrored her widow mother's titter, but, Molly found, could be made to really laugh – at which point she'd give a much-harboured giggle and bat Molly on the arm with her fan. Nathan and Charlie dispensed gallantries, and even Kingston was enjoying himself, laughing all the more for the astonished glances sent his way. Only Benedict remained sullen and quiet. Molly thought of him pointing to the ducking stool. She shook her head, trying to dislodge this feeling that some play was losing its script.

'Are we to have frogs hopping free from our pies tonight?' asked a guildsman.

'No frogs this Twelfth Night, sir,' said the Mayoress. 'Last year, we were forever finding them all through January and February. It may be a laughing matter to have them entertaining the prisoners awaiting justice, but a frog in my husband's robes amuses nobody – but myself!'

Tom leant forward, one elbow on the table. 'Who do you have in the Dark House tonight, madam?'

The table's laughter dipped.

'A wayward wretch, sir,' said the Mayor.

Tom reached for the silver bowl of walnuts. He cracked three in his hand. 'I hear the cells are so near upon the court, in this magnificent building, that a jailed man is in earshot of his judgement at all times.'

'As a guilty man always is, sir,' said the Mayor, 'for he is always in the earshot of God.'

The table banged: 'Hear, hear!'

'That he is,' said Tom, brushing his hands of shells. 'In earshot of feasts, too, I'd guess. And hungry.'

Molly watched the table take up this idea as if passing some foreign object from hand to hand, marvelling and worrying at it in turns, until finally the Mayoress, much moved, said, 'You are quite right, sir. We shall send food down to them immediately.' She dabbed at her eyes. 'For it is the Christian thing to do.'

The Mayor bowed to his wife. 'Has there ever been an example among women such as my good wife?'

The men and women were about to raise their glasses, but Tom cracked another walnut. 'Your staff are probably hungry, too.'

The Mayor winced. 'Yes. We shall tell them to partake of the next course.'

'That might stop them unleashing frogs on you,' said Tom, 'at the very least.'

A wave of laughter, and now the toast was to Tom himself.

Miss Binnie asked Molly if Captain West was always so kind to the poor, and Molly began a story of Tom smuggling food to a starving leper colony that existed, she assured the heiress, between Jersey and Guernsey.

In the kitchen, the footman told the maid, who told the cook, who told the pastry chef, that Tom West said they were to share in the dinner, and the pastry chef reconsidered the drop of icing that would tell the footman which slice of Twelfth Cake contained the bean.

In the hall, Miss Binnie whispered to Molly, 'Now we'll discover who is to be King and Queen of Twelfth Night.'

Molly looked between the Lord Mayor and Tom. 'Discover how?'

'The kitchen has made a cake so large it fills *two ovens* in the baking. This cake is in the shape of a fortress, with sentinels and flags, and in two of the slices there is hidden a dried bean, and a pea. Whosoever among the gentlemen discovers the bean is king until midnight, and whosoever among the ladies discovers the pea is his queen.'

'Has anyone ever choked on their ascension?' asked Molly.

At that, Tom laughed so loudly the whole table looked to him to find the source of his amusement, but he was saved answering by four footmen, who entered supporting the cake between them. The table clapped, congratulating the Mayoress.

'She will be queen,' Miss Binnie murmured, 'and the Mayor king.'

'How do you know?'

She shrugged. 'It is always so, sir.'

'Then what's the point?'

'Artifice,' she said. 'Artifice is its own point.'

The table hummed – 'Who shall be king?' 'And will he be a kind lord to us?' 'We can only hope he'll lower the taxes.' 'Oh, no, then what would Captain West do with himself?' – and the footmen cut the cake, and counted heads, following as many round from the dot of icing as the pastry cook had instructed, until each guest was served, and Tom inspected his slice, which seemed to be the treasury of this great sponge fortress. He chuckled, and picked up his small silver fork, considering just what he would have given to bring home this tiny amount of silver to his mother as a boy – and then he almost cracked his tooth.

Tom spat, and the coffee bean clattered on to the fine china.

The Mayor flushed the same crimson as his robes.

A footman stumbled forward, as if to whip the bean from Tom's plate, and then froze.

Tom gave the Mayor a sympathetic smile. 'Crowns,' he said. 'Slippery things.'

The Mayoress hemmed, and then gathered her glass. 'To the king!'

The ladies and gentlemen chorused: 'To the king!'

'But who shall be your queen?' said the widow, Mrs Binnie, looking about the table at each woman's cake with the eyes of a hawk, Molly thought. They intended to house-train Tom, she realised, until the origins of his riches were forgotten.

The Mayor was glowering. He expected the pea to be in his

wife's cake, of course. But it might be somewhere else. Molly looked down at her own plate, and felt the bites she'd already taken turn to stone in her stomach at the idea of the hard little pea skittering from the cake, and all eyes turning to her, and one of these grand people saying, *But you're not a girl – or are you?* Her eyes watered.

'A man can only dream, ma'am,' said Tom, bowing to the Mayoress.

But the pastry cook had a greater sense of his own preservation than that, and in her next bite Miss Binnie – the most prized heiress in Totnes – gave a genteel cough, and discovered the pea in the palm of her hand.

The widow Binnie knew her role. 'Sir,' she said, 'a mother can dream too. Only, a mother dreams a little higher.'

Tom gave her a wicked grin, lowering his voice, but not so that the whole table couldn't hear him – rather, inviting them to lean in, which they did, for here was the most daring thing to happen in months. 'I'm yet to find a man who stands higher, Mrs Binnie, though ceilings do present me a problem.'

'And what do you do then, sir?'

Molly thought, Blow a hole in the roof.

'I make my bow,' said Tom, to applause, as he rose and did just that to the new queen.

Next would be the eggs, and King West could choose who was granted the first throw – for they would pelt each other with rosewater shells, Miss Binnie told Molly, until the queen – herself – chose a winner. Molly caught the look on Benedict's face. Sick. Benedict looked sick. He rose suddenly, weaving around the footmen and their tray of eggs.

The yard was thick with snow, shivering in the plane trees. Molly crunched around the curving lane, careful on the steps, and then under East Gate, sliding down Fore Street, past Tudor fronts and new slated houses loud with their own feasts, past black shop windows, to where Benedict sat on the Brutus Stone, the granite slab slick with ice.

'What's wrong?' Molly asked, turning up her new velvet collar.

'King,' Benedict said, drumming his heels against the stone. 'They made him king.'

'Were you hoping for the honour?'

'Hypocrites. They're all hypocrites. Welcoming us while we're worth something. You think they'll anoint him king in the end?'

'The end of what?'

Benedict sniffed.

'Come inside, Benedict, and be merry,' said Molly, bouncing against the cold. 'They're not hypocrites. Devon's full of dissenters, one way or another. It's good to see them enjoy it. Taxes are too high. It hurts their trades, too. Maybe Tom is a kind of Robin Hood.'

There was such disgust on his face, Molly's stomach turned lumpen once more.

'I don't understand. What upsets you?'

'He does,' spat Benedict. 'Robin Hood. King Bean. God's blood.'

'Benedict . . .'

'What? I can say it, too. I can be as ungodly as the lot of them. You don't know what I'm capable of.'

Molly laughed nervously. 'Capable of wearing a hole in the Brutus Stone, I know that.'

'Brutus. Don't tell me you believe that story, too.'

'It's not a story,' said Molly. 'It's history.'

'History. You think so? Brutus murders his father by some error, as if that were so easy, and sails for Greece, where he bests King Pendrasu, too. So, Pendrasu grants Brutus his daughter to marry, just as Tom has been gifted Miss Binnie for the night, and Brutus journeys to Albion with her, sailing up the River Dart, not afeared of the giants who possess the land. He reaches this stone, and tells the world, "Here I set and here I rest, and this town shall be called Totnes."'

'Well,' said Molly, 'why not?'

Benedict's blue eyes settled on her, and Molly was struck for the first time by how very much Benedict looked like a painting of a saint – his dark curls and red lips, his sadness. Struck by how very beautiful he was, even in his dismay.

'You need to learn the difference,' said Benedict, 'between stories and lies. If you don't . . . '

Benedict had drawn her attention to the ducking stool as if it somehow applied to her. Molly took a deep breath, like swallowing ice, and sat down, her leg pressed against Benedict's, feeling the jagged point of his knee. 'Benedict, what is it you want to tell me?'

Silence, in which the wind grew feathers of ice, and windows winked with candlelight.

'Did you ever hear any Shakespeare?' said Molly. 'My mama used to tell me his stories. Brutus kills the man who's a father to him in *Julius Caesar*, too. It seems to me that Brutus must have hated the fathers who loved him.'

Benedict looked away.

'Perhaps he was burdened,' said Molly, 'by stories, and lies.'

'I don't hold with plays,' said Benedict.

Molly smiled, just a little. '*Twelfth Night* was my favourite. I learnt a speech by heart, for this night. Do you know what it was?'

Finally, he looked at her, and they were sitting so close, Molly could follow the red threads in his eyes, follow the great weariness there. She took a quick breath, and held it, catching courage. Then she glanced down at his lips, and delivered the words to them, as if feeding him his line.

'I am all the daughters of my father's house,' she said. 'And all the brothers too.'

Benedict bit his lip. Frost hovered between them. 'I know. I've always known.'

Relief struck Molly, hard at first, and then a gentle balm, leaving her heart skittering, and her shoulders dropped. 'I thought you shared my game, once.'

Benedict touched her fingertips. 'It's not a game any more.'

'A play, then. But you don't hold with those.'

'You'll be found out by the crew, by someone.'

'The crew wouldn't hurt me.'

'You're becoming a lady. You ought—'

Molly withdrew her hand. 'Don't tell me what I ought. I hold the key to my nature. Not you. Not Tom. Not anyone. What makes you think you can be my jailer?'

He pulled her by the wrist. 'I want to free you, not lock you up. Don't you see? This charade – the longer it goes on, the more it offends God.'

'Do I offend you?'

A croak: 'Never that. You must listen to me. The more I see of Tom, the more I believe ... I believe I was wrong, about who—'

'Boys!'

Molly jerked away from Benedict.

Charlie Savage stood under East Gate. 'It's time for the stag!'

The pasteboard stag rose on its back hoofs, preparing to dance, or perhaps to fend off its killer, for the eyes looked to Molly like they were rolling with fear. The pretend beast had been brought into the dining room and set before the great hearth, where Tom stood, holding in one hand a knife he'd normally use to gut fowl, and in the other a bronze goblet. A footman hovered behind him, turning the silver jug in his hands. The ladies and gentlemen waited on their feet, with empty glasses. Standing next to Tom, Miss Binnie looked like she was having the most fun she'd ever been permitted to have. Molly slipped through the crowd, the delicate carcasses of eggs crunching beneath her shoes, Benedict following like a tethered ghost, until she was at the front, where Tom wanted her, giving her a nod that said, *You were right. We are Devon.*

Tom drove the knife into the stag's jugular, and there was a small gasp from the crowd, for the Lord Mayor usually made a small needlepoint, from which the claret would pour tidily. Tom had delivered a killing blow, and the claret that flowed into the goblet had all the speed, viscosity and sudden loss of death.

They cheered.

Molly leant into Benedict, whispering, 'There's nothing to mourn. Nothing to regret. I'm happy as Orlando—' But she was interrupted as a young man in purple and gold stepped into the puddle of claret, and bowed, not to the Lord Mayor, but to Tom.

His voice quivered through the company:

> *'A monarch is he, as bold as can be,*
> *Of a strong and daring band;*
> *The bullet and blast may go whistling past,*
> *But he quails neither heart nor hand;*
> *He lives and dies with his fearful prize,*
> *Like a hunted wolf he'll spring,*
> *With trigger and dirk, to the deadliest work,*
> *And fight like a smuggler king.*
>
> *'Back from the wave to our home in the cave,*
> *By the gleam of our torches' glare,*
> *He reigns as lord of the free-traders' board,*
> *And never was costlier fare.*

Right firm and true are the hearts of his crew,
And there's faith in the shouts that ring,
As they stave the cask, and drain the flask,
In good health to the smuggler king.

'They call him Tom West, and you'll know him best
By his head way o'er the crowd;
A pistol and sword are his rivals' reward,
And as for the rest we're proud
Of this son who bestows, and beats off our foes,
And protects us from duties that sting;
He shrunk Limp Dick, ho that was a trick,
So Devon, remember, the smuggler king.'

Molly flinched at the touch of a hand against hers – but it was only Benedict, twining his fingers with hers. His grip would starve her of blood.

Touching for the Evil

Richard studied the cup, tilting it towards himself, daring the milk to drip on to his shirt, or else the bed linen, and then towards the window, which had been opened against his wishes, giving the milk the pearl lustre of daybreak. Blood, yellow choler, black choler, phlegm. His humours were imbalanced, the doctor said. Black choler and phlegm built up too greatly, overwhelming his body with cold and miserable fogs, dense as sea mist. Fresh milk would drive the watery humour out of him, drive out all that was dank and cold, rescue him from this treacherous marshland and return him to air and fire: determination, contentment and calm contemplation of his lot, warding off this deep self-loathing, this dark melancholy. The doctor, Richard understood, was fond of grandiloquence, so fond he came at everything sideways, telling Richard's wife: 'Fresh milk, three times a day, and there need be no fear of the English disease.'

The English Disease: suicide. It was there in his name. He'd been born with it, this capacity that the French shook their heads over, lamenting the melancholy that reigned over England, the sombre and taciturn humour, which meant gentlemen on whom life had forced intolerable reflections, terrible maladies and anxiety, or simply general malaise, would with seeming ease hang themselves. And so great lines go extinct.

But Richard's line would not suffer for his absence. He peered over the rim of the cup to his immobile legs beneath the blanket, those unmoving weights, those rotting growths, waiting since childhood to fail him, and now, finally, dead.

The doctor reassured his mother, too. 'You have done everything you could, Mrs English. You mustn't blame yourself.'

Richard did not understand the ritual of the doctor's absolution, and his mother's relief every time the man said it. She blamed herself, he supposed, for it was well known that the sins of the mother were visited on an invalid child. So be it, then. It was his mother's fault he'd been born infirm, her fault for marrying his father and running his corrupt house. But she nursed him through those sins. While his brothers played with riding whips and tops, Richard's mother sat with him inside, humming nursery rhymes well after Richard had left the nursery. And now he may as well be back in the nursery, for the games of childhood persisted. A frog on Twelfth Night had jumped on to Richard's knee, where it waited for him to jerk it off. But he couldn't, so the thing just looked at him, and the whole company cackled, led by his father.

If he didn't ring the bell for his man to help him into the chair, his mother would join him this morning and sing to him again. And if his father heard her tune, he would stride into Richard's room, seize his foot and shake him about, saying, 'What use is a man who can't stand, can't ride, can't fight, can't fuck?' Richard's mother would cry, his wife would cry, and his father would roar: 'I should have drowned you!'

Outside, the labourers drew their pattern over the field, sweeping up the blazing flax from the sport of St Distaff's Day. Games would never cease. He would lie here like a broken child until he was an old man, while around him men with

293

vigour and good humour would play at idle games and worse, and then time would break him again – but, God, it would come as a mercy.

Richard pulled at the signet ring his father insisted he wore now he was back under his roof. He dropped it in the milk.

The jewellery of a victim of the English disease was forfeit. And so mothers looked for discarded diamonds and forgotten rubies in their sons' apartments and shrank when they found them.

Richard looked beyond the field with its pyres, to the sea.

God would never forgive him. That was true. But God had already judged him guilty, for hadn't he left, as he believed then, a young child to burn to death as he ran from the corporeal body of Grace Tucker?

And hadn't God forgiven Tom, providing from the fire a bastard son who loved him?

Tears threatened him. Tears always threatened him.

What use is a man who can't stand, can't ride, can't fight, can't fuck?

God, give me leave. Oh, give me leave.

The door opened.

He hurled the milk across the room, shouting, 'There! It's all gone!'

His wife stood in the doorway, staring down at the dripping stain on her mantua, which looked so like semen to Richard, he laughed, the tears unstoppable now.

Charlotte lifted her chin. 'Are your childish performances over, sir?'

'No,' gasped Richard, holding his blanket to his face, sobbing into it. 'No, not nearly.'

She stood over his legs, always left in the same way by his man, spread like a broken wishbone. 'Today is the touching of the evil by the Queen. I have brought you a touch-piece.'

Richard looked at the coin in her palm, at the great ship carved into it, the six sails.

'Do you think Queen Anne will visit me here, so that I may give her this piece to touch my evil, and cure me?' he asked.

'I think you will visit her.'

'I see. Will you and mother drag me to London in my chair?'

'You shall walk yourself,' she said, trying to stop herself shaking him, just as his father did.

'Sweet Charlotte,' he said, 'still believes in miracles.'

'I believe in justice.' She dropped a fold of cheap paper on to his lap. 'If you do not answer this disgrace, nobody will, and I refuse to live in shame. Justice must be served. So you must stand and serve it.'

Richard nudged the piece of paper, reading the curling hand over the fold:

> *And protects us from duties that sting;*
> *He shrunk Limp Dick, ho that was a trick,*
> *So Devon, remember, the smuggler king.*

Richard felt his blood boil, and with it yellow choler, black choler, phlegm, until he was boiling over, his whole body pouring with sweat, itching, alive. His knee twitched.

The Night Before the Eve of St Agnes

'You know, really I ought to *punish* you, not *please* you, for this downfall you've brought upon Colonel Gautier. You've left me quite abandoned.'

'I've always admired your ambition.'

Madame Rhys tied the silk gown Tom had brought as a peace offering, and span idly about his bedroom. She stroked the scabbard leaning in the corner. Tom watched her, hands crossed over his bare stomach.

'There's always the birch,' she suggested.

'Let me see.' Tom looked up at the ceiling, as if trying to recall some particular detail. 'Husbands flog their wives. Masters flog servants. Governesses, their pupils. Lawmen strip prostitutes and flog them in the streets – carrying out their orders until the girls' shoulders run with blood. Men in brothels flog whores until they have red buttocks to complement lily-white thighs. No.' He clicked his tongue. 'I don't see you or me fitting any of those scenarios. Unless you want to marry me, and then bend over.'

Rhys drew the sword and threw it on to the armchair, bringing the scabbard to the bed. She sat between Tom's legs and tapped him on the shoulder with it.

'Arise, Sir Tom,' she said.

'Give me a minute to recover after our last bout and I'll oblige.'

She laughed, bouncing the tip of the scabbard on his soft penis. He grunted, but did not take it from her.

'Marry you,' she said, stroking the inside of his thigh with the leather. 'I suppose it is the eve of St Agnes.'

'I'll oblige her, too, if you like.'

She prodded him in the knee. 'You needed a governess to flog you, Tom West. Maybe you would have learnt something.'

'So, teach me.'

'We'll be celebrating St Agnes at the bal masqué tomorrow – the bal masqué you *will* attend, this time. The eve of St Agnes is special for young women, for tonight we may gain, by divination, knowledge of our future husband.'

'You're not so young any more.'

'A *girl* may take a row of pins –' she prodded him again – 'and pluck them out, one by one, sticking them into her sleeve, singing as she does the paternoster. In her dreams, her husband will visit her. Or, if travelling into another country, she may take the stocking of her right leg –'

'This is getting interesting.'

'– and knit the left garter about it. *I knit this knot, this knot I knit, to know the thing I know not yet ...* ' She eased the tip of the scabbard beneath his testicles. Still no reaction. 'The girl lies down on her back that night, with her hands stretched to the bedhead, and her husband miraculously appears.'

'With that invitation, I'm not surprised.'

'And kisses her. Chastely.'

'That rules me out.'

She drew the scabbard from his stomach to his chest, following the line of hair. 'You're right, of course,' she said. 'You'd make an awful husband.'

'Terrible.'

'*Dreadful.* But you'll have to do as a ... patron – for now. You've practically elected yourself.'

'I wonder if Gautier knew you could be inherited so easily.'

'Colonel Gautier knows I weep for his ruin.'

Tom caught the scabbard from her hand. He threw it into the corner, but kept hold of her wrists. 'I'm sure it comforts him.'

Rhys laughed, straddling him. She glanced down. 'He arises.'

'I aim to be dependable.'

'And aren't we dependants *grateful*?'

Blood dripped down Molly's thighs. The Barbary witch had lied.

She leant against the privy wall, the pit at her feet spattered. She had taught herself to piss standing up years ago – all it took was bowing the legs and thrusting her pelvis forward. Now, she could hardly stand at all, and the stones and boards of the outhouse seemed to shake with her, the night winds unmerciful and hungry. The blood came from her in brown clots and crimson threads, clumping in the golden hair down there, so that it dangled from her in long spools. Her insides were trying to give birth to themselves, pushing out womb, gut, humours, leaving no room for bone or muscle, leaving nothing but this pain, as her body transformed right in front of her – and nothing mattered, not will, not prayers, not beseeching or bargains, not declarations, not even hope. Molly punched the wall, skinning her knuckles, and did it again. She was changed. She was alone.

She brushed her legs with moss – so hard, she knew she was bruising herself – and did her trousers up with shaking hands, stumbling away from the house, where a candle flickered in Tom's window, down to the beach. Stars shivered in standing pools, and the sand grew coarse beneath her shoes: empty snail shells. Walking on them was like the crunch of bones in her ear. Snow was yet to fall. The nearby church stood silent.

Molly wiped snot from her nose – smelling iron – and clutched her jacket closer, falling to the rocks.

The witch had lied. The witch had taken Molly's money, and promised her she'd be transformed. But it was never supposed to be *this* transformation.

Molly woke to a gentle hand on her arm. She sat up. Dawn was forcing itself on to the sky and birds swarmed over the dunes.

'Benedict?'

'Thankfully not.'

It was Madame Rhys coaxing her up. She flinched away.

'No need to be frightened,' said Rhys.

Molly brushed her trousers down – what if the blood had—? – but stopped when Rhys sat beside her.

'You slept out here, Boy?'

'No.'

'He's taught you to lie about small things, too, I see.'

'I am no liar.'

Rhys looked out at waves the same teal as the sky. 'There is so little definition on this island. However, it was hard to miss the blood in the privy. And *I* did not bleed last night.'

Molly searched the sands for a rock, for a weapon, instinct telling her, *When in danger, run to sea.* She hid her shaking hands in her pockets. 'Are you a mother, ma'am?'

'Yes. I have three daughters.'

'Where are they?'

'They live with my brother, who teaches them – rightly, one imagines – to despise me.'

Molly looked over her shoulder, to the house, to Tom's window. 'Do you miss them?'

'Yes.' Rhys smoothed her skirts. 'But I miss the pearl set I lost, too. I suppose you are thinking me an unnatural mother.'

'Yes.'

'And here was I, imagining you might know more about the questionable status of nature than most ... young men.'

Molly swallowed. 'My mother misses me.'

'I'm sure she does. Mislaid you, did she?'

'She was taken from me.'

'And who took you from her?'

'Tom,' said Molly. 'Tom saved me.'

'Our hero.'

Molly rose, trying to hold down her temper. 'He let me be myself. He's my ... I am his ward.'

'Not his child?'

'I'm his – everything.'

Madame Rhys arched an eyebrow.

'This is our game,' said Molly. 'Nobody else knows what I am. But now I've ... Tom said he'd send me away, if I was a girl.'

A gentle sigh. 'You know, it's not such a terrible thing, being a woman.'

Molly kicked the sand at her feet. 'What prey enjoys being hunted?'

'If it's sport we're talking, you'd make merry hell of them.'

A step back. 'You won't tell—?'

'Oh, yes –' Rhys carried on as if Molly had said nothing – 'a smart, saucy girl with good eyes and golden hair, and the manners of a wild schoolboy. You'd drive them mad.'

'I wouldn't. I won't.'

'Listen to a mother who misses her pearls. You're well versed in art; you even had me fooled. Time to learn a new art. I can teach you how to enslave mortal man. You have the luxury of innocence. It will be my project to show you when to meet his gaze and turn your head with confusion. When to soften your eyes – when to shine with desire. When to heave a sigh, and let a tear fall. When to give your hand to another. With what

300

melting voice and bashful tongue you may let an unguarded word reveal your love, just as his despair and jealousy for you turns to hate, and now burns for you with fatal passion. What we've lost to nature, we gain by studied beauty. What we win by beauty, we keep by art. You'll make him laugh, make him yearn, make him plead for the honour of keeping you comfortable.' Her attention flicked to Tom's window too, lingered there. 'You'll enchant them all.'

With each word from Rhys, Molly backed away, until the surf tugged at her. 'I've lost nothing to nature. I don't need any man. I'm equal to 'em. Your desperate tricks won't be mine.'

'Desperate?' Rhys studied the sand. She scooped up a small crab, which tumbled in the cup of her hand, back and forth, back and forth. 'You believe Tom will leave you to settle your own mind and body, when he discovers the change? When he sees you as a girl, with a girl's body?' She poked the pincers. 'If he's not looking already . . .'

'What's he ever done to you, to make you doubt him?'

Rhys shrugged, setting the crab down and nudging it away with her bare foot. 'Only destroyed my security.'

Molly sneered. 'Try melting him with the softness of your eyes.'

'Brave words. Yet I don't believe your faith in him.'

'Why should I care what you believe?'

'Why are you not running to him with the news of your menses?' Rhys asked sweetly.

'You're wrong. He won't think me any different. You'll see.'

'I'll believe it when you prove it.'

Molly frowned. 'Prove it?'

A smile like a twisting eel curled over Rhys's lips. 'Now, *here's* a game you'll want to play. Unless you'd rather I tell Tom about your new-found womanhood? If he knows you not, then you can trust to my silence.'

The Eve of St Agnes

I

Tom made sure his mask was secure – this time, Rhys had given him a golden mask, which was fastened to a gilt crown and plasterboard rubies. He'd told her about the King of the Bean. 'Now you'll be *le Roi Soleil*,' she'd said.

Roscoff's dancing master was leading the revel, and, though it was still early in the night, Tom could see men – if they were men – taking full advantage of their proximity to costumed vestals and virgins, to nuns, flower girls, queens, sultanas, woodwoses, conjurers, devils, women dressed as sailors, men dressed as serving wenches, and the rich dressed as paupers; white masks, black masks, sequinned, feathered, hooded, whole face, half face, held on glittering sticks. There were no shrieks, no protestations, only squeals. Colourful lanterns illuminated only so much of the ball-room, playing on Chinese murals and cascades, forgetting the grottoes into which men and women – or perhaps men and men, and women and women – disappeared. And, everywhere, the same chorus of the bal masqué: *Do you know me? And I you?*

He nodded to the small Negro boy in a turban who gave

him a glass of sweet wine, but passed it to Rhys, beckoning to another boy carrying brandy.

'I presume I'm now forgiven,' he said, 'for Gautier's unfortunate fall?'

Rhys made a show of looking him up and down in her harlequin visor, her bat of lath poised for some mischief. Her particolour bespangled hose were as tight as stockings, and her jutting hip drew his eyes. 'I don't recall you prostrating yourself.'

'A king doesn't beg his mistress,' he said, 'he lavishes her.'

'Lavish or lash?' She prodded him in the stomach, where the scar from Dick English was a ghostly pain.

He was spared replying by the appearance of a gypsy and a wise man.

'Do I know you, madam?' asked the sage.

'And I you, sir?' said Rhys.

Tom sighed. This spectacle of identity and intimacy already tired. He studied the players, fixing on a woman dressed as a soldier, her breasts straining at her woollen jacket. She could take a lesson from his girl.

Rhys's tug at his arm brought Tom back to the gypsy, who curtsied to him and begged to read the King's dreams.

'You would not like them,' he said.

'How can that be, Your Majesty?'

'Yes, do tell us, Your Majesty,' came another voice – a mock cardinal – 'and we will soothe you.'

Tom watched the cardinal bow to Madame Rhys, his half-mask revealing a young man's eagerness. Tom said, 'I do not think it is me you wish to soothe, Your Grace.'

Rhys gave a gasp. 'Sir, how could you?'

'I do sense your need to give confession, child,' sniffed the cardinal.

Tom took Rhys's arm from his, and offered her out. She cast

him a look of confusion, he thought, but still she went with the gentleman, who asked her, 'Do you know me, madam? And I you?'

Tom drained his brandy and accepted another, watching a mock milkmaid and aristocrat dance with all the fervour of a couple flouting the rules of their parents.

'Who is *that* ingénue?'

He followed the attention of the gentlemen gathered near him. Tom stopped, his glass to his lips. Now, *there* was a lady worth making up to, and the gentlemen in the ballroom knew it too. She wore a white robe of Indian damask, embroidered with blue and gold flowers, and a white mantua beneath it, sewn with gold and set with pearls and turquoise. The bodice was cut across the bosom, showing just enough to interest, not enough to spoil, the hoop so wide the men were kept at bay, and only buzzed harder for all that. A thin chain of gold girdled her waist, clasped with diamonds – a waist so small, a man could pick this sweet thing up with one arm. Long white gloves winked with jewelled rings. Golden curls piled in a tiara, which seemed real. A white half-mask, utterly blank, completed the mystery.

'Où est son chaperon?' asked one of the gentlemen.

'C'est un bal masqué,' chided another, setting off towards the Lady Virgin.

Tom searched for Madame Rhys and the cardinal, but could not find what gallery or corner they had chosen for confession. He swallowed the last of his brandy and handed it off to the Negro boy.

'Do you know whose daughter that is?' he asked the child.

'Oui, m'sieur.'

'A town merchant?'

'Mais oui, m'sieur.'

Tom couldn't place her from any of Gautier's dinners.

Maybe she'd only recently been launched. He shook his head at the offer of another glass, and followed in the wake of the gentlemen, feeling interest alive in him for the first time in . . . He straightened his mask. There was a ring of men about the bride – that was how he'd begun to think of her – and Tom waited on the outside, knowing that, with his height, even their flattery would not obscure him. In fact, in the din of it all, her attention fixed on him, those red lips plumping sweetly.

'Your Majesty,' she said, in a delicate voice. 'I did not expect to see you here.'

'Nor I you, Princess,' he said, joining her game. 'Our kingdoms have quarrelled these many years – to my heartbreak.'

She tilted her head. 'How can I mend a king's broken heart?'

'Dance with me.'

Hesitation, which the ring of men attempted to fill with their own offers, but she held his gaze. 'I do not know how, Your Majesty.'

He offered his hand. 'Don't you want to find out?'

Her gloved hand was so small in his, she seemed like she might be spun from glass, and he pulled her towards him carefully, the gentlemen falling back from her skirts. He guided her hand to his elbow – she could not reach his shoulder – and then hugged her waist, one arm pinned behind his back for the opening of the two-step. She stiffened for a moment – he could feel the muscles of her back tighten, reminding him of a filly at first touch – but then the music started, and he made the first step, and she followed, until soon the wainscot, the chandelier, the cascade, the gowns, all seemed to circle them, and all the other dancers afforded them space, recognising, he felt, the magnificence of this creature trembling ever so slightly in his arms.

'You lied, Princess.'

A small gasp.

'You *do* know how to dance.'

A laugh into his chest. 'Could it be that you know how to lead, Your Majesty?'

'Hard to lead a lady such as yourself,' he said. 'But I'm the man to try.'

She glanced up at him from beneath the mask, but only briefly – he just caught the length of her eyelashes. He freed his left arm from the strictures of the dance Grace had taught him, and caught up her other hand, spinning her beneath the arc of his arm.

'There,' he said. 'A born dancer.'

'Do you really think so, sir?'

'Born beauty, too,' he said. 'There isn't much pretence in this masquerade of yours.'

'Nor yours, sir.'

He bowed his head. Her tiara tickled his chin. He could lift her, gently, and her lips would meet his. 'I'm no king,' he murmured into her hair.

Her skirts brushed his legs, but she did not retreat. 'Even more promising,' she said.

He grinned. Played with her girdle, fingering the diamond clasp at her hip – cut, he realised, to resemble a snake's head and tail: a snake eating itself. 'You prefer your suitors in black masks?'

'If they are highwaymen,' she said.

He swept her round again, and she clutched him closer. 'What if your suitor were a free-trader?'

'Such a man – he trades in freedom?'

'He steals it.'

The music stopped, just for a moment, and they were suspended, before falling into another dance, and this time he pressed her to him, feeling her small breasts, her pointed hips.

He moved to her ear, whispering against the diamond there:

306

'I suppose you have some stern keeper who'd object to me stealing you?'

'Yes, sir. I do.'

'And would you miss him, terribly?'

'Yes, sir. I would.'

He pulled back, his hands drawing down from her bared shoulders, over the satin frill, to her white gloves – revulsion dropped like a cold stone into the pit of desire warming Tom's body.

The network of burns beneath Molly's gloves felt, as always, like a cat-o'-nine-tails braided to her skin.

He released her so quickly, she stumbled.

Tom tore his mask off, ripping the sun crown.

She did not copy him, but her voice was her own as she laughed, 'Don't you know royalty never reveal themselves until the end of the night?'

'What are you – why are you dressed like a girl?'

Molly laughed still, but nervously now. 'Isn't it a little late to ask?'

'What?' Haggard, hoarse.

'Didn't you know me?'

Do you know me? And I you?

Tom flinched as Madame Rhys slipped her arm through his, saying gaily, 'Now, here's a plot twist.'

He swallowed. 'Of course I . . . Of course I knew you.' His gaze dropped down Molly's body.

A blush crept over Molly's chest, seeped from the edges of her mask to her hairline. She said nothing. The music crashed on as Madame Rhys laughed.

II

'If you're angry—'

'I'm not,' said Tom, closing his bedroom door. 'I just want to know what – *how* this happened.'

Molly backed away, bumping into the bed. The silk had made her come out in a rash, and she wanted to scratch madly. 'It was Rhys. She found out and she ... I just wanted to show her ... She wanted me to tell you, but I couldn't—'

'Tell me what?' he said, leaning against the door.

'My blood. It came.'

Silence. Molly wondered if Benedict was listening from his room next door.

'I wanted to show her she was wrong,' Molly whispered. 'That you'd know me, and not care.'

'I almost kissed you,' he said. 'You almost *let* me. You're a child, God's blood. You're my ... you're ... '

Molly dragged the tiara from her curls, hurling it across the room, where it bounced. 'You want to know how this happened?' Shouting, now. 'You brought her here! You wanted me to learn what it means to be a *woman*!'

'Please,' said Tom, stepping forward, his hands raised.

'Do you think I enjoyed having all those men swarm around me like flies?' On her feet now, tearing at the stays, which ripped.

'*Please.*' Tom caught her hands, pulling her into him, where she fought and punched and kicked, and her gown came apart. Tom squeezed his eyes shut. 'Please. Stop. God. Please.' Tom kissed her curls. 'Please, my boy. My girl.'

She fell still, her heart beating against his body.

'You don't belong in that world,' he said. 'You belong in this one, with me.'

A small voice, as if from a great distance: 'You said I was beautiful.'

'You are,' he said. 'But you're all the more beautiful pulling riggings.' He kissed her head again. 'Don't you want to stay my powder monkey?'

'Always.'

'Then we must keep pretending you're a boy.'

'It's not a pretence.'

Tom drew back, studying her face. 'Tonight was the pretence?'

'Yes. No. I am ... I am ...'

She couldn't seem to finish, so Tom placed his finger gently over her lips. She kissed his fingertip, as she had as a bairn, when she'd suckle his fingertip dipped in milk for nourishment.

It was easy to break into Madame Rhys's house, for, though Colonel Gautier had bestowed enough bolts for a citadel on the front door, the servants' entrance had only one. Tom took the candle waiting there for the scullery maid and found his way up the back stairs to the first floor, and then the second. She would have a view, he thought, and he was right, for there at the end of a satin corridor was Madame Rhys's bedroom door, ajar. She sat at her dressing table, wiping off her paste, and, when he nudged the door open with his boot, she swallowed her gasp, turning it into a titter.

'Why, if it isn't the Sun King. What does he want?'

'After today's mischief, a court harlequin deserves a royal favour.'

She threw down the cloth. 'Did I not tell you it was punishment you needed?'

Tom set the candle down on the bureau, where she had

discarded her bat of lath, her magic wand. He picked it up. 'And tonight's display of womanliness was my punishment?'

She sat back, regarding him with contempt. 'Call it punishment, for the look on your face was painful enough. Call it a test. Is the little girl Daddy's stray shot, the captain's steady whore, or something else?'

'What was the conclusion?' he asked, shutting the door behind him and turning the key.

Her expression shored up. 'What a cliché you are. In how many awful romances does the brooding count marry his wilful yet charming ward, once all the turns and disguises have been done with, transforming him from brute to gentleman, and her from tearaway to lady?'

'You think I'm the suitor who appears in the night after the girl knits her garter?' He sneered. 'You meant to snare me, sweetheart; you should've known I wouldn't want a woman despairing enough to see a child as her rival.'

She stood up. 'You prefer your women resolute martyrs, do you?'

Tom wavered, remembering Grace in the doorway at the Pilchard Inn, come to beg him for help with none of her wilfulness dimmed.

An empty laugh. 'Then you'll be pleased to learn you've raised that girl well. Ready to throw herself on the altar of your lechery, so you wouldn't drive her away.'

He closed in on her, the boards groaning beneath him. She did not back away, and soon he was leaning over her, his fist aching, the grip on the bat that tight. 'I brought you into my home to play the mother to her, when the time came. And instead you played the bawd. You should've heeded your own words. You thought me an animal, once. You thought me dangerous.'

'And yet you're shocked by your own animal desires.'

She shrugged, planting her feet. 'I knew you would be. That's what made this evening such a good game. But I suppose it says something for you. Even if it's just that you're always wearing a mask – for the world, and yourself. If you could have seen yourself trembling to get inside that *girl*'s skirts tonight.'

He struck her across the face with the stick, splitting her lip. She staggered back, knocking into the bedpost and falling on to the mattress.

Rhys wiped her mouth. She inspected the blood on her fingertips, a hard and weary look.

Tom raised the thing again, his hand shaking.

'What are you waiting for?' she said.

Not waiting. Hoping. Be a different man.

She flicked the blood at his feet. Raised her gaze to him. The contempt there rocked him.

He brought the bat down again, and she screamed.

III

The fire ate the white mask with rapacity. Molly squatted before it in the remains of her gown. She would burn that next.

'What ritual is this?'

Molly looked up: Benedict stood in the doorway, forced cheer on his face. Rain drove against the house, filling their silence, as Benedict's eyes widened, set to swallow her whole. Molly looked down at herself, trying to see this body through his gaze: the torn corset revealing the freckled skin of her chest, the hollows of her clavicle, and her breasts, too small to cup in

311

a man's hand. Her skirts were torn too, showing the ridiculous pantalettes, hugging the calves and jagged knees Benedict knew every summer day on the ship – but never like this.

'Not a ritual,' she said. 'A foolish performance, that won't be repeated.'

'It won't?' He stepped inside.

'No.' She held her ground.

Benedict glanced to the fire, where the mask buckled and hissed. 'Did Tom see you like this?'

'Yes.'

'What did he do?'

'Do? Nothing.'

Benedict touched his throat, where there was no neckcloth. 'Madame Rhys took you to the ball?'

'Yes.'

'I suppose you had a thousand compliments.'

'Compliments from men like that are nothing more than bills of fare. They expect something in return.'

'You sound like Rhys.'

Molly snorted, standing up. She took up a fistful of her skirt, fanned it out. 'What do *you* think?'

Benedict was flushing. They were just a few paces from each other – he could reach out and brush her cheek, if he wanted. But he was trembling – not as Tom had, when they danced, when his body seemed to throb. Benedict looked afeared, his gaze stuck on her thigh.

'You look like a woman,' he breathed.

The word sounded terrible.

'You prefer me as a boy?' she asked.

A half-nod.

'Because you're like Nathan, or because you prefer me as me?'

'What do you mean, "like Nathan"?'

Molly shook her head. Sometimes Benedict seemed just as innocent as a newborn.

Then Benedict said, 'I prefer you as you.'

Relief sank into Molly's body the same way it did when they got the ship into safe harbour. She took stronger hold of her skirts, and tore. The material shredded easily; all that money, for nothing.

Benedict paled, but did not turn his back, watched her strip down to stockings – her thighs were spattered with rust, blood, just like Grace – and then watched her kick those off too.

Molly turned her back on him, saying, 'Get this off me,' aware all at once that, though they had swum together almost naked half her life, this was different, but that, as his hands shook, working at the stay, it wasn't desire. Not the desire those laughable men had shown, not the desire Tom . . . The thought bounced, light hitting a mirror. No, Benedict did not desire her – not like this, anyway. She was naked, now, her own body throbbing, throbbing as she had been for hours – unknown, inarticulate, confused – but Benedict had closed his eyes. Molly picked up Tom's shirt from the back of a chair and threw it round her. He opened his eyes then, a small smile.

'That's better,' he said.

'The ritual,' said Molly.

'What?'

She gathered up the silks and satins and brocade, and carried them to the fire. Benedict grabbed the rusted stockings falling from her arms, and joined her on the hearth.

'Are you sure you're allowed?' he asked. 'What if Madame Rhys wants it back?'

Molly raised an eyebrow at him, and dropped the bundle. Flames roared in greeting, drowning the white waves until they boiled. Molly laughed, giddy and drunk, suddenly, mad with joy. Benedict dropped the stockings in too, with

313

a flourish, smiling as if there – there, in smoke – went all his worries.

His fingers brushed her knuckles. Molly stiffened, but did not flinch away. His hand travelled her scars, as they had done countless times, applying poultice, bandaging her, the care not of a treasurer, but something like it. She leant against him, just an inch, her head at his arm.

When he kissed her forehead, it seemed brotherly. But then his lips lingered. Molly knew she should shove him away. But she looked up instead, a question. He was still shaking when he kissed her lips, his whole body communicating some wild terror, some wild want. Molly let him, imagining herself into his body, becoming his arms, his hands, becoming the man who wanted her. She kissed back.

The Morning After the Eve of St Agnes

The sun pricked Tom's skull like a needle in the hands of a furious seamstress. He shouldered through the market, until a man with a basket of rope bumped into him, and Tom seized the impudent bastard by the coat. The rapid French – and look of shock on the man's face – brought him up short, and he sent the chandler stumbling, relaxing his fist. He had to get back to Île de Batz. To the ship. To Devon.

'Capitaine! Capitaine!'

Tom choked on the swell of his throat, caught now by this little merchant in front of him in the maelstrom of bodies and horses and goats and boxes and baskets and onions and seaweed and potatoes and fish, a merchant who traded – what? He couldn't remember – and who had a skinny Negro laying a blanket down over the worst of the street for his master to make his mincing steps shit-free. The morning parade.

'Was last night's revel not the *most* ecstasy, sir?'

Tom found a grin, though he saw the Negro wince at it. 'The most, sir.'

'And your ward, sir!'

'My what?'

'Mademoiselle West, sir,' said the merchant, spinning a fob in the air. 'She is on everybody's lips, this morning. We did

315

not know you kept such an enchanting creature. How did she come into your possession?'

Tom said nothing.

'Come, come, sir! Madame Rhys teased us enough, last night. She is not your daughter?'

'No.'

'But she is yours?'

'Yes.'

'Then what is this mystery?' A mock gasp. 'Did you buy her from the Barbary?'

'No. I – she – her father was a friend. I promised to ...'

The fob whirled at the end of the man's fingers, glittering with sun. 'Oh, sir, we shall have to embellish this! Her father died in tragic circumstances?'

Tom's tongue was matted and furred, a dead rodent. 'The pox.'

'It will have to be the Barbaries! She is a great fortune?'

'Yes.' The word was said by someone else.

'How old?'

'Fourteen.'

'You will have the young bloods baying at your door, sir! When shall we see her again?'

'She's returning to Devon.'

'I shall call on her when I next make port in Plymouth.'

'No!' Tom grabbed at his own neck. 'I mean – she won't be returning to Devon for some time.'

A sly smile. 'She will stay here, without a protector?'

'She's going to make a stay with family in ... Spain.'

'Then I will look for her when we next have the gift of your presence.' The merchant bowed. 'Look most eagerly, I assure you, sir. You are to be complimented.'

Tom bowed, feeling some hand at the back of his head, forcing him to bend.

*

Tom took the path down to the house, trying to calm his heart, to let the sight of Benedict and Molly playing at swords with sticks in the front garden soothe him – so like little boys, both of them, for Molly was back in her usual clothes, now. There was no sign of the unplucked girl who had danced in his arms, nor the wild girl flinging her props at him. Just this child, laughing with Benedict – and then wavering, seeing Tom at the gate.

'What happened to your face?' she asked.

Tom put his hand up – felt the scratch across his cheek. 'Hell hath no fury.' He brushed the dried blood from his fingertips. 'I need to talk to you. Both.'

Benedict was flushing the colour of yew berries. 'Something amiss?'

'Inside.'

They sat at the table, Molly and Benedict looking guilty, Tom thought, as if they expected to be scolded. He poured himself a brandy. He should sit down, take her hand, stop her bolting. But he lingered by the decanter.

'What you were, last night . . . ' He stopped, studying the cut crystal.

'I should go,' said Benedict.

'No,' said Molly. Even without looking at her, Tom knew the ferocity on her face. 'What I was last night, I won't be again. Benedict knows – our game. Knows and will keep it quiet. So will I. So will you.'

That made him look around – that note of command. Made him proud. She'd learnt that from him. So, Benedict had seen her in that gown last night, and either acted shock, or divulged – what? And what had Benedict made of her, the Virgin Lady? It explained the shame on his face. And the fear.

He'd learnt fear from Tom.

The brandy surged back up his throat and Tom thumped his chest. When he spoke, it was as if his voice were escaping from some chink, some undefended crack in him: 'We can't.'

Molly stood up, fists at her sides. 'What do you mean?'

'Rhys told the town you're my ward. When we're in Roscoff, you'll have to dress as you did yesterday.'

Hail rattled down the chimney.

'Then we won't return to Roscoff.'

'Our fortune is here.'

'Our fortune is Devon.'

'A free-trader makes his transits and follows them. He doesn't sit still.'

'I won't.' Certainty in her voice – and, beneath it, a waiting sob. 'I won't wear a gown again. I won't leave the ship. I won't leave you.'

He passed to her, taking up her fists, unfolding them. 'You won't. I promise, you won't.' He caught Benedict's eye – Benedict looking at him as if he were watching something rotten unfold. 'We'll tell the crew. Tell them you're Orlando sometimes, and Molly others. They'll live with it. I'll make 'em.'

She looked up at him, nothing but trust in her face. 'Do you promise?'

He brushed a tear from her face. 'But you'll have to oblige me something.'

'Tell me what it is first.'

He laughed. 'No blank notes from you.'

'You taught me that.'

'I did.' He stroked her cheek. 'I did. You'll have to put up with men's empty words, now. You'll have to dress in a way befitting a beautiful heir—' She tried to jerk from him and he held her closer. 'There ain't no choice,' he said. 'You'll do this, unless you want to leave me.'

'No! No, I'll just live on the ship, I won't ever leave the ship!'

'You have to, little wildego. The town thinks I have a girl in my possession. If you're never seen again, it will raise too many suspicions. You have to play this part for me.'

Two Days After the Eve of St Agnes

L ilac. Cornflower. Burgundy. Silk. Satin. Damask. Pelisse. Hoops. Bonnets. A sixteen-inch waist. An eighteen-inch bust. Elbow-length gloves for the lady, in all colours. Do you suffer this rash often, mademoiselle, or do you have a reaction to one cloth over another? I can accommodate.

Molly stood on the dais in the back of the clothier's with her eyes closed, refusing the mirror, refusing the materials, refusing the girl's question, flesh crawling every time a gown was pulled and tugged and fastened around her swollen stomach. Tom was talking with the dressmaker beyond the curtain. If Tom could only see her face, he'd stop this torture, which made Molly want to cry. She was feverish with shame and confusion, for every time she was shocked into opening her eyes, there was a girl in the gilded quicksilver, a girl Hellard would have said was fuckable at six paces, but here, when she closed her eyes, there was just Molly, desperate, desperate.

Benedict watched this from the tradesman's entrance, the door ajar, burning to save her, stuck on the threshold, held fast in time. He knew this feeling. He'd been here before.

'If he dresses her in that pale green, I'll simply have to *scream* murder. It's quite wrong for her complexion.'

Benedict jumped, twisting to find Madame Rhys in the shadows of the alley. As his eyes adjusted, his fingers groped for the door and closed it softly. Gulls laughed overhead.

Madame Rhys's face was brick red and royal purple, one eye swollen shut, her upper lip puffed like cauliflower, cheekbone jutting out, as if moved across her face – as if God had sought to rearrange her.

The scratch on Tom's cheek. *Hell hath no fury.* No fury like Tom's.

'No shock? No tears of sympathy?'

'There's a code,' someone said. Himself. 'You don't cross Tom.'

A laugh that seemed to hurt. 'Revenge was never less sweet, believe me. There is nothing like losing one's face – which is all one has, when a lady moves in my circles – to prompt a little soul-searching. I came to warn you, Mr White, as you seem to dote on her. One day, he'll turn the key for ever. And, on a day soon after that, her face will look like mine.'

The conversation of men beyond the door – Tom chuckling.

'Tom would never hurt her,' whispered Benedict.

Rhys stepped into the light. 'Do you really think I'm the first woman he's done this to? Do you think I'll be the last?'

Dizziness gripped him. Benedict saw Grace between blinks, crushed on the floor by Tom's fists, her hand reaching out, as if imploring Benedict to see it. To see the truth. He remembered Molly as a child in Tom's arms those minutes after, how her toes recoiled from the pistol stuck in Tom's belt, as if the metal were hot.

'You must be the gallant, now. If she won't save herself, you must do it. Save her from him.'

Rhys almost tripped as she ran through the dark of the alley and out into the light of the harbour. Benedict watched her go, picturing Tom hurling Grace's journal into the sea, though he'd kept it all those years he pursued justice; though Dick English still lived; though Tom swore English was the killer.

Benedict sought some purchase.

It couldn't have been Tom. It wasn't possible.

But still, between blinks: Molly, suffocated by the corset, losing breath.

I die by inches.

Leaf

To INTERLEA/VE. v. a. [*inter* and *leave*]

To chequer a book by the insertion of blank leaves.

One night, in November 1859, Charles Dickens arrived at George Eliot's house in Wandsworth for dinner.

Dickens is one of the few writers who needs no introduction: we feel we know him as well as we know Shakespeare, or Jane Austen (though, in truth, we don't know either of them very well). In these lectures, I have followed the story of Tom, Molly and Grace through literary history. When I found a trace of them in Dickens' work, I looked at him more closely, and realised I should have taken heed of his words in *A Tale of Two Cities*:

> A solemn consideration, when I enter a great city by night, that every one of those darkly clustered houses encloses its own secret; that every room in every one of them encloses its own secret; that every beating heart in the hundreds of thousands of breasts there, is, in some of its imaginings, a secret to the heart nearest it!

323

I had known the benevolent avuncular figure that entertains us at Christmas, and the heroic figure that rescued fellow passengers from a train wreck, and the campaigning figure that set up a petition to secure support for victims of domestic violence.

What I didn't know was Dickens' darkly clustered heart, kept from his adoring public. In the late 1850s, Dickens left his wife and the mother of his ten children, claiming to have never loved her, and to have been tormented by her for the whole of their long marriage. When she died, she would leave all of his love letters to the nation, showing him at the very least to have had an extremely bad memory, and at the very worst to be a man who suddenly found himself in love with a teenage actress, and wanted justification for his actions. He began to deliver public readings of his own books, something looked on with suspicion as rather *common*, and to act in his own plays. Dickens gave a reading in Exeter, where he secured a new home for his parents, not too far away from the hotel where Hester Thrale had to put up after breaking her hip in her nineties – when Piozzi was dead, and Cecy had married a man who would almost kill her.

George Eliot may need more introduction. She never enjoyed Dickens' publicity or everlasting popularity – my students often start by presuming she's a man. Born Mary Ann Evans, George Eliot pioneered realism, and in her lifetime vied for the position of the nation's favourite novelist with Dickens. It was a battle of styles as much as sales. Melodrama was on the way out. Realism was in (though Eliot's love of violent scenes often made other realists shake their heads).

George Eliot wrote under a man's name for two reasons. Firstly, she was living with a married man, George Lewes, who was not married to her. Her real name was poison. Secondly, the habit of taking up a man's name as a female writer had doubled in the late nineteenth century. In this era of widow's weeds and bridal veils, George Eliot lived publicly with a married man, had no children, and changed the course of the novel. She preferred to be called Mrs Lewes, though she knew whoever did the calling was well aware she was no such thing.

On the November evening Charles Dickens visited George Eliot for dinner, he knew her secret. George Eliot was a woman, and *that* woman. He alone had figured it out. And he wanted something from her.

(Notes for a lecture on women and writing to be given at Girton College, Cambridge, on the anniversary of Virginia Woolf's lecture series, 'A Room of One's Own'.)

I Protest that A Woman's Mind
has got into Some Man's Body

1859

Mrs Lewes & Charles

There was no pleasure to be found in witnessing Mr Lewes's face at the door. It was with good reason that Jane Carlyle called him 'The Ape'. There was, though, a sparkling voraciousness in the man, which Charles had always enjoyed, along with their many conversations about acting, Greek, Goethe, blank-verse tragedies and women.

'Mr Dickens,' said Lewes, offering his hand. 'An honour, sir.'

What a juncture to speak of honour! But his own late wildness checked him, and he shook Lewes's hand happily. 'Glad to shadow out this mystery! I said to myself: If I be wrong in this, then I protest that a woman's mind has got into some man's body by mistake that ought immediately to be corrected. I must tell you, *Adam Bede* has taken its place among the actual experiences and endurances of my life.'

Lewes was still gripping his hand. 'A word, sir. Before you meet Mrs Lewes.'

Amused, Charles looked over his shoulder at the yellow brick faces of the houses, the white porticos, waiting for one to give a theatrical *Shhh*. 'Yes, sir?'

Lewes dropped Charles's hand, in order to wring his own. 'About this proposition to publish Mrs Lewes's next book in your journal. You must know, sir, that anxiety is a monstrous vulture to Mrs Lewes: easily enticed, and put off only with great effort. If she were to give you her work, she might well bankrupt her publishers, with whom tensions are already high, as the news of who George Eliot really is – with such concerns, her writing can come to a full stop.'

'A delicate hand needed at the reins?'

Lewes cleared his throat. 'I would suggest leaving off mention of serialising her next novel in *All the Year Round*. You and I can discuss it after dinner.'

'I hope I do not flatter myself when I say my journal could bring George Eliot an even vaster audience than she now commands, and one she very much deserves. I know my plan is a good one – because it is mine! You must know I am conscious that *Mr* Eliot's last book gave mine a run for its money. I gain nothing by her ascendency. I act only out of admiration, an admiration I assure you is most real, and not for personal gain. At least, not primarily.' He raised his right hand. 'And all the rest is business, just business. I promise to conduct myself with all the niceties my admiration commands. There, now. Look relieved, Mr Lewes.'

But Lewes was tugging on his ratty beard. 'I wouldn't want to raise your expectations. Mrs Lewes views serialisation as a nightmare: a cramped space in which she has no room to turn.'

Charles gave his best smile. 'Mr Lewes, you've kept me standing like a telegram clerk long enough, have you not?'

Lewes jolted. 'Of course. Though I hear you can stand for a reading for six hours or more, sir.'

Charles followed him inside, saying: 'Until my audience faints, sir, until my audience faints.'

Lewes gave a nod that managed to be jittering and gratified all at once, something Charles was used to, for people responded to his celebrity these days as if his very presence sent them jittering.

But Mrs Lewes was not jittering, and nor did she look set to faint, at ease in this charming book-lined parlour. She looked, rather, like she was sitting for a portrait, so still was her aspect and her frame. And what an aspect! Pitiably like a Pre-Raphaelite horse. And this a face to cast aside the last shreds of social respectability for!

But then the gunmetal eyes locked on him, and this woman surrounded by fussy upholstery and gleaming surfaces suddenly seemed as hard and brilliant as diamond from coal. Yes, what a woman for whom to cast aside the last shreds of respect. And what did she gather, with her piercing assessment of him? It could only be his imagination, of course, but Charles felt he read disappointment in her face, as though she were telling him, *An actress not yet twenty – what a thing for which to cast aside your reputation. And you the father of ten children, father of fiction, father of the nation.* But then her look softened, a current of sympathy, as if she too knew what a burden a wife could be.

'What a charming spot in which to write, Mr Eliot.'

A slight upturn of the lips, and he felt admitted. She gestured towards her desk: the notebook marked *Quarry*, the stand of purple ink. 'Thank you, Mr Dickens. Please, won't you have a drink before dinner?'

He settled by the fire, glancing out at the grove of stars over the neat rectangle of garden. But how much freer the flowerbeds were than Mrs Carlyle's.

'I suppose Mrs Carlyle has bothered you incessantly with advice on your new home?'

Mr Lewes fumbled the decanter, and Charles kicked himself. Of course, Jane Carlyle played hostess to Thackeray, Mrs

Martineau, Darwin, but *Mrs Lewes* would never have crossed her threshold.

He pushed on: 'Best to leave her advice, I'd say, and avoid her confidences. *Wonderful* at attracting secrets, and terrible at keeping them! You might be amused to know she is certain George Eliot – of whom she is a great admirer, as are we all – is a middle-aged man with a wife, from whom he has got those beautiful *feminine* touches, a good many children and a dog. Alas, I see no dog. She also insists you are, if not a clergyman yourself, brother or at least first cousin to a very good man of the cloth.'

Mrs Lewes looked to Mr Lewes for help, Charles thought, beginning to see the dynamic here was something like Thomas and Jane Carlyle, but reversed, for in this house it was the man midwifing the woman's hallowed genius. But she surprised him by saying lightly, 'I told you we should get a dog, George.'

Of course, Mary Ann already knew Mrs Carlyle's views, for Mrs Carlyle had written a letter of praise to her publisher. She resisted the urge to tell Mr Dickens this – to throw up into the air all of her many letters from Elizabeth Gaskell, too, to prove she existed in the world just as much as Charles Dickens – display both the parts and the sum of herself, rather than let him add it all up, with his hand in his pocket, his outstretched leg and his confidence, as he devoured the vulgar indulgences of her domesticity, devoured the whole house, this tall cake with a garnish of holly and laurel. Admirable as his capacity to maintain a courteous neutrality of eyebrow might be, she was let down by the paucity of benevolence in his face, which suggested little in his heart.

But still, he seemed to *know* her as birds know the morning, something that pierced her, for she was not a little despondent now and then to think of old friends lost or dead, and herself robbed of the power to make new ones by the world's wife and her busy tongue. Haunted by headaches, too, and always this feeling that a great procession had been sweeping by her since childhood;

that the last notes of music would die away, leaving her alone with fields and sky, while the credit for her work went to any man who dared to bear his arms on her shield, and she could not correct them. Mr Dickens had thrown up his imperious hand and called for the procession to stop; he had turned to find her at the back of the crowd.

She smiled. 'You are lately returned from touring, sir?'

That made him wince. 'Not touring, precisely, not touring. Just a little reading. Well, you know, a little acting, a little reading. Had to raise money for Jerrold's widow, of course, that's what started me. Then the Queen and the Prince came for a private show at the Gallery of Illustration. Had to decline her summons because I was already made up for the evening's farce – Her Majesty felt, I later heard, that my acting surpassed all. I was mighty glad I carried the point – a man does not wish to meet his Queen looking *too* much of an ... of a clown.'

'What a lot of energy it must require, sir.'

'One simply juggles the day's business and the night's – correct the proof in polar costume, get *Household Works* out, play in *Frozen Deep*, preside at supper, make no end of speeches, four hours sleep and rise again. As your public comes to know you, I am certain you will be similarly called upon.'

Despite years of writing with the rapidity of a printing press under the names of the men in her life as they commissioned her to cover their collapses, under her own name (or some version of it), and finally the signature George Eliot, she now heard herself say, 'Much of my time is occupied in being a wife, sir.'

A lurch. 'I'm sure. I'm sure.' She watched him pull himself back as if it were a physical effort: his shoulders high, the cords of his neck standing out, his beard twitching. 'I wish you readers such as mine. The outpouring of love from my audiences, while elsewhere in my life I suffer – though, of course, they know nothing of that. Still, their love quite unmans me.'

'A mistake,' she said, 'that ought immediately to be corrected.'

A pause, during which she heard the hitch in his throat, and then a chuckle. 'Did I say that in my letter to you too? Yes, I rather suppose I did. Yes, yes. But still, it seems there *is* something manly in performance, for though I greatly admire my ... actresses on the stage, there seems something terrible in girls standing up before drunken men who may shout anything at them. Not that such hooligans attend my readings. Why, I remember my audience in Exeter – a wonderful night. It was a prodigious cram and we turned away no end of people. But not only that; I think they were my finest audience. I don't think I have ever read, in some respects, so well, and I never beheld anything like the personal affection which they poured out upon me at the end. It was really a remarkable sight, and I shall always look back upon it with pleasure. I can see no better thing to do that is half so hopeful in itself, or half so well suited to my ... *restless* state.'

Mr Lewes sat forward, the thrust of his body a dash introducing a new subject to Charles's sentence. 'I understand you settled your parents in Exeter, sir.'

'Alphington. A charming cottage, though of course that was no guarantee my father would approve of it!'

'We spent a wonderful summer in Ilfracombe, in North Devon. Mrs Lewes wrote much there.'

'Just a review of Heinrich Riehl and one of the belles-lettres,' she said.

'Your fiction,' said Lewes. 'That was where you began to think about your fiction.'

'I was reading Riehl's *Natural History*,' she said, glancing away. 'I began to see parallels ...'

Charles waited, his heartbeat loud in his own ears from his mangled confession of his restless state.

She addressed an empty corner of the room. 'In being so

331

delightfully at liberty in Ilfracombe, I felt free to pay attention to seaweeds, to ferns, to hedgerows. To follow lanes and desire to know the Latin name for all things about me, and their relationship to the people who lived among them – it was a tendency growing in me to escape from all vagueness and inaccuracy into the daylight of distinct, vivid ideas. The reality. For painters, idyllic ploughmen are jocund when they drive their team afield; idyllic shepherds make bashful love under hawthorn bushes; idyllic villagers dance in the chequered shade and refresh themselves, not immoderately. But no one who is well acquainted with the English peasantry can pronounce them merry. I began to wish for artistic truthfulness.'

Charles felt Mr Lewes's desire to interrupt Mrs Lewes, and Mrs Lewes's decision to utterly disregard him.

'I sought fiction that avoided the transcendence of unreality, whose only merit is the precious salt of humour, but even *that* compels the author to reproduce only a character's *external* traits, and only serves in *some* degree as a corrective to the same author's frequently false psychology: his preternaturally virtuous poor children and artisans, his melodramatic boatmen and courtesans, his encouragement of the miserable fallacy that high morality and refined sentiment can grow out of harsh social relations, ignorance and want. The aristocratic dilettantism which attempts to restore the "good old times" by a sort of idyllic masquerading, and to grow feudal fidelity and veneration as we grow prize turnips, by an artificial system of culture – none of which can coexist with real knowledge of the people, a thorough study of their habits, their ideas and their motives.'

As the clock struck, Charles said mildly, 'Well, I don't know how Spencer, Carlyle, Mr Disraeli or myself can ever recover. You've quite wiped the board clean of us and our methods, Mr Eliot.'

She caught her breath. 'Oh, no,' she said. 'The public would never forgive me. For who then would entertain them?'

Lewes clasped his hands together, then released them as Charles laughed.

'Tell me then, Mrs Lewes, what can we expect next from Mr Eliot?'

She squirmed, tried not to. 'Rivers. I have been thinking greatly about rivers.'

Charles waited, but it seemed she was swallowing her admissions. 'I will have to visit Ilfracombe,' he said. 'Maybe I'll be so inspired. I'll tell you, though, of a tale of Devon that inspired me. Smugglers. A girl known as Molly West, bound by society to ignore her nature; and her master, Captain Tom West, corrupted by his nature, though loved by society. The girl dressed as a boy and took on a man's name, it is said.'

She shared a smile with him. 'All the world's a stage.'

'And each must play her part. It gave me an idea for a very odd story, with a wild, picaresque fancy in it – for it was said Tom West murdered the girl's mother and married the girl, once she'd cast off her boyish disguise. "The Bride's Chamber", I called it. About a wife-murderer, narrated by the ghost of the murderer himself. The murderer had been guardian of the girl he would marry since she was ten, and formed her in fear of him. Reduced her to a weak, credulous, incapable, helpless nothing, and then willed her to death. But she is revenged by her young lover, and the murderer hanged. Every year, he is cursed to recount the story of her death to whoever occupies the bride's chamber, now a travelling inn.' He turned to Mr Lewes. 'Don't you wish sometimes you had been born in the days of ogres and dragon-guarded castles? Nothing would suit me half so well as climbing after a princess to the heights of a great mountain, sword in hand, and either winning her or being killed.' He puffed his cheeks. '*There's* a state of mind for you.' A shrug. 'I am aging, I suppose.'

'Did you discover why Molly West lived as a boy?'

'I was told that all evidence of her has long since washed out with the tide, and I did not seek to follow it. I'm afraid I am destined to disappoint you.'

'If Charles Dickens could give us psychological character, their conceptions of life and their emotions, with the same truth as their idiom and manner, your books would be the greatest contribution art has ever made to the awakening of social sympathies.'

'From the very start of my career, I have written to illuminate tales of distress and misery, of broken fortune and ruined hope, of unrelieved wretchedness and successful knavery.' He was gripping the arms of his chair. 'I have rallied against factory conditions and slum housing, I have campaigned for public health, I have housed terrorised women, I have fought for education, employment and children forfeited to the workhouse.' His voice betrayed a rising note. 'I have not hidden away my talents and withdrawn them from the world.'

Lewes stood up, but made no further movement.

She tilted her head. 'Perhaps, if you had followed Molly West down the tide, you might have discovered what it is to have a man's force of genius in you, and yet to suffer the slavery of being a girl. What it is to have a woman's force of genius in you, and yet to *get into the body of some man* and need to be *corrected*.' Mr Dickens stiffened, but she ploughed on: 'There is nothing I want more than for my writing to rouse the imagination of men and women to a vision of human claims. And there is nothing I want less than to be a silly woman novelist. Neither do I wish to be a suffering angel or an uncomfortable goddess forever carrying musical instruments about with me. Perhaps your Molly lived as a boy for similar reasons. We don't ask what a woman does, Mr Dickens. We ask whom she belongs to.'

A quick sniff, like a hound at hunt. 'And do you belong to your publishers, Mrs Lewes? You whose writing has got into the very heart of me – might you join in a partnership with the *other* writer of Queen Victoria's reign?'

334

She smiled at him. Mrs Lewes, it was now. 'I am a heathen, sir, and an outlaw. I am George Eliot, and I cannot give you my work. But I am *also* Mrs Lewes, and dinner is ready, if you would be quite happy to go through now, my dear sir?'

BOOK FIVE

1714–15

WHO AM I TO YOU,

AND WHAT ARE YOU TO ME?

Hunter's Moon

A column of steaming men and steaming horses, velvet finery and equally fine words, passed through Luscombe Cross, Harnaford – where a gentleman joined them from the ancient mansion by the river, and another from Luscombe House, and more from Great Englebourne and Hazard and East and West Leigh. Hawthorns popped red, a bounty that promised, according to custom, a hard winter. The gentlemen now saw the brown-grey fur of a red stag flash through the woodland, but it was gone before any man could remember the hunter's moon and think of bringing it down. Blaming each other with good cheer, they followed the pull of their hawks over Morleigh Mount, through Storridge Wood, Hazel Wood, to Blackdown Rings.

The earthworks had lasted, it was said, since the age of hut circles on Dartmoor, and, in centuries before this one, the great plateau had seen forts turn into castles. Now, the moat was empty but for puddles, its banks home to sessile oaks cowed by the wind, and twisted silver birch clinging to the exposed hill like seaweed streaming from rocks in the tide. Dry-stone walling ruptured from the banks, veined grey and white, and thick with long blonde grass, looking – to Tom, on horseback – like the corpses of women pushed up from their graves, marbled but preserved. He shrugged the image off, putting it down to the talk of All Hallows' Tide. He shrugged off, as well, the old blood of bronzing ferns, snapping a yellow flower from matted gorse as he urged the animal to trot on.

Here, hungry dormice and fieldfares tamed the hawthorns, which were draped in wool and crusted with pale contusions, their blaze of fruits snuffed by the winds so high above Aune Valley. Tom looked over the hedgerows glowing saffron and tangerine, the garnet bracken, to the silver brushes of wintering trees falling away below, past the close-packed copper and cardinal clusters, all the way south to the horizon, where sun minted the ocean. Behind him, Hay Tor waited, but he did not give the moor his face.

The hawk was flying too low, too fast, as if possessed by a manic desire to seize the very earth in its beak and shake it until limp. It would surely crash, surely snap and crumple. Molly waited for the thump and crunch, sitting astride her horse, which twitched, too, in the sight of death – and then the hawk soared upwards, reeling towards the treeline.

'Your bird ain't got the docity, Mayor,' said Tom, holding his reins too tightly, Molly thought. All this waiting.

A hard day's riding, Molly and Benedict following in Tom's stretching shadow, jostled by the families and staff of the Totnes Lord and Lady Mayoress, Dartmouth's Collector Blackoller and the Justice; by the Lord of Dartmouth Castle and the squires who joined them for today's sport, men who this month would be collecting rent and tithes, or, if the harvest was poor and the farmers and labourers had empty pockets, giving their tenants over to the poor rate. Since coming to port, Tom had visited the unluckiest of his venturers, and made sure they had enough money to keep their footing – money that would end up in these gentlemen's coffers. He'd delivered new shoes on St Crispin's Day, and tea leaves and cakes on Sundays. In days gone past, Tom had joined bitter cottagers in cursing the names of many a landowner, but now, three years after being anointed King of the Bean, he rode with them.

What would his people say, Molly wondered, if they could see Tom now, this confusion of signals, the slender sword of a gentleman, the pistols of a gamester, his coat, funereal black, embroidered with wedding silver, but still no wig on his head? She'd heard a butcher boy whisper, just last week, *When they hang Tom West, it will be with a rope of silk.* Still, others would say, *Hasn't Tom West endowed alms houses with bread, and given four hundred pounds annually to poor artificers, and another four hundred to poor maidens, so they might have a dowry, and given coats to all the boys at Kingsbridge Grammar?*

'I've promised Richard English we shall bring him a token of today's sport,' said Blackoller.

'I'm sure he took that kindly,' said the Justice.

Tom's smile struck Benedict as gored. As they'd set out that morning, it became clear Tom was occupying a place in the hawking once taken by Dick English, who still lay most days abed. His spine, they said, knuckled red from his back. It was not clear who shared these naked particulars of Dick English, only that every inch of him remained up for sale, in exchange for Tom's mirth, Tom's blessing, Tom's business.

Benedict looked to Molly, glorious in green and yellow velvets, nearing eighteen and dressed as a young courtier – dressed as Orlando.

Molly returned his look, she thought, of affection. She steered her horse from the line, letting it feed on the grass. Benedict followed. Molly pointed his attention to the slender mushrooms nosing from the earth.

'Hungry?' she asked.

'Poisonous,' he said.

'Like you're the expert,' she laughed, clicking her horse on across the clearing, over leaves like coins pouring from a cut purse, the cold wind between her shoulder blades, the sun a reprieve on her cheek. They entered the moat, just the two of them, a shrunken valley hidden by this colonnade of birch and stunted oak, bare silver and purple branches interlacing overhead. Molly studied the back of Benedict's head, the stripe of his bare neck, willing for him to turn, to see her – as what? As he desired to see her – however that was.

An uncomfortable truth, how very much she was a mirror now, attempting to show the man who studied her the thing he desired. She did not quite think herself a woman in Benedict's company, for when she raised her skirts for him, he lost all his desire. He liked her halfway, in-between, a girl in petticoats and shirts. He liked her ... She caught on the idea. Did he? He loved her, he had said more than once since the night of the masquerade. But, oftener and oftener, he looked upon her with dread, and he had never brought his penis between her legs, not even to brush or rub against her there. Perhaps it was fear of Tom, fear of discovery. He brought himself to finish with a cold spurt over her ribs or breasts, some finish that did not seem ever, to Molly, to be truly released. And she herself knew only a kind of rising wave, which never crashed, was never brought to burst. It surged in her sometimes in her sleep, so that she'd wake on its tide, as she had that morning, dreaming, just briefly, of kissing Tom's bottom lip.

'We shall become lost in here and they will never find us,' said Benedict.

'Until bluebells fill the moat,' said Molly, letting go of her reins.

'Bluebells? Do they make a show here?'

'Yes,' said Molly, suddenly rocked. These last few years she had chosen selves with all the fierceness of seizing metal from a fire, put them on and off as fast as costume changes at the theatre. Now, the backcloth fell.

'I didn't know you'd been up here in spring,' said Benedict.

Molly fixed on the purple gulley, remembering it flooded with flowers, remembering the richness of garlic, and searching, searching her memory, for some walk with Tom, his boots overgrown with crisp petals, but he had no place here. Instead, a woman urged her through the bluebells, which rose to her chin, so young, so small, before she left the beaten paths of Bantham for Tom's bounds – before she knew herself as anything other than the twin of the woman standing over her, the woman clapping her progress. Mama. Resplendent. Her mother, resplendent, yes, something about her resplendent, as if the whole world ought really to applaud her, ought to be fascinated by her, as Molly was fascinated by her, as hungry for her as Molly was, reaching after her hand – and falling.

Her mother lifting her from the ground and brushing black stains from Molly's pinny, telling her, *I'm here. I'm here.*

'Molly? Are you crying?'

All Hallows' Tide

The harvest moon dripped blood over Burgh Island, and spirits walked abroad. The full moon demanded ritual, demanded people shed their hair, to make themselves anew. Remembering mothers or grandmothers giving them trims on a full moon as a matter of clockwork, the men had taken to cutting Molly's hair each month – short enough to be a man's, long enough to curl like a woman's beneath a cap or bonnet –and then their own, throwing tangled and matted locks on to the deck with her golden rings. For Prell and Laskey, Jarvis and van Meijer, this ritual was in deference to Tom. For Pascal, it was an eccentricity, accepted with a shrug. All the more for Kingston, who, when Tom had got through with his announcement, simply passed a salutary gaze to Molly, as if to say, *Neatly done*. For Nathan, the ritual was completed with a smile, a secret tucked into the corner of his mouth, that sometimes flowed through him, prompting him to put his arm around Molly's shoulders and squeeze. The crew swapped the knife between them, now, at the Pilchard Inn, laughing as they did that perhaps the dead would rise and wear their tresses as a dreadful wig – but it was laughter edged with fear, for, on this last night of October, the middle day of All Hallows' Tide, the dead held a lot more weight.

Molly took a fist of Tom's hair and drove the knife through his black curls, flecked silver now.

Tom tipped back in his chair, winking up at her. He was bloodshot; he'd been drinking since first light, as if trying to purge some ill humour from his gut. 'My thanks, Delilah.'

Molly blew into his eyes, scattering the fallen hairs. He had spoken quietly, she noted, glancing about the packed inn. Only the crew knew her breeches were empty. Molly imagined the villagers' reactions, wondering whether Charlie Savage would be witty or kind or both. Or neither. Secrets were never safe, no matter how she strapped her chest and deepened her voice.

'What spell shall we cast?' asked van Meijer, sweeping all the hair together like a pile of sodden leaves – for the rain had caught them – before the fire.

'Your witches are nothing to those of my country,' said Pascal. 'Your witches burn too quickly.'

'Do not make jokes about witchcraft tonight,' said Kingston.

'Don't want no jokes about your mother, eh?' said Jarvis, elbowing Kingston.

'Who will try their luck?' said Benedict, setting a stick over a beam. An apple dangled on a thread from one end; from the other, a lit candle stub.

'Mr Savage,' called Molly, 'you're a lucky man.'

Charles bowed. 'I am flattered you think so, young sir.'

'Care to keep my good opinion?'

Benedict sent the stick spinning.

'How might I do that?'

'Take a bite while saving your wig from catching alight,' said Molly.

Tom clapped, and that seemed to seal it, for Charles Savage rose. Then Charles winked at Molly, plucked his wig from his head and threw it into the cuttings.

'That's cheating,' said Molly.

'The good opinion of Tom West's heir is worth too much to risk on honesty,' said Charles.

'You've a prettier tongue every day, Charlie boy,' said Tom.

'Sir, flattery will get you no more than three inches o'er the knee.'

The room laughed. Tom didn't.

The crew took turns lunging for the apple with their teeth, Kingston and Pascal getting chunks, Laskey and van Meijer smeared only with candle grease. Still, the apple clung to its string like a tooth from a dead nerve.

'Your turn,' said Charles to Molly, across the room.

Molly had remained behind Tom's chair. She reached down now, pulled Tom's pistol from his belt – primed, as it always was – raised, and fired.

The villagers ducked, but the crew didn't, knowing she was a better shot than all of them. The apple dropped into Benedict's waiting hands.

As the clap of powder subsided, Charles brushed himself down, saying, 'That's cheating.' He locked eyes with her. She'd never fully appreciated his eyes before – how alive with intelligence. Nor had she seen him without a wig. He had wild curls, somewhere between rust and iron. He looked like he'd be a lot of fun, if you got him away from a counting office.

She said, 'I hope I've earnt your good opinion, sir.'

'I'd back you in a bet.'

'Even if you can't hear a damn,' said Tom, rubbing his ear.

Molly laughed. 'If you condemn my docity, Tom, you only have yourself to blame.'

Tom's mouth was suddenly as dry as chalk. The day's whisky – which for twelve hours had refused to have any effect on him – now bled him like the moon. Spirits walked abroad tonight, and here, in this girl – now gaily begging Nathan for the last of the roast nuts, as if she were ignorant of devils – here, in this girl, was a spirit come to haunt him. Tom reached for the whisky. He must not dream.

The landlord gave Tom use of the attic, and Molly climbed to bed once the villagers had stumbled home and the crew passed out. In the parlour, Benedict fed a last log to the fire, hoping to lull Tom deeper into sleep as he slipped by him.

Tom grabbed his arm. 'The devil . . . '

Benedict shook free, pink in the face, and tiptoed upstairs. Molly had left the door open – an invitation, or the brazen assurance of a girl who knows herself protected? The one time a crewman tried to enter her room on Île de Batz without her desire, Molly cold-cocked him with a pistol, and then had the satisfaction of watching Tom drag him by the throat from the house. It was Shaun, and Shaun had never been seen since.

Tom didn't know Benedict visited Molly at night when Tom and the rest of the crew were at the palais de putain in Roscoff. Benedict and Molly only loved each other in France, for on the ship Molly shared Tom's cabin. But tonight, maybe tonight they could stake a claim to Devon. He nudged the door open, waiting for her smile. Molly sat up from the bed of sacking, holding her shirt around her. Her breeches lay abandoned in the corner of the room. A single candle cast wayward shadows. Benedict searched for her naked legs under the blankets.

'Where's Tom?' she said.

'He won't know I'm up here.'

'He should, though.'

Benedict closed the door. He shrugged from his coat and lay it over Molly, sitting down beside her. Molly moved so he could wriggle under the blankets. 'You know he'd never be happy, you letting a man . . . '

'Letting you what?'

Benedict looked for mischief in her face, but there was none. 'Love you.'

Molly kissed him, breathing in fire smoke, rain, need. She lingered there, safe. 'He'd be happy if it were you.'

'We've talked on this. He'd kill me.'

'Don't say that.'

She looked like she was about to get up, revealing her legs, and Benedict grabbed her arm. 'Please. Trust me.'

The smile returned, just. 'I've trusted you my whole life.'

'Th-then –' Benedict swallowed the stammer that always seemed to interrupt him with her – 'you'll stay with me, and accept a gift.'

'What gift?'

He pulled the apple from his pocket.

'Ha.' Molly took it, glossing it between her fingers. 'You didn't steal this, now, did you?'

'Not me.'

Molly leant on his shoulder. 'Tell you what, then – I'll share it with you.'

Benedict looked about the attic. 'Shame there's no mirror in here.'

'What do we need a mirror for?'

'On All Hallows' Eve, if a girl eats an apple before a mirror at midnight, her future husband will appear in the mirror behind her, and take a bite.'

She looked down at the apple. 'Benedict.'

'Yes?'

'You know I ain't ever going to marry, don't you?'

The patter of mice filled his silence. 'Because of Tom?'

'Because I can't be any man's wife. Or any woman's husband.'

'You don't know yourself.'

The smile was different now. 'I suppose you know me, though?'

'I'd give everything for you. Risk everything. I already have.'

'Risk Tom's wrath, you mean?'

'Yes.'

'For me?'

'Yes.'

Molly turned the apple. 'You sure you ain't risking his wrath in the hope of incurring it?'

'You don't think I want you for the reasons I say?'

She said nothing.

'Tell me, then,' said Benedict. 'Tell me what you risk it for, if not for love. Tell me this isn't because you want some way to defy him, a first step to freedom—' Benedict yelped when she grabbed his chin.

'*I am free.* I am loved. Because of him. And I won't let any man bring him down, nor any woman. Not you. Not Rhys. Not English. Not lies, not myths, not rumours. And, if you persist with this, Benedict White, I won't be trading anything with you.'

Tom stood on the ragged edge of Burgh Island, the tide creeping back to him, his pistol at his side. A woman, pregnant with the moon, walked down the beach towards him, ready to deliver her vengeance. The pistol shook his hand.

Guy Fawkes' Day

'Pray remember Dick English!'
  'Penny for the Dick!'
  'Please to remember the bonfire!'
Knowing himself in the cool way a man who contends with constant pain must, Richard gave thanks to the whisky he'd drunk, and to the special saddle his man had made to keep him strapped to his horse, for it stiffened his spine in the face of this. The contraption had allowed him to ride from Kingswear, over the mercilessly exposed Scabbacombe Head, to Sharkham Point – where, below, great seine nets closed around hake and cod, and drift nets picked off pilchard, and, further out, the *Venture* lay at anchor in the deep – to clamber down to Brixham Quay, where all of Devon knew Tom West was to set him ablaze at sun down.

And there he burnt. The black creek that stretched a half-mile inland shuttered by wharves and jostling rowboats glittered with the flames. The pyre had been raised at the water's head, and folk from Brixham Quay and Higher Brixham, from Hillhead and Churston, even from Paignton and Totnes – and, yes, Richard's neighbours from Dartmouth – showed themselves to be riotous, skipjacks of no faith, no repute and no credit, neither fearing God nor caring for man. And certainly not caring for him. The straw man writhing atop the bonfire wore a Revenue jacket, and his straw hand was bound by wire to a fine walking cane.

Tom West sat on a cheap throne, built from ship timber and sinking in the mud. His people cavorted and clapped, cheered frays and commotion, gulped French brandy and feasted on cured pilchard from hogsheads. It was not simply spite that made Tom attend this Guy Fawkes celebration over others, Richard guessed. It was Brixham itself, for it was here that King William, Prince of Orange, landed when Richard and Tom were both young men. It was a high spring tide, Richard remembered, and two days after a new moon; William had all of his troops ashore within a few hours. A Brixham man, Mr Varwell, waded into the water and helped carry the future King of England to dry land. The same man shared a cup of wine with Tom West now, and, though there were not then enough free printing presses in the country to write up the King's arrival in Exeter, tonight a cheap poet sat by the fire, writing up another ballad of Tom West, which would be copied, reproduced and allowed to litter the hedgerows.

They gave Captain Richard English to the flames, and sang the arrival of a new king. No one turned to consider the figure on the horse at the edge of their lewdness. Richard wore a hooded cloak, but imagined, if he cast it off – cast it right on to the fire – they would still not look up. For they were in Tom West's thrall.

A pistol itched at Richard's hand. November was the suicidal month. Great winds prompted ancient Saxons to lay up their keels and keep to shore. Droves of cattle all over Europe would now be slaughtered and salted for winter use. Winter meant death. The English disease came to men in November, until they took a pistol to the skull and joined the dead earth.

Tonight, Richard planned to give Tom West the English disease, a thought that made him laugh, and not mind he only shared jokes with himself these days – all days, for he had never found a place in this world. He'd shoot Tom West dead in his throne, and Tom would lose the place he'd won with such gratuity.

Richard eased the weapon free. A fiddler changed his tune, and the fire painted two men in each other's clutches, shaking Richard's fixity. There was no end to the grossness at play. The men danced together like lovers with no audience, one about thirty, the other not yet twenty, it seemed, and very narrow in the body. The light played over the boy's face. Richard stiffened. Grace Tucker's orphan and Tom West's borrowed son, when Richard himself had never been blessed by a child. He stroked the trigger.

In the heat of the bonfire, Nathan twisted Molly under his arm, and then held him close – he still struggled to think of Molly as a girl. He pulled the pretty thing's curls, rueful about the shudder that went through him when Molly nudged him in the side.

'You are a troubling thing,' he murmured.

'I don't mean to be.'

'No, I don't suppose you do. It's we who are troubled.'

'We?'

'Aye,' he said, looking over Molly's head to Tom, and then Benedict, who glowered at him. 'We.'

'What trouble do I represent to you?'

'Only a temptation.'

'Because I'm a girl?'

He wiped whisky from his stubble. 'Aye.'

'Because you can make love to me nice and pretty, and the crew will reckon it's because you're lonely for a woman.'

Words fled from Nathan. He gripped Molly tighter.

'But really it's because I look like a boy, and making love to me nice and pretty, and me obliging, assuages your loneliness.'

'And here was me thinking it was just carpentry I was showing you.'

'I know a fellow player.'

'That's what you're doing?' he asked. 'Acting?'

'Yes.'

'Which part?'

The fire's warp and weft doused Nathan in darkness. There was only Molly's voice: 'I don't know any more.'

'Which part is it that has Benedict looking on like a lost lamb?'

'He doesn't approve of tonight's entertainment.'

Nathan glanced up at Dick English's buckled face, charred and caving. 'He can't have any love for the Revenue.'

'He doesn't like me cheering on such a display. He thinks it shows a lack of moral character. A lack of *womanly charity*. Cruelty, I suppose.'

'But English ... Well, your mother ... '

'Yes.'

'Then ain't his humiliation your right?'

Molly said nothing.

'You don't want justice?'

'I don't call this justice.'

'What do you call it, then?'

He felt Molly look beyond him to the destruction. 'Small.'

He couldn't tell if she meant this humiliation was too small for justice, or whether she felt something like pity for the man who murdered her mother. She did know forgiveness, whatever Benedict thought of her womanly charity. After all, Molly had immediately shrugged off Tom's drunken, sudden temper the other night – a frequent occurrence, these days – which left her with a black eye when Tom swiped the air with his fist and caught her instead. It seemed to Nathan that the man left most unmoored by Orlando's transformation into Molly was Tom himself, who muttered, these days, deep in his cups, how very much she looked like her mother.

'So, do you love the young swain?' asked Nathan.

'Benedict?'

'Aye.'

'It is hard to love him,' said Molly, 'when he does not know me. Somehow – he refuses to know me.'

Nathan nodded. 'Then do him a favour, and cut him free. Or he'll end up like Shaun.'

Benedict felt Nathan's glance on him, and slunk away from the fire. The sudden chill of the night air splashed his face, shocking him awake. He squeezed through the men hanging about the brandy, and accepted a cup. He didn't want to be awake. If he was awake, the inertia of the last three years was real. The cowardice, that he'd watched Molly lull and soothe Tom, as something inside Tom rattled against its cage – watched, and did nothing. That he waited to become the hero, and never did.

Richard charted the bullet's course. It would strike the son between the shoulder blades, explode his chest, before piercing the Gomorrhean's stomach. Then what? He'd let Tom experience the full blow of grief before he shot him, too. Richard wondered if he'd have time to load once more and kill himself, or whether his neighbours might do the job for him.

His horse shuddered. Some idiot blundering into him. A thick-mouthed apology, and then the boy peered up, and his eyes shone so wide Richard could pick out their blue. Tom's spotsman, the young lad who always looked guilty.

Richard sneered. 'You thought me up in smoke, perhaps?'

A hasty step back to the pyre. 'It wasn't our idea.'

'I burn and yet I live. I suppose that makes me a witch. I must have done something to deserve your hate, though I cannot think what.'

A whisper: 'You murdered Mrs Tucker. You will not deny that.'

Richard flinched. Grabbed the reins. 'I will.' He pulled the horse, and himself, away from the boy's pleading stare.

A crowd had gathered on his drive. Richard reined in his horse, finding tenant farmers among them, the apothecary, his surgeon, and his mother, wife and sister, all in dinner clothes. The manor glowered at them, smoke pouring from the kitchens. The dining bell rang and rang. Richard's father and brothers, along with a handful of men, were running from one door to the other, trying to find a way in, but at each attempt were driven back by a wall of flame.

Richard's knee jerked when someone touched his leg. He looked down.

An unknown man with a vulgar aspect to him, but he said, politely enough, 'Captain English, as was?'

'Yes, sir?'

'Tom West instructed me to tell you – stay down. You have so much more to lose.'

Richard wanted to snap back, but the bell was bouncing about his skull, and the man disappeared into the gawpers and sightseers. Richard was still immobile when his father shouldered through his wife and mother and seized Richard by the jacket, hauling so hard all his tethers snapped, the saddle and its ties splitting apart. Richard landed in the dirt, and couldn't scramble away when his father's boot came down on him.

'You brought this on us!' his father shouted. 'How many times were you warned not to invite that devil into our house?'

'You've made a deal with every devil going! You and your back rooms and blind eyes—'

His father dragged him up with one hand and slapped

him with the other. Then whispered close, 'I've employed a devil or two, it's true, but I've never been fool enough to let one own me.'

He released his hold, and Richard flopped back into the mud. He lay and watched the fire play with the roses his mother had planted over the south wall. He could hear his wife crying. Nobody moved to help him find his feet.

St Nicholas's Day

I

Hedgerows keep secrets.

This was Benedict's prayer as he gained ground over Dartmouth. Just as the towering hedgerows blocked the winter sun, leaving rain to pool in mud liable to swallow Benedict's shoes whole, let them also keep any farmer from seeing him climb to the home of Richard English. The lane cut a jagged suture across the hillside, so that sometimes Benedict looked over his shoulder and saw the waiting storm chase the East Indiamen and Newfoundland fishing vessels across the harbour, and sometimes he was buried in the leaking hedge-banks. The fear that it would not be enough – that winds had bent the short oaks, and left the branches bare – kept the pulse in Benedict's neck twitching. He scoured the silver-green lichen shivering among the blood-red hawthorn, the tangle of yellow gorse and ivy, the blue-black berries the colour of Madame Rhys's face. Benedict jumped as a robin crashed from the browning ferns.

It had taken Benedict a month after the burning of the Guy to find an excuse and leave Tom and Molly's side, to follow English's word: *will*. I will deny it. Why? Because English wouldn't confess, or because it wasn't him? Benedict had prayed for guidance, and that's where Tom believed him to be now: praying in church for St Nicholas. Benedict remembered the medal Molly stole in Roscoff. *Pray for us.* What frightened him the most was telling Molly, and her questions, and his answers – that he'd watched Tom beat her mother, and never said a word. *Do you really think I'm the first woman he's done this to? Do you think I'll be the last?* The berries were the colour of the bruise on Molly's cheek, too, only now faded.

Benedict found a man too old for labour digging in the walled garden. When he asked where he might find Richard English, the man stabbed the earth with the shovel.

'Chapel. Beyond the puzzle.'

Benedict picked up a shovel himself, swinging it over his shoulder as he cut through blank vegetable patches to a garden door with hinges that announced his presence to the terrace of yews beyond. But there was no one there.

The manor would have been one of the grandest he had ever seen, were it not reduced to charred bones, the smell of which coated Benedict's tongue.

Benedict followed the ornamental canal, kept high by run-off from the waterlogged hillside – he imagined it emptied by the efforts of staff to put out the fire – to the puzzle. A sad maze, drawing loops around an empty loveseat beneath an oak, its turns blurred by long unkempt grasses. Benedict drew a line through it from west to east.

The door to the chapel stood open.

The traceried window cast a repeating shadow over Richard English's bent back in the front pew.

Benedict stepped inside.

The shadows slid from Richard as he turned, and swallowed. Then a look of exhausted amusement lit his face. 'The last boy came to shoot me. Now, you come to bludgeon me.'

358

Benedict stared at his hands, wrapped around the shovel. He lowered it to the flagstones so quietly, the metal and stone only whispered.

'My name is Benedict White. I am Tom West's spotsman.'

The smile stretched on one side of Richard's face, tugging his mouth, arching an eyebrow. 'And what have you spotted, Benedict White?'

The chapel was small, built for a family, and it only took Benedict a few steps to draw equal to English. He tried to keep his gaze from the man's legs. There was a blanket over his lap. Fear and revulsion dropped in Benedict's stomach: what was underneath?

Richard twitched the cloth. 'Would you like a peek?'

Benedict said, in a strangled voice, 'The Lord restores those who are penitent.'

Richard pulled on the thread: 'That they may hereafter live a godly, righteous and sober life. You're quite right, sir – it must have been all my drunken carousing that lost me the power of my legs. I sit soberly and await restoration.'

'God gives every man an armour of light.'

This said with a wobbling persistence that caught Richard – perhaps this boy wasn't lapsed in faith, merely in discourse. He said carefully, 'If we have the grace, yes.'

Benedict blanched, retreating to the pew across the nave. His foot caught on a hassock, which had been left on the floor. Picking the cushion up – it was damp; Benedict glanced up to the eaves, which must be leaking – he intended to put it aside, but instead played with the frayed edges. 'Do you remember me, sir?'

'Should I?'

A pattern had been pricked in the hassock by the mother or wife. It certainly wouldn't have been Richard's father, though the prayer inscribed in careful punctures was 'The Father's Prayer'. Benedict searched for his own words.

359

A sigh. 'You are the impudent boy that accosted me by the bonfire.'

'That's all you know of me?'

'Do you want to be known?'

It was said gently. Benedict looked up, finding a softness on Richard's face.

'Then I know you, sir. You were educated by the mercy of monks. Your father dreamt you would be a clerk for the Church. You were corrupted by Tom West when you were but a child.'

'How?'

'It's my job to know.'

'And that's all?'

'Pray, do tell if my records fail me.'

'We met. On the night of the Great Storm.'

Richard linked his hands. 'You were on the tidal road?'

'Yes, sir. I watched my friends die at the hands of the Revenue. And then I followed Tom to Grace Tucker's cottage.'

Pigeons shuffled in the shadows. 'I met you at the door?'

Benedict nodded, could not trust his voice.

'Then it was you, with Tom and Hellard, who left me to burn to death. That is, the *first* time your merry gang attempted to burn me to death.'

A whisper: 'I followed Tom's orders.'

'I see the benevolence of the Church in your youth did nothing to instil you with the fear of God.'

'That's not true.' There were tears in his eyes.

Richard released the breath jostling in his chest. 'What have you come here for, Mr White?'

'I need to know.'

Richard looked to the windows, where the path of a buzzard in the sky was bisected by the crumbling stonework. 'I do not know rest myself, but if I can aid you in finding it, I shall. Though, I should warn you, sir – I do not think even the most merciful of priests would forgive you for standing idle as a woman was slaughtered, and then allowing her son to idolise the butcher.'

Benedict squeezed the hassock. 'You believe ... ' The Father's Prayer: *sweet innocent thou pledge of love, may Heaven now spare thy life, protect though then of God above, the babe and much loved wife.*

'I believe Tom West is the devil.'

'That's what he says of you.'

Richard flung the blanket from his lap, revealing trousers that hung from wasted muscle and bone. 'Tell me what else the great Tom West has to say of me.'

Benedict bent into the nave and saved the silk velvet from a furrow of water. The cloth was claret, decorated with white roses. Just the size to swaddle a baby. Benedict looked from it to the hassock. He imagined Richard's mother trailing him to the chapel, tucking his christening blanket over his knees and the Father's Prayer beneath his feet. A mother's love. 'He says you murdered Grace.'

Richard gripped the pew and rose by an inch or two before crashing back down. He heaved a breath. 'I will not answer for *his* crimes. Yes, I compelled the foolish girl to help me capture Tom. Yes, I promised to take her child if she did not. Yes, I knew that, if Tom discovered the truth, he would kill her. But *I* didn't make her love a monster, and *I* didn't make Tom a murderer. He was that already.'

'Hellard said you fired at Tom and Grace stood in the way. You've already proven you did not care for her safety.'

Richard snorted. 'And how is Hellard, these days? Strange, I've not seen him up and about lately.'

Benedict traced the flowers. *Roses round the door mean you love your mother more.* Molly said that. He was only half in the chapel. The other half of him was stuck in time.

361

'When I entered the parlour,' said Richard, 'the girl was black and bloody, and Tom could hardly catch his breath. I was going to shoot him, but my powder was wet. Don't you think I would have fired on sight, if I could? That's when Hellard struck me from behind. When I awoke, she lay dead beside me. I tried to drag her body from the cottage, but the flames were too great. I left her there. And that is the sum of my heroics.'

The flowers danced in and out of Benedict's vision.

It wasn't Hellard. *I'd love to take the credit, but, sadly, that credit belongs to someone else ...*

And it wasn't Dick.

'You surely knew,' said Richard, softly. 'You must have seen him beat her before I arrived.'

'I saw ... ' What had he seen? What had he seen, all these years, and been too blinded by fear and devotion to name? 'She cannot stay with him. She's in danger every minute she is with him.'

Richard leant across the nave, gripping Benedict's arm. 'She's already dead, son.'

Benedict sat up. He pushed the blanket into Richard's hands. 'No, she isn't. She didn't die in the fire. Tom took her. She loves him. She believes she can trust him.'

Urgently, now: 'Of whom do you speak?'

'Molly Tucker. You know her as Orlando. Tom West's powder monkey.'

Colour rushed to Richard's face. He dug a hand into his pocket and squeezed the coin his wife had given him, touching for the evil. Squeezed so hard, it pricked his palm. 'He disguises her as that bastard boy? The blasphemous wretch.' Richard slammed his fist into the pew. He turned from Benedict, a long moment. 'You must tell me, Benedict, how he has treated her.'

Benedict thought of the bruise on her face. 'He loved her, when she looked like a boy. Now, she looks more and more like Grace . . .'

Richard hauled himself into the nave, falling to his knees at Benedict's feet. He clamped Benedict by the shoulders. 'You must listen to me, son. You must tell the girl the truth. You must save her from him, and bring her to me.'

'Tell her?'

'You *must*, it is the only way she will break from his influence. You must clear her eyes. *You* can save her, Benedict. Only you.' Richard's breath was quickening. 'You must sign a confession, witnessing all you have seen. You must do it now.'

'I cannot . . . I have to see Molly, first. I must find out what she wants . . .'

Richard forced Benedict's hands together in prayer between his. 'Don't you see, Benedict, she can't know what she wants? You must sign a confession, now, and bring her to me. You are the Lord's instrument. You must save her. Before it is too late.'

Benedict shook himself free, stumbled to his feet. 'I cannot be your witness against Tom – not now. Let me talk to her, and then . . . then I'll bring her to you, and sign whatever you wish. If you promise we'll both go free. You'll let me take her away.'

Richard seized Benedict's arm, still on his knees. 'You can take her anywhere you see fit. The girl will be yours to keep safe. We did not save the mother, you and I. We can save the daughter. God be praised.'

363

II

It had always been too small for him: the cluster of cottages, the slanted square, Hope Cove at low tide, sand charcoaled with the mirror image of trees. Fishermen's boats havered between the shelter of the cove and open water, laziness and peace netting everyone on this first Sunday of Advent. Tom pretended not to notice the stare of children who should have been weaving crab pots, recalling Hellard's refusal to learn the same art. He shrugged that off, along with the mothers hiding their daughters, or pushing them forward. One lass came with a pie, which Molly accepted, steam curling from her mouth as they squeezed down the small lane fronting Tom's mother's house, a line of five cob cottages, and escaped to the hillside, climbing once more.

Tom said, 'I remember telling my mother I was after adventure. She wept. She thought all adventure was chance, and I'd been born unlucky.'

'Why?'

Tom jabbed his chin back in the direction of their roof. 'Kitchen caught fire, night I was born.'

'Beat it, didn't you?'

'Something unnatural about beating the odds, to my mother. Outgrowing God's plans. But,' he said, putting his arm around her shoulders, patting the fine serge of her jacket, 'natural's what you make it.'

She leant into him. Gulls cried above, seeking, seeking. They climbed the field in silence, watched by cattle, and then dropped into a sunken lane over the crest, so narrow Tom walked behind Molly until they came to a gate and an avenue of beeches. Through the trees, Molly could see a tight quarry.

'Whose land is this?' she asked.

'Patience.'

The avenue opened on to a garden bound by high walls. The wind was up: it got inside the walnuts and cypresses and thrashed. Molly checked at the sight of a labourer crossing the path, but Tom whistled her on. She followed him around the bend to a great slate house. Before she could ask another question, Tom led her inside, where oak timber had been put to use for new floors and fresh wainscoting, and the ceilings had been replastered with ships and waves. He steered her into a parlour, with a fireplace big enough to burn a young tree, and an old plaster mantelpiece where the coat of arms faded between yellow and green.

'You can change the crest, if you like,' he said. 'Make yourself one.'

Molly turned to face him. '*I* can?'

Tom flushed, feeling ridiculously like he was courting again. 'Consider it a birthday present. You don't like it?'

Molly retreated from him, bumped into a chair and sat down. 'It's beautiful. A beautiful house.'

'The master bedroom looks o'er Hope Cove,' he said, 'and all your land.'

'My land?'

He pulled the deeds from his jacket and opened them for her.

Molly took the paper. It said that Molly West owned this house and the surrounding thousand acres. 'I don't understand,' she said. 'Nobody knows me as Molly, here. I'm not Molly, here. I live on the ship.'

'You've just become one of the wealthiest unmarried women in the South Hams.'

'But—'

Tom squatted before her. 'If anything were to happen to me, I want you to have your freedom.'

365

Molly's face cleared. 'Nothing's going to happen to you.'

Tom smiled. 'That's right.'

'Then,' said Molly, bending the paper one way and then the other, 'you're not sending me off the ship?'

'No,' said Tom, brushing a curl from her forehead. How long would it be before her body betrayed her completely, and he'd have to keep her here? 'Though you'd make a fine lady of the manor.'

She laughed, but she was still fraying the paper's edge. Tom took it from her, folded it up and slipped it into her coat. She tensed at the coldness of his hands, and did not look back up.

'The more you have, the more they can take away,' she murmured.

'No one'll take this away. It's yours.'

Outside, a couple of labourers were wondering if the day's work would survive the winds.

Tom was about to get to his feet and tell Molly they should go before the woods became dangerous, when she said, quietly: 'It was Dick English's kitchen caught fire first, I heard.'

Tom cleared his throat. 'I heard that too.'

She shifted. 'Burning his figure wasn't enough?'

'The folk there invited us for Guy Fawkes, they rigged him up before we arrived. I suppose they thought it would amuse. Which it did. But I don't think Dick took it in the spirit intended. He was there, that night. Watching.'

'You didn't tell me.'

'Listen.' He took her hand. 'Floods, storms, fires – they plague Devon more'n any other county in the land. South Molton lost more'n twenty houses in the Great Storm to fire. Honiton's been visited by two deadly fires in my life. Tiverton's lost more'n a thousand houses from the last days of the Tudor queen. First time, it was a woman cooking up pancakes over a straw fire. Killed fifty people, they say.'

'I doubt the English family seat is thatched.'

He smiled, despite himself. 'I doubt it, too.'

'And I doubt the kitchen staff were making pancakes over a straw fire.'

'You don't need to think on this.'

'I ain't afeared o' no tinder and spark. I just want to know, plain: did you set fire to Dick English's house, with all those people inside?'

Tom was about to withdraw his hand, but she was gripping him now, holding him fast. 'I had my man warn the staff first,' he said.

Nothing in her face: no relief, no condemnation. Had he made her so hard?

'If you'll burn his house to the foundations,' she said, 'why not shoot him between the eyes at the bonfire? It's what you swore. Everything I know in the world, Tom, is what you've sworn.'

A crash of a branch outside. 'All of Devon, all of Roscoff, and every league in between, it's ours. There's no one left standing. Dick English, he isn't standing any more. We've found happiness, you and I.'

The smile he loved so much, a flower that bloomed between day and night, in the cusp of things. 'Yes, we have.'

'Then can't we call it peacetime?'

'Are you capable of peace, outside the two of us?'

The question shook him, for it showed, as these questions of hers always did, how very much she understood him. 'Yes,' he said.

'And Dick English – is he capable of peace?'

'He's capable of defeat. I promised you justice, once. You've got it.'

'A life for a life,' she said. 'That's justice. That's what you told me.'

He fought against the bucking frustration in him, the desire simply to order her: *You'll believe justice is what I say it is.* 'You had the chance to take his life, and you didn't. Don't tell me he drew faster. You're something better'n me. Something purer. Don't argue.'

'You once told me you'd die for me, and kill for me.'

'I would.' *I have.* 'And will again. But it's got to stop sometime.'

A small frown. 'What does?'

Hellard sinking fathoms deep, not even a tombstone for his own brother, who he'd nursed to health in Hope Cove, holding cloth to his wounds. Shaun thrashing beneath the water. It had been low tide, when Tom dragged Shaun from the house on Île de Batz and down to the beach. He'd drowned the man in six inches of water. 'Let us be at peace.'

She looked at the empty hearth, seeming to calculate something. 'I am happy, with you. Happier now, on the ship, than I ever have been. Happier here, in Devon, with our people. And Roscoff – dressing like a girl and amusing old men really is more tedious than you can imagine. But I like being in every part of your world. You're my whole vision. You always have been. But nothing stays the same.'

He cupped her chin. 'What is this talk?'

'Soon, I won't be able to pass for a boy. I've made a deal with every devil and every saint, and none of them have honoured their pacts. So, now what?' Another look around the room. 'Do you mean this for my dowry?'

His grip tightened on hers. '*No.* The most freedom a woman can hope for in life is to become a wealthy widow.' Those were Grace's sentiments, once. 'You don't have that fate. You have power *now.* You always will. You won't marry. You're mine.'

She seemed to hold her breath. 'Your what?'

An old ache flared in Tom's head. He bowed his head over her lap, kissed her hand. 'My – everything.'

'Tom ... we don't keep things from each other, do we?'

He sat back. 'No.'

'There's something ... ' She shook her head. Lifted her gaze to the ships on the ceiling. 'The woman making pancakes. I bet no one ever asked her to make 'em again.'

He laughed, but still felt her current tug away from his. He held her hand all the tighter.

Snip! Snap! Dragon!

Here he comes with flaming bowl,
Don't he mean to take his toll,
Snip! Snap! Dragon!
Take care you don't take too much,
Be not greedy in your clutch,
Snip! Snap! Dragon!

The Sun King was setting over France, and burying his people with him under the weight of taxation. François Fénelon called the country one great hospital with no food in it, the King's people dying from famine, land going uncultivated, cities empty, trade and commerce shuddering. And all for endless skirmishes, victories, retreats; all to own Europe. Where, before, the glory of Versailles glittered in the heart of every Roscoff man, now it seemed a pale joke, and they looked to another Sun King. Louis had once been frank, handsome, imperious, ambitious: everything Tom West was, now. So he was an Englishman. The English had beaten Louis with a Dutchman on their throne. There was no natural order any more. Louis preached divine right, but God smiled on this free-trader, born of nothing, this man who ensured trade found life where none other could be found.

The town gathered about Tom, now, like courtiers in the Hall of Mirrors: where Louis' courtiers once put on His

Majesty's doublet and hose, buttoned his embroidered vest, buckled his sword, now men of great wealth fought to perform any duty they could for Tom. They had arranged this English mummer just for him. He stood in the grand suite of apartments of the latest mademoiselle to require something from him, and watched the performance of George and the Dragon play out before the curtained wall. The actors were boys from the town, dressed up in a confused arrangement of allegory: St George and his merry men, one of them sporting a feather belly as Father Christmas. They beat drums, carried holly boughs and wassail bowls, and danced around the town's beauty: Molly, the star of the show, a slim silhouette tonight in a red mantua embroidered with black buds. Her breast glistened with pearls. Egg whites powdered her face, washing the sun-blush of the sea, and her lips shone cherry red.

Tom accepted another sherry, knocking it back, and shook his head at the tray of food he couldn't identify. He was finding it hard to swallow. He watched Molly fiddle with the branch of mistletoe, her eyes downcast, but shimmering still beneath the blaze of the chandelier: eyelashes beaded with tears. She had told him, as he drew the stay tighter about her waist that night, that she'd never forgive him this indignity.

'You will,' he'd told her, gripping the back of her neck and shaking her a little.

'You're sure of yourself.'

'You'll enjoy it. I promise.'

But she wasn't, he knew. As a boy swept through the curtain and on to the makeshift stage, wearing a dragon mask and carrying a bracket of fire, Molly flinched, a blush rising over her chest, like the rashes she used to complain about. The dragon wormed about her, roaring, and the audience clapped.

The curtain twitched again. 'Do not fear, my lady. I will save you.'

Tom smiled as Benedict entered stage left and bowed to Molly. He was dressed as the Grand Turk, wearing knight's armour and sagging a little under the weight of a broadsword.

Happiness flashed over Molly's face, and the crowd cheered the look of love she gave her knight for joining her in this mortification. But then, as Benedict charged the dragon, Molly's expression faltered, and Tom saw her gloved hand seize the branch of holly, as if considering driving it into the hide of the dragon herself.

But she remained bound to the spot, watching Benedict save her, upstage.

'You owe me an enjoyable evening,' she hissed.

Tom rested his hand on Molly's back, preparing to present her to the next lady. He murmured, 'And I can think of nothing more gratifying than obliging you.'

She fired a look up at him. 'I do not speak of *your* gratification.'

He bowed, picking up this game, stretching back to the bal masqué. 'A man can hope.'

'So can a fool.'

'You mean to make a fool of me, Princess?'

'That depends, sir.'

'On?' he said.

'On whether you deserve mercy,' she said.

A hitch in his throat. 'How can I persuade you?'

'Keep your promises.'

Her archness fell away as she played her part with the gentlemen and ladies of the town, coquettish here, naive and innocent there. Tom kept his hand at her spine, watching Benedict, on the other side of the room, talking to the middle daughter of a middling landowner. Counting how many times

Benedict's attention returned to Molly, something clawed at Tom. Benedict had wanted to be her knight.

But how little he knew the wild thing next to him, Tom considered. She didn't want a knight. She wanted an enjoyable evening.

Tom took the elbow of the gentleman beside him. 'Let me tell you of another English custom.'

Word was sent down to the kitchen, and the chef – muttering about the madness of Englishmen – selected a silver tureen, filled it with raisins and doused them with brandy. A footman carried the dish upstairs, tempted to scoop the brandy in one cupped palm and have a sip. But he resisted, edging around the crowd until he was at Tom's side.

Tom pulled his pistol from beneath his coat, drawing a gasp from the lady telling him about her years in Paris, and struck the flint, dropping the seed of fire into the bowl. Flames leapt up at him, blue and hungry. The footman holding the tureen veered back, arms trembling.

'What is this English tradition?' asked the lady, fanning herself more rapidly. Where her fan had communicated her interest in him, now it signalled fear.

'A Christmas sport,' said Tom. 'A man puts his hand through the flame, and takes hold of a raisin in the dish. The bigger the fistful, the more courage the man.'

Tom nodded the footman on. He gratefully set the dish down on the punch table, and backed away.

'It is called snapdragon, mademoiselle,' said Molly, following Tom to the table, her hand in the crook of his arm.

'A new entertainment is most, most welcome,' said a monseigneur with grey curls stretched down his back, like sheep's wool caught in a fence.

'The first hand is yours, sir,' said Tom.

The monseigneur rolled up his laced sleeve and removed the

373

ruby and sapphire rings from his fingers. He bowed to Molly. 'Perhaps mademoiselle would do me the honour of safeguarding these?'

Molly accepted his jewels, and Tom could see her calculating their worth. He pinched her arm. She glared at him. The people were hot around them, now – excited, daring. The monseigneur drank the attention, plunged, yelped, and drew out a single raisin.

Younger gentlemen copied him, but nobody emerged with a fistful the size of the jewels in Molly's palm. They were waiting for Tom to show his skill, believing that this was, after all, the point of the performance. But he kept one hand on Molly's arm and one hand behind his back, waiting, waiting. Raisins swirled in the flame. Benedict did not put himself forward.

'I cannot believe this is all the courage Roscoff can offer,' said Tom. 'Why don't we raise the stakes?'

He released Molly's arm.

That gleam of fun returned to her face as Tom tipped her hand. The monseigneur's rubies and sapphires dropped into the bowl with a splash of fire. The monseigneur swore, teetered on outrage – and then clapped, insisting he would give Tom the greatest honours of France if he could but save his fortune.

'Not me.'

The merriment of the hall lurched, and then Molly stepped forward.

Tom checked Benedict's lunge with his shoulder, sending the boy stumbling.

Molly did not remove her glove, did not hesitate, just squared her shoulders and reached into the flames.

Mistletoe hung over the door. A log rumbled in the hearth, promising, Tom remembered from his youth, to burn out all a man's wrongdoings and heartbreaks. He sat in his armchair in the house on Île de Batz, with legs stretched towards the fire, and Molly in his lap, holding up the sapphire ring the monseigneur had given her as reward.

'You are forgiven,' she said. 'I enjoyed every second of that. Especially the look on their faces.' She turned the jewel, letting the light caress it. 'The beginning of my own fortune.'

Tom pulled at her pearls. She hadn't wriggled from her gown upon returning home, as she usually did. 'You don't need your own fortune.'

'Something no man has ever said to another,' she told him, closing her hand about the ring.

'You don't look terribly like a man right now, my sweet.'

'What do I look like?'

He tilted his head, mirroring her consideration. His smile faded. Then, more hoarsely than he'd intended: 'A lady.'

'Bah.'

He chuckled. 'How ladylike.'

Tomorrow – very nearly today – it would be Christmas, and they would glutton themselves on geese, capons, pies of carp tongues, frumenty, mutton pies, plum porridge. The crew – at the moment, sleeping in various corners of the house – would sing and play, and at the heart of their mischief would be Molly, Lord of Misrule for another year. 'You look like the future,' he said.

'What does that mean?'

'It means you don't need to worry about securing nothing. It's done.'

Molly rolled her eyes, but laid her head on his shoulder.

Tom shifted, moving so that her weight was even across his legs, and in the process glanced up and caught them both in the mirror.

He froze, one hand on Molly's hip, the other stroking her arm.

What do I look like?

A glass merchant had told him tonight that his ward was enough to inspire ravissement – ravishment: defilement, violation, ecstasy, a pleasing violence on the mind. 'Seventeen, and not even promised! Mais, non, you mean to keep her for yourself?' Grace had called him a ravisher once, a man who takes anything he wants by violence. But not, he'd assured her, a man who takes a woman by violence – only delight. He played with the rose buds stitched into Molly's skirts. It was a long time since he'd ravished any girl in the brothel; he had found himself bored by their forms of rapture. But he was never bored with Molly, and, as he studied their bodies twined together in the mirror, he could not avoid what his reflection showed: that the desire which had flickered to life in the pit of his body at the bal masqué burnt in him still.

Is this Daddy's stray shot, the captain's steady whore, or something else?

Something else – *something else* – what if it was something else? The only girl to ever love him and not be disappointed. Rhys said it was like a bad romance, a poor man's fairy tale. But there were plenty of men his age – especially among finer folk – who married girls as young as her.

She was his ward, his boy, his girl, his everything, always. And she could stay his everything, willing to follow him into everything.

He glanced down at her head of curls. She seemed sometimes to flirt with him, as if casting out a line for some special attention, some guarantee.

What did she want from him? And would it be so evil? Coldness washed over him.

Yes, it would. For she was willing to do anything he bid her, out of fear of losing him. And willing under fear was not willing. He'd never wanted any woman to fear him. But they always had, in the end.

He should have stopped her coming into his bed years ago. He should stop her finding his arms like this. Stop clutching her to his side. Let her grow.

But he could not hurt her with another loss. He could not let her go. He did not know what would happen to him if he did.

Tonight, watching her flourish as both bold and bound, he saw a line of compromise, a way to let her keep her wild nature, while holding to a woman's body, here in Roscoff, and soon in Devon.

After all – he hugged her closer – wasn't she his, mind, body and soul?

Our Joyful Feast

So now is come our joyful feast;
Let every man be jolly;
Each room with ivy leaves is dressed,
And every post with holly,
Though some churls at our mirth repine,
Round your foreheads garlands twine;
Drown sorrow in a cup of wine,
And let us all be merry.

The poem turned in Molly's mind as she pulled the ivy garland from her hair at her dressing table – *each room with ivy leaves is dressed* . . . She wore her best green suit, for they did not expect callers, and felt herself. It had been the finest Christmas in Molly's memory, the crew a complete and entire family, following her in the games she invented, the joy she conjured. Tom had joined her mischief, too, and Molly felt his contentment like a finite treasure, harbouring it, wishing she could blinker time, and herself. *Drown sorrow in a cup of wine, and let us all be merry* . . .

A knock at her door. Benedict smiled from the threshold, twirling a sprig of mistletoe in his hand. A rare smile, these days. For the past month, he had watched her with panic in his eyes, waiting for something she could not name. He was flushed, now. 'I haven't given you your present.'

Molly nodded to the sprig. 'Do you hope for a kiss in return?'

Benedict closed the door, glancing as he did over his shoulder, towards Tom's bedroom. He dropped the mistletoe on to Molly's table, and then pulled a box from his pocket.

Molly drew apart the ribbons, and hesitated.

'It's a bobbin,' said Benedict. 'Decorated, you see, with a love heart and our names.'

'Why would you give me the love token of cottagers surviving by making lace? You aspire so low for me?'

It was said lightly, but his face darkened. 'You do not like it.'

She tried to order her words, but he went on:

'You have no problem bearing Tom's love token. That coin you wear – lovers exchange those. And you've kept it on your breast these many years.'

'My mother gave it to me. It's not that kind of love.'

'You don't know what his love is. Yet you harbour it. You accept anything from that man. Any gift, any word, any act. Any violence. You didn't even ask what happened to Shaun.'

Molly stood up, closing in on him. 'Why should I care what happens to a man who breaks into my bedroom, promises me I'll like it, and proceeds to do his best to persuade me? A man who wouldn't have stopped—'

'Tom promised you'd like the Christmas play, though you told him you wouldn't. And so you dressed up according to his fancy, as you always do.'

'You think you're protecting me,' Molly said, seeing him clearly for what felt like the first time.

His voice shook. 'I've always protected you.'

'But don't you see I can protect myself?'

Benedict took her hands. 'You can't, not from him.'

'You think I'm – what? A charmed snake? That I am not my own person, my own body.'

'Molly, I-I want you to be *my* person.'

379

The look on his face was so sweet, Molly smiled. He didn't understand her – would probably never understand her. But he did love her. Or some shadow of her. Molly drew the coin from her neck. 'Then this is my present to you. A love token, for yours.'

He kissed her, beside her lips. 'What does this token promise?'

A shiver of desire. 'What are you prepared to take?'

He gripped her waist. 'I must tell you ... I've been trying to tell you ... '

Molly tiptoed, pushing herself into him, encouraging his trembling hands, swallowing his trembling kiss, feeling herself shake with him. She cleaved to him, love pulling her, love searching for a channel.

Then Benedict jerked away, a last clumsy kiss on her forehead, and Molly was left breathing hard, and alone.

New Year's Eve

'I thought you wiser than this,' said Tom. 'Surely you intend to wound and hurt yourself with such a hazard. I see a bullet through the head coming on.'

Kingston was unfazed. 'My pockets are deeper than you know, Cap'n.' He tossed the rest of his bet into the centre of the table.

'Embezzling from me, are you?'

A soft smile. 'That's just the half of it. Are you going to bet?'

'You're worse than a country shopkeeper who goes hunting on market day. I *grieve* for you, honestly I do.' Tom shoved his pile forward. Tapped the oak. 'Benedict, I trust you'll be a more sincere judge of yourself. No fraud against your own reflections, now. Come on, son.'

Benedict tried to laugh, turning the change in his pocket over.

It was then Tom caught a glance of the token, sifted in Benedict's palm. He wasn't sure, at first, that it was the same token, deep into gambling and drink, while outside Molly and Nathan were describing a great ship in the bitter air with their hands, working on some invention for more speed. But, after another brandy, Benedict began to play with the thing, turning it in his fingers beneath the table, and Tom saw in flashes the *T* he had scored in his love for Grace. At first, Tom thought Benedict had taken it from Molly. But Molly would never let it be taken. Benedict had no way of owning the coin, unless Molly gave it to him. He slumped in his chair at the head of the table, staring out the window, where Molly bent over her work happily. As if there were nothing to speak of. She'd almost told him something in the new house, but had steered clear of it, the same way she'd steer clear of rocks if Benedict's transits failed. So, there was something to tell, something that now flashed between Benedict's fingers, but she'd kept silent. Lied to him. And done it well. Like her mother.

Church bells drifted over the sea. The old year rang out, the new year rang in. High tide, hungry for the house. The moon looking away. Benedict stood in the hall, unable to do the same, his hands on the walls, frightened he would not be able to keep his feet. The view into Molly's room was just a few inches, the door left ajar: an easy mistake to make while you rush in to change your shirt, spattered with red wine, an accident after a day of mad excess, as if it were their last ever, led by Tom, who seemed to be careening between joy and grief. An easy mistake to make, yes, when you know a man often passes in the corridor.

Benedict swallowed. Did she know? Had she left the door open purposefully, to discover finally what her whole body would do to him? And did she know it was him, standing here? He watched the twist of shoulder, the turn of her hip. He felt his body wind up. Dancing with shadows, she looked over her shoulder. He met her eyes. She did not cover her body.

Benedict heard Tom's tread on the step. He turned, trying to shield Molly's door, trying to arrange his face.

'What's got you excited?' asked Tom, but there was no teasing in his voice.

'Tom, I wasn't—' But before he could finish, Tom seized

him, lifting him bodily from the floor and hurling him into his room.

Pain split Benedict's body as he landed, back bent, over his chest. He heard Tom lock Molly's bedroom door, heard Molly shout at him to stop.

Then those hands hauled him up, only to punch him to the floor.

'Please, Tom, I wasn't doing anything.'

'Don't lie to me!'

'No, wait, I didn't mean to—'

'Don't get up,' Tom snarled, kicking him back to the floor.

'Please!'

'You fucking worm. You snake.'

Tom's boot came at him again.

'I ought to burn your eyes out!'

Benedict tried to sit up. Tom was undoing his belt. Would he truly, finally, blot his eyes? Lord, clothe me in an armour of light. Give me courage.

'I know it was you,' Benedict said. 'I know it was you who pulled the trigger.'

Tom seemed about to fall. Then a sneer disfigured his face. 'Took you long enough.' He doubled the belt over.

Benedict pressed his face into the floor. He began to scream when he realised Tom was not going to stop. He was aware of the taste of tears in his mouth. He could hear Tom panting with the effort.

'I ought to fucking kill you.'

Benedict managed to clutch at Tom's boots.

'Stay down. Don't fucking move.'

Molly was tugging on the door when Tom opened it. She stumbled back, but did not move quickly enough before Tom locked

383

it again. Molly could hear Nathan and Kingston running up the stairs, calling, 'What's happening?'

'What did you do to Benedict?' she said.

'Whore,' he breathed.

She backed away. 'You told me I'd never be that.'

'Too late.'

Molly pulled on a shirt. 'You don't have to buy my love. You have it.'

'Do I?' He was struggling to breathe, weighing the belt in his hand. 'So, what does Benedict have?'

Nathan's shouts on the other side of the door. Benedict's sobs. Kingston's soothing murmurs.

'Nothing that matters,' she said.

'Just your body?'

Molly set her shoulders. Breathed. Cool air crossed her skin. 'My body's always been for sale. You've had me contort myself every way I can for you. And I've done it.'

A hiss: 'You let him see you, like that.'

'Why shouldn't I?'

'You're mine.'

'Your girl? Let's have it, finally. Your girl for what?'

'I love you like a daughter. You don't know what a man—'

'A father does not look at his daughter the way you look at me.'

'You don't understand.'

'What do you see,' she pressed, 'when you stare at me like I'm a ghost? Who am I to you, and what are you to me?'

'Stop it. Stop talking. Cover yourself.'

'Or what? Go on. Show me what love is.'

The belt caught her cheek. Molly gasped, and then her fist came up. Tom caught it, shoving her on to the bed. She tried to stand, but his arm wrapped around her stomach, and then she was pressed face down into the mattress. The belt struck her back. Molly yelled, cursed, tried to buck free. The belt came again. She wriggled away, was held down as the belt caught her hips, her buttock. The sheets filled her mouth, she could not breathe, could not scream. Finally, an arm came free and she drove her elbow back into his gut. It was enough to make Tom give an inch. Kicking, she turned on to her back, legs flailing between his. The belt came down, but she darted back and it struck the bed. Tom gripped her shoulder, trying to spin her on to her front again, but Molly seized his wrist.

'Coward! Look at me!'

The belt fell, dangling limp from his fist.

Molly wiped tears and blood from her face.

Tom was draining from red to white. 'Molly,' he breathed. 'Molly. I'd never ...'

His hand came up, fingers moving to brush the cut on her cheek, but she flinched.

'You've never let me have any key to any room I sleep in. You took my knife and never gave it back. You don't like me to carry a pistol no more. You've kept me disarmed, long as you can, and I've never wanted to see it. Because you saved me, and gave me freedom, and gave me love, when I'd lost everything. Because ... God, because I love you, Tom, and there's no prison for a woman like love. At least, that's what you taught me.'

The door rattled. Fists beat on the other side. A tempest swelled outside.

The year tipped.

Tom fled.

New Year's Day

1715

That forget-me-not blue hour between midnight and dawn. Kingston stood ramrod in the doorway, gaze steady on the hall, arms crossed over his chest. Molly sat among the looking glasses, the fans, the neckcloth, this room of cheap props. Nathan knelt at her feet, dabbing her lip with a cloth. It hurt, but she had nothing with which to tell him to stop, or to thank him. He had guided her into a gown, the first thing he'd found, and now drew a blanket about her.

'You're a brave one,' he said.

'No,' she said, and would have added, *Just lost*. But she knew the words didn't match, and wouldn't come, anyway.

'Strikes me you got all the docity a man could ever claim. And more. But you'd know best.'

I don't know anything at all – the thought cut through all others. I don't know anything at all.

'Where's Benedict?'

'Not sure he's up to talking.'

Distant: 'I don't care.'

When she next looked up from the blood pattern on the boards, Benedict was haunting the boards before her. He looked like a nightmare. He sat down, took her hand. His fingers were splintered.

'I told you,' he said.

Molly looked to the window, to the starless sky: the muteness of the waiting world. 'You knew he'd do that?'

'Yes,' he said, the conviction in his voice almost petty.

'How?'

Silence.

'Benedict? How?'

Still, he said nothing. Molly studied his puckered right eye, the awful obliteration of it; she studied his crisp and removed beauty. Benedict had watched them all from some righteous plateau all these years, she realised, afeared of stepping down.

'You knew he'd be angry enough to kill – so close to it, he had to run,' she said slowly. 'But he didn't kill either of us. Just like he hasn't killed Dick English. He's not the man you'd have him be. A violent man, but not a murderous man. And yet, you'd have him that way.'

Benedict dropped her hand. 'So, he showed an inch of mercy, and that undoes everything? Look at me. Look at you.'

'Then you won't forgive him.'

'Forgive him?' He stood up, turning in the tight space between bed frame and window. 'No. And I won't love him or lie for him, not for another minute. I'm leaving. And you're coming with me.'

Molly held herself. 'What lies, Benedict?'

He paused.

'If you're leaving, don't you owe me the truth, whatever it is you're not saying?'

Benedict wet his lip, wincing at the pain of it, the pain of his whole body. Molly watched him, as he'd always watched her.

'You've looked after me,' she said, 'though you didn't want to. You weren't quite a brother to me, nor were you quite a friend. You were a reluctant keeper, and then a reluctant lover. But you did both, anyway, maybe even fooled yourself into believing both were your own desires. You've been fighting something all these years. And I deserve to know what it is. I deserve the truth, finally, from someone.'

His fingers twitched, as if grabbing at frayed ends, frayed strings. And then he spoke, dragging words from the floor, from the end of those strings, which seemed miles long.

'I am a witness,' said Benedict, 'to your mother's death. I watched him beat her until she could hardly stand. I watched –' a cry broke from him – 'and did nothing. And I've done nothing every day since then.'

Molly's feet were ribboned purple, bruises wound in winter. She studied the blotches now, but couldn't feel the throb. 'You never told me that.'

'He did it. He killed her.'

The points of her body and all the pain in between. Navigating arms like knotted ropes, chest locked and rattling, ribs and hips sharp as glass, sapling legs: steam and bend them until they curve. 'You don't mean Richard English, do you?'

'No, I don't. I mean Tom. Tom murdered your mother, after she betrayed us to the Revenue. He shot her. He killed her.'

High tide ate Molly. She stood up, fell up.

'I thought it was Hellard that did it, until the night Hellard died, when he told me—'

'You didn't say anything.'

Benedict rushed on. 'And then I thought it was Dick – but . . . but it wasn't. You should have seen Rhys's face, after he beat her. It was Tom. The way he tore Mrs Tucker apart . . . I didn't want to see it. But I've known – since Rhys, since before. I've always known, I think.'

Molly said again: 'You didn't tell me.'

Benedict was frantic now, fumbling for cloaks and gowns.

'You have to pack. I went to Richard English. He'll protect us, if I sign a statement against Tom. I'm going to save you.'

'You went to English.'

Benedict paused, almost dropping the tangled cloth. 'You have to come with me, Molly. We'll be safe. We'll be happy. You'll see. We'll get married, and—'

Molly's voice floated between them: 'You watched him beat my mother, and you never told me. You believed I was living with her murderer. Hellard, then Tom. And you didn't tell me. You didn't just damn yourself. You damned me, too. And I'll never forgive you for it. Get out.'

Leaf

To INTERLEA/VE. v. a. [*inter* and *leave*]

To chequer a book by the insertion of blank leaves.

Charles Dickens is dead. For two days, his grave lay open in the Poets' Corner of Westminster Abbey. The public came in their thousands and dropped so many flowers the grave bloomed and overflowed. George Eliot is old, and will soon die – a suggestion will be made that she should lie with Dickens and Defoe in the Poets' Corner, but the Church will refuse: George Eliot they could permit, but not 'Mrs Lewes'. In 1878, Virginia Woolf's father, Leslie Stephen, writes to Robert Louis Stevenson:

It has occurred to me lately that you might help me in an ever recurring difficulty. I am constantly looking out rather vaguely for a new novelist. I should like to find a Walter Scott or Dickens or even a Miss Brontë or G. Eliot. Somehow the coming man or woman has not yet been revealed. Meanwhile I cannot help thinking that, if you would seriously put your hand to such a piece of work you would be able – I will not say to rival the success of Waverley or Pickwick – but to write something really good . . .

I'd love to know what Virginia Woolf – the new novelist her father was waiting for – would make of that 'even a Miss Brontë or G. Eliot.' But, for now – would it be Robert Louis Stevenson?

With *Treasure Island* in 1883, R. L. S. went from a moderately successful travel and short-story writer, to a sensation of the new publishing wave, boys' own stories and boys' magazines. He showed, everybody agreed, great promise – but promise of what? This question followed R. L. S. his entire life, as he refused to enter the law profession his parents hoped for and set off after bohemia. And would he live to write another book? R. L. S. had suffered from a chronic lung disease since childhood. In September 1885, we find R. L. S., his wife Fanny and his cousin, Katherine de Mattos, marooned in Exeter after R. L. S. haemorrhaged.

R. L. S. and Fanny, an American artist and writer, had recently published a book together, *The Dynamiter*. R. L. S. was now trying to finish *Jekyll and Hyde* and return to a book he'd set aside: his first novel, *Kidnapped*. Katherine was a writer, too: a poet, short-story writer, translator and critic.

This might be the last time the three were together. Not long after, their friend, William Ernest Henley, accused Fanny of plagiarising a story of Katherine's, though Katherine said she didn't want it mentioned and couldn't rightly remember who wrote what. Henley broadcast the accusation anyway, to all who would listen. R. L. S. sided with his wife. Katherine was no longer welcome, and her portion in R. L. S.'s will was reduced.

While in Exeter, Fanny and Katherine made use of the library, where they found the tale of Tom, Grace and Molly, and read it to R. L. S.

(Notes for a lecture on women and writing to be given at Girton College, Cambridge, on the anniversary of Virginia Woolf's lecture series, 'A Room of One's Own'.)

Women Were to be Excluded

1885

R. L. S.

Henley, my dear boy –

I am boxed in. Imagine me, if you will – and even if you won't – trapped in a body, which is trapped in a bed, which is trapped in a hotel room, which is trapped in the New London Hotel, which is trapped, not in London, but rather fancifully in Exeter, which itself is trapped between the winding silver of the Exe and some place at the end of the world, where I stayed as a boy with my mother when she was ill, and returned to in my imagination for the opening pages of *Treasure Island*, and now cannot stir from. I have been nearly six months in a strange condition of near collapse, and upon arrival to this city – where lamps glimmer like carbuncles, the streets drown in fog, and the only victors are motley roofs and the stately towers of the cathedral – I duly complied, and collapsed.

I suppose I shall learn (I begin to think I am learning) to fight this vast, vague feather bed of a monster that lies over me and smothers me; but, in the beginnings of these conflicts, the inexperienced wrestler is always worsted, and I own I have been thoroughly beaten. I am held captive in this bed like a limed sparrow. Around my bedside, my faithful wife nurses me and my patient cousin keeps me company with unseasonable japes to lift the cloudy vagueness: around and around they go, while I, quite dizzy from such a carousel, hold on with what strength is left to me, and try to come slowly and partially into possession of myself, as a child might fill a sandbag with little handfuls.

I thank you for sending on the reviews of mine and Fanny's *Dynamiter*. Fanny and I think it too entertaining to see these arguments of who wrote what chapters, and to see readers proclaim trousers where they should enjoy skirt, and detect skirt where they should smell trousers. I should note it is rather less amusing to see critics complain I should never have partnered up with my wife, and calling this a lesser work. Poor Fanny. I do happily own my stories in the main are stories for boys, as was *Treasure Island*, written of course for Fanny's son. Women were to be excluded. So, there I am, I suppose: R. L. S., Author of Boys' Stories.

My new story, *The Strange Case of Dr Jekyll and Mr Hyde*, is done. Showed it to Fanny, and found her unimpressed. So: to the fire, to ashes and all! Thermometer in mouth, I moved the story from Edinburgh to London, and altered the radical division. Now, of the two natures that contend in the field of Jekyll's consciousness, if he could rightly be said to be *either*, it is only because he is radically *both*: an ordinary man of rage without restriction. For man is never truly one, but always two.

Fanny turned it from an allegory to a story. If I am where I am, it is thanks to that lady who married me when I was a mere complication of cough and bones. She can make anything, from a house to a row, to great and stunning proportions. In company, she presents the appearance of a timid wife – you look for the reticule. Among her clan: an infinitely little body, insane black eyes, boy's hands, tiny bare feet, a cigarette in mouth, hellish energy. She dreams dreams, and sees visions, like I do, and if she turns out to be not an artist in her soul, still I love her for it.

394

Now, back to *Kidnapped*. Early in the year, I drudged at it and hated it. Now, Katherine has brought me a set of books from the library, a tangled web of stories. One thread has caught me, giving me fresh inspiration from a real kidnap and a rare adventure at sea, in which a man teaches a boy how to become a man, and the boy teaches the man how to become a hero. Something in it stirs me. I think my characters will now take the bit in their teeth; all at once, they will become detached from flat paper, turn their backs on me and walk off bodily, and from that time my task will be stenographic – it will be they who speak, they who write the remainder of the story. In the meantime, here is an ugly gnome by name of *Jekyll and Hyde* – ugly, but interesting, I think, and from a very deep mine.

I wonder what our friend and foe Mr Archer will make of it. I cannot thank you for informing me of what he intends to print. To call me modern of the moderns – well, if it's a compliment, I'll take it. But to suggest I have a love of literature for literature itself, at the expense of moral good – that I am an athletico-aesthete, a malingerer in the brave gymnasium, who lives life in long walks, leaky canoes and lingering sentences, that I am all enjoyment, that I have faced no test of spirit, body or mind – to this I must and will object.

I quite understand Mr Archer not caring to refer to things – my status as invalid – that are his private knowledge. But why then take for his hypothesis something he knows not to be true, and hinge an argument upon it? For he has, as it were, invalidated my invalidism; and what a tiring thing for an already tired man, to contemplate communicating his pain to others in a way they will understand and accept. For Mr Archer is aware that I have not seen a canoe nor taken a long walk since '79. Yet he charges me, it would seem, with being a back-slidden communist who will go to hell (if there be such an excellent institution) for the luxury in which he lives.

I am disposed to believe Mr Archer has not had enough sorrow in his existence. Otherwise he would not be so foolish as to claim that writing literature for the joy of oneself and one's reader is mere frivolousness – well, that could never be written by a man who had tried what unhappiness was like. I see a universe where any brave man may make out of life that which shall be happy for himself, and, by being so, beneficent to those about him. A man drowning in pain may yet help others swim. And, if he fails, why should I hear him weeping? I mean, if I fail, why should I weep?

And, if I want to keep the blood on this pillow to myself and so not be defined by it – well, what of it? I have been obliged to strip myself, one after another, of all the pleasures of life – strip myself of myself, in truth, until the box-frame I feel is a coffin, and just at the edge of my hearing, my friend, there is the man with his hammer and nail.

I am a verbose letterist – you will forgive me, and be assured: I like my life all the same.

Yours, in sickness and in wealth (he can still joke) –

R. L. S.

Fanny

Dearest Henley –

It is now a week since we left home, and we are no further away than Exeter. Louis was taken with a dreadful haemorrhage, only less bad than the one at Hyères. It did not last long, but was more violent. Had it continued but a little longer, it would have strangled him. We are, in consequence, here indefinitely.

Louis believes he wearies me; he says he cannot ask me to love him (as if he must ask); he worries I am ill. If I tell him my nerves were shattered by the terrible suspense I endured at Hyères – well, I shan't, and you must promise to burn this letter.

I know Louis's friends (you excluded) think me brown-faced, tyrannical and possessive. I know they think I married him for his money (wouldn't that be nice?). They do not know the years spent frantically putting up scaffolding, until I am blistered and sore and tearful. What a thing it is to have a 'man of genius' to deal with. It is like managing an overbred horse. Why, with my own feeble hand I could write a book that the whole world would jump at. (If they could forget I am Mrs R. L. S. As it is, my name on *The Dynamiter* is a lit fuse.) But, forget that – if I keep his hand steady, he will write a book the whole world will remember for ever.

We are not disappointed in Exeter. I am making a quick study in watercolour of the West of England Insurance Office, a quite imposing structure. Katherine and I have agreed to both write a short story, and read our efforts to R. L. S. He says he will burn the loser's manuscript, as he burnt his first draft of *Jekyll* for me – for me! Well, we shan't argue.

The doctor here tells me that, if Louis seizes again, I am to call him and retire myself to another room. Retreat? I was never a coward in my life and never lost my presence of mind in an emergency, and I have met some very serious ones. I will not sink so deep the sun can only find me in the hour of noon. I will dance barefoot for Louis, until our laughter rings louder than the bells of Exeter Cathedral.

Yours –

Fanny

Katherine

Hello, Henley, my old friend –

I could give you a charming description of an excursion from Exeter to Fingle Bridge, where the river threads between hills in close cahoots with coppice, clothed in flowering heather like so much clotted cream spilt over raspberries – but I'm sure Louis will give you enough purple prose in his letter (and him so set when my husband left on writing book reviews in my name to get me some money – imagine his relief when I sit and read my reviews to him, and they actually stand up. I am sparing him my poems, for which I am also paid – too harsh to ask a man who cannot eat to eat his own words).

Do not fear, I say as much to his face, and so we totter on together in what he calls the whoreson brink of sense, begging my pardon, for he forgets he is talking to a lady. My chatter, he says, means nothing, is blankly insignificant, like his own chatter, our friendship now getting on in years – it must nearly be of age, he says, and more valuable to him every day. Well, if I can be serious for a moment, his friendship means everything, as I watch it, and him, almost slip away from me, called back by Fanny's human cyclone of sound and fury in the face of death. He lives in art, he says, and art lives in him, and he will not leave it. As well it may be, God willing.

But, as for inspiring him to pick up his pen again, credit must go to the Devon and Exeter Institution, where I borrowed a collection of pamphlets that has most engaged him. One is a slim book, *A Wild & True Relation of A Lady Shipwright and Free-Trader*. The librarian told me it was left in a hotel by Mrs Hester Piozzi, who was convalescing there; you'll recall stories of her – the Bluestocking who invited eight hundred people to her eightieth birthday at the Bath Assembly House and danced until dawn. The book made its way to the library. Whether it was written by Mrs Piozzi, or is indeed by a female smuggler, is unknown to me. With it are folk tales seemingly inspired by the original, though where the truth lies I cannot discern. The endings differ – in some, the lady Molly prospers; in others, she dies. In some, Tom West redeems himself; in others, Molly or the boy Orlando kill him; in others still, Tom and Orlando are heroes together. It strikes me as similar to walking the halls of a gallery and seeing so many portraits of a lady unknown.

Louis promises he will dedicate *Jekyll and Hyde* to me with a poem. I might like to resist a dedication to a book such as that one, but Louis promises it will be dedicated by one who loves me: Jekyll, and not Hyde. Well, I love all of him, as do you, I know, as do we all. If only love were enough to lift him out of bed.

And so back I go to my own pen. You may tell me criticism is regarded as worthless, that I live in Louis's superfluous mansion – but it is a room of my own.

Yours ever –
Mrs de Mattos.

BOOK SIX

1715

I DON'T FEAR DEVIL OR MAN,

AND I CERTAINLY DON'T FEAR YOU

A New Year

I

Molly sold the snapdragon ring to a Roscoff jeweller.

Molly tried to buy passage to England. The first ship refused, because my lady had no protector. The second agreed.

Molly was told my lady would suffer the sea less if she stayed below, in her cabin.

Molly looked down and realised she was dressed as a girl.

Molly was surprised to find she still had a body.

Molly stayed below, in the womb of the ship.

Molly landed at Plymouth.

Molly bespoke a carriage.

Molly refused armed riders who would protect my lady from highwaymen, but the men insisted, and took a high price.

Molly refused food or drink at the coaching inn, but the men insisted, and took a high price.

Molly sat alone in the parlour, given over for my lady's use.

Molly looked down and realised she was dressed as an heir to a great fortune.

Molly dismissed the coachmen at Bigbury.

Molly crossed the beach at low tide, the cornflower blue

of her skirts trailing in the sand like a dead animal lolling from a brace.

Molly was swallowed by mist, a mist that consumed Burgh Island, consumed the bloodied headland, consumed the narrow sea.

Molly walked to Bantham.

Molly crossed the bed of the Avon, her stockings dyed algae-green.

Molly found the swollen ruin of Grace Tucker's cottage, sans door, sans roof, sans windows, sans everything.

Molly picked through shells, driftwood, the rotting ends of furniture.

Molly stroked the hearth, left standing though cracked with shoots of time.

Molly sat down in its embrace, cold body and cold stone.

Molly watched the Avon fill, watched mist lift, watched the river twist into the land, watched sunlight gild the trees.

Molly knocked door to door in the village. Some of the women were too frightened by her grandeur to talk to her. None of the men recognised Orlando West. No one remembered a Grace Tucker, and, when they did, they said she had been a fancy woman, who kept to herself, and finally went back to her people. The only friend they could think of was Mrs Weatheridge. No one gave voice to Tom West's name, only said it with their look-away eyes. No one would hear of Molly riding to Thurlestone by herself. A woman insisted her husband take Molly in his cart, begging my lady's pardon, for it was the best they had to offer.

Molly bumped in the back of the cart to Thurlestone.

Molly watched the sun wink in the arch of Thurlestone Rock.

Molly breathed in the slick ferns and dripping trees.

Molly offered the man money, but he refused.

Molly knocked on Mrs Weatheridge's door.

Molly bowed to the old woman, a woman like the Barbary witch.

Molly refused tea, accepted something stronger.

Molly asked what the witch knew.

Molly shook off the witch's curiosity, the witch's comfort, the witch's understanding.

Molly accepted the witch's knowledge: Grace and Kit Tucker hailed from Widecombe-in-the-Moor.

Molly watched the witch take her hand and impart comfort.

Molly listened to the witch's confession, listened to how she had brought Tom West into the world, how she always knew him to be from hell's own fire, and how, later, when Grace Tucker disappeared, she knew it was Tom's fire that had consumed her – how she prayed for the safety of Grace Tucker's little girl, a little girl the witch had solaced in her first moments.

Not first, said Molly. It was my mother who cared for me in my first moments. And not second. That was Tom. And not in any of the moments after Mama was killed. That was Tom, too.

II

Dartmoor was a different country. Gone, red soil and soft green hills. Gone, the lick of sea on the air. In its place, here was a chain of bog-black hills rolling with wind, whose bowels might be rich with tin, but whose face was barren; grasses choking and waterlogged, rusted bracken pouring with run-off; streams and rivers that would fructify the valleys of the South Hams, before disburdening themselves into the narrow sea; and others, by long wandering, who would seek the Severn.

The valley seemed swollen with mist, until Molly realised she was climbing towards the heavens, and that the scuds and waves were thick clouds billowing from treetops. She had set off in the dark, and would return in the dark – and felt, still, in the dark. The wastes were menacing, only tolerating her – and yet she belonged to them; her mother belonged to them. The cry of a horse echoed across the bleeding and broken crowns of granite and cresting heath. Widecombe was white with snow, and, as the cold met her searching face, Molly remembered Mama pointing to distant hills in winter and telling her, *The fine folk on Widecombe are picking their geese, faster, faster, faster.* Molly checked her stained robe, her gown, her curls.

The manor hunkered on the banks of East Webburn River, as the witch had said. Molly instructed the man at the reins to follow the drive. Tom had told her once that the loyalties of country gentlemen could be traced by their trees. Those who supported William III set lime avenues, while Jacobites planted Scotch firs. And those loyal to Tom? They balanced glass bottles in their treetops, as if the trees themselves flowered with sapphires and emeralds. Here were many Scotch firs, and cherry trees, and a terrace of ancient yews, but no cracked and rimed bottles that reeked of beer slops when the sun turned on them.

The house was eight bays wide and three storeys, with stubby pavilions and a much older gable, all built from unsmiling granite. She bade the coachman wait for her, and stepped out, conscious for the first time that she did not know how a lady asked for entry to a house. Molly brushed her hip with her thumb, where no knife waited.

'May I assist you, my lady?'

Molly flinched. A footman at the door, studying her with consternation. She searched the ground for her voice. 'I am here to talk to Grace Tucker's mother.'

The footman looked like she had blasphemed.

'I only want to speak with her,' she said. 'And then I'll be on my way.'

He was turning the same ash as the brick.

'Or perhaps I should ask my questions in the village, instead.'

He choked, then hurried her inside. The warmth of the fire in the hall caught her off guard. She heard dogs bark somewhere, and a voice call. The life of a home. Except the curtains were too heavy, and the furniture too dark, and the eyes of servants following her too suspicious, as if nothing unsanctioned or unexpected ever passed through this place. She was rushed beyond a library – wanting to linger there, to see what books Mama may have enjoyed in childhood – and guided into a salon decorated in violent pinks.

'Pray to wait here, miss.'

Molly sat on a cushioned seat by the window, her muscles tensed. The elegance made her knee jerk up and down. So, this was where women shared tea and conversation, and circumscribed their worlds. Maybe this was where they plotted to change the world, too.

'Who are you?'

The question made her stand. A woman checked on the threshold, a woman about the age her mother would be now, except this woman lacked all the humour Molly remembered in her mother's face. She was a flower pressed between the pages of a book, and forgotten. And she was staring at Molly as if she were a ghost.

'My lady, I did not wish to startle you,' said Molly, aware as she spoke that the gallantry in her voice did not fit the clothes she wore. She tried to find the tones she employed in Roscoff. 'I have come to speak with Grace Tucker's mother.'

Another lady arrived, and they edged inside together. This woman, too, seemed drained of blood. She was a little younger, and wore, Molly saw, a wedding ring. Both carried bags of knotting. Both looked over their shoulders, as if some frightening force followed them.

'Who are you?' said the first lady again.

Molly lifted her chin. 'I believe I am your niece.'

'Impossible,' breathed the first lady.

'You cannot speak with our mother. She died, nearly ten years ago.'

'I apologise,' said Molly. 'Perhaps you might answer my questions? Or your father?'

'Impossible,' said the first lady again, almost sitting down and pulling out her knotting, and then stopping. 'He will not talk with you. It is not possible.'

Molly kept her voice calm, coaxing, hearing in it Tom's charm: 'I'm sure you can oblige me just as well. Better, most like.'

'No. No.'

'Sister,' said the younger lady, 'surely we could—?'

'We did not have a third sister,' said the first lady, gripping the back of a chair. 'There was never such a lady as Grace Tucker.'

'I see.' Molly looked away, to the portraits on the wall. One did not hang straight. A lady from the last century, with the martial look of a woman who would defend her lands. In neat, golden capitals, near concealed by the frame, was the name *Wildegos*. 'Who is this lady?'

The younger sister squeezed her knotting. She breathed: 'On our mother's side.'

Molly recalled the number of times Tom had called her a wildego. He must have known her unruliness was in her foremothers' name.

The older sister straightened. 'You must leave.'

'Yes.' Molly curled her lip. 'I see that, too.'

The sharp air was a mercy. Molly stood on the drive, waiting for the front door to close behind her, but it did not. The younger sister slipped out after her.

'What is your name?' she whispered, clutching Molly by the elbow.

'Orl— Molly.'

'You are truly my sister's daughter?'

'Yes.'

'My name is Constance. Grace was only two years older than me. We were such dear friends.'

Molly glanced up at the dark windows of the house. 'You never visited her.'

'Our father – you do not know him. What became of Grace? I always hoped she and Mr Tucker travelled far away and were living some exotic life, like one of her stories.'

'She died,' said Molly, flat, almost cruel. 'The night of the Great Storm.'

'Grace died in the storm?' Constance looked like she might cry. 'Father always said God would punish her.'

'She'd done nothing evil. And it wasn't God who punished her.'

'Oh, you mustn't ... Oh, please, Miss Tucker, do not think ill of me. I have prayed for Grace often and often. Please, forgive my sister and me. Please, come again. I will – yes, I will speak with my husband. You can visit me. I am sure my master will allow it, and my father need never know. My master may even intercede with him on your behalf. Please. It would be so comfortable to know and cherish my niece. I would do Grace that justice.'

Molly studied the lines of fret around Constance's mouth, and the eyes that bulged and did not blink, as if trained to some clever trick. She pulled her arm free.

*

Molly got down from the coach outside the forge, and walked past the Old Inn, the laughter inviting her in from the dusk, inviting her back to her old life. Widecombe-in-the-Moor was arranged around St Pancras Church and the Church House. Molly crossed the bowling green, remembering Mama talking about the Storm of Widecombe, a story that most likely came from the grandmother Molly now knew to be dead. Lightning had struck the church tower, tearing through the stone wall into the stairs, rebounding with even greater strength against the side of the church, and piercing the high window, before striking the north wall like a cannon ball. Three hundred people were inside. The lightning dashed one man's skull. His hair stuck fast as lime and sand to the timberwork, and his brain slopped backward into the seat behind. A woman's gown and linen burnt clear off her body. Mama had related these details to Tom one night, imagining Molly asleep, she supposed, for she was horrified when Molly began to cry. 'Hush,' she had said, 'hush, it was only the remonstrance of God.'

Father always said God would punish her.

Molly opened the gate to the churchyard, the tors behind soft in the gloom. She walked among the stones, ignoring the heavy door of the church. She came to know the dead.

When she found the Tucker family vault, she knelt in the frostbitten grass, her skirts collapsing over the earth. She read the names of her father's fathers: Joseph, John, George, William, Owen. And Christopher Tucker. Buried, she knew, in name only, just as she really knew him in name only. She could seek out his family next. The tiredness in her bones, after hours of bumping over the road, after those minutes in the parlour, told her: *Yes. Seek shelter. Seek protection. Seek home.*

But she would find none of those things, she knew. She would have to build them.

410

And, if Mama were to ever have true justice, she would have to see to that, too.

Molly looked up at the first blush of stars.

There had been such a lady as Grace Tucker.

Yes, she would see to justice. No matter the cost. Justice would be the last man standing.

III

A gentleman was only permitted to give his ticket to a ball to a lady, and, as Molly had nobody to vouch for her as a lady, there was no way to gain legal entry to the assembly. There had been reports of prostitutes dressing up as fine ladies and insinuating themselves into polite company. The notion of dressing up as that kind of free-trader made Molly smile. The reality that she could not walk through the front door of the great house, but that Charlie Savage could, made her laugh out loud.

But front doors were for people who observed rules, just like God was for people who observed Him, as Tom said – 'and you only need observe me, son.' Well, she had observed. Wrapped in a cloak, Molly walked with purpose through the kitchen, stepping aside for staff racing between pantry, larder and coal cellar, and climbed to the ground floor. Here, she laid aside her cloak, a coarse thing she'd snuck from a taproom, and continued on past the coffee room and the coach office, her heavy mantua rustling against the boards – the familiar smells of smoke and drink, the smells of men – glancing down into the stables and coach houses at the back of the assembly rooms, where windows sweated and strained with the heat of the dance.

Molly opened a serving door and stepped into the tea room. The ceiling thrummed with feet, and the chandeliers shuddered. From next door: the crack and laughter of billiards. Crowds of ladies sat together at vast tables, each attended by one or two gentlemen. Molly squared her shoulders and pressed on, squeezing through conversations about the fashions of the evening, the possible development of a new assembly room at Dock, the winter subscription for concerts, the new play, and town life over country.

'For heaven's sake, Renwick, who is that lovely creature?'

'I am sorry I cannot inform Your Lordship, but sorrier I cannot inform myself.'

Molly glanced behind her at these words, looking for the woman the two Corinthians were discussing, and met their eyes. They were discussing her, and, at her frank stare, they looked shocked, but not ashamed, instead advancing through the crush. Molly tried to retreat, but found herself stuck, and then the lord had her hand in his, and was kissing her fingers.

'You are a sweet pretty creature,' he said, 'and let me but enlist you in my protection, and I will be the happiest man on earth – for where is your party, my dear?'

No knife. 'I have been separated from them, sir.'

'Then let her walk between us,' said Renwick, taking Molly's other arm.

Both men wore the look of bored dissipation: seeking distraction from themselves. Molly knew it well. 'My party is expecting me presently, sir.'

'Whither so fast, my love?' said His Lordship. 'We will see you safe.'

Molly tensed her arm, testing Renwick's grip: he would be the weaker of the two.

412

'To whom are you promised for the next dance?' said Renwick. 'For you must give us the honour.'

'I am already promised, sir,' said Molly, 'to Mr Savage.'

'Never heard of the fellow,' said His Lordship.

'Oh. Did they let him in? Bad as a shopkeeper, I say.'

'And yet, sir,' said Molly, 'a lady must keep her promises even to shopkeepers. Do you know where I might find him?'

'Oh, yes,' said Renwick, 'I just saw him.'

'Then, may I beg your protection in finding Mr Savage, sir?'

'I would die a thousand deaths and be happy, sweet lady,' said His Lordship, 'could I do you but one favour.'

Molly gave him a smile. 'Just one death will do.'

'Ha! Did you hear that, Renwick? Just one death will do! Come, let us take the pretty bird to her shopkeeper.'

The men remained either side of her, taking claim of her arms, and none of the red-faced gentlemen or quick-fanning ladies glanced up as Molly was steered from the tea room into the smaller refreshment room, where she looked for Charlie – but he wasn't there. The men pushed her on towards the courtyard.

'Do you believe Mr Savage to be among the horses, sir?' she said.

'We will find him, dearest dove, we will find him.'

'But, pray, good lady,' said Renwick, 'what party of ladies accompanies you?'

Molly tested his grip again. 'I am of Miss Tucker's party, sir.'

'Miss Tucker? I do not have the honour of her name.'

'She has the honour of yours, sir,' she said. 'Gentlemen, I have no cloak and will be cold in the courtyard – please, if Mr Savage is outside, ask him in to me.'

'We will keep you warm,' said His Lordship, his hand now sliding to her waist.

'Sir, I must protest at this insolence.'

Both men stopped, wavering at the door. His Lordship breathed into her face, the smell of Tom's best wine. 'Insolence?'

'I had a claim of protection from you, but you mean me no such protection.'

'A lady would not say such a thing! I am pained, sweet creature!'

'This lady would. What's more—' Molly broke off, for there, passing from the billiard room into the refreshment room, was Charlie Savage. 'Mr Savage!'

Charles paused, looking over the ridiculous headgear of the ladies about him, until he found an even stranger tableau at the door: Lord Stanbury and Sir Renwick, both giggling like schoolboys, and an unequalled beauty wearing a horribly worn French gown and a face of thunder. Charles strolled over and made his bow.

'My Lord, may I assist you?'

'This pretty creature says she is promised to you, Mr Savage,' said Renwick. 'I suppose you don't know how strict our hostess is on gentlemen giving their tickets away to actresses.'

'Actress?' said Charles, almost taking a step back at the lady's look of scorn. God, he'd not seen scorn so scorching on anyone but Tom West – Charles felt his balance go. He glanced down at the lady's arms: her tanned bicep was squeezed white and red by His Lordship's grip, and her glove had slipped down her forearm, revealing a lace of scars. Charles cleared his throat. 'If this lady is playing a part, sir, it is the part of patience itself, for I have kept her waiting e'er too long, and can only beg pardon. For what else you may be insinuating, sir, I am mortified to know I must correct you, but correct you I must.'

'Eh?'

'Do you not know who this lady's father is?' said Charles.

Orlando's look would have shrivelled a buffalo.

'Father?'

'Sir, I will say no more, but thank you for offering your protection, which I can now ably provide.'

'No need for that,' said His Lordship, 'for we have her in hand. Go on, sir, we will conduct the lady from here.'

Charles glanced at the growing bruise on Orlando's arm. He moved a hand to the ornamental sword at his waist. 'I must insist, sir.'

A snort. '*Shopkeepers.*' Then Lord Stanbury and Sir Renwick reeled away.

Molly stopped herself spitting after them, and tugged her gloves up. Then there was nowhere to look but Charlie Savage's calculating face. She sighed. Above, the music crashed on, and, around them, the trade of wit and wealth.

'Thanks, Charlie boy.'

'If you want to thank me, never call me that again.'

Molly grinned. 'As you wish, Charles.'

Charles urged her into the courtyard, guiding her around mud and horse shit –with a compliment on her silk shoes – to a quiet corner. His breath curled between them. 'While we're bandying names, might you acquaint me with yours? For I'm fairly certain it isn't Orlando.'

Her grin faded. 'It's Molly.'

'Molly West?'

'Molly Tucker.'

Charles rocked back on his heel. He cursed himself. 'Yes. I see.'

'You do?'

He pulled off his coat and draped it around her shoulders. It swamped her. He gently tugged her hair from the collar. 'Dick English told me a tale once. I should have believed him.'

Molly thumbed the silk lining. 'I'll get to him.'

'What do you mean?'

Nothing.

415

Charles summoned his nerve. 'Mrs Tucker turned on Tom to keep you with her. Dick English said he'd throw you on the parish. You were the most important thing in the world to her.'

Molly hunched into Charles's coat, burying herself in its borrowed warmth – wanting to bury herself in the warmth of those words for ever.

His fingers drummed on his sword. 'Where's Tom?'

'He ran away.'

Charles laughed. 'Tom, run away? From what?'

She looked him in the eye. 'Me.'

Charles couldn't help his gaze dropping to her body. She had twisted her girdle like a rope about her fist, as if to say, *You may go hang yourself for me.* He said gently, 'Yes, I can see that a man might be terrified by such a sight.'

'He was.'

A smile. 'More fool him. Or, perhaps, more fool us, little actress. All this time, I thought you were a boy. I'll be damned. Or someone will, at any rate, God's truth. And what are you doing here?'

'Looking for you.'

Charles rattled his sword in its scabbard. 'If I can help you, I will.'

'We'll get to that.'

'Still some man in you, I see. You're not here alone?'

'I am.'

Charles blew out his cheeks. 'Well, what do you expect but to attract the attention of men like Renwick and Stanbury, walking without a protector?'

'A man can walk alone with impunity, wherever he is.'

'This new character doesn't suit you. I suggest you go back to the role you've so lately departed.'

'I may anon. But I won't hide my nature any more – no part of it.'

416

'You can't be all things to all men.'

'I can be all things to myself. And you are going to help me.'

'Oh, am I, Captain?'

'Yes.'

'Why's that?'

Molly narrowed her eyes. 'Because you've moved to Plymouth to grow your standing, but have no advantage but your dubious charm. You can bet on the men of Plymouth or you can bet on Tom West, but neither one is as good a bet as me. I'm the better gamble. And you're a gambling man.'

He took a step closer. 'And what is it I'm gambling on?'

'I have the designs for the fastest ship on the sea, and I know how to make it even faster. You are going to introduce me to the Commissioner of the Navy Board, and I am going to share my knowledge with him. In return, he's going to commission me to build it. I'm going to be the most successful shipwright Devon's ever seen. And you're going to broker the deals and keep the books. I've got the goods. You have the sums and the connections – and, frankly, the balls. Pardon the talk of an old sea-hand. We're going to make a lot of money together, Charles Savage.'

'Do you realise how long the odds are on that scheme?' he asked, unable to resist mirroring the smile turning the corner of her lips.

'Yes,' she said, feeling something like enchantment – and, for the first time in her life, she wasn't the one in thrall. But she was enjoying it.

'And do you realise what Tom will do to us both when he discovers we sold his ship to the Navy?'

Molly touched his arm. 'Tell me he's not used you badly, too.'

Charles shook his head. 'It's not a novel experience. I let him. I have a strong sense of self-preservation.'

'What are you preserving yourself for? You think Tom's going to give you a fortune for your virtue?'

Charles chuckled. 'No. I don't. But what you're asking – it's a reckless gamble, death or the making of me. What on earth makes you think I'd agree to it?'

'Because you've known me as a woman for five minutes and you've not yet suggested a less decent proposal, and neither have you laughed at me. Because you've been playing joker to a king long enough, and you're burning to become something more. Because you're smarter'n any man around. Because you've watched me these many years, and know I am capable of running any odds I'm given. Because you *know* me. And I know you.'

Charles read the constellation of her eyes. He'd told himself, all his life, that he was waiting for the right moment, the right chance. And here she was. 'God's blood, what a wild hazard you are. Yes. Yes, I'll hazard with you.'

The Ides of March

I

Molly was glad for the lack of stays. She considered saying as much to Charles – thanking him for buying a suit of man's clothes, without a word of instruction, alongside another gown – but the climb up Mount Wise stole her breath, even without the binds. She stopped, hands trailing in the tall grasses, to look down on the inlet of the sound separating Plymouth and Dock, following Stone House Pool to Stone House Lake to Mill Lake, to the dockyard. Ships being refitted jostled in the basin. Men tacked between the building slips at the dry dock and the sail loft and ropehouse. Behind, the officers' residences on the new Fore Street gleamed white. The beer shops were already busy, too.

'You'll remember to tell them they won't have no scandals from me,' she said.

Charles took off his hat, wiped his forehead. He was going to replace it, in deference to the lady, and then remembered himself. He kept it off. 'You already are a scandal,' he said.

Molly snorted. 'The Navy's canvas contractor and yard sail-maker have both been done for supplying bad materials for bolt ropes. And the Navy's own storekeeper was embezzling from the stores. They won't have none of that from me.'

'If you're not on the take, how d'you expect to fill your pockets?'

'Don't piss on your own front doorstep.'

'I don't tend to.'

Molly grinned at him. 'No need to be on the take when you own the place.'

Charles wagged his head. 'Sir Nicholas Morice owns the place. The Admiralty lease Dock from him, and so will you.'

'Sir Nicholas Morice is a child. He'll *give* me Dock. I can convert him faster'n I converted you.'

'I don't know whether to be flattered or offended.'

'Be whatever you like. You're a free man.'

Charles watched an avocet lift off from the salt meadows below and struggle against the wind, and then followed Molly up the hill. 'I've got a notion a man don't remain free very long, around you. But, if you don't know how bewitching your words are, I'm not going to enlighten you. Tell me, then, how do you plan to buy Dock from Sir Nicholas?'

Molly reached into her jacket and drew out a folded piece of paper. 'I want you to sell this.'

'And what are we selling, now?' he asked, careful with the stiff thing, which had obviously seen little use. Then he stubbed his toe. 'You're as rich as . . . as rich as—'

'Can you sell it?'

He pulled his wig off, too. 'I can sell anything. But, heaven help me, why would you want to sell such a house, when you could live off these acres and be a great lady?'

'It's not mine.'

'It's got your name on it.'

'That's not my name,' she said.

He blew out his cheeks. Sat down in the grass and read it again. Tapped the paper. 'What is your name, then?'

Molly sat beside him. 'Wildego. The name of my mothers.'

He cast a close and gentle look over her face. 'You wear it well. Consider it sold, Lady Wildego.'

'Your tongue gets prettier every day, Charles Savage,' said Molly, before realising who had said those words first.

But he didn't baulk or pull away. He only smiled at her, open and plain, and said, 'Maybe I care to keep your good opinion.'

Rain brushed her. She folded the paper, and pushed his hand towards his pocket. 'You'll remember to say they can rely on me?'

'I'll tell 'em, but I reckon they'll be more persuaded by the thing itself. Not dressed like that, of course.'

Molly tried to hide the dread that sprang up in her. She looked south-west, to Mount Edgcumbe, where a mansion was rising. A buzzard circled. 'If you think it will help.' She looked at him. 'And, yes – I do know how bewitching my words are.'

Mast house, timber basin, saw pit, building slip, timber shed, smithy, model loft. Molly picked among them all, holding her train up from the slick stone and mud, without once turning to meet the curious stares of the men at work. *Don't just walk like you belong*, Tom would say. *Walk like you own the ground you're walking on.* The clash and clangour and sharp smell of tar and paint felt like home. She passed the victualling office, glancing in at stores Tom would make a fortune on, and came to the Commissioner's, a humble building – they were building him a larger house on Fore Street to replace this one. That's where she'd live, too. Molly repeated this to herself, holding on to her ambition like a lifeline in a storm.

Charles came out, and looked relieved to find her there. Had he thought her nerve would fail? He crossed to her and took her arm.

'They're interested,' he said, 'perhaps more curious.'

'You didn't tell them who I am? Not a word about Tom?'

'Far as they know, you're a lady shipwright from North Devon. But they want a demonstration.'

'Demonstration?'

'The design,' he said. 'You can draw it, can't you? The ship design?'

'What do you take me for?'

Commissioner Lark sat at a desk far busier with papers than Tom's had ever been. Around him, officers hummed and hemmed, tittering. Curiosity? More like amusement. The Commissioner, a grey-headed old man used to tolerating Sir Nicholas Morice's tantrums, rose now and bowed.

'Madam. I understand you are quite the lady shipwright.'

Molly remembered to curtsy. 'Thank you for your time, sir.'

'I would never deny a lady.'

Molly raised her eyebrows. 'I'll hold you to that.'

More tittering. But Lark smiled, too. 'We've been hearing rather large claims from Mr – ah – Savage.'

'He's good for them,' said Molly.

'The more pertinent question, if you'll excuse me, miss, is whether or not *you* are good for them.'

'Do you have a sheet of paper and some lead?'

The Commissioner clicked his fingers. An officer snapped to, gathered a scroll of paper and laid it across a free corner of the desk. Molly took the lead, meeting the officer's gaze dead on until he retreated, and then she licked her fingers, moistening the tip.

'This, gentlemen, is the fastest ship on the English sea.'

Charles watched, standing at the centre of the Persian rug. He watched the bow of her head, the tensing of her arm, the concentration in her whole body as she drew the *Venture*, as she gave up her home. She took her time. She wouldn't be hurried by the disbelief on their faces, by the shock. God, he hoped he'd been right in bringing her here. What if they had better? What if they laughed? What if she was destroyed, in more ways than one? She was an eccentric, that was for sure. Eccentrics were only permitted if they amused the powerful. And she wanted to do more than amuse. She wanted the power.

Finally, she dropped the lead and straightened up. Charles wanted to take a step forward, wanted to see what she had produced, but was anchored to the spot. He watched Lark study the design.

The officers were holding their breath, waiting to laugh.

Then, the Commissioner pointed to something and said, 'I've not seen this before. What is the benefit?'

And Molly leant into him, until their heads were almost touching, and began to explain.

The held breath was wasted, and the officers began to relax, some crowding round, others hanging back, put out.

'But this, here, miss, I don't quite understand – you have left this section blank.'

'I don't give blank notes.'

'Aha. I see. Am I to understand, then, that you do not wish to *sell* us this design, but rather to build it for us?'

'Yes.'

'And we are to commission you – at what rate?'

Then she turned to Charles, lifting an arm, and said, 'Mr Savage can answer financial questions.'

Charles nodded, and stepped forward.

Molly tapped a knuckle on the paper, once, twice, and made a fist.

II

'Ring that bell and you'll be ringing in your own death.'

Richard hesitated in his reach for the nightstand. The figure at the window held the pistol with a steady hand. He knew that voice. 'You were too slow in the church, Master West, and you will be too slow now.'

'I wasn't too slow, I was too virtuous, and that's long behind me.'

'May I see the face of my accuser?'

'If that sort of thing matters to you.'

Richard pulled himself upright. The curtains of the bed had not been drawn, nor the shutters on the window, for his man knew that sometimes Richard could not sleep, and instead watched the racing of the stars. The girl had an unrestricted shot from the windowsill. She wore the raiment of a young man of wealth. Richard would die in his nightshirt, a final indignity at the hands of Tom West. He tried to care, as he watched her climb into the room and perch on the edge of the desk. Outside, Dartmouth raised no alarm, for, if it knew Richard was in trouble, it did not care. Inside, he did not hear his wife stir in her room, nor any of the servants below or above. He was alone, with Grace Tucker's godforsaken daughter, a weapon that was out of reach and legs that failed him more than they served him, like everything else in his life.

'I suppose you've come to kill me at last,' he said. 'Where's Tom? Doesn't he want to watch?'

Molly weighed the gun in her hand. 'Do you ever have news from Plymouth?'

'What news could I want?'

'Of a lady shipwright.'

'Yes. I had heard there was a new naval contract with a lady of means.'

Molly curtsied. The pistol stayed level.

'But you are a child. A devil's child, at that. You mean to tell me you bewitched the Navy and the Corporation, as Tom bedevilled the Revenue and all besides?'

'I've sold our ship design to the Navy. I've agreed to build the same ships for the Revenue, too.'

Richard pulled off his cap. 'I've been waiting for Mr White to deliver you from evil. I suppose you weren't interested in being saved.'

Molly swallowed her snarl. 'I'm glad my life can afford you some amusement, cooped up as you are.'

'Watch your tongue,' he snapped.

'Watch yours, Dick, or I'll cut it out.' Molly shrugged off the heat of violence. 'I want to know your part in it.'

'I had no part in it,' said Richard, grabbing the sheets in his fists. 'I only tried to do my duty, and look at me!'

'I am looking at you, Dick. I know you're only alive because you daren't do it by your own hand. Because you fear hell. Well, I've called hell home these many years, and I don't fear devil or man, and I certainly don't fear you. So, you can keep your tantrums to yourself and tell me what I want to know. Your part in it. My mother's death.'

'I was trying to save her. I warned her about what he is!'

'What he is, is not for you to decide. Charles Savage had a story to tell me. You made her turn against him, though you knew the consequences.'

Richard sneered. 'Maybe she saw the truth of him, as you now have. Maybe she came to me, as you now have.'

Molly drew herself up. 'I remember a man, a man with pride like ice, who visited our cottage. That was you. You pressed her. You scared her.'

'What do you hope to gain by this confession?' he said. 'A clean conscience when you shoot me?'

'Justice is always clean, Dick. The rest is niceties.'

Richard felt all the air leave him. He sat back against the pillows. 'I told Mrs Tucker I'd take you away from her, if she didn't give up his route. That is all.'

The pistol was heavier than any cannon ball. Molly's finger did not move on the trigger. 'What was she like?'

'Have you no one else to ask?'

The blood drained from her face.

'No, I suppose you don't,' he said. 'She was a misguided, fool-ish woman. More than that – her journal would have told you. *A True Relation of My Life and Deeds*, she called it. As if anybody cared. Maybe she knew you'd care to know, one day. But Tom destroyed it, I imagine. Destroyed her body, then her soul, then her voice. And yet it's me you come to threaten in the night. Will you slay Tom West too, or do you plan to let me down entirely?'

'Worried you'll see him in the next life?' said Molly, hoarse at the effort.

Richard smiled. 'We are not going to the same place.'

Molly's finger twitched, but still the trigger did not yield. 'I'll leave that to God, some way down the road.'

Richard wiped sweat from his eyes.

'You didn't kill her. All these years, I thought you did. But Tom could have forgiven her. There's a code, but codes don't apply to him. He could have forgiven her.'

A nod.

'He brought me up to hate you. And I do, for your part in it. I hate you and wish you to hell's fire. But I hate him more.'

Richard knew false conviction when he heard it – knew, too, what it was like to live for revenge, because everything else was too painful to bear.

'I am going to destroy Tom West,' said Molly. 'I'm taking

his seas, and I'm going to take his lands. And you're the only man in Devon who wishes to see him brought down. Tom has trusted me, like a master trusts a dog. I know his every movement of the last ten years. I will sign a statement testifying to Tom murdering my mother. Testifying to his crimes as a freetrader, and his bribery and blackmail of justices, controllers, mayors, sheriffs, lords and ladies. I'm going to give you enough dirt on all of them to make them comply. You are going to arrest him. You are going to try him. And then you are going to hang him, in the name of my mother.'

Richard's nerve endings were firing: a pleasurable crawl up his legs. 'And then?' he said.

'And then I'll get to you.'

III

Molly had taken a house on Fore Street with a bow window that filled with the sea, looking over the ropehouses and storehouses of Dock. She sat at her desk now, midnight long past, listening to the whip of wind over the basin and the strain of ships in the dry dock. When she heard the heavy boot on the stairs, she knew it wasn't Charles come to bandy words with her. She rose, and lit the lantern on the table that ran down the middle of the room.

'Hello, my girl.'

Molly turned, one hand in her pocket, where the snug pistol waited. Tom stood in the doorway at the top of the stairs. It had only taken three months to forget his size. It was a shock, how falling from his orbit had made her forget his gravity so quickly. And how lonely she was, without the warmth of his firmament – lonely as a lost ship – and how very, very cold – that came as a shock, too, as if she'd lost everything all over again, as if she'd been punched in the stomach and all air was gone from her. The thing she wanted most in the world – wanted with so much force, it was like wanting to breathe under water with the surface out of reach – was to run to him, and bury herself in his chest, and feel those heavy arms close about her and never let her go.

She stayed where she was. Told herself to study instead how ragged he'd become, how his face had pouched with drink, his eyes had sunk with sleeplessness, his body had run to ruin.

He let her stare. It was good to be under that stare again. She wore fitted trousers, a loose shirt tucked in at the waist, curls that fell to her shoulders, neither one thing nor the other, but still all his. He could see it in her eyes, and the relief cracked his chest. He glanced about the room: the rug from Persia, the fancy paintings on the walls, the tools and papers, the smell of power. Yes, that's my girl.

'I heard you'd docked here,' she said.

'From who?'

'Charles Savage.'

Tom frowned. Closed the door behind him. 'You've developed friendly terms, I see.'

'He introduced me to Commissioner Lark,' she said.

A grunt. 'I didn't think he had it in him.'

'I know you didn't.'

Tom came closer – to the end of the table, where he flicked at a scroll. 'I suppose you'll be stealing Nathan from me, next.'

'Nathan doesn't belong to you. He can't be stolen.'

'You've already stolen from him. But I suppose everything can be bought.'

'Not everything,' said Molly, breathing in the sea-salt smell of him, which still comforted her, though she tried to shake it free. 'Not forgiveness.'

'That I'll give you for free.'

Something between a laugh and a gasp fell from Molly, and she closed the distance between them in three strides, drawing out the stubby pistol. Tom caught her arm and twisted until the weapon dropped to the floor. Then he let go. Molly stumbled against the table. The lantern wobbled.

'I didn't come here to hurt you,' he said, bending down and picking up the pistol. He put it in his coat, then brushed his finger against Molly's curls. 'I came here to explain. I know what Benedict told you. I was going to let you cool off. But when I heard about this deal you've made—'

'Don't touch me.'

Tom snorted. He lifted her to sit on the table, and then leant over her, kissing her head. Molly tried to shove him away, but it was no use. She was about to draw the knife from the small of her back when he surprised her by dropping gently to his haunches; his hands remained clamped to the table either side of her. He looked up into her face.

'You'll listen to me,' he said softly. 'One way or another. The how of it is up to you.'

'There is nothing you can say to explain yourself,' she said.

'There's a code, my girl. Grace broke it.'

'What about the code between you and her? She trusted you. And – what? – you couldn't hold your damn temper for one minute to find out if her betrayal might have been for a cause bigger than yourself?' Her voice rising, now. 'She was trying to *protect* me. And you killed her for it. And then you lied to me every day and every night, though I trusted you as if we were one soul. You left me nothing of her.'

'You have to understand. I didn't have a choice. She made me do it.'

'If you believe that, you're even less than I thought you were. I won't come back to you, if that's what you're here for. I'll never look at you with anything but contempt. You might be bigger than me, and you might be stronger than me, but you'll not stop me building those ships unless you kill me now, and you'll never again command my loyalty, nor my forgiveness, not while I have spirit left in me. You can't scare me, you can't inspire me and you can't bribe me. I don't want *anything* from you.' She caught her breath. 'Apart from the word *sorry*.'

'I'm sorry.' The words seemed to fall from him. Tom shook his head, rising to his feet. He paced the carpet. 'I'm sorry if you feel betrayed, but you don't know what you're saying. She made me do it. I raised you. I've given you everything. I've given you my heart.'

Molly stood up. 'What use is a hollow muscle?'

'What use is *sorry*?' Tom spat. 'What, you seek to unman me?' He waved at the papers. 'I don't care what you've sold to the Navy. I don't care what you've sold to the Revenue.' His voice could scatter fleets. 'I love you, I want you with me – and, God's eyes, I'll *have* you with me. And that's more mercy than I've ever shown any being alive!'

'I know,' said Molly quietly. 'My mother knows it too.'

Tom wiped his mouth. 'She told me to do it. She told me to be a man.'

Molly picked up a steel pen, just to be holding something. The split tip jabbed into her palm. 'And you think *that's* what she meant?'

Tom rocked on his feet. 'You won't get an apology. Whatever else you'll get remains to be seen.'

Molly breathed out. Bowed her head. 'You're right.' She lifted the lantern and placed it on the windowsill. 'But it won't be you who decides it.'

'Since when?'

'You should never have come here.'

He boxed her in. 'What do you think you can do to me?'

'I can wreck you, Tom. I have.'

The door opened. Twelve armed men filled the room. Tom drew his sword and his silver pistol. Molly stepped back as the men surrounded him, but still, still he looked huge – a beast, caught and confused. There was the slow bump of sticks on the stairs. Tom span towards the door, levelling his pistol at Dick English, and the two men propping him up.

'Tom West,' said Richard, his nostrils flaring with the intensity of satisfaction, 'I am placing you under arrest, for the murder of Grace Tucker, and the crimes of free-trading and breaches of justice, as witnessed by Molly Tucker.'

A jolt seemed to pass through Tom. His arm shook. The pistol dropped. He turned to her. The shock on his face made Molly sink against the wall. She waited for justice to strengthen her marrow, but there was only the same emptiness she'd lived with since Benedict told her the truth. Loss, heavy and hard and cold, as Tom was dragged away, roaring her name.

In her mouth, justice had the same copper bite of blood.

She heard the screams of her mother, as Tom beat the life from her.

She swallowed the blood on her tongue. She'd live with it.

Tom wouldn't.

IV

It was the batmen who first heard the news and tried to free him. Chained in the back of Dick's own carriage, Tom heard the noise – knew they were somewhere on the road to Exeter, but couldn't place where, the maps he lived by bleached of names and compass now – and felt his heart sinking. Drowning. Don't save me.

He was thrown to the side of the carriage as the man at the reins swerved to miss some violence, and he could have kicked at the door, found earth beneath his feet, but didn't, for, though blood spilt above his eyebrow as the horses hurtled on, it didn't hurt. He wasn't really here, in this map with no names. He was still standing on Molly's carpet, in Molly's house, staring at his girl, his boy, his – his – and Molly was watching him wreck upon the shore, with hollow eyes.

No. That was a lie. Not dead eyes, not dead of love. That would have made it easy.

It wasn't until men pulled him from the carriage that Tom realised they had veered into Totnes, escaping the batmen. There was dawn suffusing the Dart with its desperation. There was the guildhall. There was Dick English, shouting at the guards to make haste. Small men. He could have thrown them off. He let them push him beyond the church to the low door. Let them gather themselves in the court with its pretend throne. Let them push him towards the cells.

It wasn't until he was on the threshold of the Dark House that Tom felt the surge of gut and blood, the kick of the hollow muscle Molly didn't want – he roared and reared, but the men swelled against him, and cheered as they managed to knock him into the hole and slam the door on him.

Darkness.

Tom tried to stand up. He smacked his skull on the ceiling. No light. No window. He pounded at the door. It did not give.

V

The masthead lantern still burnt, though day seeped over the folds of Plymouth and slicked the water until it gleamed like a dead man's marbled skin. Molly set the oars down and peered up at the *Venture*, waiting for a voice to hail her. The red body of the ship was bruised and flaking. Next to her, Charles Savage looked ready to hurl – whether from the chop that baulked at them or because Molly had insisted they deliver word of Tom's fall to the crew of the *Venture* in person, Molly wasn't sure. But no greeting came. No shout of alarm. Molly drew up the rope coiled beneath her seat.

'What's this? Are we to be boarded?' It was Kingston, leaning over the gunwale.

Molly shielded her eyes. 'Unless you want to surrender?'

'No need to surrender to the captain,' said Kingston, leaning out further – his smile changed, Molly thought, from one that seemed painted on, to something that went deeper. 'I thought you'd be with Tom, runaway.'

'Just me. Well, and Charles.'

'Thanks for that,' muttered Charles.

As Kingston pulled Molly over, the old weightlessness came back to her, the feeling she could fly, as she'd always felt among these men and on this ship. Her shoes hit the deck, and Kingston steadied her, but there was no need for it.

'What omen's this?' said Nathan, coming out from the stateroom, hunched and bullish. She'd never seen him angry before.

Charles clambered aboard and straightened his coat. 'Whatever omen you want,' he said.

'You'd go on selling coal in hell, Charlie boy,' said Nathan.

433

Charles adjusted his neckcloth. 'It's not him I serve. Not any more.'

Molly tried to bind the relief surging through her at the sight of Nathan: worn, careful, but Nathan all the same. 'I've come for a word,' she said, 'with the best ship's carpenter I ever knew.'

Nathan clicked his tongue. 'Ain't that your own self, now? That's how I hear it, anyway.'

Laskey and One-Eyed Jarvis came up from below. Prell, van Meijer and Pascal appeared behind Nathan.

'It was a shared idea, and I've got your share,' said Molly, 'if it's a share you want. But I've come to offer a lot more than that.'

'Where's the captain?' said Pascal.

Molly blew out her cheeks. 'Ain't you going to offer me a drink?'

The crew stood back and let Boy precede them into the stateroom – they didn't know how to lead this wildego, they realised. Only Tom knew. They exchanged looks when Molly took Tom's seat, but said nothing. After a moment, Nathan sat down at the foot of the table. Charles moved to the corner, standing behind Molly's shoulder, as she or Benedict used to square up behind Tom. The crew orbited, waiting for the wind to show its direction.

'Where's Benedict?' asked Molly.

'Where's Tom?' returned Nathan.

A beat, until Kingston said, 'I heard Benedict went to North Devon. Another runaway.'

'I didn't run away from anything,' said Molly. 'I ran towards something.'

Van Meijer shook his head. 'So, you've come back to tell us another of your stories.'

'No amount of stories ever set a people free,' said Pascal.

Kingston tilted his head. 'I want to hear what story this child is telling.'

'It starts with a theft,' said Nathan. 'That I know.'

'I'm sorry,' said Molly. 'I never meant to hurt you.'

The ship shifted. Nathan studied his hands. Then opened them, as if offering Molly what was cupped inside. 'So, paint the scene for me, storyteller,' he said. 'You and the Admiralty. You – what? – promised them a ship on words alone?'

'No,' said Molly.

'You promised you'd bring them a ship's carpenter who could draw the fastest ship in the narrow sea?'

'I drew it for them myself.'

Nathan sat forward. 'From memory?'

'From understanding.'

'I've never seen a sight so beautiful,' said Charles, 'as those old battleships going pink afore this girl.'

A smile flickered over Nathan's face. He drummed the table. 'I begin to envy you, Charlie boy.'

'Molly Wildego, lady shipwright of Devon, is contracted to build ships for the Navy and the Revenue,' said Charles. 'The sun is going to rise and set with this one.'

Molly sat back, feeling Charles's warmth on her neck. 'Dock is mine.'

'No need to look for Tom,' laughed Pascal uneasily. 'I think I hear him, now.'

Molly inclined her head. 'I learnt all my lessons well.'

'I can see that,' said Nathan. 'Yes, I can see that. But where is Tom? He meant to bring you back. And here you are, and no sight of him.'

'You have sought justice,' said Kingston. The words seemed to shut out the sun, for the cabin grew storm-dark.

Molly gave a single nod of the head.

'God's eyes,' said Pascal. 'You've got some docity coming

here. You know the code. You think we'll let you off this ship alive?'

'I know codes are convenient, until they're not,' said Molly. 'Benedict didn't betray Tom. And Tom beat him near to death. You think he holds you any higher?'

Pascal seemed to baulk at that.

Molly looked out at the hammered sky. 'Tom is currently in the custody of Dick English. He'll hang for the murderer and traitor that he is.'

'What did Tom betray?' asked One-Eyed Jarvis.

'Me.'

Jarvis spat. 'You're a hard bitch.'

Molly shrugged. 'Or a man with conviction.'

'That's over now,' said Jarvis. 'You're just a wench born wrong. Nothing soft or warm about you.'

Molly sighed. 'Nothing stopping you making for land, Jarvis.'

'I won't let some girl chase me from my ship.'

'Ain't your ship.'

'It's the captain's,' he said. 'We'll have him back afore the sun sets.'

'No, you won't. I've forged a lock stronger'n you can break. Nobody in Devon wants to see Tom West walk. I've shown 'em their sins. And they've blushed for 'em.'

'You think we care if some mayor is embarrassed?' said Pascal.

'I think loyalty comes at a price. Tom is never going back to his throne. You'll never see a profit with him again. I'm set to turn a profit bigger than any shipwright in Dock. Come work for me.'

'Why should we?' said van Meijer.

'Because Tom West killed my mother.'

'And?' said Jarvis.

Charles whistled. 'You're a hard bitch, Jarvis.'

Molly almost smiled. 'Some of you have hearts, rusty as they might be. Some of you value me, as I value you. As for those who don't, you'll be free to go. But not on this ship.'

'You're seizing it?' asked Nathan.

'I'm sinking it. It's diseased. And it won't sail no more.'

'Come and work for you, how?'

'Don't tell me you're thinking on this,' said Jarvis. 'Look at her!'

Nathan narrowed his eyes. 'I am.'

Kingston pushed off the wall. 'Me, too.'

'Aye,' said van Meijer. 'I've seen uglier sights.'

'I haven't,' said Molly, grinning at him, 'but I'm used to you, and there's a comfort in that. I need a master shipwright. I need caulkers and sailmakers. I need men I can trust. Here's my proposition. Leave Tom to the prison he's made for himself. Leave Tom to the past. Build the future with me.' She looked at Nathan. 'You'll be completely free, to live as you'd like.'

Nathan smiled. 'No hiding, eh, Boy?'

'Not any more.'

'If you go with this strumpet,' snarled Jarvis, 'you'll be buried like Wade and Kirby, buried so deep no one will ever find you.'

Molly looked beyond the frenzy of construction at Dock, towards Plymouth, and Charles Church, where Captain Wade and Captain Kirby lay in lead coffins beneath the pulpit, unmarked. The two men had abandoned Admiral Benbow to die off the Cape Santa Marta. When they reached Plymouth, they were greeted with execution warrants. Molly remembered Tom telling her how Wade and Kirby had knelt on the deck of HMS *Bristol* in Cawsand Bay, how the firing party didn't hesitate. Devon had loved Admiral Benbow, as it loved Tom.

Devon would love her more.

'You fear Tom,' she said.

'You're looking for a spanking, girl,' said Jarvis.

Molly smiled. 'Try it.'

Nobody moved.

'Tom once told me, when you're captain of a crew, you're father to gentlemen of fortune. The crew fear their father and love him, in equal measure, and they enjoy it. He told me I'd have to cultivate your fear for your loyalty. But I don't want you to fear me.'

'Then you won't be disappointed,' said Jarvis.

'I don't know, Jarvis. I don't see you reaching for a paddle. But, that aside, there are men among you I love. And there are men among you who love me.' She looked at Nathan. 'You're my family.'

'You offering to keep house for us?' asked Pascal.

Molly rolled her eyes. 'Not likely. But I am offering you a home.'

'With you at the head?' asked Pascal.

'That's right. If such a choice appeals to you, come back with me. If it doesn't, row to Cornwall. Those are your choices.'

Nathan looked over Molly's head to the crest she had carved into the door. He traced the compass, the arrow pointing west. 'I'd be proud,' he said, 'to join you.'

Molly closed the door to Tom's cabin. She'd told the men who planned to follow her – Nathan, Kingston, Pascal, van Meijer, Prell – that she'd only need a minute. She knelt down by the sea chest. It wasn't locked. She kept her eyes averted from the seascape she'd painted inside the lid and searched instead among Tom's flotsam and jetsam, her heart trembling like a weathervane. There was no journal here. But there was her knife. Molly weighed the bone-handled thing in her hands. She sat down on the bed, stroking the red blanket, with its scratchy threads of gold.

You belong here. You're mine. Do you understand?

Molly drew the blanket up around her, as she used to as a child. The mattress reeked of nightmares. There was her depression, in the shadow of Tom's.

She had asked Tom if Wade and Kirby closed their eyes before they were shot through the head. *A coward always does*, he'd told her.

Molly stabbed the knife into the mattress, and drew it up, gutting the bed.

She wouldn't blink.

VI

The door opened. Tom rose to one knee, blinded, but still ready to seize the man and shatter his skull against the wall – but was checked as pistols edged into his vision, protecting a girl. He tried to speak, but he'd had no water, and so was saved from calling Molly's name, for it wasn't Molly. It was a kitchen girl, who dropped something soft into his lap, and then the door clanged shut. Tom's fists closed on the thing: the loved wool, the precious threads of fine metal. The blanket he'd drawn over Molly for the last decade and more. He fell back. There was no one to see him hide his face beneath this scrap of defeat. She'd taken his ship. And no one to see him cling to this scrap of love.

VII

Molly controlled the yawl past the mouth of the Yealm, which licked at the land between the open jaw of hills. She checked her transits – Benedict's transits – Revelstoke Church, facing the surging sea alone, and then Beacon Point. She hauled the tiller, leaning against the wind. To stand poised over the tipping world and not tip herself was a relief. She would feel nothing, think nothing. She would keep the boat aright. She would not fall.

Charles watched from the seat in the stern, gripping the board; it seemed she was possessed by a great torment, and he stayed quiet as they took the stretch of Bigbury Bay, passing on to Smuggler's Hole, Colbury Down, Stair Hole, the howling billows of the Channel lashed into a fury by a south-west wind rolling hitherwards with all the rage of a wounded man, or all the grief of a widow. Molly handled the waves expertly, just as she handled Tom's crew, Dick English, the Navy Board and Charles himself. But he didn't think there was any artifice to her hand at sea. She belonged here, belonged to this wild coast, ravined by landslides and crowned by seabirds, belonged to the majesty of Bolt Head, the unforgiving face of mica slate fissured by purple heather and yellow lichen, the petrified forest of hazels banking North and South Sands. He didn't know where they were going – imagined she didn't know either, for, now he got a look at her, as she loosed one rope and tied another, he saw there were tears on her cheeks, as surprising and as natural as water on the hard face of Dartmoor.

They crossed the inlet, resisting the tidal pull of Kingsbridge. Charles called to Molly: 'Tell me a story.'

She pointed to the castle: 'Sir Edmund Fortescue held that four months against siege, in duty to his king.'

Striking now for Prawle Point, a monstrous heap of weather-worn rocks that looked ready to maul them, Charles squeezed the bench harder, praying beneath his breath as they swung by cliffs of crumbling slate veined with quartz, towards Start Point.

Molly turned her back on the shorn rock, finding the lonely tower of Poole Priory. Dartmouth next. She didn't want to land there, didn't want to keep on in this fret. She had nowhere to land. But that wasn't true – there was no one to chase her at Dartmouth. This ship was sanctioned. She was sanctioned. She pulled the yawl in towards Gallants Bower, beneath the castle.

Charles looked up at the tower and swallowed, but held his nerve as Molly brought the boat into the surf and then jumped out. He followed, pulling the thing up on to the beach against the grab of the waves.

'If you mean to maroon me,' he said, 'I beg you just drop me off at the castle yourself. I am not that hard to shake off.'

'You talk as if you're an unwanted shadow,' said Molly, looking about at the shaving of sand left to them by high tide, and the thread of trees climbing the rocky hill.

'You don't need me,' said Charles, wiping his hands. 'Not really.'

Molly looked up at him. 'But I want you.'

She walked to the edge of the wood and sat in the shade. The trees spared her face from the sand whipped into the wind. She tugged off her boots.

Charles sat beside her, elbows on his knees, trying to see the angles on that sentence. *I want you.*

Molly closed her eyes, tilted her face towards the sun. She remembered doing the same with Benedict, as he trained her in his routes. Remembered doing the same with Tom, as he taught her to handle the tiller. It stung. She swallowed, besieged again by this urge to leave her body, fly from it, flee from this pain. To not be a body, so that the muscle and bone of her was only a useful prop, a limp and ragged nothing, a puppet of sorts, she supposed, that she – or some other entity, let's call it ambition, or survival – would tug on, and make her dance to its own tune, a tune she would claim was her own. But in truth all of life would be just this dance, this performance. In truth, she would be dancing for Tom, to show him how little she cared, and she would be dancing for Mama, to show her what she'd won back. Molly heaved a breath.

'Are you all right, Moll?'

She jumped a little. Molly considered the concern on Charles's face. She considered Charles. Sun-bleached eyebrows and eyelashes, more so than they ever were in the days he worked for Tom. She was dragging him from his counting office. Strength in his arms and lively intelligence and kindness in his eyes, green like the land. She searched for some dissembling, some pretence, some greed. There was none. Only acceptance.

Molly pulled her shirt over her head.

'What are you about?'

The wind sharpened her nipples. She stood up, and dropped her trousers. She wore nothing underneath, and felt the wind everywhere.

Charles stared up at her, his mouth open. He was going to tell her to cover herself, and then realised he very much liked her uncovered.

Molly offered her hand.

He brushed her fingers.

She knelt between his legs. She stroked his jacket, and then pulled him closer. The kiss went through her like wildfire.

Charles pressed her naked body to him, feeling the jut of

her hips, the point of her ribs, the softness of her small breasts. The hunger of her. The power of her. He struggled from his jacket. His erection was bulging his trousers shamefully, but she didn't seem ashamed by it. She was tugging at the buttons. Charles cupped her cheek and kissed her again. God, he'd kiss her every day for the rest of his life, if she'd let him.

His touch blazed over her body. Throbbed through her. Molly urged Charles's hand to the split of her body. She moaned aloud, into the wind, which gave her cry to the sea. The sea cried back, beating the shoreline, rocking the yawl, licking Charles's boots and Molly's curving back. Molly squeezed Charles's fingers, pinning him to the sand. She rutted against him, fucked him, loved him, sought him, breached him, tears on her face, breaching herself.

Leaf

To INTERLEA/VE. v. a. [*inter* and *leave*]

To chequer a book by the insertion of blank leaves.

The name Katherine de Mattos disappears from biographies of R. L. S. – and the history of literature – after their rupture. She assumed a man's name, the rather wonderful Theodor Hertz-Garten, to publish two stories in a series of books known as the *Pseudonym Library*. Katherine also published 1,300 reviews over twenty-two years in *The Athenæum*, a literary journal with a policy of anonymous reviewing, which employed women in great numbers, and whose secret credits included Virginia Woolf and Katherine Mansfield. Literary criticism was the last frontier for female writers – in the words of eighteenth-century Bluestocking Elizabeth Montagu, it was the region of literature men were most desirous to reserve to themselves. Where novelists are subject to critics, critics are subject to no one. Among Katherine de Mattos's reviews is one of *A True Relation*, the first bestseller by Elizabeth Wildego, author of over fifty historical romances, set from the early days of the eighteenth century to the closing days of the Regency. Elizabeth Wildego has recently been revived by Virago after falling mostly out of print. Katherine's review draws a link between the novel and a tale she discovered in Exeter. She was on the money. *A True Relation* features smuggler Tom West, his ward, the wilful Molly, and a ruined cottage on the Bantham Estate, which Elizabeth Wildego walked every day as a child, and later bought with the success of her books.

Bantham House – known sometimes as Bloomsbury-on-Sea – was also home to Elizabeth's younger half-sisters, the writer Blyth Radclyffe and the painter Blanche Levy. You will find a portrait of all three sisters by the photographer Erich Zille hanging in the National Portrait Gallery, in a room bracketed by the cavalry soldiers of the Great War and the refugees of the Second World War. Elizabeth, Blanche and Blyth sit working in a library. The bottom of the picture is blocked by a man's shoulder, the camera leaning over him, following his gaze. It is the only surviving colour photograph of the Wildego sisters, and appears tinted, make-believe. The caption explains that Blanche pioneered the modernist style, particularly in her paintings of empty rooms, and that Blyth brought stream of consciousness to fiction. If you visit the portrait on a Tuesday at one o'clock, you might hear a tour guide tell stories of Blyth's love life, and Blanche's breakdowns, and how both of these things overshadowed their work until feminist presses and galleries revived them. You're not likely to hear much about Elizabeth. On the day the photograph was taken – Thursday, 11 October 1928 – the name of a film producer is listed in the Bantham House guest book, now preserved by the National Trust. He stayed for a long weekend.

(Notes for a lecture on women and writing to be given at Girton College, Cambridge, on the anniversary of Virginia Woolf's lecture series, 'A Room of One's Own'.)

A Vast Network,
Unsuspected, Overlooked

1928

The Three Bees

'Would you forgive a question?'

Bee arched an eyebrow at the American. 'I had supposed that to be the idea of you being here.'

'I didn't mean *that* question.'

Bee turned back to the indoor bulbs. She had left two hyacinth bowls and a bag of charcoal in the armchair to deter the Yankee Doodle from lingering, but, in disappointingly Yankee spirit, he remained resolutely leaning against the conservatory panels, with sweat dripping from his ears. It seemed silence would not deter him either, for after a minute he pressed on.

'Why'd you end *A True Relation* with a wedding?'

'Why shouldn't I?'

'The history books are unclear on whether any marriage took place.'

'They also dispute whether Molly even existed,' said Bee. 'A wedding is what my readers want. It was also the primary concern of most women of the time.'

'A who-wedded, not whodunnit.'

'That's very clever, Mr Hall. Did you come up with that yourself?'

He smiled at her, pleasant and open. She supposed he'd been warned about her sharp tongue.

'You grew up without all this, right?' He gave a wave. The conservatory wrapped around one corner of Bantham House, and his wave took in, at one end, the doorway to Blanche's studio – he could see the corner of a beach scene, blocks of blue and yellow paint – and, at the other, the front hall, with its black marble floor inlaid with waves of sea glass. 'I read that you walked by this place every day as a little girl, and, when you sold the film rights to *California Cross*, you offered the owners for it.'

'You make me sound like a frightful American dream. I didn't *offer* for Bantham Estate. It was for sale.'

'You weren't happy with how *California Cross* came out, were you?'

'What do they call American actors doing Cornish accents? Mummering? It's even worse with Devon accents, believe me. It makes one lose all faith in the prospect of *talkies*.'

'Which is why, when we adapt *A True Relation*, we'll hire a strictly British cast.'

'Haven't you forgotten something?' she said.

'Your husband thinks you should do it.'

'And he did spend so many years slaving away at the typewriter. All right then, pass the papers over.'

'Really?'

Bee snorted. 'If you don't give your sense of humour a dust, this weekend is going to be a dead bore.'

Mr Hall put his hands in his pockets. 'D'you always garden in diamonds?'

Bee waggled her fingers at him. 'One has standards, Mr Hall.'

He grinned. 'One does, Mrs Wildego.'

'Mrs Grenvil,' she corrected. 'Elizabeth Wildego writes

448

historical romances. Mrs Sebastian Grenvil orders the meals, makes the laundry list every Monday –' she jammed the trowel into the butler sink she'd repurposed for ferns – 'and fails to manage the housekeeper. Twenty years younger than me and I never win.'

'Why d'you keep her around?'

She laughed. 'And buy one of those vacuum cleaners?'

'Well, why not?'

'Who would do the vacuuming?'

'Mrs Sebastian Grenvil, I suppose,' he said, thinking about his mother, who had been an Upper East Side lady's own Gladys, and never had time or energy to also do something like write historical romances. He tried to picture Elizabeth Wildego at work with a vacuum cleaner, a cinder sifter, a patent mop, but failed. And that, he supposed, was an achievement on her part, in and of itself.

Max lit a cigarette, and flicked his lighter towards her, feeling warmed himself as the glow washed over her face. He watched her bend over the plants, her cigarette pinched between her fingers with the air of a pen, mid-thought. The firm body of a morning swimmer. Dark hair, for the most part. A few silver strands showed when she tossed her head over the cacti – a plant, as far as he knew, that needed even less care than a kitchen cat. He'd pricked her, he realised, with the question about the novel's ending. Or maybe she was just prickly.

Before the war, she'd had a life of committees and causes, the vote, the welfare of Devon's working horses, the conditions of factories for women in the sweated industries. Boy, it was incredible what industry a mind like hers could get up to when graduating from university and taking up a profession was out of the question. If the suffragists hadn't advocated going into the Red Cross to show England their worth when France took on that churned-mud look, she probably would have continued playing mistress to her father's house, after her mother died in the loony bin. Instead, she put on a uniform and played the Front Line like a skipping rope, across Turkey, Syria, France. Her nursing campaign got her a British War Medal, a vote and, perhaps most surprising of all, a fiancé. The widowed Major, willing to overlook, it would seem, the fact that his bride was thirty-four and her father had already landed his fortune on his nearest nephew. Max didn't pretend to understand English class systems or English inheritance laws. But he understood a make-it-on-your-own story.

Sheltering in YMCA library huts while sniper shots chirped like birdsong, Elizabeth Wildego wrote a bestseller about a girl in trousers on the high seas. As far as he could work out, *A True Relation*, and all the success that followed it, paid for this whole estate, along with Blyth's writing, Blanche's painting, the Major's shooting, and sundry cousins doing whatever it was cousins did. In the decade since, there had been highwaymen, privateers and black sheep. There had been heiresses, runaways and governesses. Each and every one ended in a wedding.

He stubbed his cigarette on the sole of his shoe. 'So, why'd you invite me down?'

'Mr Grenvil is of the view that the golden goose might one day stop laying eggs.'

'So, him being so friendly, introducing me to everyone down here as Max—'

'Oh, no one does surnames on a Saturday-to-Monday any more.'

'It's Thursday. But I guess you don't use the word *week-end*, either?'

'Terribly non-U, Max.'

'I think that's just you, Elizabeth. Everyone else seems to like me fine.'

She laughed, and it was only partially at him. 'Bee. Call me Bee.'

'Bee, short for Elizabeth? Oh, I get it: Betty.'

'My name isn't Elizabeth. We are three queen bees in this hive, Mr Hall: me and Blyth and Blanche.'

'So, what's your name? Don't tell me you're a Bernadette. Papa Bernard Wildego can't have been *that* cruel.'

'Can't he?'

Max looked over his shoulder, through the steamed pane, at the magnolia. 'He wanted a son?'

'He wanted three. And his surname was Thomas.'

'*Bernadette Thomas.* Well, I'll be. How'd you pick Elizabeth for your pen name? Wait, I'll guess. I know I have the body of a weak and feeble woman, but I have the heart and stomach of a king...'

'One day, I'll write Queen Elizabeth a novel. It won't be light comedy stuff, like my other novels. It won't be romance and swashbuckling. It will be a serious historical work.'

Max said softly, 'I'd miss the swashbuckling.'

Bee watched Connor and Blanche dance to the latest gramophone record. The Steinway sat under covers. Seb had gone up to bed – *I'll leave the young to be restless* – and Erich was showing off his card tricks to Max and the cousins.

'I hope you don't mean to eviscerate him,' said Blyth, sitting on the arm of Bee's chair. 'At least not without letting us watch.'

'I suppose you're against the film?'

'Oh, you'll do what you like.' Blyth blew smoke up at the new electric chandelier. 'I saw his luggage when Davies brought it up from the station. So many books, he hurt poor Davies's back.'

'When you say you saw his luggage ...'

'I may have popped my head into his room. He's brought every one of your adventures with him. He might be your biggest fan.'

Bee poked her sister. 'I thought *you* were my biggest fan.'

'He's got a copy of *Manners and Rules of Good Society*, too,' said Blyth. 'I think we've got a travelling salesman on our hands.'

'Does that make you like him more, or less?' asked Bee.

'A thousand times more. In fact, if you don't catch his eye and encourage him to ask you to dance, I will.'

Bee twisted her rings – then realised she was doing it, and stopped. 'I'm past dancing. I'm on to the artichokes.'

Blyth laughed. 'It's come to me, you know. Tunnels. My characters are like tunnels: the surface of the mind is a cave entrance, and, in the gloom, there are memories and desires that root deeper in time, until we reach the dim impressions of childhood. And these tunnels meet, as the women's lives map on to each other. There is a vast network, unsuspected, overlooked. And that is where the story is. How about your trouble?'

'My trouble? Oh, yes. I got it last night. Woke me up. As a young man, the duke shot his calf-love's brother in a duel, ruining his honour – of course, he should have let the whelp kill him – and went into exile, a perpetual Grand Tour.'

'And how does he meet your heroine? He comes back to Devon for his inheritance?'

'He's already got his inheritance,' said Bee. 'And gambled it away. No, this one won't be set in Devon. It will begin in Greece.'

'Your readers will mutiny.'

'I want to write about women on the Grand Tour. No one writes that.'

'Don't look now – our beau is advancing.'

Pocketing the crown the magician had pulled from his ear, Max crossed the carpet and made a quick bow.

'Don't suppose your dance card's empty?' he said.

'Does he charm or offend?' asked Blyth.

'Depends which you prefer,' said Max, looking at Bee.

The armchair seemed to be swallowing Bee into its fussy cushions. She tried to shake them off, regain the posture of dances from her debutante years – but she had never managed to attract a partner then, either – and, in the pause, Blyth put her hand out, and Max took it. Bee yanked at her rings. Blyth's wedding ring seemed no problem. Blyth's husband – currently doing heaven knows what in Berlin – saw no problem in it either, while Blyth's lover, Corinne, believed it entirely a non-starter.

'Will Mrs Grenvil dance?' Max asked Blyth, after two tunes. 'Not that I'm against having you in my arms.'

'Careful, I'll swoon,' said Blyth. 'Bee's at the artichoke stage of life, now.'

'Excuse me?'

'Don't let *Manners and Rules* down. Artichokes are verboten to young ladies. Simply no way to eat them elegantly. Cheese, too. Middle-aged ladies get to eat all the artichokes they want, while they watch us dance.'

Max's hand almost slipped from her waist. 'I didn't realise my room was also a lending library.'

'We're simply *agog* about you, Mr Hall.'

'I take it you're not a fan of the pictures,' he said, trying to catch Elizabeth's eye across the room.

'Cinema has failed to connect with what we are pleased to call reality. The eye licks it all up, and the brain, satiated and titillated, settles down to watch the battle or the birth without bestirring itself to think. Lacking a language and stories of its own, cinema falls upon literature with rapacity, and subsists upon the body of its unfortunate victim. Here is *Anna Karenina* in celluloid: a kiss is love, a smashed chair is jealousy, a smile is happiness. Death is a hearse.'

'You're worried I'll turn *A True Relation* into a moving children's picture book?'

'It is a children's book,' said Blyth. The gramophone shuddered to its end.

'And what you write is worth so much more?' asked Max.

Blyth shrugged. 'Yes.'

'Says who?' asked Max.

'Modernity doesn't need a ticket for entry,' said Blyth. 'It doesn't need a book of manners. It simply is.'

'What about your sister's heroines?' said Max. 'They strike me as plenty modern.'

'To a point. A fatal point, and then they faint in the hero's arms. Bee's books don't ask the reader's brain to do any more than swallow them.'

'I don't believe that,' said Max.

Blyth kissed him on the cheek. He breathed her in – gin, Cointreau, lemon, smoke – as she whispered into his ear: 'Neither do I. But that's just between you and me.'

The breakfast gong swelled through the house, like rising water. Max resisted panic – the alarm, trapped inside the ship's lower decks, still burrowed in his bones.

The entrance hall smelt of mulched leaves. Two pairs of muddy boots waited for someone to do something about them by the umbrella stand. The more persuasive aroma of sausages drew Max towards the dining room, but an open door beyond pulled him off course. He realised the dining room adjoined a library – breaching the threshold, he nearly jumped, for the silence of the room was embodied.

No sister looked up at him. Elizabeth – Bee – sat in a corner armchair, winged by bookshelves. Her feet were bare and blue as her Delft china, but she didn't seem to be aware of the cold, for there was a bright blanket over the armchair and she did not call on it. Next to her was a rather masculine desk, with a bronze lamp and family portraits. No pens, no paper, no typewriter. She was reading a library book, a pair of glasses on the tip of her nose. She held the book in one hand; in the other, a sheaf of papers – what looked like telegrams, bills, thank-you notes – all stapled together. She was making notes between the lines with a pencil so stubby it reminded Max of an out-of-work actress's eyeliner. Her concentration – this chance to see her working, to watch a character grow in the faltering thought of her pencil, after so many years of her keeping him company in moments when he had nothing else to make him smile – he flushed with sudden and unlooked-for desire.

Max tried to shake it off, switching his attention to Blyth, curled in a red armchair with ill-fitting covers. She was partially shadowed by a folding screen painted in dull golds and blues. Beside her, an earthenware pot struggled to contain white wood asters. She was writing in a notebook. Smoke curled from a forgotten cigarette pursed between her lips. Across from them both, lying on a sofa, Blanche supported a watercolour pad on both knees. Max had a view over the top of her head – he was briefly distracted by the surprising delicacy of her neck, and the idea that she'd be very easy to pick up and launch into the air: that she'd probably float on the wind like a kite – and saw she was working in pastels, sketching in a loose way the morning light striking the flowers, and Blyth's cashmere, and Bee's diamond rings.

The companionship between them was sacred; there was a frequency to it that hummed through Max's body, a feeling of being touched by something sublime, the way temple used to feel when he was innocent and had belief, long before he changed his surname and stopped attending, long before his bar mitzvah, even. It was something—

Shutter fire made Max flinch.

He snapped about, before being seized by a wash of shame, as Erich smirked at him, lowering the camera, which, Max realised, had been pointed over his shoulder, looking in at the three women.

A sigh. Bee: 'There goes the morning.'

Blanche craned around, clutching pastel and pad in one hand. 'Oh, it's you, Erich. Must you, darling?'

'I must,' said Erich. 'The moderns – in living colour, no

less.' Then, looking over to Bee, he added, 'And of course you, Mrs Grenvil.'

The laughter ruined it all. Max could see Bee's laughter was patient, even maternal. He backed away. Now, she probably put him on the same level as Erich, there to snoop and document, there to take away from it all, when really ... Max scratched his head, sidling into the dining room and hesitating between the hotplate and the sideboard of tongue and game pie. Major Grenvil was reading yesterday's *Times*, his legs stretched out. He was bare-foot, too, with a towel wrapped around his toes. His ankles were sticks, as thin as Max's wrist, and his legs jerked at the knees, a perpetual motion that didn't seem to worry him. Nerves shot, or maybe just caught in a trap that wouldn't release. Well, they were all injured. But, still, all hunger left Max. It was the Major's bare feet that bothered him. It was the idea that the Major and Bee had walked out in the rain together, before the house woke up, like crew members sharing a smoke at the back of the lot before the actors arrived with their demands, and their games.

A good hostess, Bee knew, kept people amused without making them feel too organised. She had arranged for Mr Hall to go shooting with Seb and the boys, lunch and female company brought to them in the fields; she had arranged tennis, jigsaws and music; she had arranged cream tea on the lawn, chased in by rain; a swim in the plunge pool, followed by a reading from her latest manuscript around the wood-burning stove in the boat house. But she hadn't, she knew, given Max what he wanted.

Finally, though, she had broken. Max was leaving the next day, and his look of quietly borne defeat over the coffee eclairs, coupled with Seb's disappointed sighs, induced her to ask if he'd enjoy a walk to Grace's cottage. So, now, they stepped out together, Max complimenting her on the rockery, and Bee declining to see it all through foreign eyes, declining to name the Chinese rice-paper plant and the giant viper's bugloss, saying instead that there was a lot of work to be done, and she was being kept from it far too much lately.

Silence engulfed them and they dragged it down the drive, the wind in the trees too loud for talk anyway, passing the North Lodge and stepping down into a sunken lane. Bee clung to it, thinking that any minute he'd comment on the crowning elm hedgerow or the white-letter hairstreak butterfly that hovered over his shoulder like a better angel, but he seemed to know his audience.

As the lane let out into open field – tumbling down towards the red cliffs and the sand dunes, the sapphire brilliance of the Avon at high tide gorged on colour, hairy with ferns and bedraggled beech – Bee glanced Max's way, and saw that he wasn't sulking or stewing: he was content. The low sun made his eyes sparkle like coal, and he did seem to be kindling, as he took in the cautious cattle and the whitewashed cottages, the coastguard station, the smithy, and then stared out across the water to Burgh Island. But still he didn't say anything – was leaving her, she realised, to herself. The thought made her shoulders drop.

Beginning to feel the betrayal of a smile, she committed to it, for it was lovely to feel that he'd relinquished the claim of wants, so she could relinquish the duty of providing, could let her edges loose, blur a little, without fear of blurring into him, something that seemed so impossible at home, where one's limits must always let themselves be run upon by the borders of other people, where one was domestic but intellectual, maternal but childless, wifely but attractive, managerial but submissive – and then was accused of not handling it all very well, and being too much at the mercy of Gladys, or humouring Blyth and Blanche too much, or minding Seb's particular dreads like a well-trained border collie.

If Seb would just drop this film idea . . . They'd made such a terrible mess of *California Cross*. Those exaggerated gesticulations and shrill screams for help. That wasn't how she'd written Annabelle at all. And the actors' mouths kept slipping ahead of the actual sound. There was no easy lilt to it, no rhythm. No sex. And it was all sex, her dialogue, though of course that was unmentionable.

'Afternoon, Mrs Grenvil; how'd 'e do?' One of the farmers from the Bigbury side, taking his hat off to her as they passed.

'How do you do,' she said, nodding back.

That seemed to give Max some permission, for he took out his cigarettes and offered her one. She looked back after the farmer, and shook her head.

'My company at home was hoping to join up with Archie Nettlefold on your picture,' he said, nodding towards Burgh Island. 'We'd have to shoot around the hotel, of course. I guess you know Archie's a big fan of yours. But his people say we'd have to make Tom West Molly's father. To sort of sanitise it. And make it believable, him caring for her so much when she's young and not his baby. I said nix to that.'

'My knight in shining armour,' said Bee. Archibald Nettlefold, another film producer, had bought the island a couple of years ago. His art deco hotel was almost complete. Bee shaded her eyes, considering its white shell. 'It's all changing here.'

Max took her arm as she mounted the stile. She told him to mind out for adders. They followed the track, which wound like a corkscrew through the dunes, until reaching a muddy plateau looking on to the river, and there was the thatched boathouse clinging to the corner of the cliff, and the remains of Grace Tucker's cottage.

'Happy?' she asked, more irritably than she intended, or even felt.

'Can we get down there?' he asked.

'It's a bit of a scramble at high tide.'

'I'm sure you'll catch me if I fall,' he said.

'Whatever gave you that idea?'

They followed the steps hacked into the rock face, and then slid down the brush to the back of the cottage, clambering into the bones of the old building, which perched over the water like the ribcage of an animal left to bleach. Bee sat down on the low wall, picking at the stones as Max ran on: 'So, Grace would have planted her vegetables here ...' He dropped down the bank towards the lapping line of water, asking if the cottage ever flooded now, like the night of the Great Storm, when the wind blew so fierce, windmills caught on fire and became blazing fists in the night.

'Why does all this mean so much to you?'

Max turned around. 'It means a whole lot to a whole mass of people. Look at your rings. One for every book?'

'That's not what I asked.'

'I guess you could say you saved me. I borrowed *A True Relation* from a YMCA reading hut in '18 and never gave it back. You and I spent some very close nights in foxholes together.'

A blush scratched Bee's clavicle. He was waiting earnestly for her reply. She'd dreamt about looks of love like that. She studied her heavy tweed skirt. 'You're very kind.'

'I can be.'

She pulled at some ivy. 'The trouble is, Max, I can't agree to the film. It's Molly and Grace. I can't let them become damsels in distress.'

He came to stand before her. Dug his boot into the bank. 'I understand.'

'I am grateful to you, though, for all your ... your passion.'

A warm breeze passed between them. 'It's yours, when you want it.'

Bee pulled at her ring. 'That's never quite been my experience.'

'I wish you'd given me your answer this morning. You see, I've done something that's ... well, it was supposed to persuade you.'

'If you're planning to abduct me in your smuggling ship, you're going to be sorely disappointed. I am hard to sweep off my feet.'

'I've invited an actor up here. The man we'd tapped to play Tom West.'

'Oh, God. Who?'

'Geoffrey du Laurier.'

'You've invited Peter Pan to my house for dinner?'

'Think of him in his role as Christian Fletcher.'

'No, I don't think I will.'

Tom West got out of the deckchair on the front lawn and bowed over Bee's fingers. She felt her heart flutter like a schoolgirl's at his black crown of hair, the broad shoulders under his jacket, the sword at his hip – before the evening gave up its illusions to the light spilling from the house, and she saw his grey hairs, the thickness of his stomach and the pasteboard jewel on his pommel.

'A pleasure to meet you, Sir du Laurier. And all dressed up for me.'

'A *thrill* to meet you, Mrs Grenvil, a *thrill*. May I say what a great admirer I am?'

Bee glanced over at Blanche, who smirked at her, and then at Max, who looked sick as a drunken captain.

'You may,' she said, and pulled her hand back. His breath smelt of whisky and loneliness.

Unlike, Max imagined, thousands of fans, he had never secretly fantasised about seeing Geoffrey du Laurier drop his trousers, but that was what was happening now. The king of the West End got up wobblingly on to the dais in Blyth's studio, and asked her how she'd like him. Blyth put down her drink, picked up her brush, and told him she liked him simply marvellously as he was.

Max hauled himself out of the wicker chair – past midnight and past drunk – dragged himself upstairs – what a carcass he was, what a stinking carcass – but, wait, this was the wrong floor. Attic door. Max leant his forehead against it, and the door pushed open.

Bee was sitting at a captain's desk under a small window, punching at a typewriter by the light of a candle. The room was all books. All books and notes and postcards and paintings and shawls and empty cups. She turned around, raised an eyebrow.

'Haven't you disturbed me enough?'

'I never meant to,' he said, adding, 'I'll go,' as he sat down on the chaise longue. A green sea chest stood open, the inside of the lid a landscape painted in crude blocks. The chest was awash with a quilt of note pages. Max stroked them, uncovering a battered leather book: *A Wild & True Relation of A Lady Shipwright and Free-Trader.*

'It's real ...'

Bee turned around.

'Does she end it with a wedding?'

A sigh. 'You're already conspicuous by your absence.'

'I'm sorry.'

She hesitated, her mercury quelled by the look of awful regret on his young face. 'Yes,' she said. 'So am I.'

'I just wanted you to like me. To like the film – idea of the film.'

'I know.'

'You see, I love you. Your books.'

Bee became very still.

'I wouldn't let them be screamers,' he said. 'Molly and Grace. That's what you have to understand. They're more. They're real. To me. Tom's real, too. My father was a Tom. My mother was a Grace. That's what people have to understand. How hard Grace tries. And how she'll never be allowed to succeed. And how Molly isn't a Pamela, or a Clarissa, or ... or ... How hard it is to write a woman who isn't *their idea* of a woman. Probably impossible. Your sister understands that. I know she does, even if she won't say it ... But, me: I understand it. *Me.*'

He was sliding off the battered sofa. Bee got her arms around his shoulders and pulled him up. Brushed his hair from his eyes.

'I know.'

Max tried to focus on her eyes, but couldn't. There were her lips. 'I read that article by Hugo Spencer in the *Spectator*. "The three sisters can be found putting on a pretty display, but it is nothing more than window dressing. They suffer from vacuity, whether in painting or prose. Their work confronts no central problem."'

'Yes, well. It can be awfully difficult for a man to concede he might be the central problem.'

Max laughed. 'You should write to the *Spectator*. You should tell them that.'

'You're drunk,' said Bee.

Max clutched her hand. 'Say yes. Yes to the film. Stop shouldering the sky for everyone else.'

'I don't do that.'

How she wanted to believe that. Bee eased her wedding ring free, and then jammed it back on. But, still, she found herself leaning in to him. It was a lie, of course. She never could be done shouldering the sky. Nobody had ever taught her how to shrug.

'Yes,' murmured Max. 'Just say yes.'

She squeezed his hand.

BOOK SEVEN

1715

WIDOW'S RIGHTS

A Passage of Seasons

I

'Marry me.'

'Please, do not ask that.'

Tom pulled away. His instinct was to snap, *I wasn't asking, I was telling.* But Grace's expectation that he would offer better than his worst instincts held him back. They were in her garden, Grace sitting on the bench with her sewing now put down beside her, and Tom on a low stool at her feet, the slope of the garden forcing him to look up at her for once. Above, seagulls cried and span, and, above them, a buzzard mounted the heavens in patient circles. It was such a bright day, Grace's roses looked violent – blood spatter.

'That a no, then?' he asked.

'Why must you propose such a thing?'

'You know, Grace. You know what I feel for you. And Molly.'

'Will you cease to love us, if I refuse your offer?' – said curiously, as if there were no stakes attached.

'No, but—'

'Then to what end do you ask?'

Tom grunted. He wanted to shake her out of her coolness. He wanted to stand over her, cup her cheek, kiss her; he wanted

to peel away the layers of her mantua and touch her skin, redis-
cover what he had only witnessed and held the night he pulled
Molly from her, more than a year ago. He kept his hands in
his lap. 'I want to protect you,' he said.

'You do protect us.'

'Look after you,' he said. 'A fine house, fine clothes. A proper
kitchen to run. Silk stockings, silk coverlet for your bed.' He
grinned at her laugh. 'And all the books you could ever want.'

'I have a house. I have food, and clothes. I kept hold of it after
Kit left, and when he . . . And, when I was afraid I'd have to go
on the parish, you helped me and Molly. And you still help us,
when we need it. I could use more books, though.'

'I shouldn't help you. Not so abroad as I do, anyway.
Without Kit's body,' he said, fearing her reaction and so pushing on harsher than he intended, 'you won't be a widow for
another seven years. If your neighbours tell the court you're an
adulterer, you'll be forced from Kit's house – and, before you
tell me it's your house, my girl, it's Kit's in the eyes of law, and
so it will remain until you have widow's rights. An adulterer
has no widow's rights.'

'I am not committing adultery,' she said calmly.

And there it was. 'Your neighbours don't know that,' he said.

She smiled at him. Brushed his knee with her bare foot – her
skirts rising, showing him the slender turn of her ankle. 'Tom
West, the lawyer,' she said. 'Tell me then, esquire, as I am not
yet a widow in the eyes of the law, how do you imagine I am
to marry you?'

'I can make you a widow in a day. You might laugh, but the
law is my friend.'

'I am not laughing.'

Then he realised what he'd said: *I can make you a widow in a
day.* And he had. Tom looked off, to the kitchen door – inside,
Molly was sleeping by the hearth – and then to the stack of

firewood Grace walked for miles to gather, though he told her he could have her fuel delivered weekly. Finally, he said, 'It doesn't bother you, this loss of your reputation, Molly growing up in censure?'

'I cannot abide it. But I can live with it.'

He brushed her skirt. 'Both those things can't be true at the same time.'

'So speaks a man.'

'I don't understand,' he said, ignoring the bee that now drifted close to his face, drunk on heat. 'Are you not desirous of marrying me?'

'I do not desire to marry anyone,' she said.

He batted the bee away. 'Of all your rebellions, that is the maddest.'

Grace picked up her sewing. 'You have a vast deal of experience beyond mine, Mr West. But you have not lived as a wife.'

He straightened. 'I'm not Kit.'

'It wouldn't matter if you were Kit returned to me by God's grace. I am a widow, and, when the law acknowledges my rights, I will have the freehold of this house and this small plot of earth, and, when I die, I will name Molly in my will. This is my land, my walls, my water, and I will not give it away to a husband.'

'That's all?' Relief swelled in him. 'You think I want to take this hut from you?'

Grace's hand shook on the needle. She said again, not so evenly this time: 'So speaks a man.'

His gladness turned to stone. 'I didn't mean it like that. I don't want to take anything from you, Grace. You asked me, once, why I keep coming back to you. It's for *you*, not for what you possess in this world, whether it be this home you've built and held on to through every storm, or a grand manor. And not because of what I possess already. But because of what I don't.' He swore under his breath. None of it was right. Then he stilled her hand, holding her and the needle in his grip. 'You know I am not for words, as you are. I am for action. I want you, for all you are. I *want* you.' He held her searching gaze – God, that gaze could burn a man. 'I am proposing marriage, because I am yours – and because a lady cannot ... would not ... ' He shook himself, shook off these courtly nothings. If his wooing was baser, so be it. 'There can be no wedding bed without a wedding. I will always feel what I do for you, and Molly. Whatever you answer me, neither you nor Molly will lose anything of my help, I swear it.' He stroked her cheek. 'But, God's truth, Grace, I want more than a kiss. Do you?'

She flushed as red as her roses. She would not look him in the face, fiddling instead with the cuff of his shirt. 'You said a *lady* wouldn't – I suppose other women would?'

Hoarsely: 'Other women do.'

'Without a loss to their reputation?'

'Depends on the woman. The man usually marries her in the end. At least, she expects he will.'

'What if she knows he never will; what if *she* will never marry *him*?'

'Then she is fun, while it lasts,' he said. 'And then she is a figure of fun.'

Grace guided his hand to her calf. God, the heat of her, even through her skirts. He remembered, the night of the birth, how she shimmered and throbbed.

'And, if I refuse you a wedding,' she said, 'would you respect me for also refusing you a wedding bed? But lose all respect for me, if I wanted – if I want?'

Desire hit him like lightning, racing up his body, stiffening his spine, crackling across his jaw. He eased her skirt up, just an inch. Underneath, her legs were bare. 'You mean you would ... with a man, though he was not your husband?'

At last, Grace met his eyes. He'd never known that look on a woman before – as if her own passion equalled his own, even outweighed it.

'I would with you.'

He slid his hands up, having his full of her – the damp backs of her knees, the quivering muscle of her thighs – as, still, someone (himself) persisted: 'To what end?'

Grace gripped his shirt, brought him to her lips, whispered there: 'You show me.'

He cupped her bare buttock, dropping to his knees between her legs and pulling her to him, drawing kisses over her breasts, drawing gasps from her, these sounds of her pleasure as he kissed lower still, and then easing inside her, brushing a tear from her cheek, asking if he should stop, but she said they were tears of happiness, said, as he bent to kiss her, that she loved him—

Something crawled across Tom's face. He jerked, striking his head on the wall or the ceiling, he knew not. He tried to swallow – thirst came on him like a demon. He collapsed, holding his head. Hunger was the next devil to mount and ride him, and he trembled under it, his stomach popping like fir in fire. He wouldn't cry out. In the ice water of the cell floor, flailing for her touch, the warmth of her garden on his bare back, the urgency of her hands on him, the trust of her open body – he struck himself again – floors, walls, ceiling, pitch cave, ocean floor – he would not cry out.

But somebody was crying. A howl of pain and shock from his boyhood years – his father was taking him apart with his grandfather's cane, and his mother was screaming, and nobody answered her, no neighbours came to pull Josias off his son – and the screams continued, the screams of a bairn for her mother, Molly's screams. If fear and fury could give a body strength, the child would have broken down the door and stepped between the thunder of Tom's raining fists and her mother's body. But a little girl's need was nothing, and the pounding at the door continued, and Tom could not break the tideline between sleeping black and waking black.

'He will stand before justice.'

'I don't reckon he can stand at all, sir. Look at him.'

'He will stand, if it kills him.'

'Sir, have pity. Look at him.'

'Look at *me*, and tell me to pity this devil again.'

Hands on him. Laying their hands on him. Tom lashed out – except his arm didn't follow his fist, and the muscles of his stomach bit on nothing. He opened his eyes: a nail through the skull. Light tore through him.

'Here, Cap'n, drink this water.'

'He is *nobody's* captain, and you will not address him.'

The dam broke. Water, cool, clean water, flooded him.

'That's *enough*. On his *feet*.'

The water was gone. He flailed for it, but it was gone. He wanted to sob, but all that came was an empty retch, and then the hands of men – gentle boys, like Benedict – were gathering him up. He leant into them, eyes streaming. His toes bashed across the flagstones. Sun broke him at the hinges, took apart the last of his frame, and he was going down, despite these boys, when a hand seized him by the forelock and yanked his head up.

Dick English's blue eyes bore into him.

'Time to cut you down to size.'

Tom knew these were words of consequence, but couldn't whet his focus enough to meet and parry them. He needed more water. He needed to sit down. His legs were land-bitten. They would not carry him on the usual circuit of the court, and the guards seemed too afeared to force him. So, he gripped the wooden bar before him – his wrists blazed, the cross-hatch line that joined forearm to hand, once knitted with the barrels he'd hauled, now clung redly to the bone, and his veins bulked like swollen tributaries. He could not make a fist. Lice jumped from him, rats from a drowning ship, all souls lost, and the bite marks were visible too, festering and yellow, through the rips in his shirt. He stank worse than a fish market at high noon. All of this came on him as a fresh assault by God's light. The Mayor and the Sheriff and the squires arranged around the court shrank as if his fall were contagious. He searched for his crew – for Nathan or Benedict – but they had forsaken him. He searched for Molly. She had abandoned him.

So, take the bit between your God damn teeth. He gripped the bar with both hands, and held himself even-keeled in the headwind of the judge's words. Dick English sat hard by, with the look of a man who'd finally had his cock sucked. Tom spat a bloody circle that landed, the size of a guinea, between him and the judge, who hesitated for a moment and then hurried on. The crime was free trading, intimidation, bribery, and discourse with a foreign enemy in a time of war. The penalty for these crimes, if the prisoner were found guilty, would be, first, the pillory – here, the judge faltered, for really the pillory was meant for miscreants, but Captain English had insisted on it, and the Kingsbridge pillory, too, on some personal point – then execution, and hanging in chains. His body would be dismembered, tarred and hung in gibbets across Devon, from sea to sea. If he were found guilty, of course. Did any man wish to add to these crimes? No? Then the trial would commence.

Tom felt Grace's gentle finger follow the line of his jaw,

curve beneath his chin and draw him into the court. Outside, gulls bayed.

'Murder,' he said.

'Does the prisoner make so bold as to threaten the court?' asked the judge, as shrill as if Tom's hand were already at his throat.

'The death of Grace Tucker,' said Tom. 'Are you not to rule on who is to blame for that?'

'No.' Dick English spoke primly, and, as Tom swung about to face him, was dusting off his red jacket. 'No,' English said again. 'We will not be dealing with incidentals.'

'Such tales of your terror,' said the judge, too loudly, 'have been greatly exaggerated, and the court is assured no such murder of a woman can have taken place while the good justices of Devon stood idly by. Now, if that is all, the court has waited several months on this case – *most* inconvenient to the town of Totnes, as we have been unable to move you to Exeter, as would be proper, due to the threat of your *ruffians* staging a rescue – and, while various parties concerned have been ... that is, have fully recollected their memories, we will not endure *any* more delays. We will move quickly through the formalities, gentlemen. We have the affidavit of one – ah – Molly Tucker, *lady* shipwright, if I am not very much in error?'

Tom sheered about against the wave that rose to sink him – but she was not here. Dick English was unfolding a piece of paper.

'I will be reading the statement from Miss Tucker, already witnessed by the magistrate.'

'Very good. And what will we be hearing?'

'A true relation,' said Dick, grinning at Tom, 'of wretchedness, vile appetites and even viler heart. For, where Devon may think she sees a hero of the people, the sworn oath of Miss Tucker shows us a violent villain, who cares only for the destruction and possession of any who are cursed enough to cross his path.'

Rage shook Tom's muscles. 'You didn't *cross* my path,' he snarled, 'you've dogged it. And now you've betrayed the only oath you could have sworn to induce her to put me here. Why? You can't let her win? You don't want justice, because you know it would come down on *you*, whether from this fool or from God. You just want your own satisfaction. You are the curse, you two-faced coward, and I'll see you in the ground before it closes on me.'

Dick English waved the paper at him. 'Miss Tucker doesn't seem to see matters that way.' He dropped his voice. 'And, as for Mrs Tucker – well, we can't ask for her estimation of you, now, can we?'

Tom lost his grip on the bar. He would have fallen, but for one of the boys who reminded him of Benedict, who caught him about the waist. As Tom tried to right the world and his place in it, his vision gave him the shape of a man to the side of the court, a hooded cloak drawn about him. He wore gleaming boots. Charlie Savage. When he realised Tom had seen him, the hood twitched, revealing his face. Charlie's jaw set to working, and then he made a bow, cut to perfection, his eyes not quite dropping to the floor, but instead levelling on Tom's waist. Tom followed his gaze, and realised his trousers were stained with his own piss.

He turned his back on Charlie, shrugging off the little man, who had come here perhaps as Molly's eyes – wanted to shrug him off, but found there was nowhere else to go, and nothing else to fill his ears with but the voice of Dick English, delivering Molly's toll of his crimes – without once saying Grace's name.

II

Charles pinched the rim of his hat: once, twice. 'They're going to kill him. Tom is going to be executed, dismembered and hung in chains, so his soul may not rest.'

Terrible rushing flooded Molly's ears. The din of the hold filling with water. She couldn't see, eyes salt-stung and blind. A hand at her elbow. Nathan. Molly waved him away. Charles took a few steps after her – seemed ready to catch her, as if he thought she might faint. She turned to face the evening sun melting over the Hamoaze and West Mud, the trees on the bank blazing the same red, soon to fall. Molly followed her feet down the slip. The tide came in and hit the pebbled bank: a great sucking roar that drained all other sound from the world, as if she'd put her head under water. Then the tide pulled the water back out, and the pebbles trembled and knocked against each other like the rattle of a thousand dice boxes. She released her breath.

'Then there is justice in the world,' she said.

Nathan flinched.

Charles shook his head. 'Not for your mother.'

The din came at her again.

'He's not going to be punished for your mother's death. Dick English cut it from your statement.'

'He can't do that,' said Nathan.

'He has.'

'But why? Surely, murdering a woman—'

'I made him feel small,' said Molly, her gaze passing over the knots of chains, the wall, the wet basin.

'If you made him feel small,' said Nathan, 'it's because he *is* small.'

The gulls were deafening. Molly closed her eyes. 'When?'

'He's to be pilloried in Kingsbridge on Thursday. Tomorrow. He'll be executed on Monday morning.'

'God's blood,' said Nathan. 'English is a man of his word, when it suits him.'

Charles took Molly's hand. 'You'll know it's justice, even if no one else does. You'll know, and the Lord will know.'

That taste of blood at the back of her throat again.

III

'Well, now,' said Blackoller. 'First time in your life you are getting what you want, I'd warrant, eh, son? To your satisfaction, I hope?'

Richard grunted. His father wasn't here. In the sleepless nights he'd spent imagining locking Tom into the Kingsbridge pillory, as he'd promised at the fair, when Tom was King and Richard only court fool, he'd always pictured his father watching. But, of course, his father hadn't come, nor his wife, nor even his mother. Just Blackoller, who looked on with tolerance, as if permitting an errant boy to torture a spider.

Richard wouldn't let that throw him from his seat, not when the Lord had delivered unto him this final justice. Fore Street was as busy as it had been for the fair, and, just as then, shop-keepers and butcher boys and seamen and squires and servants and smiths and fishermen's wives and farmers' wives and sons and daughters had brought to a halt any traffic on the hill, edging between the water tanks and the butcher – and, yes, just like then, they gathered about Tom West at the pillory, but now he was not their shepherd, and no one sniffed at his heels for scraps. Now, the Revenue were the sheepdogs, lining the streets in pressed uniforms, and Richard was master, lifting a hand now to signal to his man, who told Tom to kneel at the pillory.

Tom made no response. The mob stirred. Couldn't they see he was starved and plagued, not even a shadow of himself – that he did not kneel because he hadn't heard the command, had become as insensible as a mad vagrant?

Richard snapped his fingers.

'I bade you kneel,' repeated the officer, adding, 'sir,' to a titter from those nearest.

A mill owner smirked at Richard. Swallowing a curse, Richard drew a finger over his throat – surprised to discover he was slick with sweat.

The officer kicked at the back of Tom's knees. A swell of discontent from the mob. Damn them all. Richard strode forward – or wanted to stride forward, but his canes caught on the cobbles. He swung himself into centre stage, under the horrific mockery of these servant girls and hedgerow boys.

'Lock him in,' he snapped.

The officer pushed at the back of Tom's head, handled his arms, then swung the pillory closed and winched it shut.

Still, Tom did not stir. His head drooped. Richard seized his black curls and dragged his dull head up.

'I like you this way.'

Tom gave no sign of having heard him. Richard was about to shake him again, when the clack of hoofs on cobbles made him look up. A gentleman was coming over the brow of the hill. Except she was no gentleman. That bitch still had the temerity to travel abroad while perverting her nature in the raiment of a man. Arriving on horseback, too, straddling the saddle, as if this was all a show for *her*. Though, she did not look amused, as she pulled the horse up and studied Tom from behind. She

476

looked scared, as if it took all her courage to twitch the reins once more and bring the horse around to the water tank, where she stopped in the shade, just out of Tom's sight.

Richard yanked Tom's head aside and hissed in his ear: '*Stay down.*' He jerked Tom's head again, so he could see Molly. 'For you have so much more to lose.'

Tom's head grew heavy in Richard's grip as the devil sagged, locking eyes – Richard saw – with the whore's daughter. Then Tom tried to rise, tried to lunge for Richard's neck. The pillory shuddered back to earth, and Tom's arms remained hooked and his head remained cowed, and the world refused to move to his will. Richard laughed.

Tom's anguish made Molly wince, and she had to seize the reins to keep the horse from skittering. She wasn't sure what had finally triggered Tom, but when he'd snapped awake and made Dick English rear with fright, and herself too, she'd wanted to cheer. She didn't want to see Tom tamed. And, though she told herself this was only what he deserved, the shreds of his clothes hurt her; the waste of his muscle, his bones pushing palely from his skin like porcelain; the red sores and blue fingers and yellowing boot print on his neck; the stench of him on the air – the desolation of him. She knuckled tears away – foolish, bitter grief.

The people gathered to watch wanted more from him, too. A murmur of pride buoyed each wave of men and women forward to see what feat Tom West would pull off next. They glanced at the tiled building facades and rooftops, at the spine of St Edward's, searching for the man who would shoot Dick English, perhaps a warning shot through his hat to make them laugh, or perhaps a final killing blow, the last card turned in this game. And then Tom would spread his empty hands, grin at Blackoller and say, *It wasn't me* – and all of Kingsbridge would applaud. Then, one by one, men in the crowd would toss off cloaks and hats and step forward to be counted as Tom's crew. They would free him, and bring him an ale, and clap his shoulder, as Tom made the officer who kicked him kneel in the pillory and count his sins. Or maybe he'd show mercy, and be loved all the more.

But none of that would happen, because Molly had failed to make it happen. She had taken his ship and his crew and his influence, and even the batmen watching on, mutinous, would not mutiny without the backing of Tom's crew, not against this new, powerful Dick English. The tide had drawn back and never returned, against all odds and laws and prayers. Molly waited for a surge of satisfaction, but there was only this sickness in the pit of her stomach, this sense of having betrayed.

He beat your mother to death with his bare hands, and I watched.

Had Benedict said that? Bare hands? She remembered the sinking in her body more than the words.

He shot your mother through the head.

Had he said that? She wasn't sure.

It was as if the same uncertainty gripped the people, for they swayed foot to foot, and whispered and waited, but nobody threw their rotting apples or fish bones. They refused their part in the ritual. Refused the ritual altogether. Tom West had committed no treason against them. He'd given them life's dignities. Tom had made them their own men, and, if he'd made himself king at the same time, hadn't he earnt it?

But Molly did remember this: hurling herself against the door, while on the other side a monster smashed and hurled and destroyed, and her mother cried, *Stop, stop! Let me get to Molly! Stop!*

She remembered that with the cold clarity of falling overboard.

Molly edged the horse forward. The pistol nudged against her hip. None of these people knew the real Tom West. Dick

English had seen to that. And, even if they did know, perhaps the fish guts and apples – the juvenile arsenal of a puppet show – would remain in their baskets. They wouldn't care. For what was the life of an unknown woman – any woman – against the power of Tom West? Molly gripped the cold metal thing.

Then he looked at her. It was the same look she'd catch on the ship, as she tarred or polished. As if, just for a moment, her presence in his life was a miracle. As if, just for a moment, without fear or guilt, she only now understood he loved her.

And that was the real Tom West, too.

He was just as capable of love as he was of terror. He had both tacks. And he'd killed Mama. He'd loved her – had been capable of it – and he'd killed her. Then, surely, he'd been capable of making some other choice. Capable of not killing her. And he didn't feel any sorrow. He felt, instead, that he had some right to Molly's love.

She drew the gun.

The weathervane on St Edward's rattled, and Tom saw the wind was due west. His chuckle was a rasp. He was going to be sick. The wink of buttons and buckles and swords blinded him, the same way his vision would burst when his father took a belt to him. But Dick's belt was limp, and Molly had come to see him. He chuckled, coughed up black humour on to the cobbles. The street did not rise to hit him back.

Another wink of metal caught his attention. Coins. Dick English was passing coins to the butcher boys, three or four giant lads – Tom's neck was searing, his arms were plucking apart at the ligaments – he couldn't count. But he saw the butcher boys muscling through the audience now. Flies billowed and flapped about them. Cook from the mill and Lamble from the King's Head looked disgusted as they peered into the butcher boys' baskets. Blue sleeves, white aprons and bloody baskets. The first boy's hand came out of his basket red. Guts and offal and sheets of muscle. The audience murmured. Tom shut his mouth. Closed his eyes. The first throw struck his face. The viscous grit dripped down his cheekbones. Shards of bone peppered him. He gagged, a red globule that hit the butcher boy.

The audience cheered again – he wasn't sure if it was for him, or this rat bastard.

'I'll eat your insides next,' he growled.

The butcher boy snorted. He dipped his hand, threw again. Nobody cheered when Tom choked. He'd threatened a nobody – and everybody knew his threats weren't threats, they were promises – and this nobody, this *boy*, had laughed. Tom tried to shake off the blood as the boys pelted him, but it didn't help. The blood was pouring in. He was drowning.

Molly watched Tom gasp for air. He was the same vivid red of the ship. The same vivid red as his hands must have been. When he opened his eyes, they were great white circles in the mask of blood. Her grip went slack; the pistol dropped back into her belt.

She found Dick English in the shade of the opposite water tank.

He looked happy.

IV

It was not difficult to find the Bideford meeting house. Dissenters lived in full glare, now. Not because there was nothing to fear, Molly thought, but because they dared to claim independence. A service had just broken up. Passing down the streets, inspecting the worshippers' sombre serge and wool, Molly felt their bullish satisfaction – a current of freedom, which coursed through the priest, who was shaking hands and swapping tales with his congregants. He reminded her of Tom. The door was open. She slipped inside. Immediately, the thick walls fell about her like a shroud.

It wasn't like any church she knew. There were no pews, only chairs. There was no rood screen, no stone pulpit. No colour. There were books. And gathering them, standing in a shaft of light, as pale as an icon, was Benedict, cloaked against the cold in blue serge; cloaked in independence, and self-possession.

Benedict dropped the Bible. It fell, wings splayed, like a struck bird. The strike echoed through the meeting house. He wanted to shout: *Go away. I've come this far. Now leave me.* But she had already crossed the threshold, and the door was already closing behind her – he could see the priest and the congregants, and he urged them to see him through the crack and pull him out – but the door closed, and he was stuck in here with Molly. Then, the sad absurdity of it all came on him, the absolute tragic jest his life was, and he smiled at her.

'I suppose I'm next?' he said.

'Next?'

'Tom West will die, the day after tomorrow, as the sun rises. It's all anyone will talk about, even here. They think Dick English has ruined him, but I know better. Dick English never had the mettle. Dick English is only a marionette. Once it's done, you'll cut the strings and strangle him with them.'

Molly flushed. 'I should show him mercy? Dick English locked my mother in a cage with a tiger, and didn't care.'

'And I watched. Hellard's already dead. That leaves me. So –' he bent down and picked up the Bible – 'am I next?'

Molly wanted to slap him. 'I thought you'd be happy.'

'To see you?'

'No,' she spat, pushing into the circle of chairs, into the smell of his body. 'You wanted me to turn against Tom. You wanted me to see the truth of what he's done.'

A fog was swallowing him. 'Did I?' he asked. He couldn't remember what he'd wanted now.

'I am giving my mother justice,' she said.

'We all greet justice in the end,' said Benedict. 'God has a plan for us. He will deliver his judgement, on a day known only to him.'

'I don't have that kind of time.'

He laughed. He remembered. He'd wanted *her*. And, just as swiftly, he remembered the revulsion that made him now turn away from her and place the Bible in a case.

Molly watched the shell of his ear bloom pink. Her blood was running, urging her to ride roughshod, to trample, to kick. But then the coo of pigeons and doves in the eaves, the lap of water a street away, took her back to an early summer evening by the Dart, jumping into the water with Benedict as sheep bayed angrily on the hill, and the river jostled about them, and they laughed, and Benedict sank into the muddied blue, as he was now – how the trees crowded the bank and watched on – how she'd plunged below the stirring surface in search of him – and the thrill as she folded about his body. Molly unclenched her hands.

'I know you're not to blame,' she said.

He twisted to face her.

'You were just a boy,' she said. 'I know Tom. I know there was nothing you could do. I don't blame you. But why couldn't you tell me, Benedict? What you knew, what you suspected. You could have saved me so much.'

He was crying. Suddenly, there were tears. 'I didn't want to lose you. I thought I could make amends by loving you.'

482

'So did Tom,' she said.

'We were wrong.'

'Were you?'

He tugged at a fold of shining skin at his right eye, pulling the lid shut, then open. 'You've come here for my permission, haven't you?'

She said, 'They're going to tar his body and hang him in chains. His soul won't rest.'

'The savageries of the law are a blasphemous mockery.'

Molly tossed that aside with an impatient sigh. 'Don't you understand? They're going to mock him in death.'

'Isn't that what you wanted? Burning for burning, wound for wound, stripe for stripe. He will be punished for what he did.'

'No, he won't,' said Molly. 'Dick English had the murder of my mother struck from the record.'

Benedict linked his hands. 'Just let him die, Molly. It's the only way to be free of him. Please. Free us from this. Whether it's for your mother or not; whether it's for Revenue men or wreckers or Frank Abbot or Shaun, or even Hellard; whether it's for free-trading and nought else – just let him die.'

Molly took another step towards him. 'She *must* be counted. She must count for something.'

'She does for you.'

Molly swayed. 'That's not enough.'

'The world is not yours, Molly, to direct. It never has been, and it never will be.'

'Then Dick English wins.'

'That's not your war. It's Tom's.'

Molly broke. 'I can't.'

'Why not?'

'I just can't. Not like this. I'm going to get him out. I want your help.'

He laughed again. Gestured around him. 'Don't you see,

483

Molly? There's been no peace for me, no life for me since
I became Tom West's spotsman. Tom West's witness. Since I
became your – whatever we are. I can't keep existing for you
alone. I'm not yours any more.'

They had surfaced from the Dart laughing, but it hadn't
lasted. His hands had fallen from her waist. His smile had
fallen from his face. She wanted, now, to summon contempt, or
bitterness, but could not. There was the familiarity, and scar,
of his eyes. The knowledge of him in her bones. There was the
truth of him, in front of her, unshuttered. She nodded.

V

Once it became clear she could not be steered from her
course, Charles and Nathan agreed to her plan. Then Pascal,
van Meijer, Prell. Molly assured them Tom would exact no
vengeance. They did not believe her, but nor would they let
her go alone. Only Kingston said no: he would not die for
a white man. He caught Molly's arm: 'And you should not
die for this man, either.' She told him she had no intention
of doing any such thing. Nathan sent Isaac to Yeovil to tell
the batmen, who told the fishermen of Brixham, who told
their wives, who told the lime men on the river, who told the
farmers, who told the mill men and the salt men, who told
the wreckers, who told the crabbers of Hope Cove, who put
down their baskets and picked up the steel of their fathers. As
Molly took her boat around the headland into Dartmouth, on
Tom West's last night in his body, in this, his world, she found
an armada gathering at her back, too, and it surged through

her veins, despite everything, this proof that, together, they *were* Devon.

The blood itched, a cracking mask across Tom's face. It didn't matter how much he scrubbed and scratched. Even when he hunched to the floor of the cell and rubbed his cheeks against the ice, the mask remained. The Dark House had closed about him once more. He was desperate for air, the stroke of a warm hand. But Grace's hand was so cold on his cheek, so cold on his back, as she coaxed him to lie down. Cold from the earth? The water? He'd taken her life, and left her body, and not once prayed for her soul, but she was with him all the same. She'd opened her home and her bed to him. She'd trusted him. She'd packed all her books and her lace and her plate. She was going to leave him. Betray him, then leave him, because she'd loved Molly more, because she'd trusted to herself. And she was right to. She could have conquered the world. At least found some room in it, somewhere. Molly was proof of that. Grace had almost been free.

Dick English had ten men pacing the lane that curved between St Mary's and the guildhall. Another two score lingered inside the hall. They'd been instructed not to sit on the court room chairs, but perched there anyway, on the very edge of the wood, rocking a little. Tom West was roaring at ghosts again. They did not make eye contact with each other. They were scared of Tom West's ghosts.

Charles knew Molly had planned to be invisible, but, with nigh on forty men and women waiting on her orders, there was no chance of that. And how had Molly taken command, exactly, this chit of a girl in boy's clothes? None of this lot knew her significance, exactly; perhaps they might have placed her as the boy who grew up at Tom West's elbow. In her jacket and trousers, they certainly couldn't place her as the lady shipwright of Plymouth. But, whatever it was, they followed her up the swell of Fore Street. Windows opened over shops, spilling candlelight. Molly waved people indoors, and they obeyed. There might be something of a witch's blood in her. But there was none of the devil.

Still, he hung back when she halted her army before the crest of the High Street and told half to split further in two and bottle the guardsmen they found in the churchyard: block off the narrow lane that slipped from the High Street to the guild, and block off North Street, so they may not run to the castle. Allow no hue and cry. Allow no bells or shots. Tell them Tom West walks abroad tonight and, if they wish for his mercy, they should lie down among the tombstones and play dead. But – this she seemed to add as an afterthought – don't kill 'em, unless your own life be at stake. She charged Nathan to lead. He looked seasick in the pale light of the stars, but determined, as if aware of his own folly and shaking his head over it. Then Molly led Charles and the other half of her army between two houses and into an orchard, curving ever-round to Priory Avenue.

Charles caught up with her, his breath hardening on the air in quick bursts. 'Moll, what do you mean to do when you reach the Dark House?'

Her face was a white blur against the dark. She looked away. 'What do you think any of these good people mean to do?' she said.

'I know what *they* intend,' he said. 'I asked what you intend.'

They'd reached the old wall of the long-gone priory. Molly was unlooping a rope from her belt.

'I don't think you mean to free him,' Charles persisted, wanting to clutch her to him. 'English has refused you justice.'

'What of it?' she said, tying a knot, just one of many languages of hers he was trying to learn.

A murmur: 'I think you mean to kill him yourself.'

Nothing. Around them, men and women slung ropes over the wall. Eventually, so quiet he almost missed it, Molly said, 'So?'

Charles bit down on his leap of frustration. 'So, what do you think this mob will do, when they realise the ends to which you've put them?'

Molly lifted her eyes. 'That's what you're worried about?' she said.

'Of course.'

She touched his jaw. And then she was gone.

Tom covered his ears as an almighty crash sounded. The Great Storm was tearing down lighthouses. He held Molly closer, but she was so small, there was almost nothing to her – he'd lost her. Another bang beyond the door. The door. The Dark House. He raised his head from the sheet of ice and shit. Another crash. Tom stretched out both arms and wedged himself between the walls, using them to get to one knee, then both, and then to his feet. Head smacked the ceiling. Reeled, almost sick. Listened. A fight. Swords. Curses. Fear. And, cutting through it all: 'Let no man leave!' His Molly. That was his Molly.

The court had filled with smoke from the first pistol shots. Nathan had managed to bar the door, but a dragoon had smashed a window and was now trying to climb out. Charles

487

caught him by the ankle, dragged him to the floor and pressed a sword to his throat. Molly rushed on. Two dragoons had taken up a defensive position in the short corridor leading to the Dark House. They'd fired their shots and had no time to reload, but were keeping Pascal and van Meijer at bay with their swords. Molly waited for Pascal to lunge and, as the dragoon parried, she dropped to the floor and weaved beneath their clashing blades, rising to meet the next. She shoved an elbow into the man behind – who stumbled, and was hauled out by Pascal – and then met the blow of the man before her, almost thrown off balance, the man built like an apple barrel. She managed to stay upright and present him with her left shoulder, catching his stab on her forearm and then jabbing beneath, pinking him in the stomach. He made a surprised, choking sound. Molly kneed him in the groin. He went down. She climbed over his limbs, but checked as around the corner from the women's cell came another dragoon, who had not yet fired his shot.

VI

The bullet struck Molly in the right shoulder. For a moment, she felt nothing. Then fever ran through her bones. The dragoon dropped the pistol, raised his sword. Molly told her arm to lift her blade – move – *move* – and then she met his thrust and countered, bouncing into the wall as the sword ran for her head, and all she could see was the blade. She slashed up, desperate, and his blade careened off course, but the dragoon she'd kneed to the floor had recovered. A slide of minutes:

she was holding off both, one nicked her forehead and she was blinking through blood, and then somehow there was an opening, a dropped guard, and she stabbed the first through the calf – had never felt that fat pinch of resistance before – and twisted the sword out and around to punch the other man with the hilt.

Tom backed up as far as he could, but was still hunched in this too-small coffin. Then there was a crack, a pistol shot, a lock breaking. The door shuddered under the pressure of a boot – once, twice, three times – and then gave. Smoke poured in.

Tom waited: a friendly word, an executioner's impatience.

Both came.

'Hello, Tom.'

Molly stepped through the smoke. She pulled a pistol from her trousers. Polished silver. A walnut grip. Tom's pistol. Unused.

He smiled. 'That's my girl.'

The same rushing in her ears, as if she were under water. Molly shook her head. She'd never breathed air so foul. Yet somehow the walls meant nothing, as if Tom were wearing them and could choose to cast them off. But all he did was stand there.

Molly said, 'It was a choice. Code be damned. You had a choice – to kill her, or not. And you killed her.'

His voice came with no cracks or hesitation: 'I know.'

Molly rocked back.

'So, do it,' he said.

So, do it. Outside, the clamour of pointless violence. She stretched out her arm: levelled the pistol at Tom's chest. Closed her eyes – remembered the heat of her desperation as she'd hammered on the door, trying to get to Mama, the unbearable frustration, the pitch of her terror, and the screams: Grace's screams. She edged her finger on to the trigger. Opened her eyes.

He looked at her with love.

She couldn't.

She couldn't.

'I can't.'

Then he moved – was towering over her – his fist closed over her hand and the pistol, and his finger joined hers at the trigger. He was shaking her.

'*Do it.*'

He was crying. She could feel his tears in her hair.

'I can't.'

'Moll, we've got to go, *now*.' Charles, pulling at her arm. Nathan, diving inside, wrapped his arms around Tom and hauled him out. Pascal and van Meijer and Prell crowded around him. The roar of a riot outside. Charles again: 'Now, now, *now*.'

VII

They split up on the road. Dragoons or soldiers – Molly didn't know – pursued them down Fore Street in a clatter of armour. Nathan and Charles said they'd lead a merry chase down the Dart, and Molly got Tom on to a horse. She mounted before him, told him to hold fast to her waist, and plunged into the night, as, behind them, the Brixham fishwives and the salt men defended the quay, allowing Tom West's crew to escape, they thought, with the smuggler king.

Rain bounced in the trees, and then the heavens opened.
Tom panted by her ear: 'Where are we going?'

'Home.'

The first sign of morning: a sky scrubbed blue by the night's
rains, coaxing long shadows from the trees. Molly urged the
tired animal down into Bantham village, its hoofs desultory on
the track, and then into the sand dunes, until the horse baulked
and would go forward no more. Molly slipped off, shook Tom.
He fell into her. A sudden gasp.

'Where are we?'

'Bantham.'

He stiffened, pulled back. 'No.'

She took his arm – God, the memory of just that – and urged
him on, through the banks of ferns, the folds of sand, on to the
steps hacked into the cliff. They stumbled down to the comma
of beach together. Grace's cottage was a broken silhouette in
the early light. Molly pushed Tom through what had once been
Grace's back garden, then through the stone shell, to the front
of the house, where a yawl stencilled its copy into the water.
Molly and Tom stood for a moment, holding each other up, as
a seagull stretched over the water, and a phantom gull followed
below it. Then Tom lost his footing, and Molly braced, keeping
him standing.

For a moment, he knew only insensibility, and then he saw
the ruptured parlour wall, the fireplace, where he counted a
neatly folded blanket, a cup and pan, a book, an ink pot and
a quill. Molly came here, then, to write, and this was Molly's
little yawl.

'Can you kill me here?' he said.

'No.'

So, she was better than him. Well, he'd always known that.

'Molly. I am sorry. Sorrier than I am about anything else in my life, unless it's losing you.'

The stir of water, the white ridges of a briefly broken current.

'I was never yours,' she said. 'Not truly.'

'I know.'

She leant into his chest, just for a moment, and then pushed him away. 'I can't kill you. But I can't live with you either.'

He stumbled in the ancient ruin of Grace's garden.

'Devon's mine,' she said. 'You can have Île de Batz. Devon's mine.'

Tom felt his heart founder. He put a hand to his chest. He was ragged to the core, blown through with holes, riddled with rot and howling. His heart hurt. But he didn't have any bluster left in him. He just nodded.

Molly waited for him to argue, to seize her, to shake his world into her. And then she realised it wasn't going to happen. She'd won. If this was winning.

And now she had to say goodbye.

'You can take my boat,' she said.

He nodded again. He couldn't trust his words. Or his hands. He took a step towards the water. The river was swollen bronze-green, the hills drenched and glistening. The sea waiting, wide and unforgiving.

'I'll miss you,' said Molly.

Tom squinted against the flare of sun. Glanced back at her. Blood had stained her face. She was supporting one arm. Her sleeve was red too. He thought of telling her she'd be better off without him, but she knew that. He went to speak anyway, but it emerged a choke, so he turned away and waded into the water. It was a miracle against his infested legs, then a sharp scraping pain. He clambered into the boat, drew up the line. *When you are a danger, run to sea.* Just like his father.

Except, she was there to witness him go. She'd survived him.

492

So, not like his father. Not even like himself. He hoisted the sails. Himself. He knew he couldn't survive himself.

Molly watched him take up the oars and cast off, waiting for a pucker of wind. He'd find fresh water and a bundle of food in the stern. When she'd left it there, she'd lied to herself about the reason. The river was quick this morning, and he was taken away swiftly, as if it didn't matter.

'You are not so clever as you think.'

Her heart clenched. Dick English leant on his sticks, his horse steaming in the dawn air behind him. He no longer had that infuriating – but reassuring, she now realised – air of a holy man about him. He burnt with righteousness, but it was his own righteousness now.

'You're too late,' she said. 'Tide's going out fast. He's gone.'

She looked over the crumbling wall, and Dick almost fell as he twisted, following her gaze. Tom didn't look back as he spilled into the sea. Molly watched him all the same.

Dick shook as the yawl strained around Burgh Island. Purple blotches crawled over his lime-white face. 'I'll get to him.'

'That really bothered you, didn't it?' She had one unspent shot in Tom's pistol, and her sword. But she'd had enough of murder. 'You cannot think to arrest me,' she said. 'I make the ships for the Navy. I dine with Commissioner Lark. I make Sir Nicholas feel like a man. I fund the Plymouth Corporation.'

Dick snorted. 'Like father, like son.'

Molly looked him in the eyes.

He pursed his lips. 'Like mother, like daughter.'

He hurled one of his sticks at her. It fell uselessly in the sand. He collapsed against the wall, breath hard won.

Sun slipped into the cottage. Molly followed. The hearth welcomed her. She'd scratched a title into the cover of the book: *A Wild & True Relation of A Lady Shipwright and Free-Trader, by Molly Wildego, after Her Mother Grace Tucker's True Relation and*

Very Faithful Account of a Brave and Wonderful Life, and Her Sad and Dreadful Murder at the Hands of a Smuggler. She weighed the journal, her arm throbbing. Water had pooled in the flagstones, and she skulled it, then ran wet fingers over her face. Molly studied the cottage. Remembered the feeling of safety, here, once. Justice is the last woman standing.

Run to Sea

The waves were gentle: the tick of the drag and then the small splash. Sometimes a deep crash, if they scrolled and gathered together. The semicircle of pale blue, of nothingness, fringed by heather and brush grasses and lavender. Clusters of rocks close to the shoreline. Tom sat at the dining-room table, watching the beach, the small edge of Île de Batz. The windows were open. Molly called that rock Stretching Lion Rock. Benedict called it the Rock of Supplication. Molly had laughed at him.

He studied the seaweed: how the sea came to it, a pool seeping between the bobbly mass that spread, moss-like, over the beach. No dividing line. He would stand up, lock the door behind him and pocket the key. He would fill his pockets with stones. He would walk into the ocean, and it would knock on his heart, and he would be free.

So, run to sea.

A gentle touch on his shoulder. Tom looked around. Nobody.

But, still, a voice telling him: *Be a man.*

He dragged air into his chest. Covered his face.

Be a man?

Walk into the water, and remove himself from the world.

Or: live out his years here, alone, with his sins. Own this name, this body. Wake each day himself, with the same story, which he could not make himself the hero of, and the same ghosts, which he could not bury. Wake each day himself. Discover, if he could, a new self, but always know what manner of man he had once been.

Be a man.

'As you wish.'

He stayed in his chair. The sea drank only sand, and rocks.

Leaf

To INTERLEA/VE. v. a. [*inter* and *leave*]

To chequer a book by the insertion of blank leaves.

Elizabeth Wildego said that Bantham House was 'the loveliest place in the world – it quite takes my breath away.' It still is the loveliest place in the world. The National Trust maintain its spectacular beauty and its homeliness. Every day, hundreds of people wander through the dahlia borders, taking photos on their phones of the magnolia trees, the peach house, the vinery. Wasps frenzy around the stables, where a café serves cream teas.

The doors to the house open at 10.30 a.m. A game of dominos waits on the coffee table in the morning room, sheet music on the Steinway. In the library, a table inlaid with mother-of-pearl glitters, a book left on it casually. A wall tapestry is faring less well; a small card paperclipped to its edge exhorts with shaky capitals: *LIGHT RECORDING IN PROGRESS. PLEASE DO NOT MOVE.* Everywhere there is a feeling that 'the three Bees' have just stepped out, and are expected back soon. A first edition of *A True Relation* sits on a shelf above Elizabeth Thomas's attic desk, protected by a neat cross of wires forbidding curious hands. And, beside that, the script for a film that was never made. Production began just two days before the Wall Street Crash.

I arrived ten days ago, for a writing residency. I am staying in the servants' quarters, where ice boxes like oversized coffins sit empty, along with travelling trunks labelled *GWR, Grenvil*. I am here to finish a lecture series for Cambridge, about the literary life of one legend, and the man it remembered, and the women it forgot. A groundskeeper asks me which Bee I'm writing about. I tell him: the Queen Bee. He seems pleased, telling me over the leaf blower, 'She's my guilty pleasure.'

She was my great-great aunt. This house was my childhood refuge. That's my copy of *Five Go to Smuggler's Top* carefully preserved on the table of the magnolia bedroom. That was my bedroom. I wrote at the window. Now, tourists take selfies at the desk, and I write in the vinery, listening to the drumbeat of rain on the roof. It was in this house that I outgrew playing as Enid Blyton's George and started playing as Aunt Elizabeth's Molly.

I thought it was only a story Aunt Elizabeth told me, a vital secret we crossed our hearts over. Then I forgot it. I grew too old for games when she grew too old to share them. After she died, I discovered she was only the centre of my life. I had more luck finding Aunt Elizabeth's books in Oxfam than in my university library. When the cousins sold my childhood refuge to the National Trust, I decided to find out how much truth there was in Aunt Elizabeth's story that we are the descendants of Molly Wildego. I have been researching Molly's life since, hunting for her journal, which she wrote when her mother's was obliterated. I've found folk songs and ballads, footnotes and ellipses. I followed them to Exeter City Library, where Molly's journal seemed to pass from the possession of Hester Thrale back into the hands of Devon. But the library was destroyed in the German Baedeker raids, with one million books burnt. The 'Phoenix Plan' for rebuilding the city was displayed in the library's ruin. I discovered Aunt Elizabeth donated most of her books to the city in an effort to help the library rise from the ashes. I searched her shelves in a room known as the Cage, where dust clings to the spines of books as one clings to memory, but the Cage stayed silent.

Aunt Elizabeth left me the contents of her green sea chest, with the provision that the chest and all its contents would not leave the house. Today, as high winds keep visitors away, I climb into the attic and step over the red cord. The chest is locked. I take the key charm off my wrist – my thirteenth birthday present. I should have visited the green sea chest years ago. Let's just say this: sometimes, what we inherit from our foremothers seems a burden, until we realise it's a gift.

Dust plumes, and the landscape painted inside the lid seems to come alive beneath it: clouds driven by a stormy sea.

The chest whispers with her papers. The blue loop of her pencil, trembling with age in the first layer, flows in neat waves to the bottom, time spooling backwards. I land on a book. The spine creaks. Gilt shimmers in the evening light. Inside, there is a stamp: *Ex-Libris Exeter Library*, purchased at a book fair in 1920.

A Wild & True Relation of My Life and Deeds, by A Lady Free-Trader and Shipwright.

Inside, there is a clipped review of *A True Relation* by Elizabeth Wildego, and a note headed with my name in fragile blue on the back of a shopping list: *For the next writer in the family.*

(*Notes for a lecture on women and writing to be given at Girton College, Cambridge, on the anniversary of Virginia Woolf's lecture series, 'A Room of One's Own'.*)

BOOK EIGHT

1762

PEACE

Cast Away

It seemed to Charles that the long curve of white houses over Dock, so recently put up with such pomp, had already lost their shine. But more likely, he knew, it was just the day. For all of Dock – now Devonport, he kept forgetting – seemed pallid to him: the twin sentinels of the furnace towers looming over North Yard, the hollow clamour of beaten meal booming from Dry Dock, the three hundred men (and women, Molly never satisfied with just one scandal) at work refitting the cruisers, all of the money it represented – all of it failed to gladden him today. Even the sight of Grace, all grown up now and arguing outside the beer shop with Kingston over the merits of some new poet only made him shake his head.

Beside him, Nathan was just as quiet, tugging at his clipped beard, which was bone white against his sun-gold face. The soft lap of Sutton Harbour played over his reed-thin voice as he turned to Charles and said, 'I always had the feeling she built it for him.'

Charles breathed in so sharply, it was like swallowing salt. 'Dock?'

'Don't be a fool,' said Nathan. '*That* she built for herself. The hospital.'

Charles watched a young Negro dressed in surprising finery go inside the ward. 'You reckon she knew?' he asked. 'Knew he'd come home to die?'

'I reckon she knew he couldn't go, without taking her leave.'

'As long as that's all he expects,' said Charles, crossing his arms.

Nathan laughed. 'Ever the gallant, Charlie boy.'

Charles snorted. The Negro came out again, looking like he'd seen a ghost. Maybe it was over.

Inside, Molly set her book down by her chair. She glanced at Benedict. Almost time. He stepped out of the shadows and came to stand on the other side of Tom's bed. Molly looked past his dog collar to his eyes: still the blue of the Virgin Mary's robes, and still as wide, but the horror in them had faded, leaving only understanding. He touched Tom's elbow.

'Heavenly father,' he said, 'bless this—'

'No.' Tom's voice was as harsh as a rusted chain letting down an anchor. 'No. Molly – Molly . . .'

'I'm with you.'

'Fire . . .'

'There's no fire, Tom.'

'I can smell it . . .'

'Stonehouse,' said Benedict.

For a moment, Molly didn't understand: her world had narrowed to this room, this bed, these men, her book, and the spirit of Grace. She thought Benedict might be speaking of a chamber in hell – but then sense came back to her.

'The Admiralty built a hospital at Stonehouse,' she said. 'First night, a fire swept through one of the blocks, destroyed everything in its path. They're rebuilding now.'

Tom smiled. The same kindling warmth when he looked at her, the same pride and promise of adventure, the same strength of feeling – a feeling she'd barred these many years. He reached for Benedict.

Benedict touched his shoulder and said, 'You won't die to fire, Tom.'

'No,' said Tom. 'No.' He nodded at Molly – a nod of gratitude, she thought.

She wanted to answer him, but was afraid of the convulsion
waiting inside, the break.

'Benedict, my boy. My witness ... '

'I'm here, Captain,' said Benedict.

'You've always been there. Watching me. And I never told
you. I'm sorry, for that.'

Benedict held his breath. Bowed, and kissed Tom's cheek.

Molly's heart ran like a hare. She needed some gesture, some
act, like that. Something that would allow her to communicate
the contradictions that riveted her, even now. But it didn't exist.
Instead, she stroked Tom's swollen fist, the map of damage.

'I cannot forgive you,' she said.

Tom murmured, eyelids fluttering now. He was almost gone.
He would be gone, from her, for ever. The tales of him would
not comfort her.

'But I can wish you – peace. I know you loved me, as
you could.'

I love you still – this, she could not voice.

His hand tightened on hers. He was hardly breathing, now.
He said something – it might have been 'Thank you'; it could
have been anything – and then there was strength in him
again, and he raised her rope-worn hand to his lips.

Molly and Benedict were losing shape, losing firmness, blurring, becoming ship's lanterns, becoming lodestars. Benedict's
eyes. Molly's curls, like golden wood shavings from a planed
deck. He touched her hand to his lips again. Sighed. Let
go. Let go.

His fist was marble in her hand. Molly studied his face. His
stubble was as silver as evening sun over open ocean. His jaw
had kept its strength. His cheekbones and his nose showed their
blows, pounded metal. He wore the endurance of his years in

deep sea-lines around his eyes, which she closed now, drawing shut the smile that seemed to wait there. A tear slipped on to his cheek – his or hers, she didn't know. His hair was sheep's wool, grey and matted. He'd smuggled wool out with the owlers as a boy. He'd beaten the world into a shape of his choosing; he'd beaten himself, misshapen and awful; he'd made lives and taken lives. He'd killed her mother. He'd come back to her to die.

Molly gripped his hand a last time, and then freed herself.

Thanks and Acknowledgements

In the eighteenth century, writers prefaced their books with notes of 'gratitude, admiration and affection' for their patrons, in the words of Frances Reynolds. I would like to end this book with a note offering my gratitude, admiration and affection to the following fine organisations and people, for their support and encouragement in the writing of this novel since 2009.

My research was made possible by the collections of public libraries, archives and small museums across the South West, and the generosity and expertise of their staff. My thanks to Kingsbridge Library and the Kingsbridge Cookworthy Museum; Salcombe Maritime Museum; Dartmouth Castle and Dartmouth Museum; Totnes Library, Totnes Guildhall and Totnes Museum; Exmouth Museum; Exeter Library; South Tawton and District Local History Group, whose meticulous archive is kept in the cupboards of Victory Hall, South Zeal; Devon Rural Archive; Bath Central Library; and Bristol Central Library. Beyond the South West, my thanks to Dr Johnson's House; the National Portrait Gallery; the Museum of the Home; Greenwich Maritime Museum; the British Library; and the National Archives. Many of these organisations have suffered funding cuts in the fourteen years since I began writing this book, and I would like to underscore how vital support of our libraries, archives and museums is to the creative and educational lifeblood of our country.

I was further enlightened by the generosity and expertise of historians and research groups. Many thanks to Professor Steve Poole at the University of the West of England, whose work and insight into eighteenth-century crime in the South West was invaluable. Many thanks to Miriam Al Jamil and Gillian Williamson, both members and driving forces behind the Women's Studies Group 1558–1837, a multi-disciplinary group formed to promote women's studies in the early modern period and the long eighteenth century. The study of women's history has often occurred despite lack of institutional support, and the history and ongoing work of the WSG is inspiring. The group is open and inclusive, and I would encourage anyone interested in the period to attend its fantastic workshops and seminars.

If you are interested in the history of women's writing, and are curious about the gaps in your curriculum or your bookshelf, I would recommend Joanna Russ's *How to Suppress Women's Writing* and Ellen Moers' *Literary Women* as landmark starts. If you'd like to know more about women writing in the eighteenth century in particular, I would suggest *Dr Johnson's Women* by Norma Clarke as another pivotal starting point.

I received support and time from Libraries Unlimited, the University of the West of England and the University of Edinburgh. I was awarded the Authors Foundation Grant by the Society of Authors, which enabled me to carry out my research. I am especially grateful to the National Trust and Greenway House for inviting me to stay in Agatha Christie's home. I finished writing the novel in her gardens one twilight, and will forever be grateful for that memory.

Fourteen years is a long time to keep a novel alive, and I am grateful to all of the people who offered a friendly word and hand on the journey. Dame Hilary Mantel and Andrew Miller, thank you both for your encouragement at crucial points. My agent, Sue Armstrong, a guiding light; and my editor Rose Tomaszewska, literary kin. The whole team at Virago.

My friends. Lauren Fried and Eleanor Stewart-Pointing, who discussed ideas and read drafts. And my family. Thank you to Roger Squire, who took me out on the water. Thank you to my sister, Rosie Sherwood, who walked and talked along sunken lanes and estuary beds. Thank you to my husband, Nick Herrmann, who has been with these characters as long as I have. And finally thank you to my mother, Ellie Baker, who held on to the story when I couldn't, and never set it down.

In the words of Virginia Woolf, novels 'are the outcome of many years of thinking in common, of thinking by the body of the people, so that the experience of the mass is behind the single voice. Jane Austen should have laid a wreath upon the grave of Fanny Burney, and George Eliot done homage to the robust shade of Eliza Carter . . . For we think back through our mothers if we are women.' This book is my wreath.